HOLLY'S HEART

Collection One

BEVERLY LEWIS

HOLLY'S HEART

Collection One

◆ BETHANYHOUSE
Minneapolis, Minnesota

About the Author

BEVERLY LEWIS, born in the heart of Pennsylvania Dutch country, fondly recalls her growing-up years. A keen interest in her mother's Plain family heritage has inspired Beverly to set many of her popular stories in Amish country, beginning with her inaugural novel, *The Shunning*.

A former schoolteacher and accomplished pianist, Beverly has written over eighty books for adults and children. Five of her blockbuster novels have received the Gold Book Award for sales over 500,000 copies, and *The Brethren* won a 2007 Christy Award.

Beverly and her husband, David, make their home in Colorado, where they enjoy hiking, biking, reading, writing, making music, and spending time with their three grandchildren.

Books by Beverly Lewis

GIRLS ONLY (GO!)*
Youth Fiction

Girls Only! Volume One
Girls Only! Volume Two

SUMMERHILL SECRETS†
Youth Fiction

SummerHill Secrets Volume One
SummerHill Secrets Volume Two

HOLLY'S HEART
Youth Fiction

Holly's Heart Collection One†
Holly's Heart Collection Two†
*Holly's Heart Collection Three**

www.BeverlyLewis.com

*4 books in each volume   †5 books in each volume

HOLLY'S HEART

Best Friend Worst Enemy

To Dave,

my heart-mate, best friend,

and very cool husband.

Chapter 1

"Is it hot in here?" I whispered to the boy sharing my music folder.

Tom Sly's eyes bulged. "Holly Meredith, you're turning green!"

That's when it happened. Halfway through our seventh-grade musical, on the second riser, in front of half the population of Dressel Hills, Colorado, I felt dizzy. Faces in the audience began to blur. Heat rushed to my throbbing head. With a mouth drier than Arizona, I gasped for breath. Then my knees buckled and . . . I blacked out!

My best friend, Andrea Martinez—better known as Andie—witnessed this embarrassing scene and filled me in on the details later. She jumped off the risers and hightailed it over to help me. Tom Sly dragged me behind the risers and across the newly waxed gym floor to the janitor's room. Jared Wilkins followed.

When I came to, I was lying on the floor in the musty janitor's room. The first thing I saw was the adorable face of Jared Wilkins, the new boy. He smiled down at me, fanning me back to life with his music folder. In my half-dazed state, his blue eyes seemed to dance dreamily. *Maybe this fainting stuff isn't so bad after all,* I thought, squinting through the haze.

"Holly," Jared said. "Can you hear me?"

"Uh-huh," I whispered.

"Hang in there. Andrea went to get your mom." He glanced at Tom Sly, who leaned against the doorway, fidgeting.

Jared helped me sit up next to some mops and a bucket. I still felt a little out of it, but not so bad that I couldn't enjoy being the focus of his attention.

"Are you feeling okay?" he asked.

"I think so," I said weakly.

"That's good. You just take it easy till your mom gets here, all right?" Smiling, he sat beside me, leaning against the wall. "What a cool way to get out of a boring musical!"

"Speak for yourself," I said, feeling a bit stronger. "You didn't just faint in front of the whole school."

"But it's very romantic, being rescued by two men, don't you think?"

I was about to tell him that two seventh-grade boys didn't exactly qualify as men when Mom and my little sister, Carrie, burst into the room, followed by Andie.

"Holly, honey, are you all right?" Mom leaned down to touch my forehead while Carrie frowned.

"I think she's going to be okay," Jared said, smiling at me again. "It just got a little too hot up on stage."

"Well, let's get you out of this musty mess and into some fresh air," Mom said. "Thank you for your help, boys."

"No problem," Jared said.

Tom gave me a weird grin.

Mom led me down the hallway and settled me into a chair in an empty classroom. Then she and Carrie went to search for a glass of water. As soon as they were out of earshot, Andie sat next to me. She twisted one of her dark curls around her finger. When she does that, I know something's up!

"Holly," she whispered, "you'll never guess what happened when you were out cold."

"What're you talking about?" I asked, still feeling a bit woozy.

"One of the boys tried to give you mouth-to-mouth resuscitation."

"What?" Suddenly wide-awake, I grabbed Andie's arm. "*Who did?*"

She shook her head and looked away. "I, uh, shouldn't tell you."

"What do you mean *shouldn't?*"

"Oh, Holly," she whined. "I shouldn't have said anything."

I grabbed her other arm. "This is embarrassing. I *have* to know!"

She pulled away from me. "Don't do this, Holly."

"Do what? We're best friends, remember?"

She folded her arms. "I can't tell you."

"Why not?" I was desperate. "Did his lips actually touch mine?"

Andie nodded solemnly. "Your first . . . uh, kiss—well, not really—but, you know. And you weren't even awake for it," she said.

"Andie!" I howled. "Don't you dare joke about this. Who was it?" I was dying to know, but just then Andie's parents poked their heads in the door.

"Ready to go?" Mrs. Martinez asked. "We told the baby-sitter we'd be back by nine."

"Okay, Mom," Andie said. Then she whispered to me, "Call me the second you get home."

"Don't worry," I replied.

Mom returned with a glass of water and made me drink it. Then she held my arm while we walked to the car. Carrie opened the door for me. During the drive home, Mom kept pampering me.

"Are you feeling better, Holly-Heart?" she asked. Flicking on the inside light, she stroked the top of my head. "The color's returned to your cheeks. That's good."

Carrie giggled from the backseat. "You looked like a ghost up there."

"Did I? Did everybody see me faint?" I was mortified. Not only had I been semiresuscitated by a boy while unconscious, but a whole auditorium full of parents and kids had watched me keel over!

"Now, Holly, things like this can happen to anyone," Mom said. "There's nothing to be embarrassed about."

"But, Mom, that's not *all* that happened." Then I told her about the unneeded attempt at resuscitation.

"I think someone was trying to help you, Holly. That's all."

"But don't you see, Andie won't tell me who! I guess I wouldn't mind it if it was Jared, but Tom Sly, well . . ." I felt queasy at the thought.

Mom asked, smiling, "Does Jared happen to be the cute new boy you've been talking about? The one who spoke to me tonight?"

I nodded, and Carrie caught on and began to chant, "Holly and Jared, sittin' in a tree, K-I-S-S-I-N-G—"

"Mom!" I protested. I didn't need trouble from my eight-year-old sister, too.

"Carrie, *please*," Mom said. "Don't tease your sister."

I could hear Carrie snickering softly, but I let it go. It was enough for Mom to glare at her in the rearview mirror.

We pulled into the garage, and I could hear the phone ringing as we got out of the car.

"It's Andie!" I guessed, getting out of the car. I made a mad dash for the house and the phone. "Hello?"

It *was* Andie. "What took you so long?"

"Nothing," I said. "We came straight home." Quickly, I retreated to my favorite telephone stall—the downstairs bathroom. No one could hear me there. I lowered the toilet lid and settled down. "Okay, I'm ready for the whole story," I said.

She began to reveal what happened when I blacked out. Everything except the thing I was most eager to know. Then she said, "What do *you* remember about tonight?"

I was cautious, keeping the most private moments with Jared to myself.

"So . . . that's it?" she asked. "Nothing else?"

"Nope!" I said impatiently. "Now, when are you going to tell me who brought me back to life?"

She sighed. "Like I said, I can't tell you."

"Why not?" I demanded.

"Honestly," she said, "I wouldn't keep my best friend in the dark unless—"

"Unless what?"

"Unless it's for your own good."

"Don't make me crazy, Andie. What good is not knowing?"

"My lips are sealed. True friends must shield one another sometimes."

"C'mon, don't get weird on me. Tell me!"

"I can't, I really can't."

"Okay, I'll just ask Jared. He'll tell me the truth."

"That's not a good idea," she said.

"Why not? He was there. He should know."

"You're getting too hyper, Holly."

"No kidding!" I was ready to pull my hair out. "Look, Andie, I refuse to talk to you until you tell me everything you know."

"But, Holly, I—"

"Good-bye, Andie." And with that, I hung up.

What a nightmare this was turning out to be. The most mysterious thing that had ever happened to me, and my own best friend wouldn't even talk about it!

Chapter 2

Fortunately, I had two whole days to get over my fainting episode. I would have died of embarrassment if I had to go to school the very next day!

I spent Saturday morning writing in my diary. Ever since third grade, I'd kept a journal. My secret wish is to be a writer when I grew up. That is, if I survive seventh grade.

My hand shook as I wrote the date: Saturday, January 16. Then I described the whole humiliating evening. Right down to Andie's awful secret. What *had* happened while I lay there, dead to the world? I imagined several scenarios and wrote them down. In one scene, Tom tried to get near me and Jared bravely pushed him away, protecting my innocent lips.

Carrie called up the stairs, interrupting my thoughts. "Holly! Andie's on the phone for you."

"Tell her I'm busy," I yelled back.

"She won't believe me!" she said.

I went to the head of the stairs. "Tell her I'm out."

"No, you're not."

"Okay!" I said, exasperated. "This is the truth: Tell her I refuse to talk to her until she tells me in person what happened last night."

"Have it your way," Carrie snipped.

Tiptoeing downstairs, I observed my sister telling Andie what I'd just said. When Carrie hung up I asked, "What'd Andie say?"

"She said, 'Over my dead body,' " Carrie repeated, snickering.

I tromped back to my room. Enough of Andie's nonsense. "This means war," I muttered.

♥ ♥ ♥

At church the next day, I made a point of snubbing Andie. Sure, my conscience hurt when the minister talked about forgiveness, but I tried very hard to push the sermon out of my mind. I was still too upset to deal with it.

♥ ♥ ♥

On Monday at school, I arrived early to Miss Wannamaker's gloomy English classroom, hoping to have the chance to talk to Jared or Tom. The walls in the classroom were a sick gray, a sorry color for a room where some of my best creative writing happened—assigned by one of my favorite teachers. Miss W was one of the largest women I'd ever seen, but she had the face of an angel and the heart of a saint.

The classroom slowly filled up, but before I could catch either Jared or Tom, Miss W herself arrived. "Dear class," she began, like a letter. That was her way every day. "Turn to page 249 in your literature books." She faced the chalkboard and wrote a "pithy" quotation, as she called it. The flap of skin under her arm jiggled as she wrote.

"Hey, Jared. How much to call Miss W the *B* word?" Tom Sly whispered behind me.

I glanced at Jared, who sat across the aisle.

"Do you mean . . . *blob*?" Jared blurted out.

Miss W whirled around. "Jared. Tom." They looked up from their desks, shocked. "You will both see me after class."

Her tone meant trouble—*big* trouble. I didn't feel sorry for Tom. His show-off routine had finally caught up with him.

But Jared? That was another story. . . .

Two months ago, right before Thanksgiving, Jared Wilkins had moved to Dressel Hills, our ski village nestled in the Colorado Rockies. I often caught him watching me when I peeked at him. I secretly hoped *he* was the one who had come to my rescue, like some fairy-tale prince.

"Dear class," Miss W began again, "I'm returning the quizzes from last week."

The papers came around. I got a ninety percent—not bad for last-minute cramming.

"Now for Thursday's assignment," she said. We all groaned, but she ignored us. "I want each of you to write a short story—two pages typewritten, minimum." More groans. "The main character must have something in common with you—your personality, hobby, or a special interest. Otherwise, the sky's the limit."

I jotted notes in my red binder and sneaked a look at Jared. He gestured that we should talk after class. I smiled yes.

Out of the corner of my eye, I saw Andie scrunch her eyes at me like a snapping turtle ready to attack. I turned my back and ignored her. True to my word, I hadn't spoken to her all day—even though her locker was right next to mine.

After English, Miss W gave Jared and Tom a tongue-lashing. I waited in the hallway, nervously pulling on my hair. Who should I ask about Friday night? Jared or Tom? Tom was a tease and a real pain, but at least I'd known him since first grade. I hardly knew Jared at all. Thinking it over, I decided to play it by ear.

Before long, Jared came out. "Hope you aren't in trouble with Miss Wannamaker," I said.

"Not really, but Tom's still in there." He glanced over his shoulder, and then we headed down the hall toward our lockers. "Any chance you're going to youth group tomorrow night?" he asked.

"Well, Pastor Rob said he wants kids to wait till they're thirteen," I said, my heart *thump-thump*ing.

"When will that be?" He reached for my books.

"I doubt you'll believe it if I tell you." I was actually walking down the corridors of Dressel Hills Junior High with the best-looking guy in school balancing my books on his hip!

"Try me."

"February fourteenth."

"You're kidding." He looked surprised. "Valentine's Day?"

"That's my birthday." My face felt like it had a bad sunburn. Jared had to notice. That thought made it worse.

"How'd you end up with a Christmasy name like Holly?"

What was wrong with my knees? They shook like I was up on the second riser again.

"My mom named me after her great-aunt," I said. "We share the same name, but that's where the similarity ends."

"What do you mean?"

"My great-aunt Holly became a missionary to Africa."

"Really?"

"Her life was filled with fabulous excitement—dangerous adventure that would build your faith instantly. *I'm* lucky if I remember to read my devotions every day."

Jared grinned.

"Mom calls me Holly-Heart," I volunteered without thinking. "It's her special nickname for me, because of my Valentine birthday."

"It's perfect for you. You *are* all heart, aren't you?" His eyes softened.

I didn't dare tell him the nickname my gym teacher had chosen for me. Holly-Bones was verbal abuse at its worst, I thought, tucking my shirttail into the tiny waist of my jeans.

Arriving at my locker, we found Andie rummaging in hers.

"See you tomorrow," Jared said, handing back my books.

"Okay . . ." My heart pounded as he headed down the hall.

"Aw, how—what should I say?—promising," Andie muttered inside her messy locker.

Refusing to respond, I spun my combination lock and opened the door—right into Andie's.

"Ex-*cuse* me!" Andie said, pushing my door aside. Then she slammed her locker shut and stomped off.

I shrugged, deciding to keep my word about not talking to her. But I wanted to, so I could find out what she knew that I didn't. No way would I let her withhold valuable information from me— her best friend.

Suddenly Tom was beside me, hanging on my locker door. "That was some act you pulled last Friday night," he teased. "Some way to upstage the entire seventh grade."

"Maybe," I said, rummaging around my locker, pretending to search for something. Now was my chance to ask, but did I dare?

"You were so wiped out," he said, like he was dying to talk about it.

I summoned up my courage. "What happened after I fainted?" I asked. I kept my head in my locker so he couldn't see my flaming face.

"Are you saying Andie didn't tell you?" he said.

"Not yet."

"*Ve-ry* interesting." He put his hand to his chin and stroked an imaginary beard. "Hey, I guess you'll never know then. See ya." He waved and took off down the hall.

Weird, I thought. Why wouldn't he tell me? Sighing, I knew I had only one other option. Jared Wilkins. Now I'd *have* to ask him.

I walked home from school, watching my breath float ahead of me. As usual, Dressel Hills was swarming with winter tourists. Skiers roamed the streets and crowded into shops and coffee- houses. I turned the corner away from the bustling village, toward Downhill Court. The trees, bare as skeletons, shivered in the cold mountain air.

Picking my way along the slippery street, I thought of Jared. Could someone that cute possibly like me? Could he overlook my "no-shape" and see my heart instead? Daddy had with Mom. She said she was so thin when they met, she looked like a pipe cleaner. As for me, I ate like a hippo, but nothing ever changed. Something about my metabolism made me burn up the fat. Meanwhile, all the other girls were changing . . . developing. Maybe something would happen in time for my thirteenth birthday—an eternal twenty-seven days from now.

I waved to a neighbor and plodded ahead to the tri-level three houses away, where I lived with my mom and sister. Flecks of powdery snow dusted the icy bricked walkway. I hoped we'd have another snow day soon. Andie and I always managed to get together on bad-weather days we had off school, no matter how snowy the streets were.

Then I remembered—she and I weren't talking. I kicked at a hardened gray clump of ice clinging to the gutter in front of our house. This secrecy stuff made me mad. Somehow, I *had* to get Andie talking again.

When I walked in the front door, Mom was relaxing with her usual after-work cup of peppermint tea.

I pulled off my shoes. "Love you, Mom," I said, tossing my scarf aside.

"Everything okay at school?"

I dumped my books on the sofa, scaring Goofey, our cat, away. "Andie's a total nightmare."

"What do you mean, Holly-Heart?"

"She *still* won't tell me who . . . uh, you know." I pressed my hands against my cold face. "Mom, I've *got* to know."

She nodded.

"I tried to ask Tom, but he wouldn't tell, either."

"What are you going to do now?" Mom asked.

"I don't know," I said glumly.

Three whole days had passed since I backflipped off the risers, and Andie still guarded her secret. I wondered if she'd paid the boys to keep their mouths shut, too. Sooner or later the truth had to pop out. Whatever it was.

Chapter 3

After school the next day I studied at the library while I waited for Jared to get out of basketball practice. For once I didn't have to hurry home to be with Carrie, because she was going to a friend's house after school.

I couldn't exactly study, though. I kept looking out the window, across to the gym. I pictured Jared shooting hoops and dribbling up and down the court. I hoped I could actually muster up the nerve to ask him about the night I passed out!

Just then I spied him leaving the gym, wearing gray sweats, his navy blue gym bag slung over his shoulder. Even with his hair wet from the shower, he looked great. I jumped up and was out the front doors of the school in a flash.

Jared waved, coming across the freshly plowed walkway toward me. "Hey, Holly. Glad you waited." He grinned, like he was *really* glad. He held the door for me as we went back into the building. "Got time for a soda?"

"Sure." *Thump-thumpity* went my heart.

"Wish you didn't have to wait another whole month to come to the youth group at church. I'll miss seeing you there tonight."

I breathed slowly, deeply. *Should I ask him about Andie's secret now?*

We stopped at his locker, and I waited while he grabbed his jacket and books. It was now or never.

I took a deep breath. "Jared, uh, can I ask you something kinda personal?"

"Sure, what?"

"I'm having a little trouble getting things straight."

He closed his locker and leaned against it. "What things?"

"Like what happened . . . you know, Friday night when I fainted?"

At that precise moment, Andie appeared. She marched toward us like a soldier in battle. Her dark eyes flashed. I tried to ignore her, but she came right up to me. "Holly, can I talk to you a minute?" she asked, oh so sweetly, offering a smile to Jared.

I was trapped. I couldn't be rude to her in front of Jared. What would he think?

"Excuse me," I told Jared. "Can you wait a sec?"

"No problem."

I pulled Andie over to our lockers. I'd vowed not to speak to her, and I wasn't about to now. She'd just have to read my expression. Pure disgust!

"What's with you?" she demanded.

Ignoring her, I reached into my locker for my jacket.

"Cut the jokes. Stay away from Jared," she said.

I scowled at her as I pulled my long hair out of my coat collar and flung it over my shoulder.

"Talk to me." Her voice softened. "We're best friends."

My patience with her was almost gone. I glanced down the hall at Jared, who was still waiting for me. It was useless. I had to talk to her.

"Look, Andie, you've had your fun. You've played your secretive game long enough."

"Have you forgotten our Loyalty Papers?" she insisted.

" 'Course not," I said. "After all, *I* wrote most of them." In third grade Andie and I had drawn up our first Loyalty Papers. Every possible problem in our friendship had been thought out carefully and written down, legal-like. "Devoted, caring best friends, until the final end of us" was some of the dramatic wording. We revised the Loyalty Papers every year. But the message always remained the same—pals to the very end.

"Well, you're not following them very closely, are you?" she said, looking up at me. The top of her dark head just reached my shoulders.

"Hey, Holly!" Jared waved to me from down the hall. "Meet me at the Soda Straw later, okay?"

"I'll be there in a minute," I called, nodding. Then, as soon as he was out of earshot, I turned on Andie. "You're spoiling every-thing," I said. "Listen, Andie, if you hadn't shown up just now, I'd know your secret."

She began yanking all her stuff out of her locker, hurling books to the floor. It looked like the beginning of one of her fits. "I can't believe you asked him," she said over her shoulder. "You should reread our Loyalty Papers."

"I don't see what that has to do with anything," I said. "If you'd stop being so stubborn and just tell me—"

"Look who's being stubborn!" Andie interrupted.

"I should've known better than to talk to you." I slammed my locker extra hard and stomped off. Andie was being totally unrea-sonable, and I wasn't going to put up with it anymore.

Outside, the mountain air cooled me down some, but I was still steaming inside. Andie had never been so rude before, and we'd been friends for ten years—ever since preschool, where we became instant playmates. By first grade we were true-blue best friends, and that's how it had been ever since. We'd even traded favorite teddy bears! Her droopy-eyed Bearie-O had been sitting on *my* bed for six years. My hugging had worn the tan fur off his teddy head. And my beloved Corky sat with a collection of stuffed animals in *her* room.

Maybe it's time to send Bearie-O back, I thought as I opened the jingling door to the Soda Straw. It was a fifties-style diner, with red-vinyl booths, stools lined up at the aluminum counter, and a jukebox in the corner.

Jared sat in a booth toward the back of the restaurant, his

notebook spread out in front of him. My heart did its skipping thing.

He looked up as I slid into the seat opposite him. "Still thirsty?" he asked, his eyes twinkling.

"Sure," I said. When the waitress came around, I ordered a pop.

Jared leaned forward, tapping his pen on the table. "Where were we . . . before, uh—"

"I'm sorry about that," I interrupted. "Thanks for waiting."

"Wouldn't have missed *this* for anything."

I felt my face grow warm. "Doing homework?"

"Just plotting my short story for English. Have you written yours?"

"Not yet." I couldn't tell him my mind had been focused on more important things . . . like getting the truth from him.

"I was worried about you the other night, Holly. You didn't hurt yourself, did you, when you fell?" he asked softly.

"No bruises." *Except to my ego,* I thought. Then the waitress brought my drink in a tall soda glass.

"Just glad I could help." Jared closed his notebook.

Reaching for my pop, I sipped through the straw. "Was I breathing?"

"You were breathing fine."

"Then why did I need mouth-to-mouth resuscitation?"

He smiled. "So . . . you heard?"

Br-ring! The bell on the door jingled as Andie appeared, popping my magical moment. Again!

"Hey," she said, bouncing over to our table.

Couldn't she read the secret message in my eyes? *Get lost. Get lost . . .*

Jared looked surprised. Her timing was unbelievable.

"Hi, I'm Andie Martinez," she said to Jared. "We met when Holly, uh, fainted the other night." She tipped an invisible hat.

"You two must be friends," Jared said, looking at me.

I wanted to say no but told the truth. "We're best friends."

"Can I borrow her again?" Andie asked, pulling on my arm.

"We were just leaving," he said, grinning.

"Oh, were you headed somewhere?" she asked, her voice honey-sweet. Sickeningly sweet.

"Nowhere," I said. *Thanks to you.*

Awkwardly, Jared and I stood up. Looking into his face, I realized we were almost the same height.

Andie grabbed my arm again. "I need to see you, Holly. Alone." She mumbled something to Jared about being sorry and then promptly escorted me out the door and over to a clump of aspen trees. I was ready for a face-off like in ice hockey, only this was a game I wanted to end.

"What do you think you're doing?" I asked.

"I'm ready to talk. I'll fill you in on what happened Friday night."

"Finally! You've come to your senses." I glanced back at the Soda Straw. "So talk."

"This is it—the truth. Jared didn't try to revive you. *Tom* did."

I heard her words, but they made no sense. I wanted to turn her upside-down like a saltshaker to get *all* the answers out.

"Why didn't you tell me in the first place?" I tried to erase the mental picture of Tom leaning over me, his breath on my face.

"You really shouldn't be so curious, Holly."

"Andie, give me a break."

"Figure it out," she said, her nose red from the cold. "We like the same guy."

"What?" I exclaimed. "Jared?"

She nodded.

"No wonder you're following us around everywhere," I said. "It's ridiculous."

"Don't change the subject. There's more," she said, surprisingly eager to tell me everything. "Jared grabbed Tom off the floor—away from you."

Just as I had imagined it in my diary! "Really? What did he say?" I asked.

"His exact words: 'Get up, you total loser.' "

"He said *that?*" *This was too cool!*

"Jared knew you didn't need resuscitating. You were *breathing*. Tom jumped at the chance to get near your lips," she said, studying me.

I wiped my mouth on my coat sleeve, groaning. "I was probably his first romantic moment."

"Knowing Tom, that could be."

"So, you kept that part a big secret—about Jared pulling Tom away—because you didn't want me to know how Jared feels about me. Right?"

She nodded sadly. "It's just that I want Jared to like *me*."

"I should've known."

Andie's lip quivered. "Am I forgiven?"

"If you promise one thing," I said, forging ahead.

"What?"

"Ban the secrets, okay?"

"Sure, no secrets. But I can't promise much else."

I knew what *that* meant. The battle lines had been drawn. Jared was fair game. Not surprisingly, Andie and I had more in common than ever before. Only now instead of trading teddy bears, we were playing tug-of-war over a boy.

Across the street, Jared burst out of the diner and waved to us. He crossed the snow-packed street to catch the city bus. We watched as the doors closed, sighing identical sighs. This was too much!

"I wonder if he needs someone to type his English assignment," Andie said, breaking the spell.

"You wouldn't dare!"

Our eyes locked. Better than anyone else, I knew Andie would do what she wanted. No one could talk her out of it. Not even her best friend.

"Well, gotta go," Andie said. "I've got youth group tonight—with Jared. See you later, Holly." She walked off, her curls bouncing.

I watched her cross the street and go into the drugstore. More angry and confused than ever, I headed for home. I wasn't quite sure what had just happened, but it seemed that I had traded the mini-problem of Andie's secret for a worse problem—the green-eyed monster.

Chapter 4

When I arrived home, Carrie met me at the door. "Hi, Holly," she said, looking up at me with pleading eyes. "Will you French braid my hair?"

I sighed. "Okay, but let me grab a snack first. Where's Mom?" I poured some pop and threw together a peanut butter sandwich.

Carrie sat at the kitchen counter and banged her legs impatiently against the stool. "She'll be down. She already drank her tea. Guess you missed it."

It meant the first half hour of Mom's arrival home each day. She was usually cheerful even after a long day at work.

"How are my angels?" Mom said, coming downstairs a few minutes later. She was wearing the giant elephant slippers I had given her for Christmas.

I hugged her. "You look tired."

"I guess I am a little." She sat on the sofa, handing a yellow flyer to me. "This came in the mail today from church. It's information about a teen choir audition. They'll be traveling."

I clutched my throat—this was one of my dreams! "Do you think I could audition?"

"There's a good chance, honey. I'm sure the director will realize you're *almost* thirteen. Your birthday is so close." Mom flipped a page of the Psalms calendar on the lamp table. My birthday was marked with a red heart. It was going to be the best day of my life, if it ever arrived.

"When are the choir auditions?" I asked.

Carrie pulled me out of the living room, her pink brush and comb in her other hand.

"Next week, Tuesday," Mom said.

"I'm definitely going to try out," I called.

"C'mon, Holly, braid my hair *now*," Carrie said.

I reached for her brush. "Okay, let's do it."

Andie and I had learned how to French braid early in the fall of third grade. We'd visited her aunt's beauty salon one rainy day and had come home informed hairstyle experts.

Peering down at Carrie's thick golden locks, I remembered the first time I'd tried to braid her hair like this. It was over four years ago, on the day Daddy moved out. Carrie was four, and I was eight.

I had helped carry Daddy's shoe boxes out to the car. I knew I shouldn't have tossed them in any old way. Lids and shoes scattered all over the backseat. Some helper I was. Daddy frowned at me for throwing them in. But I didn't care. That's how my insides felt—all scrambled up.

Inside the house, he put his arm around my shoulder. "Holly-Heart, you and Carrie can come visit me at my new place any time." With that, he kissed my sister and me.

"*This* is your place," I said. "And Mom's and mine and Carrie's!" It was weird—no one scolded me for yelling at him.

After Daddy closed the door behind him, I went over to Carrie, who sat huddled beside Mom on the couch. I took her hand. She followed me upstairs to the bathroom sink, where I wet her hair and tried the very first French braid. We could hear Mom's soft sobbing downstairs. *Things will never be the same,* I had thought. It was the worst day of my life.

"Make it tighter, so it won't come out." Carrie's voice pierced my thoughts. I pulled the strands carefully, making a perfect braid.

We didn't see Daddy after that. It frightened me. Things *weren't* the same. Eventually, though, things got better, little by little. Mom didn't cry so much anymore, and Carrie and I managed to live on without Daddy around.

"There you go." I finished off the braid with an elastic tie and a tiny ribbon. "You look fabulous."

Carrie ran downstairs to show Mom. I headed to my room to write the latest developments of my life in my journal. Andie and I were both interested in the same boy. And even though we were years from being able to date, that spelled only one thing: trouble ahead.

During warm-ups in gym on Wednesday, Andie asked if I'd heard about the teen choir tryouts.

"Yep. Sounds exciting," I said.

"Pastor Rob told us about it after the youth service last night." She fluffed her hair, then twisted a strand of it around her finger. A bad sign.

"Jared and I signed up to try out," she said. "Too bad you're too young."

She acted like they were a couple or something—just because they were both auditioning! "I'll be thirteen before the tour," I said.

But I felt left out. What if I wasn't allowed to audition? What if Andie and Jared *did* go on choir tour without me? I couldn't let myself think too hard about it. I just couldn't.

We practiced lay-ups, and Andie missed every time. When my turn came, I dribbled up and banked it in. There were a few advantages to being tall.

"Nice shot, Holly-Bones!" Miss Neff shouted across the court.

There it was—the dreaded nickname. Half the class snickered. It was true. I was bony all right, and there was no hiding it. I tugged on the back of my green gym suit. My stork legs barely filled out the baggy shorts. Mom had darted the suit to fit my waist, but she couldn't do anything about the hideous-looking wide-legged hems.

"Have you had your bacon and eggs today?" a curvaceous classmate joked as she dribbled past me down the court. I watched her move away gracefully. *Someday,* I thought. *Someday I'll look like that.*

"Each of us has a body clock," Mom had explained when we had our first heart-to-heart talk about womanly things. Trouble was, *my* body clock seemed to be losing time.

"By the way," Andie mentioned after showers, "Jared doesn't need someone to type his paper, but he *does* need an accompanist for his choir audition."

I whirled around. "You talked to him?" She was keeping her promise all right—no secrets between us. So how come it hurt when she told me everything?

"After youth group last night, he told me. And . . . he asked me to play the piano for him." Andie swaggered around, emphasizing her excitement. And her shape.

I couldn't compete with a fabulous pianist. Andie was moving in . . . fast!

After school I raced to my room to start the creative writing assignment for English. I titled it, "Love Times Two." It was about fraternal twin sisters who had nothing in common except the love of their lives. I wasn't foolish enough to give them names like Holly and Andie, but *I* knew what the story was based on, and so would Andie and Jared. But the story was safe. After all, it was for Miss W's eyes only.

"Hi ya, Bearie-O," I said, picking up Andie's old teddy bear. "Depending on how things go with your owner, you might not be here much longer. But before you go, you have to hear my side of the story." I began reading my first draft out loud. Halfway through the second page, Mom called from downstairs.

"Holly-Heart, Andie's here."

"Send her up," I called.

Andie dashed up the steps and plopped down on my canopy bed, snuggling with Bearie-O. "Ready to launch a writing career?" she said.

"A what?"

She slid a twenty-dollar bill out of her jeans. "You heard me."

I stared at the money. "What's that for?"

"For you, if you do a good job on my short story."

"You're joking, right?"

"Nope. I have to baby-sit my little brothers tonight. I don't have time to do the assignment."

"Andie, you know I can't do that. It's dishonest."

A frown sat on her forehead. "What'll I do? Miss W will hang me from the ceiling if I don't turn in something."

"Maybe she will, but it still beats lying," I said.

Peeking over my shoulder, she asked, "What's *your* masterpiece about?"

I shoved it safely into a folder. "You'll never know."

"You were reading it to Bearie-O, weren't you?"

"Sure, I tell him everything. Same as you—just not this."

"You're hopeless," she said, pushing the money back into the pocket of her faded jeans.

"Pals forever?" I said with a shy grin.

"Some pal you are." She stood up to leave.

"At least I help keep you honest."

She scrunched up her face and said, "You really are Holly-Heartless." She closed my door with a thud.

Bearie-O took it all in. So did I. After all, I wasn't interfering with *her* first crush. Just refusing to do her homework.

The next morning I hugged Mom before heading off for school. My clean hair smelled like roses under my knit hat. I couldn't wait to turn in my fabulous short story.

At last, English class! I slid into my seat and pulled my fiction assignment out of its shiny red cover. It deserved a top grade, no question about it. Surely Miss Wannamaker would recognize my amazing ability and my destiny . . . to become a famous writer. She might even wonder—as she read and graded the stories in the privacy of her home—from where in the world such a creative plot could have sprung.

"Dear class," she began as usual, "today we shall begin by reading our stories aloud."

I felt faint.

Chapter 5

Miss Wannamaker's eyes skimmed over the desks. For a moment they stopped at mine. I held my breath. This was it, the end of life as I knew it. Someone sneezed behind me. Miss W looked up and miraculously called on Andie. I could breathe again.

Andie went to the front of the room. She opened her folder and began. "Once upon a year . . ."

I heard no more. If Andie picked me to read next, there were only about five minutes between now and a living nightmare! The similarities between my main characters, and the boy they liked, were too obvious. Could I change the story, making it up as I read aloud? Or become too sick to read?

My face burned with embarrassment as I thought how I would feel if I exposed details of my first real crush to the whole world— or at least the Dressel Hills' seventh grade. I couldn't risk it. Not to mention Andie's fury when she discovered *she* was in my story, too.

The class applauded. Andie had done a quick job of it last night. At least she didn't get hung from the ceiling.

I'd rather hang than read, I thought as Andie's eyes penetrated me. I quickly put my head down, avoiding her stare like a firing-squad victim.

Then I heard her say, "Jared Wilkins, you're next."

A truer best friend I could never have, I thought as butterflies played tag in my stomach. I listened intently as Jared read his story. It was unique and well written—about a mad scientist who met Einstein in a dream every night for seven days, and at the end, became not only sane, but wealthy from the secrets passed to him from the old genius himself.

Jared's story impressed me. We had more in common than I thought. I made a mental note to ask him about his writing ambitions.

The applause was loud. Some boys whistled. Miss W frowned.

Jared's eyes scanned the classroom. He caught mine off guard. "I choose Holly Meredith," he announced.

A declaration to the world! Under any other circumstances, I would have been thrilled at his words. But now they felt like a punch in the stomach.

I stumbled to the front of the class. How could I have concocted a stupid story like "Loves Times Two"? I prayed for a miracle. If God could roll back the Red Sea for the Israelites, He could easily get me out of this mess.

I stated my title. Girls giggled; boys slouched.

"Excuse me, Holly, you'll have to speak up, please," Miss W said.

I smiled weakly.

Seconds from now I would reveal my dearest secret to the world, create more conflict with Andie, and maybe upset Jared.

I was well into the second paragraph of my emotion-packed composition when the school secretary tiptoed in. All heads turned toward the door.

"The principal would like to speak with several of the students," she said politely.

Several turned out to be seven—all boys. Jared was one of them. This was it . . . my miracle! Jared would miss my confession.

After the boys shuffled out, I continued reading with as little expression as possible, sneaking glances at Andie, hoping she wasn't paying attention.

Afterward, we passed our stories to the front. Miss W announced tomorrow's grammar quiz. And that was that.

I tried to dodge Andie in the hallway, but she caught up with me. I braced myself for the onslaught.

"What's up?" she asked.

"Not much." I smiled. Who cared if Andie creamed me? At least Jared hadn't heard my creative writing assignment.

"What are you so happy about?" she persisted.

"Let's just say God answers prayer."

"I know *that*. What else?"

I changed the subject. "Hey, looks like you got your story written without my help."

"I was up till midnight doing what you could've done in a few minutes." We waved at Marcia Greene, the brainiest girl in our class, as she passed us in the hall. Andie continued, "That was some fantasy you read today. It doesn't have anything to do with Jared and the two of *us,* does it?"

"Oh, you know how it is. We writers get inspiration from many sources."

"But did you have to describe me down to my toenails?" she asked.

"Hey, I do my best writing when it comes to things I know"— this in my most sophisticated voice.

"Don't you mean *people* you know?" She was accumulating ammunition. "Aren't you worried Jared will hear about it?"

"Who's going to tell him?" I said. "Besides, it's already obvious how he feels about me."

"Yeah, well, there're two sides to every story." She had that familiar glint in her eyes.

We came to our lockers. "Look at that," Andie said. There was a note, all squashed up, stuck in her combination lock.

I peeked over the top of her. "Who's it from?"

She opened it. "From Jared!" she crowed. "He wants me to

practice the audition music with him after school tomorrow. At
his house."

This was bad news. No, it was horrendous.

"He's heard I'm a piano whiz, no doubt," she bragged.

I opened my locker. No notes for me.

"Want to tag along tomorrow?" she asked.

"No, thanks," I mumbled. "I promised Mom I'd watch Carrie
after school."

"Holly." Andie's tone had changed. She sounded hurt. "Can't we
be as close as we were *before* we laid eyes on Jared Wilkins?"

I looked at her. She gazed back with pleading puppy-dog eyes.
I shook my head. "One of us has to back away from him," I said.
"That's what we wrote in the Loyalty Papers: 'If we both like the
same boy, one of us will give him up for the sake of our enduring
friendship.' Can you give Jared up for the sake of our friendship?" I
felt a giant lump in my throat. I didn't want to lose our friendship.
But I didn't want to forget about Jared, either.

Andie grimaced. "It's time to revise those papers again."

"Why?" I asked.

"Might save our friendship, don't you think?"

The seriousness in her voice convinced me. "Okay," I agreed.
"Saturday afternoon. My house."

Luckily the route to my next class took me past the principal's
office. I was dying to know what had happened to the guys who
were pulled out of Miss W's class. I rounded the corner to the principal's office. Three ghost-faced kids sat waiting for the principal.
Remnants of my English-class miracle.

I spotted Tom Sly. "What's this about?" I whispered.

"Someone saw them smoking behind the gym at lunch," he
said.

My heart sank. But I defended my crush. "Jared? Smoking? He
wouldn't do that."

"Grow up, girl. Jared's no saint. Besides, lots of kids smoke . . .
and more." He pulled me over against the wall. "Listen," he said
in my ear, "can you keep a secret?"

"You can trust me," I said. But could I trust him? After all, he had tried to resuscitate me for no reason.

"*I* was the one who caught them smoking." He snickered.

"Who else saw them?" I asked.

"You're looking at him."

"Did Jared catch you spying?"

"No way."

"You're sure it was all of them? When was all this going on?"

"Hey, don't grill me, girl," he said. "During lunch. About twelve fifteen."

The principal opened the door of his office and out came a tall, muscular boy. It was Billy Hill.

"There's one of Jared's smoking buddies now," Tom said.

"Billy Hill doesn't smoke," I insisted. I watched him head down the hall, his shoulders slumped. He was one of the best players on the basketball team, and one of the nicest guys I knew. "Billy looks so helpless," I said as he disappeared from sight.

"Not as helpless as you looked after you conked out the other night."

I glared down at Tom, who was inches shorter than I.

"Your lips were so soft. We oughta try it again," he said.

He was actually admitting it. I gave him a dirty look. "You're disgusting."

"I was your hero. I saved you," he taunted.

"Jared was the *real gentleman,* dragging your face away from mine."

"You can do better than Jared." He cracked his knuckles one after another. "Like me, for instance."

"Don't be weird. We're barely friends." I tossed my head.

"I think you're gorgeous," he said.

Oh great, I thought, *not the class show-off.*

He must've seen me frown, because he blurted out, "Is it true what Miss Neff calls you in gym?"

I got away as fast as I could, but I still heard him calling after me, "Holly-Bones, Holly-Bones . . ."

The nickname stung all the way home. Still, that was nothing compared to the news about Jared. I couldn't wait to tell Andie what I knew, even if she *was* my rival.

I tramped up the snowy steps leading to my house. The porch swing swayed as I bumped past it. Daddy and I used to spend summer nights singing our hearts out on that swing. Sometimes Mom came out to join us, surprising us with iced tea to sip on between songs. But that was light-years ago.

Carrie met me at the front door. "I got an *A* on my math paper," she announced, waving it at me. A happy face smiled at the top.

"Great!" I congratulated her. "How about a snack?" I needed to get Carrie out of my hair so I could talk to Andie.

Once Carrie was safely settled at the table with apple slices, I retreated to the downstairs bathroom with the phone. I dialed Andie's number. Mrs. Martinez answered. No, Andie wasn't home yet. She was still at her piano lesson. "Please tell Andie to call back as soon as she gets home," I said.

I hung up and paced the house, waiting for Andie's call. Finally I flopped in front of the TV beside Carrie.

"Where's Mom?" Carrie asked, snuggling with the cat. Goofey cleaned his little paws.

"She's working late tonight." I threw an afghan over our legs. "I hope she gets home soon. I'm starved." Actually, I wasn't super hungry. I just didn't like it when Mom wasn't home. I guess I worried too much. When she was gone longer than I expected, my brain kicked in with dumb things like *What would happen to Carrie and me if something happened to Mom?*

A half hour later we heard the garage door rumble open. Both of us raced to the windows and rubbed holes in the frost to peek out. Mom was home! Carrie and I ran through the kitchen to greet her.

"What do my darlings want for supper?" Mom asked as we hugged.

"I got your homemade pizzas out. How's that?" I said.

"Sounds wonderful." She removed her shoes on the way upstairs. "I'll make a salad in a minute." Mom looked worn out.

"*I'll* make the salad," I called up to her. She didn't answer. I hurried to preheat the oven. Then I pulled out a head of lettuce and began to shred it.

Carrie dropped a stack of letters on the bar. "Here's the mail."

I moved the mail to the desk in the corner of the kitchen. A blue envelope slipped out of the pile, landing on my foot.

I picked it up. My heart leaped as I saw my name written in bold black script. Who could it be from? The handwriting wasn't familiar at all.

I checked out the return address. There was no name, just a street address and state. California? The last I'd heard, Daddy lived there. My heart began to pound.

The phone rang. I grabbed it off the desk.

"You called?" It was Andie.

"Yes, and it's real important, but I'm stuck in the kitchen now, so I'll call you after supper."

"Can't you tell me quick?"

"I can't talk now."

"Just give me a little hint," Andie begged.

"It's about Jared and—" I looked up to see Mom on her way downstairs. "I promise I'll call back later."

Quickly, I hung up. Excited and nervous all at once, I hid the letter in my pocket. Should I tell Mom? I would read it right after supper, then decide.

A letter from Daddy! This was headline news. Compared to *this,* the info about Jared was "Dear Abby."

Chapter 6

"The pizza smells terrific," Mom said, sitting down at the table. I had drawn the curtains across the bay windows, and the dining room light threw a warm yellow glow across the oak table. The heat vent behind me blew warm air at my feet. Now that Mom was back, it felt like home.

We bowed our heads as Mom prayed over the food. Goofey rubbed playfully against my leg under the table.

"Long day?" I asked after the amen. Mom had pulled her hair back into a ponytail and scrubbed her face clean of makeup. Her eyes looked tired.

"Let's talk about *your* day, Holly-Heart."

"Well, to start with, you'll never guess what happened in English."

"Try me," she said, biting into a slice of pizza.

"I was reading my story about two girls in love with the same guy, when—"

"Now, Holly," she interrupted, "what kind of things are you writing for school assignments these days?"

"It's okay, Mom," I assured her. I could see this wasn't the time to share my English-class miracle with her.

Carrie jumped right in and began talking about her math test. I knew my part of the conversation was probably over. Picking the black olives off my pizza, I tried not to think about the envelope that was poking into my leg through my jeans pocket. I didn't want to tell Mom about the letter. Daddy was probably the last person on earth Mom would want to hear from tonight.

"I saw your principal's wife at the post office this afternoon," Mom said, helping herself to another piece. "Was there some trouble at your school today?"

"Uh, yeah . . . kind of." I wondered how much she knew.

"Please, Holly, choose your friends wisely," she said. It was a definite warning.

"My friends are okay, really."

Carrie piped up. "Whose night is it to clear the table?"

"Yours." I pointed to her. "I made the salad."

"*I* set the table," she hollered.

"Girls, girls, please," Mom said. "Supper was wonderful, Holly-Heart. Do you mind if I go upstairs and rest?"

"Go ahead, Mom. Carrie and I will clean up the mess."

"We'll talk later tonight," she said, leaving the room.

Carrie and I cleared off the table and stacked the plates in the dishwasher. I wiped the crumbs from the counter and picked off the dried and gooey pieces of cheese from the oven rack. Meanwhile, the letter burned in my pocket.

As soon as we finished in the kitchen, I headed for my room. Closing the door behind me, I pulled the letter from my pocket.

I crossed over to my window seat and perched there, holding the letter in my hands. What would it say? Staring at the unfamiliar handwriting, I realized I wasn't ready to open it.

I hadn't seen Daddy since I was a little girl. I'd never known what went wrong between him and Mom, and she never told me. Possibly thought I was too young. All I knew is that one day he had gone away, and after a few months, even his cards and phone calls stopped.

Soon after their divorce we started attending church. That's when Mom became a Christian. And then Carrie and I accepted Jesus, too.

I couldn't remember seeing Mom happier. She was excited about her faith, reading the Bible and talking to the Lord every day. Our new church friends helped us put our lives back together.

Now, after four whole years without Daddy, my world was comfortable again. Safe. Somehow, I had learned to adjust. Praying helped. I honestly believed my prayers would help bring Daddy to Jesus. Wherever he was.

I held the letter—a window to another world. Did I dare open it? I hesitated. No, it was safer the way things were, with Mom and Carrie and me on our own. I started to rip it up. Then I stopped.

Curiosity won out. I tore open the blue envelope and pulled out a handwritten letter.

I could almost hear Daddy's voice as I read.

Dear Holly,

   Perhaps you don't remember me very well. You must be quite a young lady by now. I would like to get to know you and your sister again. How do you feel about that?

   I realize it's been a very long time since you've heard from me. If you find that you are interested in getting better acquainted, perhaps you could come visit me during your spring break. I have remarried, and my wife's name is Saundra, and she has a son named Tyler. They would also love to meet you. Take your time in deciding this. My address is on the front of the envelope if you want to write.

   I am sorry to tell you some sad news about your aunt Marla. She is very sick with cancer. I know she is one of your favorite aunts, and since she is my only sister, I wanted you to hear about this from me.

   I love both my girls. That may be hard for you to believe, but it is true. I would enjoy hearing from you.

                                          Love,
                                          Daddy

I stared at the letter. It seemed like forever since we'd sat on the porch swing, singing into the night. And the books. He'd read tons of them out loud to Carrie and me. At bedtime, after supper, on Sunday afternoons. Tears stung my eyes as I stuffed the letter, blue envelope and all, back into my pocket.

I tiptoed to Mom's bedroom, gently touching the door. Silently it glided open. I peeked in and saw Mom sprawled out on the bed. I crept inside and pulled the comforter over her. *She'll be asleep for a while,* I thought as I wandered downstairs.

Carrie was relaxing on the floor in the family room, drawing. She was surrounded by colored pencils, markers, and several coloring books.

"Carrie, this place is a disaster." I grabbed a handful of markers. "Can't you keep these in the box?"

She ignored me. "Is Mommy asleep?" she asked, playing with the red clip on top of her head. Her blond hair gleamed in the lamplight.

"Mom's napping." I picked up a coloring book and started flipping through it.

"She's tired a lot."

"That's because she works with stressed-out lawyers all day."

"But why is she so sad?" Carrie looked up at me.

"I don't know." I wondered if Mom had heard about Aunt Marla. Maybe Grandma Meredith had called her. We were still close to Daddy's parents in spite of the divorce. Grandma and Grandpa had never really gotten over it. I remembered hearing Grandpa say, "Why is our son leaving his perfectly wonderful family?"

Guess we weren't that wonderful, I thought. Anyway, they still thought of Mom as their daughter. And Carrie and I would always be their granddaughters, no matter what.

The phone rang, and I ran upstairs to the kitchen to answer it.

"Hey, Heartless," Andie said. "How come you didn't call back?"

"Guess I just forgot." I kept my voice low. "Something really major just happened."

"What?"

"It's my dad. I got a letter from him."

"Really? Wow! What did he say?"

I told her all about the letter, how Mom and Carrie didn't know about it yet, and how he wanted to see me again. I even told her about Aunt Marla's cancer.

"That's really sad."

I swallowed the lump in my throat. "Yeah, I know."

There was a short silence. Then I changed the subject. "Did you hear why those guys got called out of class today?" I asked. "Tom says he caught them smoking behind the gym during lunch." I felt strange spreading this kind of news around, but I wanted to see if Andie would defend Jared the way I had.

"That's hard to believe," she said.

"You know what I think?"

"What?"

"I think it's one major mistake . . . or else someone's lying."

"There's one way to track it down." She sounded like a super sleuth. "Let's corner Tom at his locker tomorrow first thing, since he seems to know so much about it."

"Okay," I agreed. I wasn't so sure I wanted to talk to Tom Sly again, but with Andie around he'd never dare call me insulting names.

After I hung up, I pulled the letter from Daddy out of my pocket and folded it neatly. I went back down to the family room and curled up on my favorite spot on the sofa.

"Anything good on TV?" I asked Carrie.

Her eyes were glazed over. There was a Dairy Queen commercial on.

"Huh?" she whispered. I could see that the jazzy advertisement had won out over her drawing.

"Never mind," I murmured, reaching for my red binder containing every possible question on tomorrow's grammar test.

But I couldn't study. Instead, I daydreamed about the contents of Daddy's letter. I held the letter in my hand. It was strange reading his words, seeing his handwriting.

"What's that?" Carrie asked.

"Oh, this?" I smoothed the wrinkles out of the California letter. "It's a letter from . . ."

Fast thinking required.

"Who?"

"From someone you really don't know." It was the truth. "I have to study now," I said, tucking the letter into my notebook.

"Hi again," Mom announced, breezing into the room. She was dressed in her coziest pink robe, still wearing her funky elephant slippers. "Let's talk, honeys," she said, fluffing the couch pillows.

"Turn off the TV," I told Carrie.

"Come sit on my lap," Mom said to her. Goofey jumped on her lap, too. Mom leaned over and gave me a hug. "I've been thinking about someone very special lately," she began. "Do you remember Aunt Marla and Uncle Jack? And your stair-step cousins?"

I nodded. How could we forget the Christmas we spent in Pennsylvania two years ago? We'd chopped down a nine-foot giant of a tree. The tip of it bent under the lofty farmhouse ceiling. Our stair-step cousins—we called them that because each kid was a little older than the next—Carrie, Mom, and I took half the day to decorate the monstrous tree. It was great fun for all of us, except Daddy wasn't there.

"Your aunt Marla is very ill," Mom said softly.

"What's wrong with her?" Carrie asked.

"She hasn't been well for several months," Mom said, moving Carrie to the other side of her lap. "She has cancer. I've just heard from Grandma that some tests show Aunt Marla might not have long to live."

"I know about this," I whispered.

Mom peered at me curiously.

"Would you be surprised if I told you Daddy wrote to tell me about her?" I stared down at my hands, then up at her.

"Not too surprised," she responded. But her eyes said differently. "Grandma told me this news has changed your father."

I watched her face. "What do you mean?"

"Sometimes, when people learn that someone close to them is dying, it alters the way they view life."

"How?" Carrie asked.

"It makes them think more about how *they* want to live."

"I feel sorry for Uncle Jack and my cousins," I said.

"Let's pray that the Lord will give them extra strength during this painful time," Mom said.

We joined hands in prayer for Aunt Marla, Uncle Jack, and my cousins—Stan, Phil, Mark, and Stephanie. I prayed, too, that God would touch Aunt Marla and make her well again. Slowly, tears trickled down my face. The news about Daddy's letter and dear Aunt Marla all in the same day had caught up with me.

Mom wiped away my tears and looked into my eyes. "Do you want to talk?"

"I feel sorry for Aunt Marla. Very sad. And . . ." I drew in a deep breath. "Do you think I'll ever be able to forgive Daddy for leaving?"

"That troubles you, doesn't it, honey?"

I nodded.

"It takes a simple, honest prayer of forgiveness, and remembering each day that Jesus does the same for us when we hurt Him," she said, taking my hand in hers and squeezing it gently.

"I used to miss Dad a lot." I looked away. "Then, when we didn't hear from him anymore, I figured he was gone forever. And now . . ."

"I know, honey." She leaned her head against me. "I know."

"You can read the letter," I offered hesitantly. It seemed like the right thing, letting her see it.

"Maybe another time," she said, her voice sounding stronger.

"Is it okay with you if I write back?"

"Of course. He's your father, Holly—that won't change. If you have a relationship with him, it's because you both want it."

Carrie had been listening to us silently, her eyes wide. "So *that's* what you were hiding before."

Mom intervened. "Maybe Holly will share it with you some other time."

"Did I get a letter, too?" Carrie sounded hurt.

"No," I said. "But Daddy says he wants to get to know you, too. I bet if you write him, he'll write back."

"Will Daddy start writing letters to Mommy?" she asked.

Mom said something that was probably pretty tough to say. "Carrie, love, your daddy is married to another woman now. He has a new family."

Carrie never understood all this divorce stuff. *Who does?* I thought sadly.

"Does he have some new kids?" she asked.

"He has a stepson."

"Will Daddy ever come visit us?" Carrie asked.

"If you see him, most likely it will be at his house," Mom said.

I couldn't believe she offered that. So I sucked in some air and dropped an enormous idea on her. "Dad says he hopes you'll let me fly out to visit him during spring vacation."

Mom sat motionless. "I'll have to think about *that*." She pulled us against her. "Now, don't we have homework tonight?"

While Mom coached Carrie with math flash cards, I tried to study for tomorrow's test. But all I could think about was Daddy. Did I really want to see him again?

My notes on adverbs blurred, so I set aside my English notebook. Other things seemed more important than maintaining my B+ average. Right now, anyway.

A few hours later I was propped up in bed, reading my devotional book without the usual suggestion from Mom. Bearie-O stared straight ahead as I tucked Daddy's letter inside my Bible, marking the verse for the day. It was Psalm 46:1. "God is our refuge and strength, an ever-present help in trouble." How did the writers of my devotional always seem to know the perfect verses to choose . . . for me? For today?

I slipped under my blanket and turned out the lamp beside my bed. Bearie-O fell forward, his face pressed against my lavender comforter. I leaned my elbow against his love-scarred head.

A timid breeze caressed the aspen trees outside my window. Through the window I could see the shadowy form of their bare branches. But try as I might, I couldn't see Daddy's face, his tall frame, or those gentle blue eyes in my imagination. Only the outdated picture on the nightstand came into view, faint in the twilight.

Chapter 7

"Ready for action?" I asked Andie.

She nodded. We stood in the hallway before our first class, plotting our strategy. We had planned to corner Tom Sly and make him talk—whether he wanted to or not.

Andie grabbed my arm and we strutted down the school hallway, on our way to the stakeout.

"Super sleuths to the rescue!" I said.

We giggled.

"Got any spy glasses?" Andie said, peering around, her eyes squinting.

"Here." I handed her an imaginary pair, and she put them on with a flourish.

"Shh, there he is." Andie pointed at Tom, who had just finished unlocking his locker and was removing his jacket. "Remember, *I'll* handle this."

We strolled over and stood silently on either side of him. He slammed his locker shut and turned around. He looked surprised to see us, but he covered it quickly.

"Hello, beauties," he said, eyeing both of us. "How may I assist you today?"

"There's something we need to ask you," Andie said. "We figured you'd be the one to ask, since you know everything about everyone around here." She laid it on thick. Boys fell for her routine, and since it worked, she kept recycling her approach.

"Since you put it that way," he said, "I'd be happy to fill you in. *Both* of you," he said with a meaningful look at me.

He'd tripped over Andie's ridiculous line!

"So," she said, "what were you doing, spying on Jared?"

That's it, Andie, shoot from the hip, I thought.

"Who wants to know?" he said, getting defensive.

"Let's put it this way. It's important," Andie said.

"What do you care?" he asked.

Andie was smart enough not to tell him we hoped to clear his name.

"He attends our church, and we thought—"

"You thought he was a good church boy, right?" he jeered. "Well, *nobody's* perfect."

"Christian kids have a perfect example to follow," I chimed in. "God's Son."

"Oh, really?" he mocked.

Andie pressed on. "I thought I saw you in the gym watching intramurals yesterday during lunch."

"Well, you're wrong."

She turned to me. "Holly, you saw him there, right?"

Come to think of it, I had! He *had* been inside the gym the whole hour. I nodded.

"So maybe you didn't see Jared and those guys smoking at all. Right?"

"Back off. You don't know what you're talking about," Tom shot back.

Bingo! Andie, the genius, had touched a nerve.

And Tom looked guilty. I was beginning to suspect something was amiss.

"Guess we'll just have to get our information from a *reliable* source," Andie said.

"Excuse me, I have a class to catch." He shoved past us.

We looked at each other and grinned knowingly.

"He's hiding something," Andie said, watching as he disappeared into a crowd of students.

"Definitely," I agreed. "Meet me at lunch?"

"Okay." And we were off to first period.

The morning dragged by. I could barely pay attention in history and math. The situations with Daddy and Jared weighed on my mind. I caught myself daydreaming several times.

When lunchtime came, I was nibbling on my roast beef sandwich as Andie came into the cafeteria, carrying her lunch tray piled high.

"Check this out," she said, balancing her tray on the back of a chair. "Jared gave me some of his leftovers. He said something about having timed tests in gym. Guess he didn't wanna pig out before the tests."

"Coach really puts the guys through the ropes on those tests," I said, remembering what I'd heard last year. I slid a piece of lettuce out of my sandwich.

Andie handed over a dish of apple cobbler. "Here, this is for you, from Jared."

"Jared?" I picked up my spoon. My cheeks burned.

"You're blushing," she sang.

He was thinking of me. Still, I worried. "Is this because he thinks I'm too skinny?" I asked.

"Think? Anybody can *see* that. But don't worry. Things'll change soon." She took a bite of her sandwich. "I can't wait till after school. Are you sure you can't come over to Jared's with me for the audition practice?"

I shook my head. I didn't want Andie to know, but I didn't like being around her and Jared at the same time. So I said, "I promised Mom I'd be home on time to be with Carrie."

On the way out of the cafeteria I ran into Jared. His eyes lit up, and he fell into step with me. My knees felt like jelly. Again. But all I could think of was how to bring up the subject of what had happened yesterday.

"Good luck on your timed tests," I said.

"Thanks. Did you get the dessert I gave to Andie?"

"I wasn't sure why you gave it to me."

"What do you mean?"

"I'm self-conscious about being thin." I looked away, embarrassed.

"Holly, I think you're *perfect*. Besides, I like tall, thin girls."

Good! And that left Andie out. She was only four-feet-ten and a little on the chunky side.

"Are you ready to wow them at the choir auditions?" he asked, waving at Marcia Greene as she passed us in the hallway.

"I will be by the end of the week. Mom's going to accompany me." I hoped he'd mention that Andie was accompanying him, but he didn't. Maybe it was no big deal to him.

"Did you hear the choir's going to Southern California?"

My heart jumped. That's where Daddy lived!

"Tough competition, too," he said. "Half the youth group is trying out, and there's only room for thirty."

"Guess we'd better get our voices in shape," I said. But my mind wasn't on the auditions. I wanted to know the truth about what had happened yesterday behind the gym. We stopped near the entrance to the boys' locker room. If I was going to ask, I'd better do it now.

I took a deep breath. "Were you really smoking at the noon hour yesterday?"

"No way!" he said. "It was a complete setup. I was having lunch with my dad—you can't have a better alibi than that. Someone's trying to get me booted off the team, and I know who."

I thought I knew who it was, too. *Tom Sly*. "I bet he's threatened by the competition," I said, "and he doesn't want to share the accolades with some new kid. Totally paranoid."

"My thought exactly," he agreed, smiling. "Hey, where did you get the vocabulary?"

"From books," I said, realizing I was going to be late for home ec. "I devour them."

"Hey, I like that. By the way, I heard you wrote some terrific story for the assignment in English."

"I liked yours a lot. Ever think about becoming a writer?" I couldn't believe how much fun he was to talk to.

"It's one of my life goals," he said. "Did you have someone in mind when you wrote your story?"

Who had told him about "Love Times Two"? Surely not Andie. I played dumb. "What do you mean?" I said.

"Maybe we can talk about it sometime," he said, moving toward the locker room. "See you later," he said over his shoulder, flashing a grin that melted my heart.

"Set the record for the timed tests," I said.

"Thanks." He was about to push open the locker room door when he turned and said, "Holly, I'll call you tonight. How's eight o'clock?"

"Perfect," I said. I waved and took off down the hall before he could see the huge grin on my face. I kept smiling all the way from my locker to the home-ec room. I couldn't wait to tell Andie that Jared was cleared of the smoking charges. But the rest of our talk I planned to keep to myself.

I sprinted into class just in time. I settled onto one of the work-station stools as Mrs. Bowen began giving instructions for the day's culinary creation: lasagna. When she finished, Andie made a mad dash for the sink and started to scrub her hands vigorously.

"Hey," I said, "we're making lasagna, not performing surgery."

Andie looked serious. "Tom manhandled my arm in the hall. He's ticked. Tried to get me to quit asking questions about Jared smoking. I'm scrubbing the contamination off me."

I laughed. "Jared's not even guilty, just like I thought."

"*You* thought? We both knew he was innocent. Did I miss some more important info?" She slipped a green-and-white terry cloth apron around her waist.

"Well, I just so happened to talk to Jared himself," I announced. "He's off the hook. His dad vouched for him, since they had lunch together yesterday. Besides, Jared agreed Tom's paranoid—thinks Jared will show him up on the team. Tom's been number one around here too long. Well, move over, number one, here comes Jared Wilkins!"

The girls at the next station were gawking.

"You must be having a personality change," Andie said, eyeballing me. "I've read about things like this. Crushes do strange things to people."

"My countenance shineth," I said, prancing around, waiting for the noodle water to boil.

"My friend needs help," Andie said to the other girls. "Come along, you poor dear." She led me back to the workstation, pretending I was senile.

We fried up the ground beef and prepared the tomato sauce. After draining the noodles, we started creating the lasagna casserole layer by gooey layer.

"Whoops!" I almost spilled the tomato sauce.

"Watch what you're doing!" Andie warned.

My mind was on Jared. And Daddy's letter. I still couldn't believe my father had written to me and completely bypassed Mom. He'd overlooked the fact that she could easily veto his spring break invitation.

A few minutes before the lasagna was finished baking, a siren rang out in the distance. Because of all the ski slopes in the area, we were used to this sound. But *this* siren, instead of fading away as it climbed into the mountains, grew louder and louder. It sounded like it was heading for our school!

Andie raced to the window. "An ambulance is parked out front," she said.

Mrs. Bowen went to the window, and soon we were all there, squeezing in, trying to see. "Look, Holly!" Andie said, pointing at a woman. "I think Jared's mother is down there."

"How do you know it's her?" I asked.

"I saw her in church last week. What's *she* doing here?" Andie stared at me, her face filled with fear.

Pressing my nose against the icy window, I saw a white stretcher emerge from the ambulance. Two men wheeled it into the gym entrance. "Something terrible has happened," I whispered.

Minutes later, there was more commotion. Now the stretcher carried a tall, brown-haired boy wrapped in wool blankets.

It was Jared. Was he alive?

Mrs. Wilkins stepped inside the ambulance. The doors closed.

My heart sank as the siren sang its mournful song.

Chapter 8

The ambulance was long gone when I backed away from the window. I wandered over to Andie, a huge lump in my throat. She had removed the lasagna from the oven and was staring down at it sorrowfully. The cheese was brown and some of the noodles were burned black around the edges.

"I feel sick," I said, holding my stomach. "And not because of the ruined lasagna."

"I can't believe this!" Andie cried. "We have to find out what happened."

"Someone next period might know something," I said. "Ugh. I'll probably bomb for sure on the English test."

Andie pushed the chairs under the tables. "Who cares about English tests—Jared's been hurt!"

Tears blinded my eyes.

The bell rang as Andie put her arm around me. "Let's go to the rest room. We'll pray in there," she whispered.

I gathered up my books. Andie led the way to the bathroom. She always seemed stronger in situations like this, even when we were little girls. For me, the tears came all too quickly.

"C'mon, let's pray," Andie said, grabbing my hands. I balanced my books on the sink. Andie's prayer was long and fervent. When we opened our eyes she looked up at me, poised for action.

"Here's the deal," she said. "After school we split to my house and get Mom to drive us to the hospital."

"Okay," I said, "but I'll have to call my mom first."

A toilet flushed. The serene moment gushed away. An astonished girl came out of the stall. I guess she'd never heard anyone pray out loud. And in school, too. She turned to stare at us before making her departure. We smiled back.

"I feel better," I said.

"Me too," Andie said. We headed for English in silence.

Settling in for the test, I noticed Tom Sly and Billy Hill were missing. Rats! No chance to ask about Jared and what had happened in gym during timed tests today.

My stomach churned. I felt as prepared for this exam as a computer without a printer. The short time I'd spent studying wasn't going to earn me the kind of grade I was used to getting.

The questions on the test blurred together as I thought about Jared in the hospital.

Hospital. A scary thought. It reminded me of Aunt Marla. She was dying! My favorite aunt. It wasn't fair. She was so cool—always doing terrific things for Carrie and me, spoiling us when we went to visit at Christmas and in the summer.

Just then, Marcia Greene, the smartest kid in class, brushed past me on her way to Miss Wannamaker's desk. She'd already finished the test! Daydreaming was a luxury I couldn't afford. I gripped my pencil and filled in some answers.

After class Andie and I hung around until two boys who had been in gym during last period finished talking to Miss W. Then we headed for them like vultures.

"Hey, Jeff, do you know what happened to Jared Wilkins in gym?" Andie asked.

"Yeah," Jeff Kinney said. "He fell off the trampoline during warm-ups for timed tests."

"He was up really high," Mark Jones added.

"What happened?" I asked.

"He lost his balance and fell. The bone was sticking out of his leg," Mark said.

"I hope he won't have to have surgery," I said.

Mark shrugged. "Beats me."

"C'mon, let's go," Andie said, pulling me away. We turned and headed down the hallway.

I held my books tightly against my chest. "Mark's attitude is sick."

"You got that right."

I didn't get it. "What's the entire male population of the school have against Jared, anyhow?"

"You've seen how new kids get treated around here. We're a bunch of snobs," Andie said.

"But the guys must be *jealous* of Jared. For once here's a guy who has more than muscles and good looks. He's got smarts, too."

Andie nodded, then gave me a fierce look. "I have a feeling Tom Sly knows something about Jared's accident." She jammed her books into her locker. "And I intend to find out what."

At Andie's house, the smell of brownies lured us into the kitchen. Mrs. Martinez looked similar to Andie, with dark curly hair and sparkling eyes. "Brownies, girls?" she asked.

We plopped down at the bar while Mrs. Martinez cut two large pieces.

"Mom, there's been an emergency at school," Andie blurted out. "Can you take us to the hospital?"

"What's wrong?" her mother asked, pouring a glass of milk.

I spoke up. "We want to go see Jared Wilkins. He's been hurt."

"What happened?"

We explained what we knew of the accident, and Mrs. Martinez listened sympathetically. But at the end she shook her head. "I think the two of you should stay put and pray for him instead. I doubt you could see him now anyway," she said.

Andie's curly-haired twin brothers bounced into the kitchen. Seeing the treats, they tripped over each other to get to us.

"Me get tweet?" one of the two-year-olds asked.

"Yes, Chris. You get treat," Andie said, pulling the pan of brownies closer. She cut a small piece for each of them. Chris and Jon jammed the brownies into their mouths and went running around the kitchen. Mrs. Martinez followed them to make sure they wouldn't make a mess of things.

"Still want to get together tomorrow?" Andie asked.

"What for?" I'd completely spaced out.

"The Loyalty Papers, remember?" Andie said. "We're going to revise them. And now that I see how much we both care for Jared, I think it's urgent."

Andie's comment confused me. I thought things were actually improving between us.

Just then I remembered something else. "I forgot to call Mom." I hurried to the wall phone and punched in the number for her office. She answered almost immediately.

"Mom? I'm at Andie's. I didn't go right home because there's been an accident. . . . A friend of mine was hurt at school."

There was a pause. Then Mom, sounding quite displeased, said, "Holly, your sister's been home alone all this time. Usually you're more responsible than this."

"But I *had* to come straight to Andie's house," I said, defending myself.

She didn't buy it. "You should've called. I'll phone Carrie to let her know you're on your way."

She hadn't even asked about the accident. All she cared about was Carrie, who was perfectly able to take care of herself. Frustrated,

I said, "I don't need a lecture about this, Mom. I really don't." I hung up without saying good-bye.

♥ ♥ ♥

When I arrived home, Carrie was watching cartoons. "How was your test today?" she asked.

"Probably flunked it," I told her. "Where's Mom?"

"She's home now, and boy, are you in trouble."

"Why?" I slouched into the arms of my favorite sofa.

"Something about your disrespectful back talk." Carrie was sounding like a grown-up. Too big for her britches.

"Guess I should go up and apologize," I complained. I stood and trudged up the stairs. Mom's bedroom door was closed. I knocked and waited.

"Come in," she said.

Not daring to look at her, I plodded over to the bed and sat down. The first few seconds were tense. Then she put her arm around me. "I love you, Holly-Heart, you know that."

"Mom?"

"Yes, honey?"

"It's getting harder to be . . ." I didn't know how to tell her that I was feeling more and more rebellious—at least sometimes. "To be obedient."

She smiled knowingly. "There are hundreds of changes occurring in your body right now. Your emotions will fluctuate, swing up and down. And most of the time, you won't understand why you're feeling the way you are."

"So this will happen more and more?"

"It's part of becoming a woman," she said.

I picked up the rose-colored sachet pillow on her bed. Hugging it against my flat chest, I breathed in its sweet fragrance. "I was very sassy on the phone. I'm sorry, Mom."

"I forgive you, honey. We all have moments like that. Try harder next time."

I sighed, feeling exhausted. "You won't believe what happened at school today." From then on it was like opening a can of soda. My words poured out. I could always talk to Mom. The fiery rebellion was gone.

♥ ♥ ♥

After supper we got a call from the church prayer chain. The actual facts: Jared was stable, but he was suffering some momentary amnesia from having struck his head on the hard gym floor. As for his leg, it would be in traction until they operated. Then he'd be in a cast for six weeks or so.

So much for basketball this season, I thought. I was disappointed for him. And I was dying to see him.

"When can I visit him?" I asked Mom while I washed the pans. Carrie was drying, and Mom was putting away the leftovers.

"We'll have to call the hospital and see about visiting," Mom said.

Carrie teased, "Maybe his amnesia wiped *you* out of his memory forever."

"No chance," I said, flicking her with soapsuds. "I'm unforgettable."

When the phone rang, Mom answered it. We could tell by Mom's responses that the call was from Grandma Meredith. Carrie and I looked at each other, then watched Mom anxiously. Her smile faded, and the lines in her forehead deepened as she listened. Finally she said, "I can't leave the girls, but I wish I could help in some way." She sat down slowly.

There was a long pause.

Mom leaned her blond head against her hand. When she spoke, it was barely a whisper. "Please tell Jack and the children we're praying." Hesitantly, she beeped off the cordless phone.

Carrie and I stood like statues as Mom searched for a tissue in her pocket. Neither of us dared speak.

"Darlings," Mom began slowly, "Aunt Marla's not doing well. The docs think she has only a few weeks left. . . ." Her voice broke.

We knew.

Later that evening, when we'd rehashed the news of Aunt Marla's cancer, Mom and I made a feeble attempt to rehearse my audition piece for the youth choir. Mom made tons of errors, and it was obvious her heart wasn't in it.

Afterward, I read out loud to Bearie-O in my bed. Having him close reminded me of the special friendship Andie and I had shared all these years. But lately things were so up and down between us. Like a yo-yo, or worse.

I continued reading, but my concentration was messed up. Uncle Jack and my cousins kept creeping into the mystery novel I struggled to read. What would they do if Aunt Marla died? My worries wandered in and out of the story.

Daddy strolled across chapter three. What about a response to the spring break question?

Jared called to me from chapter five. His leg had to be amputated.

In chapter six, Andie demanded a major overhaul of our Loyalty Papers.

Halfway through chapter eight, Carrie threatened to whack off her long hair. She was sick of my sarcastic remarks and didn't want to look like her big sister anymore.

It was close to midnight when all of them finally faded away. And I fell into a restless sleep.

Chapter 9

The next morning I slept till nearly nine o'clock. Mom was relaxing with the paper when I wandered downstairs. "Good morning, Holly-Heart," she said, glancing up from the sofa. "Ready for breakfast?"

"Definitely." I was starving as usual. So Mom fixed a platter full of pancakes with scrambled eggs on the side, then sat down with me to chat.

"Can I make snickerdoodle cookies after lunch?" I asked. "Andie's coming over later. She wants to revise our Loyalty Papers, and I want to make sure she's in a good mood, you know."

"Sounds like you're going to bribe her." Mom's eyes twinkled.

"Not really." Quickly, I changed the subject before too many questions were asked. "Where's Carrie?" I asked, finishing off my last bite of eggs.

"Watching TV," Mom said. She sipped her peppermint tea, her hands wrapped around the mug to warm them.

"Did Carrie say anything to you about cutting her hair?"

A shocked expression crossed Mom's face. "No . . . this is the first I've heard of such a thing. Why do you ask?"

"Just checking," I said, recalling the parade of problems dancing across the pages of my book last night. But the problem I cared about most was Jared Wilkins.

Thankfully, Mom didn't probe any further about Carrie chopping off her hair. After we finished cleaning up the kitchen—and Mom was safely out of the room—I dashed for the phone and called Andie.

"Hi." She sounded alert and ready for action.

"Whatcha' doing?"

"This is so cool, Holly. Listen—I just found out Jared's parents have agreed to let me bring my keyboard to his hospital room."

"What for?" I asked but guessed what she was up to.

"The youth choir director wants to audition him at the hospital."

There was a long silence while I groped for something to say. Andie had one-upped me, and I knew it.

"Sounds . . . well, interesting," I said at last. The old green-eyed monster was poking its nose into my business again. "He must really want Jared in the choir."

"Good tenors are hard to find," she said.

"What about Jared's amnesia?"

"It's simple. He doesn't remember anything that happened yesterday."

"Nothing?" I thought about the phone call he'd promised to me. "What about the fall off the tramp?"

"Nope, not even that."

"How do you know all this stuff?" I asked.

"My mom and his mom talked."

Real sweet, I thought.

"When are you going to practice the song with him?" I was dying for her to ask me to go along.

"Tomorrow afternoon. He's supposed to rest during the morning. Which is probably a good idea. He's in traction, you know."

Her know-it-all attitude irritated me, but I said, "Still coming over today?"

"Yep. We've got major work to do on the Loyalty Papers, remember?"

Of course I remembered, but I secretly hoped *she* had forgotten. "Are you sure you want to revise them?" I asked.

"Sure do! Got 'em ready?"

"Uh-huh," I said, giving in. "The Loyalty Papers await. And I'm making snickerdoodles after lunch. Wanna help?"

Andie laughed. "I'll help by making them disappear."

"Fabulous," I said, and we hung up.

But I was worried about revising the Loyalty Papers. Really worried. I felt sure that the restructuring of our original documents—made between friends—might cause another major argument, especially since Andie and I were both crushing on Jared.

Upstairs, I showered, then dressed in my most comfortable jeans and my favorite old T-shirt. Counting the days till my birthday was priority on my morning agenda. In giant numbers I wrote *22 days* on the scrap paper stuck to my bulletin board. The day still seemed too far away to plan my big bash.

After lunch I mixed together some flour, cream of tartar, soda, and salt. Then I stirred in soft butter, sugar, and eggs.

Andie arrived just as I began rolling the dough into walnut-sized balls. "Mmm, yum!" she said, eyeing the cookie sheet.

"They'll be ready to eat in about eight minutes," I said. "Want some apple juice while we wait?"

"Thanks," Andie said, watching as I poured the cold juice.

I flicked on the oven light, and we watched the snickerdoodles do their thing—puffing up at first, then flattening out, leaving a crinkled top. After they were done, we let them cool. Then, piling the cookies high on a plate, we headed for my room with plenty of sweet treats to munch on.

Andie plopped down on a corner of my bed. "Ready to revamp the Loyalty Papers?"

I was glad she couldn't see my scrunched-up face as I sorted through my dresser drawer, searching for the precious papers. Finally I spied them in the legal documents holder Mom had given us years ago. The folder was a reject from the law firm where she worked as a paralegal.

Overly eager, Andie set the plate of cookies in the middle of the bed and began to shuffle through our papers. As she read, she reached for a snickerdoodle cookie.

I, on the other hand, sat on the opposite side of the bed and nibbled on my cookie, watching her face for any warning signs.

She frowned. I gulped.

"Look here," she said. "We really missed it on *this* paragraph." She pointed to the page, clearing her throat like the principal getting the kids' attention in assembly. "Page three, paragraph seven." She paused. "This is really absurd, Holly."

"What is?" I peered down at the page between us.

"This dumb idea . . . that one of us has to back away from a boy if the other person likes him, too."

"Well, we wrote that two years ago, before guys were even a blip on our radar. Maybe we should add something about whoever likes the guy *first* gets dibs," I suggested.

"Oh no, you don't. That'll never work. Besides, how could we know for sure who liked him first?" She flipped through the next two pages. "Were we so naïve to think we'd never attract the same boy?"

"Well, look at it this way," I said, trying to remain calm. "Since we're both so different—in looks, in personality, in the way we think—maybe we were on to something when we wrote that part."

She stood up, brushing the cookie crumbs onto the floor. "I'm sick of your logic, Holly. Maybe we should talk about this some other time, when you're thinking clearly."

"Wait!" I followed her out of the room. "What's the big deal? Do we really have to do this now? It's not like either of us can actually date Jared yet."

She glared at me. "Don't be dense. Liking the same guy is still a huge problem, and you know it." She was in the hallway now, heading for the stairs.

"Where are you going?"

"Home—to practice Jared's audition music. See you, Holly. Thanks for the snickerdoodles."

A lot of good the snickerdoodles did. Back in my bedroom, I stared glumly at the plate. One lone cookie was left. I picked it up and ate it. Without licking my fingers, I shuffled the pages of our Loyalty Papers. Who cared if they got messy. They were useless now.

At last, I set off for the lower-level family room. There, I joined Carrie for a DVD cartoon, trying to get both Andie and Jared off my mind. But nothing could stop me from thinking about Jared—hurt and possibly alone—in a hospital room.

After the cartoon, I purposely grabbed Mom's attention by juggling four cookies at a time. When I quit showing off, the kitchen floor was a crumby mess. Goofey licked up the sweet crumbs.

"Something's *really* troubling you, Holly," Mom said, handing over the broom to me. "You're not yourself."

"It's Jared. No . . . it's Andie. She and I both like him. And now *everything's* a disaster."

Mom thought a moment. Then she said, "Why can't the three of you be friends?" She said it so innocently, I thought surely she must be joking.

"It doesn't work that way."

"Well, enlighten me," she said, rinsing out a rag for me to wash the spots off the floor.

I got down on the floor, scrubbing up the mess I'd made. "I think Jared wants me to be his girlfriend, and Andie's totally freaked out about it." I looked up at her from all fours.

"Wait a minute—be his girlfriend? And how do you see that working when you can't date?"

"We wouldn't be dating, Mom." This was hopeless. "It just means we'd being hanging out together at school and church and, well, you know. Places we're already going anyway." I got up and tossed the dirty rag into the sink.

Mom was studying me. Hard. "Hang out, you say?"

"Right."

"I see," she said. But of course she didn't. The days when Mom was a teen were long past.

Later in the afternoon Carrie and I tagged along when Mom went grocery shopping. At the check-out, we bagged the food for her, racing to see who could get the most in each bag.

"Oops, this isn't working," Carrie said, bending over to retrieve one of the grocery sacks. Two boxes of microwave popcorn tumbled out.

"Look out!" I cried as two oranges also found their freedom, rolling under the counter.

The clerk announced the grand total, casting a peculiar look and a frown at Mom.

"Big mistake bringing *you* along," I told Carrie as I reached around the back of the counter, groping for the oranges.

"Mom! Holly's being a pain," Carrie whined.

Mom looked frazzled with stress. "Please go and wait in the car." She dangled the car keys in my face.

"Send Carrie. This is all her fault." I glared at my sister.

"I want *you* to go now," Mom said again.

"Perfect," I whispered.

Outside in the cold car, I turned on the ignition. Grandpa Meredith had let me start his car last summer when they came to visit. I'd even backed it in and out of the driveway dozens of times.

Shivering, I stayed seated in the driver's seat and turned on the heater full blast. The lights of the village began to twinkle on as dusk approached. Mom had no right to send me out here this way. What had I done to deserve such treatment?

Pulling a tablet out of the glove compartment, I began to write:

Dear Daddy. It was time for an answer to his invitation. Way past time.

When I saw Mom and Carrie coming toward the car with the groceries, I scrambled over the front seat and sat in the back, hiding the half-written note in my coat pocket.

Mom doesn't need to know about this, I thought, feeling sneaky and good about my secret.

The next day was Sunday. Once again, I had trouble concentrating on the sermon. Andie, who was sitting across from us, next to her parents, looked much too confident. Her brunette hair, perfectly in place, framed her round face. Oh, I could just imagine her playing the piano for Jared, their eyes catching snatches of each other's unspoken adoration. It was unbearable, so I tried my best to block out those kinds of thoughts.

In my Bible, I underlined the pastor's text with a red pen. Carrie cozied up to Mom in the pew, and I wanted to be somewhere else. Somewhere like the Dressel Hills Hospital, maybe in traction in the same room as Jared.

I knew there was only one reason why Andie hadn't asked me to go with her to Jared's audition: She wanted all his attention. Some best friend she'd turned out to be.

Just then Carrie peeked around Mom in the pew and flashed me a less-than-angelic grin. Her missing teeth completed the impish look.

Most of the time I loved Carrie, but sometimes I felt that Mom spoiled her rotten. Getting away from my little sister for a full week during spring break was a fabulous thought. And if I got permission to go to California to visit Daddy, I'd be leaving Andie behind for a while. It seemed, now that I thought of it, there was only one person I would miss at all. Jared.

When we arrived home and sat down to dinner, the food tasted blah. Usually I can't get enough baked chicken and onions, but Jared was on my mind and in my heart.

Later, after the dishes were stacked in the dishwasher, Mom grabbed a note pad and sat at the table. "Let's plan your birthday party, Holly-Heart."

I glanced at the calendar. "It's still too far away."

"Oh, but the days are flying by," she said, clicking the pen. "How many friends do you want to invite?"

I paused to count. "I can think of at least ten."

Her eyebrows rose high above her eyes. "Well, I was thinking more in terms of seven. Including you, that's eight. An even number is always nice . . . for games and things."

Then I said something I shouldn't have said. And in a catty sort of way. "Who cares about even numbers?"

Mom sighed. "Maybe we should talk about this later." She was exasperated with me, and how could I blame her? I'd given her a tough time on purpose.

"Why don't we just forget about this birthday? Maybe turning fourteen next year will be better!" I stormed out of the kitchen, certain that Andie was doing her musical thing right now at the hospital with Jared. More than anything, I wanted to be there. Not *here*.

Upstairs, I curled up in my window seat and wrote the remainder of my letter to Daddy. I tried to imagine what his new life was like. This, after all, was *his* house. He and Mom had fallen in love with Colorado. They'd moved from Pennsylvania after getting married, making a life together in this skier's paradise. And what a skier Daddy was! He even gave me skiing lessons, starting when I was five. After a few practice runs, the sport was like breathing. Daddy said I was a natural.

Surely his new life wasn't half as good as it had been here with us. And what about this new stepson of his? Somewhere out there I had a ninc-year-old stepbrother. How weird was that?

A knock on the door interrupted my thoughts. Mom poked her head in the door. "Holly-Heart, Andie's on the phone."

My heart skipped a beat. *News about Jared! Could it be?*

"I'll get it up here," I said, coming out of my room and going to the hall phone. Mom wouldn't allow either of us girls to have a phone in our room. "Hello?"

"Hey, Heartless, still speaking to me?"

"Why shouldn't I be? *You* were the one who stormed out of here yesterday."

"Well . . . Jared had his audition."

"How was it?"

"Jared's voice is as fine as he is."

"I *know* that. How's Jared *feeling*?"

"Feeling? Well, uh, I know you won't believe this, but our hands touched today, when no one was watching. Is that what you mean?"

"You are so not telling the truth," I said.

"Hang on, I'll get Jared to tell you himself."

"You're disgusting, Andie," I yelled. "And you call yourself my best friend? I'm tearing up the Loyalty Papers. They don't mean anything to you anymore."

"Holly, what's going on?" she said, acting innocent.

"You're ruining my life."

"What's happened to you? You've changed so much. Honestly, I thought you'd be happy for me . . . for us." She was pouring it on like honey, though her words were anything but sweet.

"You want me to congratulate you for stealing away Jared's affections?" I yanked at my shoestrings.

"But you weren't really—"

"This is truly the end of our friendship," I said, kicking my tennis shoes down the hall.

"You'll change your mind if you want to be on choir tour."

"Meaning what?"

"The director told us—Jared and me—about the theme for the tour. It's unity. 'Our hearts in one accord,' Mr. Keller said. You know—getting along. Which doesn't allow for fighting over boys or anything else."

I'd had it with her preaching. "If *you* don't make it into the choir, getting along will be the easiest thing in the world," I said, a bit surprised at how sarcastic my words sounded. And how easy it was to say them.

"I'm *in*—the choir, that is," she announced with way too much pride.

"How do you know? Auditions aren't till Tuesday."

"Mr. Keller wants *me* no matter what. If there are too many sopranos, he'll use me as an accompanist at the piano." Downright haughty, that's how she sounded. "Uh, excuse me, Holly. Jared's calling. They're bringing a tray up from the cafeteria for me. I've got a dinner date with You-Know-Who. Bye."

Andie's words stung. Hanging up the phone, I stumbled back to my room. I fell into bed and stared at the underside of my canopy, feeling terribly cheated. My best friend had trespassed— on my heart.

Chapter 10

I don't know how long I stared at the canopy, but soon I had the urge to grab Bearie-O and throw him across the room. I didn't need him reminding me of Andie. Not anymore. So I tossed him off my bed.

Mom called me downstairs to play caroms with her and Carrie. I played even though I didn't feel like it. "Please, will you take me to see Jared?" I begged Mom when Carrie's turn came around.

Then, when it was Mom's turn, she placed the white shooter on the board, aimed, and shot. "I don't know the family very well," she said.

"Why couldn't you get to know Mrs. Wilkins?" I pleaded as two of my green caroms slid into a side pocket. "Please, Mom?"

It took three more turns and saying "please" at least five more times before Mom even considered taking me. Finally, after I talked about how the Wilkins family attended our church and Jared was in the youth group, she agreed to drive to the hospital on the way to evening church.

"We'll stop there briefly," Mom said.

Briefly, momentarily . . . whatever. I was beyond thrilled.

Dressel Hills Hospital was small but well decorated. Cozy

couches and chairs were scattered around the waiting area. Potted palms and spider plants gave it a comfortable feeling. Oil paintings of local spots—mountains, waterfalls, and meadows—were spotlighted on the wall.

Mom asked for Jared's room number at the receptionist's desk. As we walked down a long, narrow hall, I became more nervous with every step. What would I say to Jared? Would Andie still be hanging around?

We rounded a corner, and I spotted Mrs. Wilkins chatting with Andie's mother in the waiting area near room 204—Jared's. So Andie *was* here. Mom shot me a glance. I nodded and pointed back at her. I wanted *her* to make the necessary introductions.

Somehow, I don't know how, I managed to smile and shake hands with Mrs. Wilkins, a small woman with blue eyes and a smile just like Jared's. "Why don't you go on in and see Jared?" she said. "Andie's with him."

"Are you sure it's all right?" I asked.

"Well, to tell the truth, he might already be sleeping," Mrs. Wilkins said. "He just had some medication for pain."

Jared in pain? My heart jumped. I wandered over to his room.

Pausing at the doorway, I spied Andie. She sat curled up in a chair, close to Jared's hospital bed, like she was monitoring his every breath. He was propped up with a zillion pillows, his right leg supported by a pulley system above the bed.

Andie looked up at that moment. "Holly!" she said in her most charming voice. "Come right in."

I approached the bed just as Jared let out a tiny, high-pitched snort. He was snoring.

Andie began to explain. "He just had some pain medication."

"I know. His mom already told me." I found another chair and pulled it over next to Andie's and sat down. A long silence settled over the room. I was boiling inside.

At last, I blurted out what I was thinking. I just couldn't hold in my thoughts any longer. "Look, Andie," I said, leaning toward her. "Jared likes *me*, I know he does."

She crossed her chubby little legs. "Maybe he did once, but this is *now*," she said. "Whatever you had, or thought you had, well, it's over. You're history."

This was beyond my worst nightmare! Jared interested in Andie? He had said he liked tall, skinny girls. Andie was anything but that.

"I know you're wrong," I argued. "You must've been dreaming—wishing it were true—when you thought he touched your hand."

"Do you want a written statement?" She leaned closer to Jared, her eyes scanning the rings and pulleys that held his fractured leg in place. "He wants me to watch over him while he sleeps."

"Oh, puh-lease." I rolled my eyes. "He doesn't need mothering, Andie. He's got a real mother for that." Then I lit into her. "You're the poorest excuse I know for a best friend."

"What about you? You didn't back away when you knew how much I liked him, did you?"

"That's different," I managed to say. "He was the first boy to accept me as I am."

"You mean skin and bones?"

A low blow! Something snapped inside me. "That's it," I shouted. "You'll never see our Loyalty Papers again."

"Whatever!" She fluffed her dark locks. "You don't know what you're saying. Your life's a big, fat zero without me."

"That's what you think," I growled. "Why don't *you* go home and leave me alone with Jared?"

"If I'm not here when he wakes up—well, I just don't know what he'd do. We have a very special bond," she said in her sickening-sweet voice.

"Well, he must be desperate, then. Just pack up your precious keyboard and get out of here."

Mom and Mrs. Wilkins poked their heads in the doorway. Mom looked puzzled. "Is everything all right?"

"Not really," I said. "Andie was just leaving."

Mom caught on quickly. "Girls, can you solve your problems elsewhere?" Then she motioned to me. I got up reluctantly and started toward her.

Jared woke up. "I . . . I heard voices," he said.

Andie jumped up to reassure him. "It was nothing. Nothing at all."

Jared's father came in, carrying a white paper cup brimming with hot coffee. He was good-looking, too, with blond hair and a mustache. He pulled a chair over next to the bed. "Thanks, girls, for dropping by to visit our son," he said.

"Girls?" Jared said sleepily. "Where?"

Mom's firm touch on my arm signaled the end of my visit. "It was nice to meet you," she said to Jared's parents. "We'll be sure to mention Jared during the prayer requests at the service tonight."

We smiled and shook hands all around. Then I headed down the hall with my family. Carrie held Mom's hand, and I moped behind. I felt like picking a fight. With Andie, with Mom—with anyone in sight.

"What's come over you?" Mom asked as we drove to church in the snowy stillness.

I shrugged. "You wouldn't understand."

"Holly?" she said in her warning voice, which meant, *You'd better shape up—or else.*

"Don't you remember?" I said. "It's all part of becoming a young woman. Isn't that what you said?"

"I've never seen you so rude."

"For as long as I live, I never want to see Andrea Martinez again," I announced as we pulled into the parking lot of the church. "Never!"

♥ ♥ ♥

Later, when we arrived at home after the short service, a strange sense of delight swept over me as I slammed the car door and stomped into the house. Like an arrow, I darted straight to my room. There, I pulled the Loyalty Papers from the special folder. I looked at them—fondly for a moment—then I began to rip each page in two. I scattered the pieces all over the floor. Finally I slam-dunked Bearie-O into the trash can, head first.

This was it. My friendship with Andrea Martinez was over!

Chapter 11

Tuesday afternoon—choir auditions! To sing with a traveling group had always been one of my dreams. But as I sat waiting in the hallway leading to the choir room at church, I wasn't so sure my dream was going to come true. The place was crammed with guys and girls. They lined the hallway, leaning against the plaque-covered wall. They sat cross-legged on the floor, each reviewing last-minute dynamics and phrasing.

Mom and I were together. She sat calmly waiting for my audition while she read a novel. Me? I pulled and twisted my long hair.

"We've practiced over twenty times," I told Alissa Morgan, the girl ahead of me, when she asked.

"That's probably a good idea by the looks of things." She stood on her tiptoes, searching for someone.

"Are all these kids in the church youth group?" I asked.

"Yep." She spotted her friend and called, "Hey, Danny, over here."

A tan-faced boy with reddish hair bounded over to us.

"How's it going in there?" Alissa's head bobbed toward the auditioning room.

"Fierce competition," Danny Myers said. "How are *you* doing? Nervous?" He touched her shoulder.

"I'll be glad when this day's over," she admitted.

"Hey, relax, you'll make it." Then, spying me, he said, "I remember you. Holly Meredith, right?"

I nodded.

"Your mom makes the best cookies ever. Snickersomething."

I smiled. "That's close. They're snickerdoodles, and they're *my* favorite, too."

He nodded. "She brought some to our Christmas bake sale. That's when I first met you and your sister. You two look so much alike."

"The tall and the short of it," I replied.

"How tall are you, anyway?" Alissa asked.

"Almost five eight." I beamed down at her.

Danny grinned. "One more inch, and you'll catch me." He had a comfortable way about him.

"Wanna get some water before you try out?" he asked Alissa.

"Good idea. My throat's so dry," she said. Danny walked with her down the hall to the water fountain.

I sighed. *Some day, a boy will treat me like that.*

Thirty minutes dragged by. A heaviness hung in the air. One girl came out of the choir room in tears. Next came a boy, smiling. He jumped up and down all the way to the end of the hallway, exclaiming, "Yes . . . so cool!"

"*He's* confident," Mom said, looking up from her book.

An older girl poked her head out the choir room. "Holly Meredith, you're next."

With as much courage as possible, I entered the choir room. I did fine on the sightsinging and my prepared piece . . . but the arpeggios. Gulp!

On the way home, Mom chattered with excitement. "You sang like an angel, Holly-Heart."

Maybe she thought so, but I knew better.

When I wrote the heading in my journal for the day it was:

Tuesday—An Alto's Nightmare. But I survived it. It was the only mention I made of my pitiful audition. The rest of the diary entry was taken up with how sweetly Danny Myers treated Alissa Morgan. I couldn't remember seeing them together before. But it wasn't any surprise, because I hadn't started attending youth group yet.

To be honest, it felt weird going this long without talking to Andie. I pulled Bearie-O out of the trash and told *him* all about my audition. He was a good listener. Never talked back. Never threw junk out of his locker, making piles in the hall. Never moved in on a friend's crush, or called me stupid nicknames, like Heartless. Even though he really belonged to Andie, after six years I thought of him as mine. I had a right to.

Wednesday morning arrived. Eighteen days to thrilling thirteen! I wrote the number on my bulletin board. The days were crawling by like snails.

Before Mom left for work, I asked her about my party. "Can we plan it tonight?"

"After school."

"Perfect," I said, chewing on the ends of my hair.

"You'll split your ends," Mom said.

I wanted to say *who cares?* but bit my tongue.

That afternoon following gym class, Andie bragged about Jared's musical genius to the girls in the locker room. The only good thing about gym today was Miss Neff didn't call me Holly-Bones. A first.

Maybe she noticed some development that I missed, I thought, standing sideways at the mirror.

My hair was still damp from a quick shower when I reached for my history book and slammed my locker. Racing toward history class, I accidentally bumped into Danny Myers in the hallway.

"Oh, excuse me," I said as he bent down and helped me pick up my books.

"Holly Meredith, right? Five eight? Look-alike little sis? Bookworm mother, right? Favorite cookie—snickerdoodles?"

"You're a walking, breathing computer chip, aren't you?"

He stopped, took a long look at me, and smiled. "That's my specialty—memory. I work at it."

I straightened my books. "It shows."

"See you at youth group next Tuesday?"

"When I'm thirteen I'll start going. A few weeks to go."

"Really?" There was that smile. "They should change those rules." And he was off in the opposite direction.

For a nanosecond I actually forgot about Jared Wilkins.

In history class, I doodled on my notebook. How long before my letter to Daddy arrived at his home in California? I had mailed it on the way to school this morning. Mom was still in the dark about what I'd decided, of course. Best that way.

The teacher droned on about the decisive battle in the Norman conquest of England. I daydreamed through class. I figured I could catch up by reading the account of the skirmish tonight.

After history, I caught up with Billy Hill heading for his locker. "Wait up," I called.

"Hey," he said, smiling.

"Any news about Jared?" I asked.

"He had his surgery Monday night. They put a rod in his tibia bone."

"Which one's that?"

He pointed to his own leg. "Shinbone."

"Is he in a cast yet?"

He nodded.

"For how long?"

"About six weeks. Bummer, huh?"

"So he'll get the cast off by spring break?"

He scratched his head. "Yeah, it should be off by then." He

looked serious. "The worst thing about this whole mess is it should never have happened."

"What do you mean?"

He glanced up the hallway, like he had to check out the turf. "Several guys were spotting Jared on the tramp before he fell. One of them was Tom Sly. When Jared began to lose balance, Tom backed away. On purpose."

This was rotten. I could hardly believe it.

But there was more. "Jared and Tom had been hassling each other a lot during practice games after school lately."

"So . . . do you think Tom wanted Jared to get hurt?"

"Who knows." He ran his fingers through his hair. "Thing is, there was major hostility between them. You heard about the smoking thing Tom tried to pull on Jared and me, didn't you?"

I nodded. "Too weird."

I stopped with Billy at his locker. There was a note taped to the outside. "Looks like a note from the coach," he said.

I peered over his shoulder as he read it. "Late practice?"

"Yeah. Things are real tough without Jared around. The team needs him."

"Looks like Tom's revenge is messing things up for all of you."

"No kidding." He closed his locker. "You like Jared, don't you?" He looked me square in the face.

I felt my cheeks starting to warm up.

"You're blushing," he said with a smile.

"Gotta run," I said, heading for my next class.

In English, I jotted down seven names on a note pad. These kids were going to receive invitations to my thirteenth birthday bash. Andie was *not* on the list.

Jared was.

Chapter 12

The back door slammed behind me as I came into the house. Dropping my book bag on the bar in the kitchen, I heard Carrie calling to me from the family room. "Jared called."

My hand froze as I unzipped my jacket. Jared! My heart pounded. I went to the top of the stairs and tried to sound casual. "When did he call?"

She came skipping up the stairway and watched as I hung my jacket in the hall closet. "He called right after school was out," she said. "He wants you to call him back."

"Thanks for the message." I picked up my book bag. Slowly, I headed toward the steps leading to my bedroom, then raced to the phone in Mom's room so Carrie wouldn't see or hear me.

"Room 204, please," I told the hospital operator when she answered.

Butterflies flittered in my stomach as I waited.

"Wilkins' Torture Chamber," a male voice said.

"Is that you, Jared?"

"Who else?" He was laughing.

"It's Holly."

"I'd know your voice anywhere." He paused. "How's school?"

"Okay, I guess. The team misses you. Everyone does," I said, thinking I was the one who missed him most. "I visited you Sunday afternoon, but you were snoring."

He chuckled. "Meds knocked me out a couple days before surgery. But Doc says I'm going home tomorrow."

"Really?" I was dying to see him again.

"How'd your audition go?"

"Let's just say I've sung better," I told him.

"Hope you make it." His voice was soft. "Choir tour wouldn't be the same without *you,* Holly-Heart."

My heart flip-flopped. "Mr. Keller's going to post the list this weekend. But you already know you made it. They need guys in choir . . . I heard that before auditions." Fidgeting, I folded my long hair over the top of my head. It hung down like a satiny curtain in front of me. "I might be going to visit my dad in California for spring break," I said.

"You can't do that . . . it's the choir tour."

"But isn't the tour this *summer*?"

"No, it's during spring break, and we're going to Disneyland."

"Guess I'll just have to visit my dad another time," I said, wondering how I could've gotten so mixed up.

Jared changed the subject. "Aren't we going skiing this weekend?"

"With your leg in a cast?" Some comedian.

"And why not?" Jared asked, laughing.

"But your leg . . ."

"No, really." He sounded more serious now. "I'll be home from the hospital on Friday, and the youth group's going tobogganing Saturday at Jake's Run. How about going along to keep me company at the lodge?"

Jake's Run—the steepest, wildest toboggan ride this side of the Continental Divide. It had a cozy, A-frame lodge with a coffee shop and a lounge with a huge stone fireplace. "How can you get around with your leg in a cast?" I asked.

"I've got crutches now. And my folks think it would be good for me to get out, as long as I'm careful. What do you say?"

As much as I wanted to go along, Mom would never agree. She always said I had to be much older—like in my twenties—and oozing with responsibility before I could even think of dating. Besides, I still wasn't old enough to go on the youth group activities yet, not for eighteen more days. I sighed. "I don't think I can," I said. "Sorry."

"Why not?"

I dodged the question. I had some doubts about Jared, and they confused me. What really had happened between him and Andie at the hospital? Had she lied about his wanting her there? Eating supper together? All of it bugged me. "Isn't Andie going on the ski trip?" I asked.

"I don't know," he said. "Why?"

"I thought you liked Andie. *She* thinks you do."

"Andie and I are just friends," he protested.

Carrie was suddenly standing in front of me. She was tugging at my shirt, even though I shooed her away. Her eyes were demanding little specks, growing wider with every second.

"Look, I've gotta go. My little sister needs me."

"I'll call you tomorrow," Jared said. "Bye, Holly."

I held the phone in my hand, reluctant to hang up. Turning to Carrie, I said, "Please don't ever do that again. This phone call was private."

"So that's why you came up here—to Mom's bedroom—to talk." Her childishness was annoying. "You were hiding from me."

"You'll understand some day."

"So you must *really* like this Jared person," she taunted.

"You'll never know." I raced her downstairs to the kitchen, where we helped ourselves to carrots and dip.

If what Carrie said just now was true, why did I feel both happy and miserable?

The next two days in school dragged on. Jared called Thursday night and pleaded again with me to go to Jake's Run with the youth group. I told him I hadn't asked my mom yet.

Before I knew it, Saturday had arrived. Sleep-in time!

Mom jostled me out of my covers. "Wake up, Holly-Heart. This is the day we've been waiting for. The choir list will be posted at church." She tossed Bearie-O at me.

I kicked my leg over the side of the bed. Slowly easing out, I stood and stared at the mirror. Was this the face of a traveling singer? A new youth choir member?

Right after breakfast the phone rang. It was Andie.

"I'm not sure I want to talk to you," I said.

"Listen, something's really crazy," she said. "It's just too awful."

"Why are you calling me? We're not talking, remember?"

"It's such a shame," she said, ignoring me. "It really is."

"*What* is?" I asked.

"Holly, I'll try to break this to you gently."

"Break what to me?"

"You asked for it," she said. "Your name's nowhere to be seen on the list for choir."

I slammed down the phone. Enough of her gloating. Mr. Keller and his precious choir could go sing in their sleep for all I cared.

Determined to ignore Andie and her nasty news, I marched to the garage. There, I found a box of lawn and leaf trash bags. I scribbled a note to Andie, pinned it to Bearie-O, and stuffed him inside.

"I'm going for a walk, Mom." I yanked my jacket and gloves out of the closet.

"Where on earth are you headed in this cold?" she called.

I slung the trash bag over my shoulder. "I won't be long, I promise."

Trudging down the sidewalk—where Andie and I had played the don't-step-on-a-crack-or-you'll-break-your-mother's-back game when we were kids—I headed off to Andie's house, only a few blocks away.

When I arrived, I noticed the mail carrier coming up the street. Perfect! In a few minutes the deed would be done. I hid behind a clump of aspen trees in front of her house till the mail truck passed by. Then, in a flash, I dashed to Andie's mailbox, opened it, and shoved the trash bag inside—Bearie-O and all.

♥   ♥   ♥

Back home, I told Mom to forget about checking on the choir list at church.

"Why's that, honey?" she said, looking up from the dining room table, where she was writing a list.

I tossed my mittens up onto the shelf in the hall closet. "I already know I wasn't picked for choir. But it's okay—I didn't want to see Andie's fat little face every day of my life during spring break anyway."

"What's going on between you two?" Mom asked, putting her pen down and staring at me.

"We're through, she and I. Finished. The final end of us has come." Then, on the heels of that, I made the cold announcement about Daddy. "Oh, by the way, I thought you might like to know . . . I've decided to visit Daddy during spring break."

She looked positively shocked. "Isn't this a bit sudden?"

"I'm sick of being around here. I'm sick of everything!" I sat down on the floor in a heap.

"Holly-Heart, you're terribly upset about the choir tour, aren't you?" She left her list behind and sat on the floor beside me, stroking my hair.

"It's that, and everything else. You . . . you just don't understand anymore."

"We can talk about it."

"It's too late. My letter to Daddy has probably arrived there by now."

"We could've discussed this. I wish you'd talked to me first."

I looked at her. "Well, Daddy must think I'm old enough to decide where I want to spend my vacations." With that, I got up and trudged upstairs. At the top, I turned to see Mom, still sitting on the floor, looking terribly sad.

In my room, I tried to think of five exceptionally creative ways to ask Mom about going tobogganing with the youth group. But after letting some time pass, and then going back downstairs to talk to her, the only thing I came up with was this: "May I please go to Jake's Run with the youth group this afternoon?"

She was sitting at the dining room table, now clipping coupons. She looked up, scissors in hand. "It's pretty short notice, don't you think?" *Snip* went her scissors.

"I guess, but I just found out about it," I said as politely as a charm-school graduate.

"From whom?" She added three more coupons to her pile. Somehow I knew *that* was coming.

"Jared Wilkins told me," I said.

"Didn't he just get out of the hospital?" There was no fooling her.

"Yes, but he needs some company, some fresh air, too." I pleaded my case upside and down. Mom was a hard one to crack.

"Your friend Jared wouldn't be foolish enough to go tobogganing with his leg in a cast, would he?"

"Oh, Mom. Be fair. We won't be outside. He and I will probably talk inside the lodge . . . wait while the others go sledding, you know."

"What you just described sounds much too exclusive. Besides, the whole idea of going with a group is to be *with* the group."

"But I've been alone with Jared before. We went to the Soda Straw and . . ."

Oops. What had made me mention that?

Mom's eyes got all squinty and she said, slowly and evenly, "You did *what?*"

"We just had a Coke one day after school, and Andie came by anyway, so it wasn't as bad as it sounded. I'm responsible. Please, Mom? Please may I go?"

"Not this time, Holly-Heart," she said flatly.

That nickname meant I was loved, but I certainly didn't feel like it, at least not now. "I wish you wouldn't call me that," I said over my shoulder as I stomped up the steps, thinking of ways to escape for the afternoon.

Five minutes alone in my room was all the time it took. When Mom was ready to go grocery shopping, I'd say I had to finish up some homework. Then when the house was empty I'd hop a bus to the church. The perfect plan!

After lunch I volunteered to clean up the kitchen. Mom seemed to be impressed. Carrie was obviously relieved.

By the time Mom was ready to do the shopping, I had convinced her to let me stay home to do a report for school. I couldn't believe she fell for it.

House empty, I slipped into my soft pink turtleneck sweater and brushed my hair. My heart pounded at the thought of the daring adventure ahead.

The lodge above Jake's Run buzzed with noise as skiers clumped in their boots across the wooden floor to the snack bar. Jackets hung on pegs, their bright colors splashed against the dark paneling.

Jared and I went through the snack bar to a quieter spot, a small room with cozy sofas and tall windows overlooking the slopes. A roaring fire crackled in a white-brick fireplace nearby. I warmed my feet as Jared showed off his storytelling abilities to the perfect audience: me.

"That's fabulous," I said when he finished. "You should write some of them down."

"Sometimes I do. But mostly they're in my head. What about you?"

"I'd write all the time, if I could."

"I think we're made for each other," he said.

I laughed, enjoying the attention. Too much. "What do you mean . . . just because we both like to write?"

"That's one of the cool things about you, Holly. You don't play games. You're honest."

I took a deep breath. He sure wouldn't be saying that if he knew how I'd lied to get out of the house.

Later, I signed his cast. In red letters, I wrote, LOVE, HOLLY. Our hands touched.

"Does this mean you're, uh, you know . . . my girlfriend?" he asked, propping a pillow under his bad leg.

I ignored the question. "Here, let me help you."

"Well, Holly-Heart?" He'd called me by my nickname again.

I blushed. "Okay."

Jared's eyes twinkled. "Fabulous," he said softly, using *my* word.

We played six games of checkers while the youth group tobogganed. What a great time I was having with Jared smiling and flirting across the checkerboard at me.

By the time the sun's rays disappeared behind the mountains, around the supper hour, I knew that Mom would know the truth.

♥ ♥ ♥

On the way home Jared said I was perfect. So what if I was tall and thin?

Happily, I believed him. This was a first crush at its very best. Well, almost. The guilt from lying and sneaking off grew more powerful as each snow-packed mile crunched under our bus.

Then, on the final mountain pass, the bus broke down. Danny and Alissa and several others got out as the driver surveyed the problem. I watched Alissa from inside the bus. She looked like a snow princess; her face glowed—half windburn, part sunburn, and a little adoration for Danny Myers thrown in.

I checked my watch. Mom would be worried sick by now. Too bad no one had cell phone reception in this rocky locale. *Maybe, though*, I told myself, *it will be better to talk to Mom face to face about this.*

My nerves told another story.

Then Jared winked at me and my heart flip-flopped. I pushed my worries away.

Three hours and a growling stomach later, I turned my house key in the lock. Carrie caught me tiptoeing in. "Mom, she's home," she shouted, throwing her arms around me.

Mom eyeballed me from the sofa, closing the book she was reading. Slowly, she stood up. Her precise movements spelled trouble. "You've been gone a long time, Holly-Heart." It was a statement, not a question.

She knew.

"I won't lie to you anymore, Mom. I went with the youth group to Jake's Run."

She squinted her eyes. "It was deceitful, Holly, and willfully disobedient. You're grounded. No friends, no TV, and no phone for a full week."

"That long?" I cried.

"There are leftovers in the fridge. Eat something before you go to bed. I'll have a list of chores on the table in the morning."

"But, Mom, I—"

"No back talk or I'll add more." She turned toward the kitchen. I'd never seen Mom this rattled before.

"She forgets how it feels to be a kid." I let the words softly slip from my lips.

"I'm gonna tell," Carrie said.

"Who cares?" I shot back, taking the steps two at a time.

Safe in my room, I wrote a heading for today's journal entry— "My perfect afternoon with Jared Wilkins." Paying for my deceit with a week's grounding was even trade for the hours I'd spent with the cutest, sweetest boy ever.

Chapter 13

The first week of February—seven days of pure boredom! Going to school was what I lived for. Jared was back, and I was his faithful helper—carrying his tray at lunch, sharpening pencils in class, and helping with his crutches in the hall and everywhere else.

Andie was furious, following us around. But Jared was polite even though it was obvious she couldn't accept the facts. Jared was my guy now.

After-school hours dragged endlessly. Even Bearie-O was unavailable for dumping my woes. And when Corky, my old teddy bear, showed up on our porch on Tuesday with a note pinned to *his* ear, I knew my friendship with Andie was in deep trouble. But I didn't care.

Finally the week of being grounded was over. Freedom! Talking on the phone was pure heaven. Best of all, my birthday was getting closer. Mom stocked up on ten toppings and four flavors of ice cream for the birthday bash. One of the flavors was bubble gum, with delicious pieces of pink gum mixed in. I couldn't wait for the best ice-cream party ever.

On Sunday afternoon I did fancy cuttings with lavender and blue crepe paper. Everything was set for my party the following Saturday.

♥ ♥ ♥

Then on the Thursday before my birthday, I came home to find a note propped against the cookie jar. *Holly: Carrie and I are at the travel agency. We'll be back soon. Love, Mom.*

I poured a tall glass of milk, stirred chocolate syrup in, and grabbed two cookies to nibble on. My imagination ran wild.

Just great, I thought. *She's planning some exotic travel adventure during spring break while I'm in California visiting Daddy. . . .*

While pigging out on cookies, I began to compose a note to Jared. I was half finished when the garage door rumbled open. Quickly, I hid the stationery.

Carrie ran into the kitchen, out of breath. "We got plane tickets, and Mom has something to tell you."

Is it Paris or Tahiti?

Mom walked in at a snail's pace, her face drawn. She pulled out a kitchen chair and sat down. I didn't want to look at her. *This is some cruel trick,* I thought. *Does she really think I'd cancel my plans to go with them instead?*

"Holly-Heart." She breathed a heavy sigh. "Aunt Marla died this morning."

I was stunned.

"We're flying to Pennsylvania tomorrow."

Carrie asked, "Do we have to wear black to the funeral?"

"No, darling," Mom said, pulling her near.

Tears began to trickle down my cheeks. I couldn't help myself.

"Your aunt's pain is finally over," she said, holding out her arms to me. "She's with Jesus now."

"But . . . what about Holly's party?" Carrie asked, rubbing her eyes.

"I'm sorry, dear, we'll have to postpone it," she said, picking up Goofey and petting him.

I pulled on my hair. "Who feels like celebrating, anyway? I'll let everyone know."

The timing was terrible. I'd never anticipated the possibility of a funeral disrupting my thirteenth birthday party plans. Worst of all, Aunt Marla was dead.

Grandpa and Grandma Meredith met us with hugs and tears at the airport. They drove us through the narrow tree-lined streets to their house. Quietly unpacking, I thought back to the happiest times in this house. When Mom and Daddy were still married, we came for week-long visits here in the summer. Uncle Jack and Aunt Marla and our cousins drove the short distance to Grandpa's house on the Fourth of July. We kids would make short order of the corn on the cob until Grandpa teased that we might turn into walking ears of corn ourselves. At dusk, we wrote our names in the air with the sparklers Uncle Jack gave us. Daddy and his sister, Aunt Marla, would kiss and hug good-bye. Very sweet.

I swallowed hard, fighting back the tears. Those days were forever past, not just because Aunt Marla was gone, but because Daddy was, too.

Carrie came in and sat on the quilted bedspread. "Mommy says our dad will be at the funeral tomorrow. Do you think he'll bring his new wife and kid?" Carrie asked.

"Maybe," I said, brushing her hair. "I wonder if he'll recognize us." I felt giddy with excitement and sadness all mixed together.

"We sent him school pictures last fall, so he should."

I stopped brushing. "Oh yeah, and mine looked pathetic because I couldn't get my hair to do anything," I said, staring at the mirror. My hair looked droopy now, too. Humidity was part of the problem. Even in the winter, Pennsylvania air was heavy with moisture.

The funeral was on Saturday—the day my ice-cream party had been scheduled. The church foyer was crowded when we arrived. People lined up to sign a formal-looking white book on a small table encircled with red roses. Mothers with young children and their executive-type husbands—probably men who worked with Uncle Jack—waited to say their good-byes to Aunt Marla.

The family was supposed to gather in a small reception room behind the church sanctuary. Carrie and I followed Mom down the long hallway to the private room. Grandma and Grandpa were sitting with Uncle Jack and the cousins. We settled into the soft chairs behind them.

Relatives I hardly knew stood around. Mom introduced Carrie and me to them. They were from Daddy's side of the family.

Behind me I heard whispering and turned to see who it was. In the doorway stood a handsome man wearing a navy blue suit. He was with a smartly dressed woman.

Four plus years of mounting curiosity hit me in the face. This man was my father.

"Holly?" he said. "What a beauty you are." He turned to the woman. "Honey, I want you to meet my daughter Holly."

"Hello," I said, suddenly shy. I reached out to touch her gloved hand.

"Holly, I'd like you to meet Saundra, my wife."

By then Carrie was tugging at me to leave. I grabbed her arm and turned her around.

"Well, hello there, Carrie," Daddy said, bending low.

She looked up at me, confused. "That's him?" she whispered back at me.

Daddy smiled. "It's wonderful to see both of you."

Saundra said, "We were happy to receive your letter, Holly."

"Yes," Daddy said. "I was planning to call . . . to set up a flight schedule. But now we can discuss the trip in person." He stepped toward me like he wanted to hug me, so I offered a quick one.

"I'll see you at the dinner for the family tonight," I said, turning to look for Carrie, who had already slipped away.

She was standing across the room beside our young cousin Stephanie, who sat, eyes swollen, leaning against Mom. It was time for Aunt Marla's funeral to begin.

The church was filled with a sweet fragrance from the many

floral sprays. The organ played softly, and voices were hushed. I touched the tissues in my dress pocket. I knew I'd need them.

♥ ♥ ♥

After the funeral, we waited to ride in one of the black limousines to the cemetery. Carrie begged Mom to let Stephie ride with us.

"Uncle Jack wants all of the children to ride together," Mom told us as we walked down the church steps.

The limo pulled up, but there was room for only two more people.

"I'll ride in the next one," I said. Mom agreed.

Another limo came around, and I got in. Daddy and his new wife climbed in behind me. He looked lousy from grief; his face was pale and his eyes were red.

I felt numb. Aunt Marla's funeral wasn't exactly the best place to reunite with my long-lost father.

The ride to the cemetery was awkward. Here I sat across from this Saundra person trying to be polite when I really wanted to shout: Leave me alone with my dad!

What was she doing here, anyway? She'd probably never even met Aunt Marla. To top things off, she began chattering about spring break and where we could go sightseeing. Stuff like that. "We've planned a delightful time for you," she said. "Next month, isn't it?" She opened her purse, took out lipstick and a mirror, and began to touch up her already bright red lips.

"The last week in March." I glanced at Daddy. "Maybe you should talk to Mom about it."

"There will be plenty of time for that tonight," he said, adjusting his tie. He was as handsome as I'd remembered. "Tomorrow is your birthday," he commented. "When are you flying back?"

"We'll get home late tomorrow night." Too late to have the ice-cream party. Too late to celebrate my milestone birthday with my friends. With Jared.

Saundra asked, "Is there something special you'd like for your big day?"

I tugged on my hair as I thought of the most special things in all the world. They couldn't be purchased by her or anyone. But there was *something*. "The latest mystery novel by Marty Leigh just came out. I'd like that."

Saundra smiled, closing her compact mirror with a click. Did she really think she could make points with me so easily?

"How are you doing in school?" Daddy asked. "Good grades? Lots of friends?"

I told him about my B+ average, but I didn't tell him about my ongoing journal writing or about Jared.

At supper, Stephie sat with Carrie and me. Her nose was red from too much blowing, but her eyes looked less swollen now. When the caterer came around to get our beverage orders, Stephie ordered a soda, then looked at her dad to see if he would disapprove. Uncle Jack didn't say a word. His usual fun-loving smile seemed to have disappeared.

"Mom would never let me drink pop at meals," Stephie whispered to us. "Things are going to be different without her."

I nearly choked on my ice water. I couldn't imagine being seven years old and motherless.

"Things changed at our house when Daddy left, but not that much," Carrie spoke up. I wondered if she truly remembered.

After the lemon angel food cake was served for dessert, Grandpa signaled for everyone's attention. "My granddaughter Holly will be celebrating her thirteenth birthday tomorrow. Please join me in singing the birthday song."

He motioned for me to stand while they sang. Relatives I'd never met and friends of Uncle Jack's sang "Happy Birthday to You" with amazing gusto. I glanced at Daddy. He winked at me. Mom, at the other end of the long table, beamed with pride. Some birthday party! I should have been eating ice cream with Jared right about now.

Suddenly I felt ashamed. Aunt Marla was gone, and all I could think about was missing a boy. What was wrong with me? What was I thinking?

Late that night, lying awake in Grandpa's big house, I stared at the shadows dancing eerily on the ceiling. In a few minutes I'd be a teenager. "Dear Lord," I prayed, "let this be my magical night." He knew what I meant.

The next morning I woke with a jolt. A small backbone pressed against me. It was Carrie's. I lay still in the quiet. The table clock's ticking soothed me. Today was Valentine's Day. *My* day.

Uncle Jack and our cousins came over for breakfast. The boys wolfed down their pancakes, and Uncle Jack said, "Slow down, fellas." Usually he would have made a joke of the boys gobbling down their food like so many turkeys, or something like that.

I remembered why we'd called them stair-step cousins. Sitting across from them was like looking at a descending scale. Stan first, then Phil, then Mark. Little Stephanie last.

Grandpa came downstairs carrying a box wrapped in bright pink-and-red paper. He planted a wet kiss on my cheek. "Happy birthday, Holly-Heart."

Inside, a huge white teddy bear stared up at me. Grandma had cross-stitched a red heart on him, and a ten-dollar bill shaped like a bow tie was pinned under his chin.

"Thanks." I hugged the bear first, then Grandpa and Grandma.

"What's his name?" Stephie asked.

"I'll have to think about it first. Let's see what kind of personality he has." I pulled out my chair for Grandpa. "How did you know what I wanted?"

"A little bird flew around and chirped it in this ear." He pulled on his left ear.

"Oh, Grandpa," Carrie said. "You're just teasing."

A few minutes later, the doorbell rang. Grandma hurried to the living room.

"Happy birthday, Holly." It was Daddy—and his new wife.

"Come in," I said shyly, inching toward them.

Daddy pulled an envelope out of his pocket. It was a gift certificate to a national chain of bookstores. "You can get that mystery book you wanted and many more," he said with a grin.

"You should be able to buy an entire month's worth," Saundra said, smiling too broadly.

"Thanks, this is fabulous." The words choked in my throat.

Carrie lost interest quickly and disappeared upstairs with the cousins. Mom hadn't ventured into the living room. I could see her alone in the kitchen, clearing things away.

"We really can't stay," Daddy said. "We have to catch a plane, but we'll be in touch."

Uncle Jack held out his hand. "Good to see you again."

But Daddy ignored my uncle's hand, hugging him instead. "Take care of those kids, Jack," he said, a twinge of longing in his voice.

Grandma kissed him and said to call when they arrived home.

"Take it easy, son," Grandpa said. His eyes glistened.

"I'll have my travel agent line up a flight for you soon," Daddy said to me. I reached for him. He held me. And then, he was gone.

Chapter 14

After Daddy and Saundra left, the rest of us headed off to Sunday school and church. All but Uncle Jack. He said he needed some time alone. I wished I could say something to make him feel better, but what could I say or do? His beloved wife had died, leaving him and the children alone. As we headed out the door, I hurried over to him and gave him a big hug. He hugged me back and kissed me on the forehead. "You're sweet, Holly," he whispered.

During church, we sat toward the back of the sanctuary, passing tissues up and down the row during worship. Why did such joyful songs now seem so terribly sad? I kept praying: *Dear God, be with Uncle Jack and my cousins. Please comfort them.*

When church was over and we were back at my grandparents' house, I retreated to the room where I'd slept. Silently, I closed the door. It was time to pour out my feelings on paper. Rummaging through my suitcase, I located my journal. In honor of my dear aunt Marla, I wrote her birthdate and death date in my diary. I stared at what I'd written till the tears came. She was too young to die—just two years older than Mom!

Our flight home was long and boring. When we arrived home,

Mom set the suitcases on the kitchen floor and promptly marched Carrie off to bed. I went up to my room and read my Bible until my eyes drooped. They felt like Bearie-O's eyes had looked. I missed him *and* his owner, my former best friend. But I didn't miss Andie's disgusting attention-getting routines. No way.

I hugged my new birthday bear to me. It had been three whole days since I'd seen Jared—the longest ever. I couldn't wait to see him again. Turning thirteen was perfect with him as my friend!

The next day at school I told everyone on the list about the *new* date for the party: Saturday, February 20. Everyone but Jared. I couldn't find him. Not in the library. Not at his locker between classes.

At last, I saw him in the cafeteria at lunch . . . with Andie! She was getting some grated cheese for his spaghetti. I waited in the hot-lunch line, seething, as she slid into the seat next to him, shaking the cheese on his plate.

I felt like hanging her upside-down by her fat little toes.

Billy Hill slipped in line behind me. "Looks like Andie's earning points with Jared," he said. "The second you left for Pennsylvania, she moved in."

"She did?" I was crushed.

"Andie didn't waste any time—helping with his crutches, running errands . . . you name it."

I stared at the two of them. They looked so cozy over there, talking and laughing. I set my tray down on the table, seething with anger.

Billy looked at me. "Hey, you okay?"

I blew my breath out hard. "Jared's a two-timing jerk."

"Funny. Andie doesn't seem to mind," Billy said.

I sat down with my spaghetti. "How could he do this to me?" I said between bites.

Danny and Alissa came into the cafeteria together. They sat

at the end of our table. Before they ate, they bowed their heads for grace.

Billy glanced at them, frowned, then got up to leave. "See you around, Holly. Hang in there, okay?"

I moved over across from Danny and Alissa. They smiled and seemed glad for the company. "Ready for choir tour?" I asked them. I'd decided that even if I wasn't going on the tour, I would be mature about it and not sulk.

Danny looked at Alissa. "*I'm* ready, except . . . well, Alissa can't go."

Alissa explained, "Yeah, things are changing for my family and me. We're moving next week."

"You are?" I said, startled to hear this news. "How come?"

"My dad's being transferred to another state." She and Danny looked sadly at each other.

While I talked with Danny and Alissa, I observed Andie talking and flirting with Jared. Worst of all, he was enjoying it. Once I even saw him reach over and ruffle her hair playfully. This was too much!

When I finished my dessert, I excused myself and headed to my locker. Inside, I was a wreck, upset at myself for trusting Jared. And furious with Andie for moving in on him while I was away.

Andie came careening around the corner. "Look out!" she screeched, dropping a load of books on the floor in front of her locker.

"Watch where you throw things," I said, sidestepping her hefty stack.

"These are Jared's and mine *together*." She huffed and puffed and opened her locker.

"Where's Jared now?" I asked.

"Waiting for me on the steps," she said, pointing down the hall.

"You just couldn't stay away from him, could you?" I snapped. "I'm gone for a couple of days, and—"

"We're starting where we left off in the hospital, before *you* messed things up. Jared said so."

"He's insane," I mumbled into my locker.

"I can't believe what you wrote on his cast," she said.

Either can I, I thought. "I'll write whatever I want," I said, kicking my locker shut.

"When *I* signed his cast, Jared's hand touched mine and he whispered, 'Does this mean you're my girlfriend?'" Her eyes glazed over. "Isn't that romantic?"

I could've told her those were his exact words to *me*. Of course, she wouldn't believe me, not for a single second. So I didn't waste my breath.

Thinking back to my efforts to spend a little forbidden time with Jared at the ski lodge, I wanted to kick myself for sneaking out of the house, lying to Mom—not to mention getting grounded. And what for? To play checkers by the fire with a complete jerk? Was I such a lousy judge of guys? Turning away from Andie, I dashed down the hall. I couldn't get away fast enough.

"Holly, you owe me money for Bearie-O," she called after me. "The fur's worn off his head. I could overlook it for a couple of tens."

I quickened my pace, ignoring her. I wasn't sure who I disliked more—Andie or Jared.

Tuesday night Mom drove me to my first youth group meeting at church. Now that I was thirteen my attendance there was like some sort of debut. Definitely a big deal. Pastor Rob introduced me to all the kids and everyone clapped. Danny and Alissa sat together, grinning at me. Andie arrived late, and she walked right over and squeezed into the seat next to Jared. I sat with some new kids on the other side of the room.

I was heading down the hallway afterward when Mr. Keller, the choir director, came out of his office. "Holly!" he said. "You're just the person I was looking for."

He ushered me into his office, and I sat down. Perching on the edge of his desk, he explained that he needed an alternate singer for the tour to take the place of Alissa Morgan, who was moving. "You have a fine voice, Holly, but I didn't choose you earlier because you were a bit younger. I wanted to give some of the older kids first dibs. However, now that Alissa is leaving, I need you. Can you attend all the rehearsals and catch up a little at home, as well?"

To sing in the youth choir I'd do anything! But then I remembered Daddy and his airplane tickets. I hesitated.

"Is there a problem?" he asked.

"Might be," I said, still surprised at this fabulous turn of events. "How soon can I let you know?"

"Two days. There are kids who would trade places with you in a flash."

When Mom came to pick me up, I told her the fantastic news. "What'll I do?" I moaned. "Will Daddy understand if I don't visit him?"

"You'll have to decide that," she said.

Carrie piped up. "You don't *really* know him, anyway."

"Speak for yourself," I shot back.

"Girls," Mom scolded. Then she said, "Holly-Heart, what about talking to the Lord about this? Pray for His guidance?"

Praying. *Hmm.* Something I should've thought of.

At home, I went to my room and knelt at my window seat. It felt good talking to God about everything again.

Then I thought of Daddy. I needed to tell *him* about the choir tour, as well. Mom was tucking Carrie into bed, so I went to her room to use the phone. It rang four times. When I heard his voice, I said, "Daddy, it's Holly. Something's come up." I told him about the choir-tour opening.

"That's wonderful news." He sounded excited.

"There's only one problem," I said.

"What's that?"

"The tour is during spring break."

There was a short pause. "I guess we could plan your visit for another time." Disappointment seemed to leap into his voice.

"What about this summer?" I suggested.

"Sure, that's a possibility." His voice revved up a bit.

"The tour will take us to L.A. So maybe you can come hear us sing during spring break."

"You can count on it. We'll be there."

We'll . . . That meant I'd have to share him with Saundra. Even the way he pronounced her name gave me the creeps. Could prayer change my attitude toward her?

I wandered downstairs, looking for Mom. She was in the family room, curled up reading a book. "Daddy said he'd come to hear me sing with the choir . . . and he agreed that maybe I could visit him this summer instead."

Mom merely nodded. "We'll talk things over."

"By the way, where's Carrie's last report card?" I asked.

"In the desk in my room. Why do you want it?"

I sat down beside her on the couch. "I thought Carrie could send it to Daddy. I feel funny about Carrie being left out of things with him. She's his daughter, too."

"How does *she* feel about it?" Mom asked, reaching over to loosen the clips in my hair.

"I'm not sure. I hope she doesn't feel jealous. Jealousy is a miserable thing."

Mom paused. "Now that your father has shown an interest again, maybe Carrie will want to know him better, too." She brushed one side of my hair while I did the other.

"Why didn't Daddy keep in touch with us more than just a note on a birthday card or tons of presents at Christmas?" This question burned inside me.

"Honey, I don't understand that, either. But I *do* know he has paid his support money to the court registry faithfully every month all these years. That's something lots of dads don't do."

She braided my hair in one thick braid.

"It's still so hard," I said, deep in thought, "but I'm more concerned with his salvation now." It was true. Very few nights had passed recently that I didn't say his name in my prayers.

"I feel very close to you tonight, Holly-Heart," Mom said, giving me a hug.

"Me too." Again, I felt sorry for Stan, Phil, Mark, and little Stephie. "Mom?" I said, thinking of their loss.

"Yes, honey?"

"I really do love you. Even though I can get sassy sometimes . . . always remember?"

"I'll remember." She hugged and kissed me, and I headed for bed.

At Wednesday night choir rehearsal, I was assigned a spot on the risers next to Jared! I couldn't believe it. I wanted to lash out at him, but I kept my mouth shut except to sing, my hands firmly gripped on the music folder.

"What a relief," Jared said between the first and second songs. "You're here. It's like a miracle."

"The only miracle I know is you haven't been found out before now," I blurted out.

"What do you mean, Holly-Heart?" He sounded so innocent.

"Don't call me that." I felt sick inside. Crushed. And fooled into thinking he was too good to be true.

We practiced five more songs for our tour repertoire before Mr. Keller dismissed us. Andie came right over to Jared, ignoring me. She acted like a mother hen, holding his crutches, helping him with his jacket.

I couldn't watch this. In the strongest voice I could muster, I said, "Jared, you're not welcome at my birthday party. I've thought about this a lot, and I'm sorry." Heading for the church foyer, I waited for Mom, holding my breath and willing the tears away.

On Thursday morning I got up really early. Quietly, I pulled a purple folder out from between the box springs and mattress of my canopy bed. I'd told Andie about destroying our original Loyalty Papers, but she didn't know there was a duplicate copy.

It was time to confront Andie with the truth about Jared. I cut out the paragraph referring to one of us backing away from a guy to save our friendship. In a hot pink marker, I circled it and wrote, *I'm willing. Jared's not worth the destruction of us!*

There, that should speak loud and clear. I folded it neatly and slipped it into a business-sized envelope. Licking it shut, I labeled the envelope, *IMPORTANT! PRIVATE!* I would slide it into her gym locker during warm-ups.

With my birthday party only two days away, things just had to work out between Andie and me. And soon.

Chapter 15

On the snowy walk to school, I couldn't stop thinking about Andie. Would she accept my note? What could I do to make her see what a two-timer Jared was?

I was heading up the sidewalk to school when I heard someone call my name. I turned to look.

It was Jared. He sat on the brick wall surrounding the courtyard leading to the school's main entrance. His bum leg was sticking out, supported by one crutch. In his hand lay a single long-stemmed rose. "Holly-Heart," he called again. "This is for you." He held it out.

"Give it to Andie," I shot back.

He ignored that. "I know it's a little late, but happy birthday. And . . . I'm sorry about your aunt."

"Not sorry enough." I folded my arms.

"I know what you're thinking," he said. "But things aren't the way they seem." He shifted his bad leg off the crutch.

"You must think I'm totally dense, Jared. I don't want any of your explanations. What you did was unforgivable. I thought you were better than that." I turned to go.

"Honestly, Holly, Andie and I are *just friends*," he insisted, holding the rose out farther.

"Is that what you told her about me?" I glanced around. "Where is she, anyway?"

Jared frowned. "What's wrong?"

"Nothing's wrong with me. You're the one with a problem." I remembered, with a twinge of pain, how perfect things were . . . just a week ago, *before* I'd left for Aunt Marla's funeral. The outside temperature added to the cold, painful reality of seeing Jared for who he really was. I shivered, pulling the collar of my coat against my neck.

"C'mon, Holly." He held the sweet-smelling rose out to me again. "I want you to have this."

The rose—his attention—was so hard to resist. But I had to. "Don't do this," I pleaded, turning to go, leaving him sitting alone. Opening the doors to the school, I refused to look back.

During PE I found time to slip back down to the girls' locker room. Quickly, I opened my locker and found the long envelope with the copy of the clipping from the Loyalty Papers. I hurried to Andie's locker and slid the envelope through the slits in the door. *Now* she'd have something to think about. Maybe she'd even call me and request a face-to-face meeting. I was desperate to get my best friend back!

After school, I noticed Jared in the stairwell. He'd cornered some girl. I couldn't see who, but it wasn't Andie. Whoever it was, I could tell they were involved in animated conversation.

Way to go, Jared. Fool someone new. Peering around the corner at them made me hurt all over again.

Billy Hill zipped past, nearly knocking me over. "Excu-use me," he said. Together, we walked toward the front entrance. "You look depressed."

"It's Jared. Mr. Flirt himself is attempting to charm yet another girl," I said, referring to the stairwell scene. "Why did *I* fall for his empty words?"

"Don't be hard on yourself," Billy said, "Jared's just some guy, that's all."

"But he's two-timing Andie. If she only knew!"

"If I were Jared, I'd stick with Andie," he said, and then, realizing he'd let something personal slip, he blushed.

He likes Andie! I thought. Perfect. I shifted my books from one arm to the other.

"The way Jared was talking in class, you'd think he was stringing you along, too." Billy was covering his tracks.

I scuffed my shoe as hard as I could. "His brain's definitely warped."

Just then a fabulous idea struck. "Wouldn't it be fun to catch Jared at his own game? You know, teach him a lesson?"

"Yeah," Billy laughed. "Like how?"

We pushed the front doors open. The smell of woodsmoke filled the air.

"I have an idea, but let's talk later," I said. We headed home in opposite directions.

Cutting through the school yard, I noticed Marcia Greene making fresh footprints in the snow. She wore a heavy tan parka. The hood was tied tightly, framing her face, and in her mittened hand she had a single, long-stemmed red rose.

So *that's* who Jared had cornered. Marcia Greene and I were destined for a heart-to-heart talk. Andie too. Wait'll *she* heard about this—precisely what I needed to convince Andie of the truth. I decided to wait until after supper to phone her. That would give her a chance to get finished with homework before I dumped the bad news on her.

When I got home from school, Carrie had stacks of artwork and old report cards piled on the table. She must've heard about my chat with Mom last night. That Daddy might like to see some of her progress.

"Carrie," I called to her, opening the fridge.

She bounded up the stairs and into the kitchen. "You're home. Good."

"Want to make a package to send to Daddy?"

She showed off two pages of artwork. "These are my favorites. Think he'll like them?"

I nodded. "If you want to keep the originals, Mom can make color copies at work."

Carrie seemed to like the idea. So I spent the rest of the afternoon helping her compose a letter to Daddy.

After our supper of chicken chow mein—yum!—I settled down at the dining room table to do some homework. I was finishing up my algebra assignment when the phone rang. I flew across the kitchen to get it.

"Hey, Holly." It was Billy.

"Hey," I said.

"I was thinking about what you said today. I saw this show on TV about a guy who wasn't happy unless he was dating at least two girls at once."

"And?"

"He not only two-timed every girl he went with, but he got messed up trying to keep things straight with the girls he'd lined up dates with."

"That won't happen to Jared," I said, determined. "Not when the word gets out about him to every girl in Dressel Hills. Beginning with Andie." I took a deep breath. "I have a fabulous scheme. Wanna help me pull it off?"

"Absolutely," Billy said.

"Here it is." I told him what I'd dreamed up on my way home from school.

Billy laughed when he heard my plan. "You're right," he said. "Your birthday party will be the perfect place to set Jared up. Whoa, Holly, you're good."

"So . . . I'll talk to you later." Excitement jitters were building inside me. I could hardly wait for the perfect moment to get Jared good.

After I hung up, I grabbed my notebook of secret lists. There were important details to plan, involving Andie, Marcia Greene, and Jared.

First, I phoned Marcia. She seemed a little hesitant, maybe a teeny bit taken in by Jared's attention (the rose probably did it), but she was willing to go along with the plan . . . for a price. I had to let her wear my purple-and-pink jacket to some ski party next week.

I agreed. That was easy.

Next, I called Jared. He seemed surprised but thrilled that I'd changed my mind about including him at my party. I didn't tell him *who* was coming, of course.

Getting Andie to show up at my party would be much more difficult. I called her last.

"Hey. It's Holly. Please don't hang up," I said.

"What can *you* possibly say that I'd want to hear?" she said sarcastically.

Praying for courage, I said, "Andie, I really want you to come to my party Saturday night."

She hesitated. "Uh, I don't know."

"Did you find the note I stuck in your locker with the clipping from the Loyalty Papers?" I persisted. "Did you read it?"

"Sort of, but I'm not—"

"*Jared's* coming to the party. I thought you'd want to come with him." It was my last ploy.

"Okay . . . sure. If he's coming, I'll be there."

I stifled the urge to do backflips. "Perfect," I said. "I'll see you Saturday night."

We said good-bye. Then I clenched my fists and jumped up and down. Mom looked at me funny when she came through the room hauling the vacuum cleaner and its attachments.

I picked up the long vacuum hose. "Here, let me help."

"Looks like we have spiders again," Mom said, waving her feather duster in the corner of the ceiling and whisking away a few cobwebs.

I shivered at the thought of the creepy things. "I don't see any spiders now," I said, fluffing up the sofa pillows.

"Not now maybe, but the proof's in the webs they spin."

It sounded like a bit of poetry and reminded me of the mini-webs I hoped to spin for Andie this Saturday night. To help her see the truth. At last!

Friday after school Billy walked me home. "Your plan to expose Jared is so cool," he said, stomping the snow off his boots.

"If we all do our part, it should be as smooth as vanilla pudding." Then I set things straight with Billy. "This whole thing is *not* about revenge, just so you know. It's about getting my best friend back."

"And there's no way it won't work. You and Andie will be friends again by tomorrow night, you'll see." His smile was so big I was curious about *his* motive.

At choir rehearsal Saturday morning I went out of my way to be nice to Jared, which wasn't easy. After all, I had been nuts about him last week. The wounds from his deception were still fresh.

"Thanks for inviting me to your party," he said, sliding over on the riser to make room for me. "I thought you didn't want me to come."

"I changed my mind." I didn't say I'd had a change of heart. That would've been a lie.

Mr. Keller chose several kids to sing in an a cappella group. Danny Myers was one of the tenors. I listened as they sang, admiring Danny's performance.

After choir, Mr. Keller congratulated us on our good blend. "When we achieve unity with our voices, our music is that much stronger—more powerful. The same is true in our lives when, as brothers and sisters in Christ, we have unity of mind and heart. United, we can accomplish more for the kingdom of God."

I thought about his words. Even though we were both Christians, there hadn't been much agreement between Andie and me lately. I hoped my plan would help restore some of that unity—and give me back my best friend.

Chapter 16

Pastel streamers and paper cut-outs dangled from the ceiling of the dining room, creating a festive atmosphere for my birthday party. The table was covered with Mom's special white-lace tablecloth. Pink napkins were lined up beside pink plastic bowls. In the middle of the table, there were ten kinds of ice-cream toppings: strawberries, caramel, butterscotch, hot fudge, chocolate sprinkles, nuts, gummy bears, sliced bananas, maraschino cherries, and—best of all—whipped cream.

Mom rearranged the silverware, lining the forks up symmetrically. "We're all set, Holly-Heart," she said. "Why don't you go get yourself ready?"

I stood back and surveyed the table. "It's beautiful, absolutely beautiful." Impulsively, I hugged Mom. "Thanks."

"Hurry along, now," she said, chuckling like it was *her* party!

I rushed upstairs and slipped into new jeans and a hot-pink wool sweater with a white T underneath. Then I went into the bathroom to do my hair. I brushed it vigorously, then parted it down the middle and made two big braids, one on either side of my head. I finished the outfit off with a pretty beaded bracelet featuring every conceivable shade of pink. *Perfect.*

At seven o'clock sharp, the doorbell rang. I greeted my first guests, Joy and Shauna, two girls from youth group and my home ec class. Two boys from the basketball team showed up next. Later, Jared and Andie arrived . . . together. I smiled and welcomed them, but neither of them looked me in the eye. I offered them seats in the living room, where the other kids waited for the ice-cream bonanza.

The doorbell rang again. I hurried to get it.

"Billy!" I gasped. "What happened to you?"

Billy, his right leg in a cast and crutches under his arms, wobbled into the living room. Marcia Greene followed close behind, watching him and holding his arm so he wouldn't slip.

Everyone circled Billy, firing questions at him. "Clear the way," I said. "Let him sit down." I led Billy to a chair and propped his leg on a footstool.

"How's that?" I asked, sneaking a look at Jared. He was sitting next to Andie on the couch, wearing a puzzled look.

"It was a skiing accident," Billy told us. "Yesterday after school. I was skiing fast down a black slope when I hit this mogul and boom—I wiped out." He described how his sister had screamed, how the ski patrol had taken him down on the snowmobile. "Lucky my mom's a doctor. She made sure I didn't go into shock," he said.

I stole another look at Jared. He was listening to Billy with interest. *So far, so good.*

"Ice cream's ready," Mom called.

All of us trooped into the kitchen, where my mother, the perfect hostess, announced the flavors. We lined up at the kitchen bar, and Mom dished out the ice cream. Then we gathered at the dining room table and picked out our favorite toppings.

Andie hovered near Jared. "What ice cream would you like?" she asked. "I can get it for you."

Marcia did the same. "Oh, Billy," she said. "Just tell me what you'd like on your sundae, and I'll take care of it."

A few minutes later Andie picked up the can of whipped cream. "Would you like some?" she asked Jared.

When she finished with the can, Marcia reached for it. "Billy," she said, her voice a tad sweeter than Andie's, "would you like some of this?"

"Sure, thanks," he said, playing the part.

Andie turned cherry red. Jared frowned.

Everyone stood around the dining room, laughing and talking as we ate our huge sundaes.

Then Billy motioned for me. Balancing on his crutches, he held his punch cup high in the air. "Here's to the birthday girl," he announced. Then he blew me a kiss. I giggled. All part of the act. Jared's eyes nearly popped out.

After Mom offered seconds on ice cream, we headed downstairs to the family room while Mom and Carrie cleared away the dishes. Tossing our shoes off, my friends curled up on the sectional facing the entertainment center, and I started a DVD, pre-approved by Mom. On the coffee table stood a tall white vase displaying a single, long-stemmed red rose, which I'd bought for myself that afternoon.

The movie was one of my favorites, *Ever After.* So romantic and sweet. But I hardly paid attention. I kept watching Andie and Jared. I pulled on my hair, nervous about what Billy and I had schemed to do.

The end of the video, when the credits came up, was Billy's cue. As soon as I turned up the lights, he whipped out a blue marker and asked everyone to sign his cast. When Marcia signed it, LOVE, MARCIA G., he grabbed her hand and said, "Does this mean you're my girlfriend?"

She stuttered, acting the part flawlessly. "I . . . I'll have to ask Jared," she said, facing him.

Andie's eyes popped.

There was a long, awkward silence. Jared's jaw flinched nervously.

Then Andie leaped up. "What's going on?" she said, scowling first at me, then Marcia. "Jared and *I* are together. What's this about?"

By now Jared looked like a trapped rat. Nearly speechless, he mumbled, "I . . . uh . . . I don't . . ."

Marcia stared at Jared and poured it on. "I thought you liked me, Jared. Isn't that what the rose was for?"

Andie let out a tiny gasp. She swung around to face Jared, face aghast. I'd never known Andie to be tongue-tied, but at this minute, she was absolutely silent.

Now it was *my* turn. I picked up the dainty rosebud vase. Holding it high, I said, "Roses are usually given to represent something important. Like true friendship or . . . love. This rose is exactly like the one Jared tried to give me. But I didn't take it." I stared at Andie, hoping she could take note of my demonstration of loyalty.

"Jared offered a rose to *me,* too," Marcia declared, "after school."

"This is nuts!" Andie looked from Marcia to me and back again. "I'm outta here." Her eyes shot fire—at me. "Meet me upstairs, Holly," she said coldly. It sounded like an invitation to a duel.

I followed her upstairs to the hall closet, where she dragged out her jacket and put it on. She pulled me outside into the bitter night. Standing there on the front porch, lit only by the faint glow of a distant streetlight, we faced each other. "What are you trying to prove, Holly *Heartless*?" she asked.

"I'm sick of Jared coming between us. Honestly, I thought this was the only way to show you what he's really like. I doubt that Jared would fill you in on how he offered me a rose, then gave it to Marcia instead. He's a two-timer, Andie. It's obvious."

"I don't care!" she said.

"You're actually going to stick with him?"

She just glared at me.

"What about our friendship—years of great times, sharing our deepest secrets, a good, solid relationship . . . the best I've ever had," I said, hoping she'd snap out of it. Hoping . . .

"You humiliated me, Holly." Her voice was shaking, and I thought I saw tears glistening in her eyes. "Our friendship's over. No more Loyalty Papers, no more teddy bears, no more nothing.

You can forget about me, Holly Heartless, because this is the last time I'll ever set foot in your house."

Before I could say more she turned to leave, running full speed down our driveway and across the street.

"Andie!" I called. "Please don't leave like this."

It was a long, cold three blocks to her house, but she kept going. Her figure rounded the corner and disappeared at the end of Downhill Court.

I shivered uncontrollably. My fabulous plan had totally backfired. What could I do now?

BEST FRIEND, WORST ENEMY

Chapter 17

Downstairs in the family room, I found the boys cutting through Billy's cast with the small hacksaw I'd hidden behind the TV for this purpose.

"Guess I don't need this anymore." Billy tossed the cast aside.

"Where'd you get it?" Joy asked, eager to know.

"My mom really is a doctor. She did a good job of making me look injured."

Staring at the signatures on the discarded cast, I felt sick inside. The scheme had blown up in my face. And Andie and I were as far removed as east and west.

Jared? He was nowhere to be seen now. Missing . . . in my house somewhere?

"He's hiding out in the bathroom," Billy said when I asked. "We sure did a number on him, don't you think?"

"It wasn't him I was after," I whispered, wishing this night had never happened. It was obvious the party was over. I thanked Marcia Greene for her fabulous dramatic skills as she left the house. Billy too.

Then, going back downstairs, I vented my frustration by yanking down all the streamers. At last, Jared came out of the bathroom, like a turtle emerging from its shell.

He picked up the vase with the rose and leaned his nose deep into the flower. "Too bad, isn't it?" he said.

I tossed a crumpled wad of crepe paper to the floor. "No kidding."

"A rose is a symbol of love," he continued. "The Bible says we should love everyone, right? I'm doing the best I can to be a loving Christian."

I wanted to choke. Was this guy for real?

"Jared, just go home. You're leading girls on, and that has nothing to do with God's love." I threw his jacket at him and pointed to the stairs.

He flashed me a wink and a grin. "See ya, Holly-Heart."

He never quits, I thought, going in search of Mom. She was in bed, propped up with a zillion pillows, reading a magazine. When she saw me, she patted the bed beside her. I snuggled in and shared the entire dreadful evening with her.

"You embarrassed Andie in front of her classmates," Mom chided. "How else would you expect her to react?"

I nodded. "It was a lousy mistake. I didn't think about how *she'd* feel, only how lonely I felt." I pulled my socks off and threw them one at a time across the room. "Now what'll I do?"

Mom slipped her arm around me. "Only one thing, Holly-Heart. Apologize."

She was right.

"It won't be easy," I said. "And Andie might not forgive me."

Mom squeezed my hand. "Oh, I don't know. Given time, you might be surprised what Andie will do."

I returned to my own bedroom, where I dressed in my nightshirt and read my devotional. Lying in the darkness, I replayed the events of the party in my mind. Over and over, I recalled Andie's reaction. How could she ever forgive me?

At church on Sunday, my conscience still pricked at me. How could I have done such a terrible thing to my best friend? I listened carefully when our pastor spoke of forgiveness of sins, and I said a silent prayer of thanks to God that He had already forgiven me. Now if I could only get Andie to do the same.

I searched right away for Andie after the service, finding her alone in the choir room. She sat at the piano, numbering measures in her music.

Standing behind the piano, I was silent for a moment. Then I said, "I'm sorry about last night, Andie. Can you ever forgive me?"

She looked up, a hint of sadness in her eyes. "Sure, Holly. I forgive you. But you should know that Jared and I are already back together."

Not surprising. Jared's charisma was hard to resist.

She went on. "He apologized to me, too. And to Marcia Greene. Jared's trying to be more up front with me now. He just wants to be good friends with *all* the girls. Really."

Some joke. If only she knew how Jared had flirted with *me* last night after everyone left. But it was pointless. She'd never believe it.

I sighed. "I hope you two get along all right." With nothing more to say, I left the room. At least she and I were talking again. But we couldn't possibly be close friends. Not until Jared Wilkins was out of the picture.

February fizzled, and March piled snow on us until I thought winter might never end. I spent most of my free time with Marcia Greene. And even though Andie and I didn't talk much, at least we were civil to each other. She continued to help Jared with his crutches and his books, standing sentinel at his locker to assist him with his every whim.

The second week in March, Jared had his cast removed. To celebrate, Andie decorated his locker door with colorful balloons. I congratulated him, hoping that now that he could walk without crutches, Andie and I could resume our friendship.

But nothing seemed to change. She stuck by him as closely

as before. And worse, Jared kept trying to flirt with me! At choir practices, in English class, at church. Even though I didn't respond, he kept it up.

At last it was Saturday, March twenty-seventh—the final choir rehearsal before we left for our tour on Monday. After numerous dress rehearsals in February, the choir had gone into a slump, but Mr. Keller was going to present a unified choir or die trying. We prayed at the beginning of rehearsal, as usual. Then he said, "Let's chat." He motioned for us to sit on the risers. "Some of you are still thinking in terms of solo work. In a choir situation"—and here he waved his arms to include all of us—"we must have togetherness. We're a group of singers, not thirty different people doing our own thing. So blend. Listen to each other. The theme of our tour is 'Hearts in One Accord.' When we sing in each of the churches on the tour, the audience must feel our inspiration, our love for the Lord and for each other." A couple kids snickered. "C'mon, kids, you know what I mean."

I glanced at Andie, who was sitting at the piano. She, of course, was gazing at Jared, next to me. *She must really care for him,* I thought sadly.

Mr. Keller continued. "Acts 2:46 says, 'Every day they continued to meet together in the temple courts. They broke bread in their homes and ate together with glad and sincere hearts, praising God and enjoying the favor of all the people.' " He asked for hands. "Let's have some input from you. What's this verse mean?"

Hands shot up.

"Yes, Danny?"

"The early Christians were in agreement. They were united."

"Exactly," Mr. Keller said. "More ideas?" He pointed to Jared.

"They looked forward to pigging out together?"

The kids laughed.

Mr. Keller nodded. "But wasn't it more *how* they broke bread together?"

I raised my hand. "They were together in everything. Like best friends."

"Now we're getting somewhere," he said, rubbing his hands together. "Think about what Holly said as we rehearse the last stanza of page forty-four."

I thought about Andie sitting there at the piano as we sang. I missed her terribly. More than anything, I hoped this choir tour would restore us to true friendship. That was my earnest prayer.

Chapter 18

Dizzy with excitement, I stood at the back of the Los Angeles Chapel, peering through the glass separating the foyer from the sanctuary. Scarcely was there a vacant seat—each pew was filled, right up to the altar. The crowd fidgeted. Young children peeked at parents' programs, and teens whispered on the far left side, segregated from the rest. I looked over rows of heads and soon spied Saundra's swept-up red hair. Where was Daddy?

I became aware of the nervous rustlings behind me—the other girls, straightening their lavender dresses.

"Ready for the concert?" Jared, my assigned escort, whispered.

Just then, I caught a glimpse of Daddy at the drinking fountain. "Excuse me," I said, moving out of line and dashing to him.

"Holly," he said with awe in his voice. "You look simply stunning." He gave me a tight hug.

I heard the musical cue and reluctantly pulled away. "Wait for me after the concert, okay? We'll talk then." I scurried back to my appointed spot.

Jared's hand touched my back lightly as he guided me to my place beside him. I slipped my hand through his elbow, and we were off. It felt weird walking down the aisle with him, like we were in a wedding, or worse, getting married to each other! Andie regarded us with a half-sarcastic, half-accusing look as we rounded the altar and walked up the steps.

On the platform, we located our place on the risers. Quickly, I searched the audience for Daddy, who was leaning forward slightly. His warm smile beckoned to me like a beacon in the sea of faces.

Energetically, we sang our opening song, a lively chorus, "Everybody Sing Praises to the Lord." It was a great start by the sound of the applause. Somehow, I made it through the next few songs, even though Jared kept inching closer and closer. I refused to respond to his immature behavior.

At the intermission, during the offering, Jared strolled through the lobby to me. Handsomely outfitted in his black suit, he was any girl's dream.

"You're going to introduce me to your father, right?" he asked, grinning.

I stepped back. "Why should I?"

"C'mon, Holly, you know Andie and I are just—"

"I've heard it before. Just friends, right?" I interrupted.

Andie materialized out of nowhere. "Flirting again, I see," she said to *me*.

"Tell that to Jared," I said. "If you're too blind to see the truth, then you deserve him!" I hurried to the back of the foyer area. Refusing to cry, I flipped through the church's brochure, attempting to read the now-blurry statement of faith.

"Holly?"

Whirling around, I found the gray-green eyes of Danny Myers looking down at me.

"Problems with Andie?" His voice had a calming effect on me. I didn't have to tell him what was wrong. The whole choir seemed to know.

My voice grew soft. "It's not her fault. She's just . . ."

"Just what?" He seemed interested. His eyes were kind—so

was his face. He was older than me and seemed wiser spiritually. I remembered the way he'd prayed even at school during lunch.

"She's being fooled," I finally said. "It makes me angry."

"Why does it bother you so much?"

I told him how close Andie and I had always been. Until now. How I preferred *one* best friend and Andie had changed all that, because of Jared.

Danny nodded and smiled as though he understood. "Sit here, Holly." He patted a chair near the deacon's room. "You can't sing with those kinds of feelings. We're here to give to people, to minister through our music. There could be people here tonight who need Jesus."

"I know," I said, tears refusing to dry up. I was thinking of one of those people: Daddy. The Gospel message we sang was for him. "I can't go back in there at all," I mumbled through my tissue. "Not looking this way."

"Let me pray for you."

I blinked the stubborn tears away.

"And we'll pray for Andie, too," he said. "She *needs* your friendship again. Can you forgive her?"

"In my heart, I can. Outside, it's not so easy."

Danny prayed a quiet prayer, full of assurance. It touched my heart. And as the choir lined up for the second half, I felt confident again.

I thrilled to the melodies we sang—slow hymns and fast gospel songs. Lost in the music, I watched Mr. Keller's every move. During the last song, I saw Daddy reach for his handkerchief. He wiped his eyes. It was the first time I'd seen him cry. A lump came to my throat. Could this concert be a new beginning for him? The answer to my prayers?

The church was nearly empty by the time all the equipment was carried out to the bus. Daddy and I were still talking in the second row. Saundra had politely disappeared a half hour before.

Daddy held my hand as he spoke. "So much about me has changed since your aunt Marla died. Losing her has been a great shock. And losing four years of your life . . . and Carrie's, well, I just wish there was a way to catch up somehow."

I hugged him, my tears falling on his suit coat. "I've been praying for you all this time," I said.

"And I love you for it," he said quickly. "We'll have lots more to talk about when you visit this summer." He gave me another hug. "Holly, will you please tell Carrie I love her, too?"

"Those words should come from you," I said.

"The right time will come." He dug into his pocket and pulled three twenty-dollar bills from his money clip. "Here, have fun at Disneyland tomorrow on me."

Something stirred in me. It was the question I had never asked him: Why had he abandoned us? My lips formed the words, but my heart squelched them. I mustn't spoil this moment.

"Thanks," I said, staring at the money. I loved *him,* not what he could give me.

"I'll give you a call when you get back from tour," he said.

"Okay," I answered. One last quick hug, and he was gone.

Staring at the empty pew beside me, I wondered why things had to be this way. If only Daddy hadn't remarried. I crossed my arms and bent over, hugging myself. The old, familiar ache of his absence had returned.

Chapter 19

The towering pinnacles of Sleeping Beauty's Castle loomed into view as our bus rumbled to a stop near the entrance to the Magic Kingdom. Mr. Keller gave some last-minute instructions. "Above all," he warned, "remain in twos. Girls with girls, and boys with boys. Stay with your partner everywhere you go."

Danny flashed a grin at me. I knew he was saying, *Go for it, Holly. Forgive your friend.* Most girls would have loved to have an attractive older-brother type like Danny Myers for a friend. He was perfect.

I leaned over the seat behind Andie. "Wanna be my partner?" I asked.

"Why not," she grumbled. "Everyone else already has one."

Inside the main gate, we raced to Splash Mountain first. The line was long, but just hearing the screams of delight (or was it terror?) as people came hurtling down the fifty-foot drop-off, doing forty miles an hour in those little log boats, told us it would be worth the wait.

So, here we were moving along the ramp, about to go on a must-do fabulous ride together, and we weren't even talking. And Andie was being a real pain about it, too, keeping her back to me the whole time.

I opened my backpack. "Want some gum?" I asked.

"Is it cinnamon?" she asked.

"Spearmint." I held it out.

"Never mind." She wrinkled up her nose. "Save my place. I want to get something to eat."

My heart sank. What more could I do? Was I trying too hard?

My journal was tucked away in one corner of my backpack. So while Andie ran off to get some food, I wrote Proverbs 17:17 in my secret notebook. "A friend loves at all times."

Hmm, I thought, *that means I should keep showing Andie I care about her, even though she's being an impossible brat.*

Soon, Andie was back with a hot dog, chips, and pop. She ignored me more than ever, talking to the girl *ahead* of us instead of me.

Forty-five minutes later, we staggered out of our log boat, having just flown down Chickapin Hill and survived.

"Wanna go again?" I asked, hoping Andie might respond.

"Maybe later" was all she said.

Undaunted, we backtracked to Astro Orbitor, a ride at the entrance to Tomorrowland. Tucked into small "rockets," we circled around planets and other riders. Then we hit the Indiana Jones Adventure, trying to decode the markings along the wall as we moved along the ramp.

Next, Andie and I lined up for some spooky fun at the Haunted Mansion.

Then I spotted Jared. He was across from us, on the docks of the river rafts, sitting with his partner and sharing sodas with two sopranos. I watched as he worked his magic.

"Look over there," I said, pointing at Andie's two-timing friend.

"What?" Andie turned to look. She spotted Jared with the girls, and her face fell.

Silently, we watched as he teased one of them, a pretty soprano named Amy-Liz. One of the cutest girls on choir tour, Amy had curly blond hair and sparkling blue eyes. Jared's foot, newly released from its cast, reached out under the table and touched hers. She giggled and pulled back a little—but not too much. Then his foot found hers again.

"They're playing footsie!" Andie screeched. "I don't believe this."

She ducked under the roped ramp and marched over to Jared. Dying to hear what she would say, I followed.

"Jared!" she called to him.

He spun around, a guilty look on his face. But as soon as he saw Andie he grinned, bowing low. "Andie, my lady."

"Cut the comedy act," she said. "What do you think you're doing?" Andie glared at Amy-Liz.

"Spreading Christian love," he said as the girls giggled behind him.

"Wrong answer. Try this: You're two-timing every girl, everywhere, all the time!"

"I kept telling you, Andie, we're just friends, right?" He turned to Amy-Liz. "Like Amy-Liz and me." Laughing, he took her hand and they left the table.

"You just wait," Andie hollered after him. "Every girl in Dressel Hills is going to hear about you. I promise!"

He waved without turning around.

"He should apply for the Disney court jester, don't you think?" I said.

There was disgust written all over her face. No tears, no jealousy, just plain old disgust. The light had dawned at last.

"Jared's out. He and I are through," she announced, studying me momentarily. "Holly, can you forgive me for everything? I mean, *everything*?"

I had been waiting for this moment. "Hallelujah! The loathsome nightmare is past, and I've regained my long-lost best friend."

"Speak English, would ya?" she said, giggling. This was it. The old Andie was back.

"Look up there," I said, pointing. "Let's celebrate our renewed friendship at the Hungry Bear Restaurant."

At once we raced up the wooden walkway. Waiting in line to order hamburgers, Andie turned me around and began to braid my hair. When we finally sat down at a table on the banks of the Rivers of America, I noticed a lumpy bump in my backpack.

"What's this?" I investigated inside.

Andie opened her bag of chips, ignoring me.

There, under my jacket and all smashed up, was Andie's droopy-eyed teddy bear.

"Pals forever?" she said, wearing a sheepish grin.

" 'Until the final end of us,' " I quoted from our now-defunct Loyalty Papers, hugging Bearie-O close.

"He's missed you, you know," she said softly. "And so have I."

My emotions soared. "I missed you, too, Andie."

She took a bite of hamburger, her eyes shining. "You're really all heart, Holly. Honest. No one else would've stuck with me this long." She leaned over and sprinkled salt on my fries.

"Believe me, I had *major* help," I said, glancing heavenward.

HOLLY'S HEART

Secret Summer Dreams

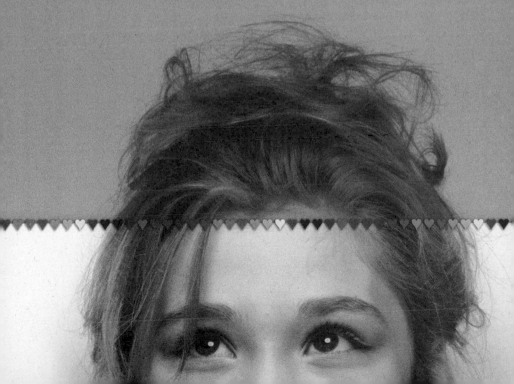

To Jane B. Jones,
my dear mother and friend,
who blessed me with her understanding heart.

And
to her namesake, my Janie . . .
dreamer of heart-dreams,
secret and not so secret.

SECRET SUMMER DREAMS

Chapter 1

"Holly Meredith!"

I awakened with a start. Andie Martinez, my best friend, was standing in the aisle of our chartered tour bus, her brown eyes wide as she stared down at me.

Jared Wilkins and three other boys from the choir were leaning over the seats, getting in on the action. They were laughing as Andie, speechless, pointed at my hair.

Then I felt something. A horrible tickling sensation, as if a giant spider were crawling step by hideous step through my hair. I froze. "Andie, what is it?" I asked through clenched teeth.

"I . . . I'm not sure," she said, her eyes fixed on my head.

The creepy crawling continued. "Get it off me, Andie!"

Jared grinned. "Someone get a tissue. I'll handle this."

"Not you, Jared," I squealed. "Don't *you* touch me."

"Where's a scissor?" one of the boys joked. "Maybe we could get the thing to crawl down her hair, and just cut it out."

"No—Andie!" I shrieked. "Please, no cutting." I wasn't sure which would be worse, losing my nearly waist-length hair or enduring this thing nesting in it.

"What's going on back there?" Mr. Keller, our youth choir director, called from the front of the bus.

"Holly has something in her hair and she's freaking out," Jared said loudly.

By now the thingamabug had moved to the top of my head. I could feel it moving around up there.

"Look, she's turning white," Andie said. "Someone help!"

"Quick, grab my camera," Jared yelled as I sat there, trembling.

A flash of light blinded me. Seconds later a box of tissues came flying. Jared caught it and tossed several to Andie. "Here, if you stuff enough of these in your hand, you'll never have to touch it," he said.

Just then Danny Myers walked down the bus aisle. Unlike most boys in junior high, his head nearly touched the ceiling of the bus. "What's going on with Holly?"

He stopped talking, probably when he spied *it*—the whatever-it-was—having a holiday in my hair. Before I could move, Danny reached over, and with a flick of his fingers, a velvety green beetle flew off my head and toward an open window.

"It's just a June bug," Danny said. "Are you okay, Holly?"

"A *what* bug?" I said, beginning to relax, feeling comfortable as usual around this boy. I shook my hair out, running my fingers all through it.

"Looks like you could use a handful of snickerdoodles," he said, smiling.

"My all-time favorite cookie." I was pleased he'd remembered. Danny was a walking memory chip. "How do you remember details like that?" I asked.

His gray-green eyes turned serious. "I make it a point to recall crucial information—such as the names of important snack foods." He smirked, then we broke into laughter.

I shivered, still feeling that creepy-crawly June bug on my head. Danny must have noticed my concern. "Don't worry, it's definitely gone." He raked his hand through his own auburn hair. "Next time, scream or something. Don't hold it in or you could pass out."

Passing out, otherwise known as fainting, was not an option

for me. Not *this* time. During the seventh-grade musical last winter I'd fainted off the next-to-top riser. Thanks to Andie, I survived the whole embarrassing scene.

Now my best friend was sitting across the aisle from me. "I'm real sorry I freaked over that bug, Holly. I wasn't much help, was I?"

"Forget it." I was still rubbing my head, trying to get rid of the tickly feeling.

"You were so cool about it," Andie said. "Me? I would've behaved like a mad woman. Shouting . . . hysteria, you name it."

I giggled. "I can just imagine."

"Can you believe it? Jared took your picture with that nasty bug in your hair." Andie got up and squeezed her chubby legs past mine and sat down at the window seat next to me.

"Let's not talk about *him*," I whispered. Our former crush, Jared Wilkins, had almost destroyed Andie's and my ten-year friendship. Before he moved to Dressel Hills, Colorado, things had always been perfectly cool between Andie and me. But soon we weren't speaking to each other. Worse, our close friendship ripped apart, and fast, the way Grandma's seam ripper zaps threads. Before we knew it, Andie and I were helplessly caught in an angry tug-of-war over the same guy.

Jared was a charmer, all right. Brown hair and blue eyes with lashes long enough to curl. But looks and charm were *all* he had. Now we knew he was nothing but a two-timing, heartbreaking flirt. Thankfully, Andie and I had come to our senses in time to save our friendship.

Things were fabulous between us now. Yesterday, we'd spent a full day at Disneyland, and now we were racing through the dusty Arizona desert on our way to the Grand Canyon, heading home from the best choir tour ever.

"Daydreaming again?" Andie asked.

"Sort of," I said.

She leaned over, whispering in my ear. "You know what I think?"

I grinned back at her. "What?"

"I think Danny Myers likes you."

"Shh, he'll hear you," I whispered, glancing up toward the front of the bus.

"Well?" she said.

"Well, what?"

Andie curled a strand of dark hair around her finger. "I bet you two skate together at the youth group skating party next week."

I rolled my eyes. "Where do you come up with this stuff?"

"Just wait and see," she said. "I've noticed him watching you, Holly. Ever since we sang at the chapel in L.A."

I stared out the window. Danny Myers wasn't like the eighth-grade boys I knew. At fourteen and a half, he was much more grown-up. More sensitive, too. He'd reached out to me when Andie and I weren't getting along. He probably thought of me as a little sister. That's all.

Andie poked me. "You're avoiding my question."

I pulled on my hair. "I *forgot* the question."

"Nice try." She inched closer. "Hmm, I think I see Danny Myers in your eyes," she teased.

"Get outta my face." I playfully pushed her away.

She giggled, pulling a brochure from her jeans pocket.

"What's that?"

"Info on the Grand Canyon," she said, smoothing the folds. "I picked it up at our last rest stop."

Just then Jared came down the aisle, pausing at our seats. "Hi again, girls." He leaned on the back of my seat and smiled. Andie and I exchanged a quick look.

"Now what?" Andie asked him.

"It's lonely up front," he said.

Andie stood up. Cupping her hands around her eyes, she scanned the front of the bus. Then, with a huge sigh, she sat down. "Looks crowded to me. Plenty of people up there."

I muttered under my breath, "Just no *girls*."

Jared ignored my comment and pointed to Andie's brochure. "Is that what I think it is?"

"Could be," Andie said. "Depends on what you're thinking."

"Looks like there are some great places to hike," he said, studying the brochure. Then, saying no more, he headed to the rest room in the back of the bus.

Andie peered at the information on her brochure. "This says the gorge is two hundred miles long. Wow! Who can see that far?"

"Daddy says he goes to the Grand Canyon when he feels like life is caving in on him," I said softly.

Andie turned toward me. "You must've had a good talk with him after the concert the other night," she said, prying in a roundabout way.

"It was weird seeing him again, you know. He's totally missed out on the last four plus years of my life. Says he wants to catch up."

Andie's dark eyebrows shot up. "How *can* he, when he lives in California with his new wife, and you and your mom and Carrie live in Colorado?"

I took a deep breath. "This summer, probably."

Andie gasped. "You're going to California this summer?"

I nodded.

"Your mother will never let you," Andie said. "And neither will I."

"*You* won't?"

"Have you forgotten that we always go camping together? Every summer since second grade? You don't want to mess things up, do you?" she demanded.

"I have to do this," I said. "For me."

Andie folded her arms in a huff.

But I stared her down. "Please, don't do this. It'll be hard enough getting Mom to let me go, without you putting me on a guilt trip about it."

"Boring . . . boring." She put on her best pout. "It'll be boring for you out there. You'll see."

"Andie, listen," I said. "Your father lives with you and your family. Mine left when I was in third grade. I know you'd be curious, too, if you were me."

"So it's curiosity, then?"

"That and other stuff," I said, reluctant to share more.

"Oh, Holly, don't be stubborn. Just tell me, okay?"

"Not now." I noticed Jared coming back from the rest room. No way was he going to overhear this conversation.

Andie ignored me, continuing her guilt campaign. "It'll be the lousiest summer of my life!"

"Shh!" Privacy was impossible on a bus, especially now that Jared had plopped himself down behind us, eavesdropping. I gave Andie a don't-you-dare-say-anything look. She smoothed out her brochure of Grand Canyon National Park while I flipped through the pages of my devotional book.

"What's the verse for today?" Jared asked, peeking around my seat.

I had already tried the polite approach, so I ignored him and kept reading. Why couldn't he just evaporate?

"Come on, Holly-Heart, give a guy a chance," he crooned. "We can still be friends. Can't we?"

Without looking up, I said, "Holly-Heart is the nickname my mother gave me. It's reserved for relatives and close friends only. Remember?"

Andie glanced over and stifled a giggle.

"Hmm," Jared said. "I don't want to be your relative. But a close friend? Now, that's an idea."

I slammed my book shut, whirling around. "Listen up, Jared. I liked you once, but that's over. Why? Because I don't trust you. Besides, you made big trouble for Andie and me."

Andie started to cheer for me. She forgot that it was quiet time on the bus. Some of the altos turned around and shushed her, and she got as red as the illustrated cliffs on her brochure.

Jared slunk back to his seat like a wounded puppy. Some act.

"Will he ever give up?" I whispered to Andie.

"Persistence is his game," she said. "Now you're a big challenge to him. Maybe if you act a teeny bit interested, he'll leave you alone."

"I can't do that," I said. "I don't want to show any interest in a jerk."

Andie refolded the brochure. "Let's talk summer, Holly."

I sighed and looked away. *She* was persistent, too.

"Please, just think about it. You're throwing our entire summer away," she whined. Andie sounded selfish. She was acting like she hadn't heard a thing I'd said before.

"Can we talk about something else, maybe?" I leaned against the headrest and closed my eyes.

"No fair sleeping. June, July, and August are coming faster than you think."

"Okay," I said, giving in. "Besides the family camping trip, what else do you want to do?"

"A raft trip," she said, sitting on the edge of her seat. "A wild and crazy white-water raft trip down the Arkansas River. I hear it's outrageous. Imagine the breathtaking thrill of Zoom Flume, Screaming Right, and get this . . . the Widow Maker!"

"Which means girls have to be pretty tough if the guys don't survive," I concluded.

"And," she said, her voice growing louder and more excited, "the minimum age is twelve, so you know it's gotta be very wild."

More annoyed looks were cast our way by choir members observing Mr. Keller's stipulated quiet time. I put my finger to my lips.

Slumping down in her seat, Andie curled her legs beneath her. She grinned. Andrea Martinez—Miss Magnificent Manipulator—had me and she knew it. Rafting was the one thing I'd been dying to do. An all-day trip down the mighty Arkansas, along with two fabulous weeks of camping with Andie and her family. Irresistible.

Mom's idea of camping was the Holiday Inn without maid service. No chance *she'd* go. But Andie's family? That was a different story. Her twin baby brothers, Chris and Jon, would stay with their grandma, then off we'd go. Before the arrival of the "double blessing"—as Andie's mom liked to call the twins—the Martinez family had gone camping every summer. Thanks to Andie, I'd been invited to tag along.

What great summers we'd had. Always camping high in the Colorado Rockies near the Twin Lakes that nestled like giant mirrors beneath soaring mountains. There, the air smelled of pine trees and the lakes were so blue it seemed a piece of sky had fallen to the earth. Wispy clouds scurried past snowy mountain peaks and the summer sun warmed the valleys. It was enough to birth the poet in me.

Andie's father, dashing and comical, kept us in stitches at all times. Summer and laughter seemed to hold hands—at least on camping trips with Andie and her family. Would spending the summer with Daddy be worth the sacrifices I'd have to make?

The sacrificial list was growing. I'd miss out on camping with Andie, youth meetings, white-water rafting, and . . . yes, maybe getting to know Danny Myers better. But I wasn't going to let any of it come between me and my secret summer dream to visit my dad and get to know *him* for the first time in four long years.

Chapter 2

"Quiet time's over. Sleepers awake!" Walking down the aisle of the bus, Mr. Keller clapped his hands to rouse dozing choir members. "We're coming close to the Grand Canyon," he said.

The Grand Canyon. The words awakened all thirty of us. Soon the bus was buzzing with excited voices.

I grabbed Andie's leaflet, tracing the path of the Colorado River with my finger. From what I'd read, its treacherous rapids and gigantic boulders made navigation barely possible.

"That's *one* raft trip we can forget about," Andie said as my finger slid along the path the swift river cut through the canyon.

"Guess you'd have to psych yourself up for a trip like that," I said.

Andie looked pleased. "So, you *are* thinking about staying home this summer?"

I flashed her a knowing smile. She was so sneaky. The little rat!

Mr. Keller announced that we were welcome to explore the area as long as we did not wander off alone. "Please take someone with you," he said. "I want to return all of you to your families in one piece."

"How dangerous *is* this place?" I asked Andie.

"Can't be too dangerous," she said. "Look at all the people."

We peered out the window as the bus inched into an open spot. The parking lot was really crowded.

"We'll see soon enough," I said, wondering if this place would be any big deal.

We bounded off the bus and headed straight for the lookout area, which was rimmed with a rock wall.

"Fabulous." That's all I could say for the next five minutes as Andie and the rest of the kids and I stood there drinking in the awesome sight.

It was late afternoon, and a golden haze lay over the canyon. Gazing across, I could see the rosy reds and gray-blues of the cliff-like formations. Dark ravines, gouged out by the river's tortuous path, made me feel small, like a speck in the universe. I felt lost in the canyon's never-endingness. Squinting, I wondered where it ended. Andie was right. Who can see for two hundred miles?

I felt Andie's hand on my arm.

"You okay?" she asked.

I felt frozen. "It's . . . it's like *forever.*"

"You're right," Danny said. I hadn't noticed him standing there next to me, but Andie must have. She threw me a look that said "I told you."

I ignored her and turned to Danny. "Makes me wonder how God keeps track of everything on this earth," I said. "He even knows how many hairs are on our heads."

"And when June bugs are gonna dance in them," Andie said, tugging playfully at my long hair. She consulted her brochure. "It says here that the park is almost two thousand square miles, and that there are 290 species of birds that fly between these canyon walls."

Danny pulled out his binoculars and scanned the rocks below. "The smallest animals live in those crevices a mile down," he said. "No way can God be nearsighted."

Andie and I laughed. Out of the corner of my eye I spotted Jared, standing a few feet away and looking annoyed. Probably jealous of the attention we were giving Danny. *Too bad,* I thought. *He had his chance, and boy did he blow it.*

Danny touched my arm. He was still looking through his binoculars, but he directed my gaze to a ledge far below. "If you look carefully, you'll see a red-tailed hawk," he said, handing the binoculars to me. He helped me adjust the focus and pointed me in the right direction. "They live in all parts of the canyon, except near damp areas or open water."

Then I spotted what he was talking about—a fierce, proud bird, perched on the edge of a cliff. Spreading its wings, it flew away, and I followed it with the binoculars until it disappeared from view.

"Thanks. That was cool." I handed the binoculars back to him. Smiling, he took them from me, then moved closer to the stone wall to peer down the edge of the ravine.

"How does Danny know all that stuff?" Andie whispered to me.

"He reads constantly," I said.

"Anyone can read. How does he remember all of it?" Andie asked.

"Photographic memory, I guess." Admiration filled me as I watched Danny. He had his binoculars up again, slowly scanning the canyon.

The group started to break up. A bunch of kids went to the gift shop to buy souvenirs and candy. Others hung around the coin-operated telescopes. Jared came over and suggested that we hike down into the canyon a short distance. "It's safe enough," he said. "And we've got a whole hour. Mr. Keller said we need to be back on the bus, ready to go, at six."

"Uh, I don't know," I said, looking down at the great abyss.

"C'mon, Holly. Don't be such a scaredy," Andie said. "Where's the trailhead?" she asked Jared.

"This way." They walked off together, leaving me with Danny.

"Is it safe, do you think?" I asked.

"We won't hike far." Danny moved up beside me. We followed Jared and Andie as they made their way toward the hiking path. "Want to wear these?" Danny asked, pulling the binoculars over his head.

"Sure."

He handed them to me and our fingers touched slightly. A

strange, giddy feeling shot like an arrow straight to my heart. Was I falling for Danny Myers?

Don't be silly, I told myself.

We hurried to the trailhead, where Jared and Andie had stopped to wait for us. I peered hesitantly down the path. The blacktopped path zigzagged down the side of the cliff, and it wasn't exactly level. In fact, it looked like a forty-degree angle to me.

"Stay close to this." Andie patted the reddish rock wall to the left of us.

One hand touching the wall, I headed down the trail, my tennies skidding a little on the steep path. Keeping my eyes on the trail, I tried not to think about the sheer drop-off to the right of me. Jared led the way, followed by Andie, then me, and last, Danny. I was glad he was behind me. Somehow it made me feel safer.

After completing several switchbacks, we stopped to gaze at the beauty around us. I made sure my back was safely up against the canyon wall before I pulled out the binoculars and scanned the slopes just below the canyon rim.

There was a slight movement. I adjusted the focus. A deer with antlers and the largest ears I'd ever seen made me catch my breath.

"What is it, Holly?" Danny asked.

"I think it's a deer, but it has huge ears." I watched as the animal moved boldly along the cliff, grazing.

Danny said, "Must be a mule deer."

"Hee-haw!" Jared brayed like a donkey. "Let's see!" He pushed between Danny and me.

"Wait a second, Jared," I said, still gazing through the lenses. The deer had lifted its head and seemed to be staring at me, its head cocked, its eyes alert. I inched forward, intent on the beautiful creature.

"Hurry," Jared said in a silly voice, pulling on the strap to the binoculars.

"Just a minute," I snarled, swinging away from him. As I did, I lost my balance. The binoculars fell from my hands and my feet slipped away from me. Desperate, I grabbed for the canyon wall. Anything to keep me from falling.

Andie screamed, "Holly, no!"

Chapter 3

For a terrifying second the sky spun above me.

Then I felt a strong hand grab my arm. "I've got you, Holly." Danny reached for me with both hands and pulled me away from the drop-off. "Here." He set me against the canyon wall. Shaking, I leaned against the rock, my hands wet with fear. I refused to look down into the great chasm below.

Andie took my hand. "Holly, you scared me," she said. "Are you all right?"

I nodded slowly, trying to catch my breath. She and Danny looked at me, concern written on their faces. Jared hung back, knowing it was his fault.

Closing my eyes, I took a few more breaths. I could still feel my feet slipping out beneath me, the sky tilting to meet me. . . .

I shivered and opened my eyes. "I'm fine, really," I said when Andie and Danny didn't look convinced. "Danny saved my life."

I pressed my hands against the canyon wall. The solid rock felt reassuring under my fingertips. Suddenly, I remembered. "The binoculars. They're gone!"

Jared held them high over his head. "Never fear, Jared's here."

"That's what I'm afraid of," Danny said, frowning. "If you

hadn't been here, clowning around like that, none of this would've happened."

"Well, let's hear it for Mr. Responsible," Jared mocked. "If Holly hadn't been looking through *your* binoculars . . ." His voice trailed off.

What a ridiculous comparison, yet Danny said nothing. The two boys glared at each other.

"Can we go back now?" I asked, still shaken up.

Jared started to argue, but Danny gave him a stern look and he stopped.

"I'll go behind you, Holly, and catch you if you slip," Danny said.

"Thanks," I said.

Jared led the way again, with Andie following. My knees still shook from the close call as I started up the trail, watching my step and staying close to the right side of the path, near the wall. Whenever I even glimpsed the edge of the trail, I shivered deep inside.

The climb up took us longer than coming down. Soon I was breathing hard.

"Can you make it all right?" Danny asked behind me.

"Yeah," I said, not turning my head. We didn't talk the rest of the way. I was still too rattled to concentrate on anything except getting out of there.

At last we arrived at the top. I turned around for one last look, and then the four of us headed for the bus.

A tassel-eared squirrel darted across our path. We stopped to watch as it shimmied over the rocks and disappeared. "What kind of squirrel is that?" I asked. "I've never seen anything like it in Colorado."

"I have an animal guide back in the bus," Danny said. "We can look it up there if you want."

"Sure," I said.

Andie flashed me a knowing smile. I knew what she was thinking.

Mr. Keller was waiting for all of us beside the bus door, counting kids as we boarded the bus.

"One more day before we head home," Mr. Keller told us. "We'll spend tonight at Flagstaff, and then we'll leave for Colorado bright and early tomorrow."

Danny offered his hand to help me into the bus. "Are you sure you're okay?" he asked, pointing the way to his seat.

I nodded, aware of my stomach flutters as we sat side by side.

From his backpack he pulled out a handbook. "You were so interested in the animals back there, I thought you'd like to check this out."

He turned to a picture of a Kaibab squirrel. Its tail was completely white, and the caption said it was rare and endangered and lived only on the north rim.

"The squirrel I saw had a gray tail with white underneath," I said. "Must not be a Kaibab." I paged through his book. "This is too cool."

"You can have it," Danny said, his eyes dancing.

I wondered why he was giving the book away. Had he already memorized it?

"Thanks," I said, holding it. "And for saving my life, uh, back there." I started to feel a bit shy. There wasn't much more to say. "I'd better get back to Andie now. See you later."

Heading down the aisle, I saw Andie give me her thumbs-up sign. She eyed the book Danny had just given me. "What's that?"

I showed her the animal guidebook. "Isn't it terrific?"

She whistled. "So tell me everything," she said as I sat down. "What's going on between you two?"

"How should I know?" I said, puzzled at my own excitement over Danny. "I mean, he's like a big brother. That's all."

"That's *not* all," she insisted. "He kept you from being a skinny little grease spot at the bottom of the Grand Canyon!"

There was no denying that. Andie was absolutely right, and I couldn't hide my smile.

When we arrived in Flagstaff, Andie and I settled into our hotel room. All of us had supper at a McDonald's nearby, then a few of the kids went swimming while others played a game of Rook on the pool patio.

I searched for a pay phone. It had been days since I talked to Mom. I found one in the hotel lobby and punched in the number for my phone card.

The baby-sitter answered. It was Marcia Greene, a straight-A student from school.

"Hi, Marcia," I said. "It's Holly. Is Mom home?"

There was an awkward pause. "Just a minute," she said. "Here's Carrie."

"Hi, Holly," Carrie said when she got on the phone. "Where are you?"

"In Arizona. We'll be home tomorrow night."

"Goody! Can't wait to see you. It's real boring here without you."

Carrie's voice made me homesick. "Where's Mom?" I asked.

"Out on a date."

I almost choked. "A date? Who with?"

"Some man," Carrie said.

"Do I know him?" I said, feeling like a parent screening a prospective suitor.

"His name is Mr. Tate. He's new at church. Mom went out with him to dinner somewhere real fancy."

I coughed. "How do you know all this?"

"Well, Mom never dresses up to go to the Golden Arches, does she?"

"I guess you're right," I said, laughing only on the outside. "Tell Mom I called. See you tomorrow night." I hung up.

What a nightmare! Mom had never loved anyone but Daddy, at least until he left us and got remarried. I actually thought she was okay with being single. But now, while I was hundreds of miles away on choir tour, she'd started to date. What on earth was going on?

Slowly I climbed the stairs to our hotel room. Andie was out swimming, so I took a long shower, then climbed into bed without waiting for her to return to the room.

When my watch beeped out the time at six o'clock the next morning, I woke up immediately. My first thought was of Mom. I couldn't wait to get back home, where I wish I could've been last night. I was desperate for a heart-to-heart talk with Mom. Where was her good sense?

I leaped out of bed and stuffed my clothes into an overnight bag.

"What's the rush?" Andie said, rubbing her sleepy eyes. "You're not homesick, are you?"

"No."

"Hey, what's bugging you?" She sat up, stretching. "You're always so cheerful in the morning."

"Mom's started dating." I bunched up my pajamas and thrust them deep into the bag.

Andie scrunched her nose. "She's what?"

"You heard me."

"Did I miss something? How do you know?" She took her brush from the nightstand and began counting the strokes out loud. Stopping at fifteen, she said, "Come on, Holly. Talk to me."

I wanted to cry. "I called home last night, and Carrie said Mom was out on a date," I explained. "Out with some guy she met at church: Mr. Tate." I swallowed hard. "I'm just upset, that's all."

"How come?" Andie looked puzzled. "You should be happy for your mom. Doesn't this mean she's growing past her pain—you know, accepting the divorce and all that?"

I shrugged. I didn't think Mom needed to grow. She seemed fine just the way she was.

Andie persisted. "Well, it *is* a good sign, isn't it?"

I didn't want to talk about this. Besides, Andie had no idea what it was like to lose a father to divorce and possibly a mother to remarriage.

No idea at all.

Chapter 4

Carrie and Mom were waiting in the church parking lot when our bus finally rolled into Dressel Hills. It was dark, but in the streetlight I could see a purple and pink balloon bouquet floating out of our car window. Grinning, Carrie was waving the balloons back and forth.

The bus came to a stop, and the kids began gathering small pieces of luggage under their seats.

"Hey, Holly," called Jared from the middle of the stampede. "Need any help?"

"No thanks," I replied. I'd made sure to avoid him ever since my near-death experience in the Grand Canyon.

Andie poked me. "Are you *sure* you don't want the finest-looking boy in Dressel Hills to help you with your bags?"

"*He* almost got me killed." I stashed the nature book from Danny into my backpack.

"You're guarding that book pretty close, I see," she teased.

"It's full of interesting stuff."

"Well, if you can't find all the facts in there," she said, tapping the book through the backpack, "I know a guy who's a walking encyclopedia." Andie jerked her head toward Danny.

I blushed.

Loaded down with backpacks, we squeezed through the swarm of kids exiting the bus. At last we were outside. We gathered around as the driver opened the huge luggage compartment.

My eight-year-old sister jumped out of the car. "Holly!" she cried, running toward me. "Look what I got you with my own money." She held out the balloon bouquet.

"What a sweetie," I said. "Thanks!"

Surprisingly, Andie's and my suitcases were among the first to be unloaded from the bus. Mom had already opened the car trunk, and Andie lugged her stuff to our car while Mom stood smiling at me. No, she was literally grinning. "Welcome home, Holly-Heart." She hugged me close. Maybe my eyes were pulling tricks on me, but Mom looked happier than she had since Daddy had divorced us. I mean, *her*. My stomach tightened. What did it mean, this strange glow?

"How was the choir tour?" Mom asked, arranging my luggage in the trunk.

"Fabulous," I said.

"Let's hear all about Disneyland," she said as Andie and I climbed into the backseat, the balloons bobbing between us.

Carrie turned around and peered over the front seat. "Did you get a Mickey Mouse for me?"

"Wait and see," I teased.

I wanted to fire my questions about Mom's new love interest, but I bit my lip. I'd just have to wait till Andie and Carrie weren't around.

When we stopped at a red light, Carrie asked, "Did you see your daddy?"

"He's *your* daddy, too," I replied.

"I don't have a daddy."

Andie looked surprised. "What does she mean?" she whispered.

"You do so," I insisted, ignoring my friend's question.

Mom tried to explain, probably for Andie's benefit. "Carrie

151

doesn't remember her father because she was so young when he left."

"Well?" Carrie wouldn't let it go. "Did you see him?"

"Uh-huh," I said slowly, not wanting to let on just how important my visit with Daddy had been.

"What's he like?"

"Carrie, honey," Mom interrupted. "Maybe Holly would like to wait to talk about this later."

"It's okay," I said, sticking up for Carrie.

Seemed obvious to me that *Mom* was the one who didn't want to discuss it. Her attitude upset me. I decided to get right to the heart of things. "I've made a decision," I announced. "I'm going to spend the summer with Daddy."

"You're what?" Carrie said.

"Wait a minute," Mom said. "We haven't talked over any of this."

"Yeah," Carrie said. "I won't let you go away all summer."

Andie glared at me. "Neither will I," she said softly.

Let me? Nobody seemed to care what *I* wanted. Even Andie seemed too close to blowing up over my decision. Fortunately, we turned into her driveway before she had time to have a hissy fit.

Unloading her luggage, she turned to me beneath the raised trunk. "Oh, Holly," her voice shook. "I can't believe you'd really do this."

"What? Like it's some horrible, hideous thing to want to get better acquainted with your father?"

"*You* know what I'm talking about," she said in a huff.

It was deathly still as Mom drove the short distance home. But as we turned onto Downhill Court, Mom said, "Holly, I understand Carrie told you that I was away on a date last night. My friend's name is Mike Tate, and he will be meeting us at home."

Tate. That rhymed perfectly with date and late. He wouldn't be Mom's date tonight, or at all, if I hadn't been so late. This mess could've been avoided if I hadn't been off on choir tour.

"Mr. Tate's coming over?" Carrie asked excitedly.

Mom nodded. "Only for a short time. We have something important to discuss. And I'd like Holly to meet him."

"Terrific," I mumbled, wondering how this guy had managed
to upstage my return home. This was supposed to be *my* night!

Our headlights bounced off a somber blue car up ahead. "There
he is," Carrie said, pointing as we pulled into the driveway.

A stocky man got out of the car and came around to help Mom
with her door. It reminded me of Danny offering his hand to help
me climb into the bus yesterday.

"Holly," Mom said, "I'd like you to meet Mike Tate. Mike, this
is my older daughter, Holly."

I shifted the balloon bouquet to my left hand so I could shake
his hand. "Nice to meet you," I mumbled.

"Well, it's very nice to meet you, too, Holly," Mr. Tate said.
"Your mother has told me a lot about you."

Like what? I wondered. I didn't like the idea of Mom discussing
me with some guy. I mean, she'd just met him, for pete's sake.

Mr. Tate gathered up my luggage, and we headed for the front
door. Under the light of our porch lamp, I saw a shiny bald spot
on his head. He opened the screen door, holding it while Mom
found her key. I could tell by the way he stood there what type of
a person he was. Polite and structured. He wasn't nearly as tall as
Daddy. Not nearly as handsome, either.

Inside, Mom said, "Holly, why don't you go ahead and unpack?
Just toss your dirty clothes in the hamper. I'll do the wash tomorrow evening."

I grabbed my bags and headed for the stairs. She sure was
in a hurry to get rid of me. When I glanced back, I saw Mr. Tate
touch the tip of Mom's elbow, guiding her through the dining room
toward the kitchen.

"We'll be in here if you need anything," Mom called.

Carrie asked, "Can I have a bubble bath, Mommy?"

"That's fine," Mom said. "Holly-Heart, could you help Carrie
rinse her hair?"

"Sure," I said. Carrie and I headed upstairs, leaving Mom and that Mr. Tate person sitting at the island bar in our kitchen. I often helped Carrie rinse the shampoo out of her hair. It was as thick and almost as long as mine.

"How much bubble bath can I put in?" Carrie called from the bathroom.

"Doesn't matter," I said, lugging my bags into my room.

"Goody." Carrie ran to the hallway closet and came back with three bottles of the bubble stuff.

"What are you doing?"

She giggled. "You said it didn't matter how much."

"Just don't flood the bathroom with suds," I said, closing the door.

Back in my room, my stuffed animals stared at me from their shelf-home near my window seat—my favorite place to think. And write.

I yanked my backpack off, pulling out a droopy-eyed stuffed animal. "Welcome back, Bearie-O," I said to the tan teddy bear. He actually belonged to Andie. Six years ago we'd traded favorite bears. A very cool thing to do with your best friend.

I sat on my canopy bed and leaned Bearie-O gently against my pillow. "What do *you* think of my summer plans?" I asked the love-worn teddy. He looked intently at me. At least *he* would listen. A good trait for a best friend. Mothers too.

"I've saved up secret wishes ever since Daddy left," I whispered. "You're the only one who knows them all." I stroked the place on his head where the fur was sparse, a bald spot made from kissing his teddy head good-night. Yikes! It made me think of bald Mr. Tate downstairs with Mom.

I reached for the mini straw hat on my hillbilly mouse. Plopping it down on Bearie-O, I prayed out loud. "Please, Lord, don't let this man mess up our lives."

I unpacked the Mickey Mouse I'd purchased for Carrie and marched down the hall. "Knock, knock," I said, tapping on the bathroom door.

"Who's there?" Carrie answered, playing along.

"Mickey Mouse."

Carrie squealed, "Really?"

I sneaked Mickey around the door and peeked him in.

More squealing.

"Do you need a shampoo, little girl?" Mickey said in a high-pitched voice.

"Nope, it's all done," Carrie answered.

It was *my* turn to peek around the door. There sat Carrie in a mountain of shampoo bubbles, suds closing in on her eyebrows.

"It's time for some expert help," I said. "Besides, you need to get to bed soon. Tomorrow's Sunday."

"Let Mickey watch us rinse my hair," Carrie said.

"Okay." I set Mickey on the sink counter, wondering what I was like at eight. I remembered a surprise birthday gift from Daddy—a shiny red bike. That was my last birthday with him.

"Do you like Mr. Tate?" Carrie asked between rinsings.

"Don't know him," I said.

"He's real nice, Holly. You should see what he got me."

I felt uneasy. Not only was he showering my mother with attention, he was buying off my little sister.

"I'll show you the present when I say my prayers." She held her breath and disappeared under the bubbles. Golden strands of hair floated up like a mermaid's.

At last her bath was done. I used the hair dryer on her long locks and braided it slightly damp to keep the tangles out, the way I did my own every night.

In her room, I was surprised to see a giant mermaid posed on her bed. "This is new, isn't it?" I asked.

"From Mr. Tate."

"That's nice."

The gift was. *He* wasn't. I knew I wouldn't let myself like this man. Presents or not, he had no business with our family.

I listened to Carrie say her prayers, then I tucked her in.

"I'm glad you're home again, Holly," said Carrie. "You really won't go off to California this summer, will you?" Her soft blue eyes pleaded with me.

"I want to get to know Daddy better, Carrie. Can you understand that?"

"What about *me*?" She curled her lip into a pout. "What will *I* do all summer?"

"We'll talk more tomorrow," I said, feeling like a grown-up.

"You can talk all you want," she said, "but it won't change my mind. Not one bit!"

I hugged my spunky sis, then left the door cracked open to let the hall light shine in a little. I hurried to my window seat for some secret list-making. Curling up, I began to write in my notebook. On the left side of the page I wrote reasons for going to California. On the right side, reasons for staying home.

CALIFORNIA	HOME
1. Get to know Daddy better.	1. Keep Mom away from Mr. Tate.
2. Learn more about my childhood from Daddy.	2. Go camping and rafting with Andie and family.
3. Stay at a beach house.	3. Make Carrie happy.
4. Prove to Mom I am grown-up enough.	4. Attend youth group and parties.
	5. Find out if Danny Myers really likes me.

So far, there were five reasons to stay home and only four to go to California.

I reached for my teen devotional. After reading it, I wrote the fifth reason: Talk to Daddy about God.

Now both sides were tied.

Chapter 5

The next morning, before I got out of bed, I wrote in my diary—
Sunday, March 28. Then I copied the secret list into my journal.
Afterward, I prayed.

"Please, oh please, dear Lord, make Mom let me go to visit
Daddy this summer. It's the most important thing in my life now.
Honest. Amen."

Feeling satisfied that I was approaching this like a mature
Christian, I went downstairs and poured myself a bowl of cereal.
After breakfast I called Andie. No answer. She must have gone to
the early service at church.

Just as I hung up, the phone rang. I could tell it was long
distance. Daddy!

"How was your trip home?" he asked.

"Perfect," I said.

"The Grand Canyon?"

I remembered the powerful feeling I had there. "I think I know
what you mean about that place," I said softly.

"It's amazing," he said. "And Holly, you'll be even more inspired
if you ever have the chance to hike down into it."

"I, uh, sort of did that," I said, recalling my near-fatal fall.

"Well, how was it?"

"Much scarier than I dreamed it would be." I didn't explain what had happened. I didn't say I nearly dropped into the Grand Canyon.

"Pretty steep, was it?" He paused, then asked, "Have you thought any more about your summer plans?"

I wanted to say Mom was chewing her nails over his invitation, but didn't. It could be a mistake to get him in the middle of things here.

"I really want to come—more than anything," I said, hesitating. "But there's, uh, lots of stuff going on here. I just don't know how it's gonna fly."

"Well, Holly, I can get your plane tickets in a jiffy, so that's no problem. Let me know when you're sure. Okay?"

"Sure, Daddy. Thanks."

"How's Carrie?" he asked.

"Spunky as ever," I said, laughing. "She missed me so much, she welcomed me home with balloons she bought with her own money."

He chuckled. "Tell her thanks for sending the artwork. I hung it up on the wall in my study."

"Why don't *you* tell her?"

"I'm in a rush," he said quickly. "Have an appointment with a client in thirty minutes. I'll talk to you soon. Good-bye, Holly."

I hung up, feeling sad that he was headed off to work instead of church. On a Sunday morning, no less.

Tiptoeing up the steps, I heard Mom singing. I went to her bedroom door and knocked.

"Come in," she called cheerfully.

As I entered, she drew back the curtains, letting the morning drift in. Dressed in her soft pink robe, Mom looked like an angel, her blond hair spilling forward on her shoulders. She sat down on the bed.

"Can we talk?" I asked.

She patted the bed beside her. "Sure, what's up?"

"Mr. Tate," I said, getting right to the point.

"Oh?"

"How long have you known him?"

She looked at the ceiling, like she was counting something invisible. "About ten days, I guess."

"You've gotta be kidding," I said. "And you've been out with him? Mom, he could be a bank robber, a serial killer, a—"

"Honey," she interrupted. "I met him at *church*."

"I've never seen him there before."

"He came from another church, he and his son."

I sighed. "So he's been married before?"

"His wife died several years ago. He's lonely." She touched my hair. "Like I am."

How could I follow up with my anti-Tate campaign when Mom looked so happy? I couldn't tamper with that. At least not now.

"Do you like him?" I asked.

"He's very nice. And his adorable little boy is in my Sunday school class. *He's* the one who introduced me to Mike."

I studied her.

"I hope you'll give him a chance, Holly-Heart, even though it may be difficult."

"Okay, I guess." I wanted to ask why he picked our church to come to, and why he was so bald. Instead, I hugged her and ran to wake Carrie for Sunday school. Maybe Mom was right. Maybe I *should* give Mike Tate a chance. But he'd better prove himself fast, because I wasn't going to give him very long.

After school on Monday I was at my locker, dropping off books and loading up my backpack, when Jared popped around my locker door. "Boo!" he said.

"Eek!" I squealed, jumping back.

"Didn't scare you, did I?"

"Get away from me," I said.

"Let's go skating next Friday, Holly-Heart."

"Don't call me that," I said coldly.

"Oh, that's right. I forgot," he said. "The name's to be used only by close friends and relatives."

"Perfect, you remembered. Now remember *not* to say it." I glimpsed Andie speeding toward us.

She grabbed my arm. "Quick, I've forgotten our English homework assignment," she said, out of breath.

"It's here somewhere," I said, flipping through my assignment notebook. "There." I handed it to her, wondering why she hadn't paid attention in Miss Wannamaker's class.

Jared leaned over my shoulder, real close. "Cool handwriting, Holly."

"You need a decoder for yours," Andie joked, scribbling the assignment on the back of her lunch bag.

Jared leaned on my locker, almost in it. "That's some ingenious essay Miss W has planned. 'Write about your secret summer fantasy—what you would most like to have happen this summer,' " he said, mimicking Miss W's sweet voice. "Where do you think she gets these wild ideas for our writing assignments?"

"She has a creative mind," I said, gathering my books and slamming my locker.

"When are you going to start writing your essay, Holly?" Andie asked. "It's due next week."

"I *am* writing it—in my head."

Finished scribbling, Andie pushed the brown lunch bag into her jeans pocket, and together we squeezed through the crowd of kids in the hall.

"Wish I could pull an *A* on this paper," Andie said.

"I have zillions of ideas," I said, rearranging the books in my arm.

"Oh yeah? What's *your* summer fantasy?" Jared asked, suddenly behind me.

I ignored him. When would he ever give up?

"Come on, Holly," he persisted. "Forget the past. Let's start over like we've never met."

Wish that were true, I thought. Up until last winter, not one guy had shown interest in me. I figured it was because I was as flat as Kansas and skinnier than the Oklahoma panhandle. Andie said it was because I was a threat to a guy's IQ. Mom said it didn't matter, since I was too young to care what boys thought. But Jared? Jared had said I was *perfect* and that he liked me just the way I was. The fact that it was only one of his many lines still hurt. A lot.

"So, Holly, what'll it be?" Jared asked, pressing against the crowd near me. "Will you please go skating with me Friday?"

"Leave her alone," Andie said. "Can't you understand English?"

Jared whined like a wounded puppy—one of his better routines. He slumped back away from me, and the crowd devoured him. I quickened my pace to match Andie's.

Outside, Andie asked, "Just what *is* your secret summer fantasy, Holly?"

"I think you already know," I said. "We've discussed it enough, and I'm not saying more till I know what's really going to happen." I was determined not to tell her I had talked with Daddy yesterday. I didn't want to get into another argument with her.

Andie sulked for a moment. Then she said, "Give me some ideas for English. What sort of summer fantasy could I possibly write about?"

"Here's one," I said. "You're on a wild raft trip, and you fall for the cute guide. Or maybe you rescue someone who falls off going through the rapids. How're *those* for summer fantasies?"

"Good deal! You oughta be a writer, you know," Andie said.

"I *am* a writer, just not a published one," I said, pushing my hair back over my shoulder. "But someday."

Outside, we skipped down the steps of Dressel Hills Junior High and headed for Aspen Street, where mobs of ski buffs mingled during the winter, waiting for a bus to the slopes. Things were much quieter now. Ski resorts had reduced their rates for spring skiing, and guys skied without shirts or in shorts, getting a jump on their tans.

Andie interrupted my thoughts. "Has Danny called you since we got back?"

"Nope. And he wasn't in church yesterday, either."

"So you noticed." She was so coy.

"Not exactly."

"Of course you did. C'mon, the guy saved your life."

I agreed. "Do you really think he likes me?"

"He gave you his guidebook, didn't he?" Andie said. "I mean, it's so cool, Holly. After the way Jared treated you, you deserve some attention from a decent guy. Enjoy it."

"It won't matter when I'm out in California this summer," I said. A California summer would be a great change from this boring town. Sun and fun, and warm breezes blowing in off the ocean. Late nights and long talks with Daddy. The way it used to be.

"Oh no. Not *this* again." Andie rolled her eyes.

I turned away, looking up at the mountains around us. The ski runs, covered with the last snow of winter, soon would be bare and brown. Ski lifts would carry hikers in shorts and sturdy leather boots instead of skiers in colorful parkas. The countdown to summer vacation had begun.

Halfway to the end of Downhill Court, I saw Mr. Tate's dreary blue Ford turn into our driveway.

Andie spotted it, too. "Looks like you've got company."

"Not *mine*." I wanted to turn and hightail it back to school. Then I heard footsteps behind me.

It was Carrie. A small boy wearing a red baseball cap trailed behind her.

"Hi, Holly. Hi, Andie," Carrie called, brushing past us.

"Where's the fire?" I asked.

"Zachary has to throw up," she shouted over her shoulder. They dashed into the house.

Andie snorted. "Where'd she find *him*?"

I shrugged my shoulders, puzzled. "Never saw the kid before in my life."

"Isn't he too young to be hanging out with Carrie?" she asked. We climbed the steps leading to our redwood porch.

"Who knows? One thing's for sure, he's new around here." I opened the front door, eager to find out what was going on.

Chapter 6

Inside, our house was in an uproar. Mom was standing outside the bathroom door, wringing her hands. Carrie was hanging on Mom, hands cupped over her ears, and Zachary—whoever he was—was in the bathroom, making horrible retching sounds.

"What's going on?" I asked. "Who's Zachary?"

Just then, Mr. Tate emerged from the bathroom with the white-faced boy.

"Er, excuse me," I said, moving out of the way.

Carrie patted the boy on the back. "You okay, Zach?"

He nodded weakly. But he didn't look okay to me.

"Let's find a place for you to rest," Mr. Tate said.

Mom led Zachary downstairs to the living room, and Mr. Tate followed.

"What's wrong with him?" I whispered to Carrie.

"Some pill he has to take," she said. "It makes him sick."

Then it hit me. Zachary was Mr. Tate's kid.

"Why are *they* here?" I asked Carrie.

"Mr. Tate's cooking lasagna for dinner," she explained.

"What?" I was shocked. Men like Mr. Tate seemed just a little too resourceful in my opinion. I didn't care to stick around and eat *his* meal.

"Can I eat at your house tonight?" I asked Andie.

"Sure!" Andie said. "We're having Stove Top Stuffing!" We giggled loudly.

"Holly, stop clowning around and come here," Mom called from the bottom of the stairs.

I hurried down, embarrassed that she had overheard.

"Please keep the noise down, and will you get a blanket for Zachary?" she said.

"And a pillow," Mr. Tate called.

Feeling like a slave for Mr. Tate's sick kid, I went to the hall linen closet and pulled out blankets and a pillow. Some gall, exposing all of us to the flu. When I came down the stairs, arms loaded, Mom and Mr. Tate were still hovering over Zachary. They didn't even say thanks.

Andie and I escaped upstairs to my room. I grabbed my notebook and a pencil.

"What's that for?" Andie asked, flopping onto my bed.

I scribbled off a limerick. "Listen to this," I said, laughing so hard I could barely read.

> "There once was a man named Tate
> With a balding pate like fish bait.
> His son had the flu.
> He threw up on cue.
> Such a terrible, horrible fate!"

Andie burst into giggles. "Mr. Tate's head doesn't look *wormy!*"

"But worms are smooth and don't have hair," I said.

Andie held her sides, laughing.

"I rest my case," I said as Andie reached for my notebook.

"Here, let's think of all the words that rhyme with Tate," she said.

"Okay, first off—*regurgitate*. It even has Tate at the end!" I scratched my head. "And it describes how I feel about him hanging around here with his throw-uppy kid."

"I know what you mean," Andie said. "If my mother were divorced and Tate was cooking lasagna for us, I'd create a scene and *agitate* him so he'd *irritate* my mother."

I continued. "Then I'd *terminate* their social life and *accentuate* the good life—which was life before Tate, who's looking for a *mate*."

Andie clapped, and I took a bow. "Hey, you're pretty good yourself. There's hidden literary talent in there," I said, knocking on her curly head.

Andie replied, "I would *hate* to see you *salivate* over Tate's cooking. Who knows, you might *disintegrate!*"

More giggles.

Andie checked her watch. "Yikes, gotta *terminate* this conversation." She staggered out of my room, giggling uncontrollably.

"You gonna *isolate* me?" I called after her.

She waved, holding her stomach as she left.

I stayed holed up in my room. No need to be around Mr. Tate any more than I had to.

"Holly, supper's ready," Mom called later.

Great, I thought as I headed downstairs, straight toward Tate's lasagna.

Everyone but Mr. Tate was seated at the dining room table when I arrived. Since my usual place was already taken by Zachary, I started to sit in the seat nearest me—the head of the table, where Daddy had always sat.

Mom stopped me. "Holly, dear," she said. "Could you sit beside Zachary? I was saving that seat for Mike."

Saving Daddy's seat for Mike? I forced myself not to grimace. Obediently I went to the empty chair next to Zachary and gave him a fakey smile as I sat down.

Mr. Tate came in carrying the lasagna between two potholders. "I think we're ready to begin." He set the CorningWare in the middle of the table, looking very silly wearing Mom's pink-and-white striped "World's Greatest Cook" apron.

Mr. Domesti-tate, I thought, smothering my snickers. Too bad Andie wasn't here to share another great pun.

Mr. Tate removed the apron and sat down. "Shall we hold hands for prayer?" he asked.

"We usually just fold our hands," I said quickly. I didn't want to hold Zachary's germy little paw. And I didn't want Mr. Tate holding my mom's hand, either!

Mom stared at me, but Mr. Tate said, "All right, let's just fold our hands tonight." He bowed his head and prayed a long and rambling prayer, something about "our most merciful, gracious Redeemer" and "thou who hast covered all our iniquities." It didn't sound anything like the way Mom prayed. She talked to Jesus like He was her best friend.

After the prayer, Mr. Tate began dishing out the lasagna. When my turn came, he said, "Pass your plate, Holly." I held out my plate, and he served me a huge helping. I was about to pull it back when he said, "Wait, looks like yours could use a bit more sauce."

Sulking, I waited while my plate received yet another gooey spoonful. Then I ate slowly, keeping my eyes down so I wouldn't have to talk to anyone. Mom chatted with Zachary, who leaned on her arm, looking pale and tired. Carrie talked to him, too, seeming to enjoy the extra people at our table.

Not me.

Mr. Tate helped himself to more lasagna. "Well, Holly, I never heard about your choir tour," he said. "How was it?"

"Fine, thanks," I said.

Mom caught my eye. Her face was telegraphing little messages. *Be polite. Say something.*

Mr. Tate buttered his roll. "Where did you go?"

"California," I said.

"See any interesting sights?" he asked, taking a bite.

"I saw my dad," I said.

Dead silence. I didn't dare look at Mom. "That's nice," Mr. Tate said at last.

"And we went to Disneyland and then to the south rim of the Grand Canyon."

He cleared his throat. "I prefer God's creation to man's, don't you? The Grand Canyon is so much more inspiring than anything human beings could ever create."

"I guess so." I didn't dare say that I thought Disneyland was just as cool as the Grand Canyon—man-made or not.

Mr. Tate changed the subject. "How do you like the lasagna?" he asked me as I scraped up the last bite on my plate.

I wanted to be flippant and say something like, "Well, I'm eating it, aren't I?" Instead, I nodded my head and forced a smile, since my mouth was full of his cooking.

"She's trying to be polite," Mom said for me. "When her mouth is empty she'll tell you what she thinks of this recipe, won't you, Holly?"

Inside, I churned with anger. Couldn't they all just leave me alone? I held a napkin over my mouth, making it obvious to everyone I was in the process of chewing . . . not talking. No way would I compliment Mr. Tate on his cooking ability. He might get the wrong idea and decide to treat us to his food—and his presence—more often.

"Daddy," Zachary whined, "I don't feel well."

"I'll take care of him, Mike," Mom said. "Go ahead and finish your meal." She led Zachary down the stairs to the family room.

Carrie finished her supper quickly, then headed down to talk to Zachary while Mom and Mr. Tate moved into the living room to have some peppermint tea.

Naturally, I got stuck cleaning up. I cleared the table, loading the plates into the dishwasher. Evidently The Cook was not ready to demonstrate his domestic skills in the area of kitchen duty. It appeared that he'd used every pot and pan in the entire house. Scrubbing them would give me time to think. And to eavesdrop on the cozy conversation in the living room.

Slopping around in the dish suds, I thought about disgusting little Zachary Tate. He'd leaned on Mom all during supper, whining. And sneezed his germs all over us. I'd heard that an only child can be a real pain, expecting all the attention, but this was ridiculous. Even Carrie got sucked into catering to him.

Maybe I could try to ignore the whole thing. Maybe Mom would soon get sick of having zillions of extra people around. But by the frequency of her smiles, who was to say what would happen?

Wiping off the table, I heard laughter. It was Mom. Slowly, with dripping hands, I peeked around the doorway.

Gulp!

Mr. Tate's arm was resting on the back of the sofa, behind my mother. And it looked like he was moving in for the kill.

I closed my eyes. *Please, God. Do something quick!* I imagined a lightning bolt descending from heaven, ripping through the roof, and frying the spot between Mr. Tate and Mom. Closer to Mr. Tate's side, of course.

Right then, Carrie screamed from the family room. "Quick! Something's wrong with Zachary!"

Mom jumped to her feet, following Mr. Tate down to the family room. The timing was miraculous. *Thanks, God, you did it.*

I ran to see what could possibly be wrong with Mr. Tate's spoiled brat.

Chapter 7

I sat at the top of the family room steps observing the situation. What *was* wrong with Zachary?

"Call the hospital," Mr. Tate told Mom. She snatched up the phone, punching the numbers as fast as she could. Carrie looked on fearfully as Mr. Tate carried Zach to the couch. He felt his face, then took his pulse. Zachary's face was a chalky white.

I inched my way down the stairs to the bottom. The minute Mom was off the phone I asked, "What's wrong?"

Mom ignored my question. Instead, she hurried to Zach's side. "The doctor wants to see him, Mike." She stroked Zach's head.

In one swift move Mr. Tate picked Zach up, blanket and all. I moved aside as they rushed past me up the steps. Carrie and I followed them to the living room.

Mom stood in the doorway peering out as Mr. Tate put his kid in the car. "I wonder if I shouldn't follow them down to the hospital," she said, thinking out loud.

"I wanna go, too," Carrie pleaded.

"All right, get your jacket. Hurry." Mom flew to her room to get her coat and purse.

Seconds later the back door banged behind them, and suddenly the house was still. I stood alone in the kitchen. "Mr. bald Michael

Tate—dissipate . . . evaporate!" I said out loud. Then I made up another rhyme.

> "One-three-five, four-six-eight,
> Dirty dishes, you can wait.
> Peace and quiet, no Mike Tate.
> Hey! It's time to celebrate!"

I ran to the freezer and pulled out a carton of strawberry ice cream. If Zach was as sick as he looked, no chance would Mom be dating Mr. Tate for at least a week. I didn't need a degree in medicine to see that *this* was no twenty-four-hour flu. With Mr. Tate out of the picture that long, I'd have time to work on Mom. Getting her to say yes to a California visit was my top priority.

Halfway through my ice-cream binge, the phone rang. "Hello?" I said.

"Holly?" It was Danny Myers! "Are you going to the youth group skating party on Friday?" he asked almost shyly.

"I'm going," I said, excited.

"Great. Then I'll see you there, okay?" he said. "Catch you later. Bye."

Just like that, he hung up. I stood staring at the phone. I wondered if he'd hung up so quickly with his former girlfriend, Alissa. She'd moved away a month before choir tour. Last I heard, Danny wrote her letters occasionally. But they were basically just friends now.

I reached for the phone to call Andie. "Guess what?" I said when she answered.

"Hmm, let's see."

"C'mon, Andie. Guess."

"You're back with Jared?" she teased.

"Get it right . . . it's something fabulous."

"Yes," she shouted into the phone. "Danny called you?"

"About Friday night," I said.

"Did he ask if you were going?"

"Yep. And he said he'd see me there. It's cool to know he cares whether I'm coming, even though it's not a date. Mom wouldn't let me go if it were," I said. "I have to be lots older before I can go on a real date."

"Me too," said Andie. "Unless someone extra special comes along, then I can crash the dating scene early."

"*My* mother will never change her mind."

"She might approve of Danny Myers if she met him," Andie said. "Get her to drive us Friday night. You could introduce him then."

I tugged on my hair. "If Zachary Tate gets over the flu by then, she'll probably have her own date."

"Which is something Jared won't have," Andie said, snickering. "He's stuck. Can't get anyone to go with him."

"Thanks to us." I felt proud of protecting the rest of the Dressel Hills female population from the likes of two-timing Wilkins. "As Grandma Meredith would say, 'He's cooked his goose.' "

"That's for sure," Andie agreed.

After we hung up, I went downstairs to read a new mystery I'd borrowed from the school library.

An hour and a half later, Mom and Carrie arrived home. Carrie looked worried. Mom looked exhausted.

"How's Zachary?" I asked.

"He's hanging tough," Mom said, tossing her purse onto the bar. "They'll keep him for a couple days while the doctors try out some new medication." Before I could ask what was wrong with him, Mom headed for the stairs. Guess she didn't want to talk much about Zachary—at least not tonight.

Tuesday after school, I confronted Mom about my California trip.

"Holly, I'm not interested in having this conversation now." She was sitting at the dining room table, sipping her peppermint tea, trying to unwind. "Let's talk about it later, okay?"

I asked her again, during supper. I was actually enjoying supper for a change, minus Mr. Tate.

"Holly, you're starting to bug me about this," Mom said.

"But you said we'd talk later," I whined. "It's important to me."

She sighed. "Your father's lifestyle is much different from ours."

"How do you know?" I put my fork down, eager for an answer.

"I keep in touch with Grandma Meredith. She's told me she's concerned that he's still not a Christian."

"Well, I'm concerned, too, but I don't see why I can't visit him just because of that."

Mom's eyes narrowed. "Los Angeles isn't exactly the best place for a young girl to spend the summer."

"I won't *be* in L.A. Daddy's house is on the beach west of there."

"Well, blame it on the beach crowd, then," she said as she reached for the basket of rolls. "Your father will be gone at work most of the time. Who knows what could happen?"

"You don't trust me, is that it?"

"Why don't you do something for me, Holly?" she said, buttering her roll. "Think about your decision for the next month or so. Maybe by then you'll feel differently."

Change my mind? She had to be kidding.

"Aren't you just hoping I'll forget about this?" I demanded.

"Of course not." But she avoided meeting my eyes and started fussing over Carrie not having had enough to eat.

"Uh-huh," I muttered. "Right."

Mom was wrong to put me off this way. It was a lousy scheme to delay my all-important decision. A month or so, she said? Well, in thirty days I'd be back with zillions of reasons why I should go. At least that many.

❤ ❤ ❤

Wednesday night, Andie and I did homework at *her* house. Andie called it the great Tate-break, even though Mr. Tate was at his own house taking care of Zachary. The kid was on some new medicine. Maybe he was allergic to penicillin, like Andie's twin brothers. Mom didn't say much about it. We had sort of an unspoken pact going: She wouldn't talk about Mr. Tate and Zachary around me, and I wouldn't talk about Dad and going to California around her.

At Andie's, I helped her with plot ideas for the creative writing assignment in English. She decided to go with my suggestion: the raft trip. While she started her first draft, I multiplied twenty-four hours times the days remaining till Friday. Skate night.

❤ ❤ ❤

After school the next day, Jared was still scrounging for a girl to meet him at the skating party. Poor, pitiful thing.

Andie baited him. "What about asking the Miller twins? You *do* know Paula and Kayla, don't you?"

Jared's eyes lit up.

"They moved here from Philadelphia. Same place my uncle and cousins live," I said.

"I heard their dad was stressed out back East and quit his executive job to live in our small town," Andie added.

"That's right," I said. "Uncle Jack suggested they move to our peaceful, stress-free ski village."

"How old are these girls?" Jared asked.

"Eighth grade," I said. "Think they'd want to hang around a lowly sevey like you?"

Jared leaned on my locker. "I could make them forget my school grade," he said, grinning.

"Fat chance," Andie said.

"So which one of you wants to introduce me?" he asked.

Andie whispered behind my locker door, "He doesn't have a chance! I already filled them in on him."

"Andie, you're wicked," I said, straightening the books in my locker.

"Says who?" She slammed her locker shut.

Jared shifted his books. "Girls, I'm waiting."

"Give up," Andie said. "You're on your own." We turned away, leaving Jared in the dust.

❤ ❤ ❤

At last, Friday night arrived. The kids in the youth group met at the church and divided up for transportation. Danny rode to the skating rink with Pastor Rob in one of the church vans. Jared, Billy Hill—from school—and four other guys rode along. Andie and I rode with her dad.

Inside the skating rink, Danny waited for me near the pop machine. "Soda?" he asked, pulling some change out of his jeans pocket.

"Sure, thanks." I watched as he selected my favorite soda pop. His light green sweat shirt made the green in his eyes sparkle.

While I picked out some ice skates, Danny grabbed his and laced them up. Then he helped with my left foot, which wouldn't budge. It was stuck partway inside the skate. I guess it would've been embarrassing with any other guy, but not with Danny.

The music swelled as we stepped onto the ice. The rink was crowded. Beginners claimed the middle areas, while speed skaters and show-offs zipped past us on the outer rink.

Danny and I circled the ice. "You're good," he said, smiling down into my eyes.

"Thanks." Butterflies swirled inside me.

After three more times around, Andie grabbed my hand and called for the others to join us in crack the whip. We got real rowdy then, especially the second time with short little Andie at the tail end. Hanging on for dear life, she flew across the ice, screaming at the top of her lungs.

Soon more church kids crowded in, and the guys speed skated together. Andie and I stayed with the girls, but secretly, I watched

Danny. His long legs made swift, sure strokes on the ice. Some of the other guys were more reckless and crazy, but he was always in control. And fast. He passed up the other guys without even trying.

Andie went off toward Billy Hill, and I circled the ice a few times with the girls. Then the loudspeaker crackled. "Couples only."

Out of nowhere, Jared zoomed up behind me. Before I knew it, he was whirling me toward center ice.

"Let go of me," I demanded, pushing away from him. I turned around and skated toward the snack bar to catch my breath.

Jared followed. "You're great, Holly. Let's try it again," he said, bowing low like a matador ready for the bullfight.

"Once was too much," I said, turning to look for Danny. Had he missed Jared's skating stunt? I could only hope so.

I spotted Andie eating ice cream with Billy Hill. They waved me over to their table. Uninvited, Jared tagged along.

"Lookin' good out there," Billy said, fumbling for an extra chair.

I glanced at Jared. "Wasn't *my* idea."

Andie held her cone up for me to lick.

"It's good you came, Billy," Jared said.

Billy nodded. "Danny's been asking me to come to these things for about a year. Thought I'd give it a try."

"You'll like our church group," I said.

I should've known Billy was Danny's guest. Perfectly wonderful Danny—witnessing, praying in public, making all the right moves.

Andie bit into her cone, staring at Jared like he wasn't welcome. "That was some sneaky action out there on the ice," she sneered.

"Are you Holly's bodyguard, or what?" Jared snapped back. Billy looked uncomfortable. Jared glared at Andie. Then he got up and went to the snack counter.

"Want to help teach Billy how to skate?" Andie asked, obviously glad to see Jared gone.

I smiled. "You're kidding, right?"

"Nope," Billy said. "It's my first time."

"Well, you're so fabulous on the basketball court," I said, meaning it. "There's no way you'll have any trouble skating."

"Hey, how can I go wrong with the two of you teaching me?" he replied.

We headed for the ice, laughing as we went. Halfway around, Billy took off skating by himself.

"Would you look at that?" Andie said. "He doesn't need our help."

"Maybe not on the ice," I said.

"You're right," Andie said. "Might feel kinda weird hanging out with a bunch of Christian kids."

She had a point. "Wait for me," I said, skating with her.

"Holly." I turned to see Danny coming at full speed. He skidded to a stop. "Want to skate?" he asked.

Sailing on ice next to Danny, I was oblivious to the flurry of activity around us. We slowed to a comfortable pace, our legs pushing off in the same rhythm. I couldn't believe this was me—Holly Meredith—skating around the rink with Danny Myers. I wanted this moment to last forever.

Then the music stopped.

"Are you hungry?" Danny asked.

"Are you?"

"Let's grab something," he said.

At the snack bar he ordered two hot dogs, chips, and pop. He even paid. Was this his big-brother routine again?

We found a table. I was so excited sitting there with him, I worried that he could hear my heart pounding.

"Mustard?" he asked.

I nodded. "Thanks."

"Chips?"

"Sure." I felt really bashful.

He opened the minibag and we shared them. Our fingers touched.

All of a sudden, things got really bizarre between us. During choir tour, Danny and I could talk about almost anything. Now all I could do was mumble stupid stuff about relishes and hot dogs.

"Something bothering you, Holly?" he asked.

"Why?" I asked sheepishly.

"You seem quiet tonight."

I looked into Danny's sincere face. When he smiled, I knew suddenly that I could trust him. I sighed. "I've been thinking about my mom lately. She's starting to date again, and it bugs me."

"I *thought* there was something wrong." He reached for another chip.

"There's more," I said.

"Yeah?"

"Mom won't let me go to California this summer to see my dad."

"Why not?"

"She doesn't approve of Dad's lifestyle. He's not a believer."

Danny took a swig of pop. "What if you go for only a couple weeks?" he said. "Can you convince her that she doesn't have to worry about you then?"

"Maybe, but Mom has this idea that California is a thrill-a-minute place and that it'll spoil me." I paused. "Or maybe it's Daddy who will."

Danny looked at me. "What do *you* think, Holly?"

"All I know is that I'm dying to get to know my father better."

"That should be good enough for your mom," he said.

Funny, I thought so, too. I smiled at him. It was nice having Danny Myers on my side—even though it wouldn't help convince my mom to let me go. At least it proved I wasn't so off base after all. Maybe . . .

Danny crinkled up his hot dog wrapper and aimed at the trash can. Bull's-eye! "Ready to skate again?" he asked, grinning.

I returned his smile. "Definitely!"

Chapter 8

Slowly, April blossomed into May. Mr. Tate was still showing up at our house. Fixing, repairing, sometimes cooking. Always hovering. Zachary came, too. Mom never said anything about why he was still throwing up. Or why she put up with it. Personally, I'd never heard of the flu lasting *this* long!

The final weeks of May inched toward summer like an old tortoise. And California called to me every waking minute. Carrie was beginning to bug me with her crying spells every time I even mentioned my trip out West. And Andie—well, she was as set against the idea as ever.

Then there was Mom. "I haven't decided yet," she would say when I tried to bring up the subject. Even though it looked pretty hopeless, I refused to give up.

Finally it was Friday, May 28—the last day of school. I was cleaning out my locker when Danny stopped by. "Did you pack up your smile?" he asked, eyeing a box filled with my junk. I was throwing things in, helter-skelter.

"No," I said, but I didn't smile.

"What's wrong?"

I explained my problem. "Mom still won't talk about California. I'm afraid if I keep bugging her, she'll say no, once and for all."

"Try looking at things *her* way. Dressel Hills isn't exactly the best place to prepare for big city life, you know," Danny said, laughing. "Who knows what evils may be lurking in L.A."

"I'm serious, Danny. There's so much I don't know about my father. I don't want to wait forever to see him again."

"Have you prayed about it?" he asked, taking a more serious approach now.

"Every single day," I said, thinking of my secret list of prayers. Danny Myers was on it, too. Not for the same reason as Daddy, though.

Danny picked up my box of things, and we strolled down the deserted hallway. The Miller twins waved at us from the drinking fountain. They waited to talk to Danny. They had been in his Algebra class last semester.

"What activities are happening this summer with the youth group?" Kayla asked Danny, ignoring me.

"You've heard about the gondola ride up Copper Mountain, right?" Danny asked them. "It's tomorrow." He gave them all the details.

"Psst!" It was Andie, sneaking up behind me. Pulling me away from Danny, she whispered, "Look what's happening here. Still want to chance being gone this summer?"

"Danny's not a flirt like Jared," I said, sticking up for Danny.

"Oh, but Danny doesn't have to flirt, now, does he?" she said. "*They're* doing all of it."

I watched the brown-eyed beauties. My box of junk was tottering under Danny's arm. Their conversation *was* lasting longer than I cared to admit, but it wasn't as if I had any special claim on Danny. We were just good friends.

Danny called to me. "Holly, you know Paula and Kayla, don't you?" he asked. "They moved here from Pennsylvania a couple months ago."

"Yes, we've met. Their dad used to work in the same company as my uncle Jack." I mustered up a smile.

Kayla told Danny, "Holly's uncle was the one who told our dad about Dressel Hills." She turned to me. "Did you know my dad's trying to get him to move out here, too, away from the rat race?"

"Uncle Jack? That'll be the day," I said, wishing he and my cousins *did* live closer.

"Well, have a good summer," Paula said.

"See you at the sky ride tomorrow," Kayla said to us. Both twins waved good-bye to Andie and me, then grinned at Danny. He and I turned and headed toward the door while Andie walked a few feet behind.

Outdoors, Andie waited beside the bike racks while Danny and I talked about tomorrow's gondola ride up Copper Mountain.

"It'll be fun," Danny said. "Maybe we'll end up sharing a gondola."

Before I could say more, he glanced at his watch. "Gotta get going," he said. "See you tomorrow."

"Bye." I waved. He headed down the tree-lined street, and I wanted to dance for joy. So much for Paula and Kayla. *I* was the one he wanted to ride up the mountain with.

Andie asked, "What was that all about?"

"Nothing," I said airily, glancing over my shoulder at Danny. He was nearly at the end of the street. From this angle, he practically looked like a grown-up. Acted grown-up, too. Never acted weird or embarrassed anyone. Danny was one of those super mature guys every girl dreams of.

But I was only thirteen. And even though Andie and I bordered on maturity, every now and then it was fun to act like ten-year-olds. So we skipped all the way to the library.

Inside, we came close to bumping into Billy Hill. His arms were piled high with books.

"Whatcha doing?" Andie asked.

"Reading some books Danny gave me."

"Like what?" I asked.

He held up one. It was about being a Christian without being weird.

"Looks good," I said.

"Danny liked it. What do *you* think?" he asked Andie.

"Hey, Danny should know. He's the preacher-man," Andie said.

I didn't like the tone of her voice. It was like she was putting Danny down.

"He's not a preacher," I said. "He just knows the Bible better than any of us. And he's not embarrassed to talk about God."

"You got that right," Billy said, heading for the street.

Watching Billy leave, I felt proud to be Danny's friend. If he could get through to Billy Hill, maybe he could give me some pointers about witnessing. I would need them this summer when I talked to Daddy about God. *If* I could ever get Mom to let me go.

At home, I wrote a note and posted it on the refrigerator. *Mom: Can we talk? Love, Holly.*

Mom had no choice but to see the note there. Strange, making an appointment with my own mother. Not the way it used to be. *Before* Tate.

Upstairs, I went to spy on Carrie. She was supposed to be cleaning the junk out from under her bed. Instead, she sat in the middle of the floor, inspecting each item before tossing it in the trash or another pile on the floor.

"Hey," I said, pushing the door open wider. "Some girls at school said their dad's trying to talk Uncle Jack and our cousins into coming out here. Wouldn't that be cool?"

"Mom says they might move here," she answered.

"When was *this* discussed?"

Carrie said, "It *wasn't* discussed. Not really."

"So how do you know?"

"Grandma Mcredith called when you were out. She's been calling Mom a lot lately."

"Really?" I sat down next to her on the floor. "I wonder why."

"I think she's trying to talk Mom into letting you go to California this summer."

I was overjoyed. Someone was finally on *my* side!

"That's fabulous," I said. "She knows how much I miss Daddy."

And she did, too. Grandpa and Grandma Meredith had stuck by us even though Daddy was their son. They never seemed to be able to put the divorce behind them. Said we were their grand-daughters, no matter what.

"Does your daddy know how much you miss him?" Carrie asked. Her voice sounded strange.

I cringed inside. "He's *your* daddy, too, Carrie."

"But I like Mr. Tate better."

"That's only because you hardly know Daddy," I said.

"Well, you don't, either," she shot back, "or else you wouldn't be going out there this summer."

"This summer is my business."

Carrie jabbered on. "You'll miss Uncle Jack and the cousins if they come. You'll miss all the fun with Stan and Stephie. And maybe Phil and Mark might get into your secret notebooks, and—"

"Stop it, Carrie. You're making me mad."

"I'm mad, too. I don't want you to go to California. I don't know why Grandma wants you to. She must not be thinking straight anymore."

"Watch what you say."

But she kept it up. "Grandma's going to be seventy soon. Old people can't think very clearly. I'm a kid. Listen to *me*, Holly."

"I've decided. That's the way it is. Daddy should be mailing an airplane ticket any day now." I wasn't going to let her beat me with her Miss Know-it-all fit. Besides, saying it might help make it come true.

"Holly-Heart." Mom was home from work.

I raced down to the kitchen, where she stood with my note in her hand.

"We'll have to talk fast," she said. "I have to go out."

"Again?" I wailed.

"Holly, please stop these outbursts." She opened the freezer and reached for some pizzas.

"I'm tired of frozen dinners. I want my mother back," I whined.

"I think you're blowing things out of proportion." She sat down. "But if that's how you feel, we'd *better* talk."

I sat on a barstool and fiddled with the place mats. "First of all, you probably won't believe it, but I've been praying about this summer. A lot." I paused to check her reaction. I could usually tell how things were going over from her eyes. Nope, they weren't all squinty yet. *Breathe, Holly, breathe,* I told myself.

I continued. "I've been hoping you'd see how important it is for me to go to California. I want to get to know my dad," I told her.

She stared at me. No comment. No squinting.

"Do my feelings count?" I asked bravely.

"Of course they do," Mom said.

"Then it's time I visit the other part of my family."

I could see the *family* word bugged her. The eye squinting started.

I took a deep breath. "I feel all torn apart."

"You're right, Holly," Mom said. "An important part of our family *is* missing, and has been for a long time."

"But he's still in *my* family," I argued.

"Holly, please don't make this difficult," she said, her voice trembling.

I brought up the other forbidden topic. "Are you and Mr. Tate . . . ?" I couldn't finish.

She brushed a crumb off the bar. "Perhaps. In time."

"Are you *serious*?"

She nodded. "I would like to get married again someday . . . to the right man, of course."

My heart sank. "You're kidding. Please say you are. I mean, it's taken this long to get used to Daddy being gone, and—"

"Holly, settle down. I'm not getting married next week. I promise you." She slid off the stool and went to the refrigerator.

"Good," I said, hoping Mr. Tate and Mom would break up. Soon.

While Mom cut into an apple, I returned to the subject of the summer visit. "I know you don't approve of my summer plan, but it's right, I know it is. I'm a good kid. You don't have to worry about me linking up with the wrong crowd out there. Beach parties don't excite me. Getting to know Daddy does."

Mom's eyes were serious. I could see she was beginning to understand. Finally she was listening with her heart.

"And there's another reason," I said softly.

She tilted her head, encouraging me to go on.

"I want to talk to Daddy about God." Silently, I waited for her to say I could go. A yes was on the tip of her tongue. I was sure of it.

Then the phone rang. She ran to get it, the way I do when I think it's Danny Myers. "Hello?" I heard her say. "Hi, Mike."

What timing! Mr. Tate's call had preempted me.

Chapter 9

Ripping the plastic off the pizzas, I slid them into the oven. Then I set the oven timer and stormed upstairs.

Carrie met me in the hallway. "Did you have a fight with Mommy?"

"Never mind."

"You gonna baby-sit me tonight?" she asked.

"You guessed it." I closed my bedroom door. Not a single second of peace passed before Carrie was pounding on my door.

"What now?" I opened the door a crack.

Tears spilled down her cheeks.

"Aw, Carrie, what's wrong?" I reached for her and gave her a big hug. She sobbed something into my chest. Something like if I were far away in California right now, she'd be stuck with Marcia Greene or somebody else for a baby-sitter.

True. But it was Mom's responsibility to look after Carrie, not mine. Carrie's fears were growing, and something had to change that. I figured that if Mr. Tate were out of the picture, we'd have Mom back. And I could go to California without worrying about Carrie.

There was one problem, though: Mom's happiness. It might disappear right along with this man . . . and Zachary.

Wiping my sister's tear-streaked face, I pulled my box of school stuff closer. "Wanna help me sort through these papers from my school locker?"

We sat on the floor, and I started digging through the box. It was full of important stuff. Like notes passed to me in history class. Other things, too. Like the English assignment titled, "My Secret Summer Dream Fantasy." It was squashed down under the end-of-the-year quizzes in math and science.

"What's that?" Carrie asked as I flipped through the pages of my essay.

"The best English assignment I ever wrote," I said, showing off the *A*-. "It was perfectly fabulous. About my secret summer dreams."

"Read it to me," Carrie begged, her nose still stuffy from crying.

"You sure?"

"Uh-huh." She nodded.

"Okay, but you have to promise never to tell anyone about this. Okay?"

"Cross my heart and hope to die, stick a needle in my eye."

"That's gross," I said. "You don't have to say that stuff." Eight-year-olds could be far from cool.

I began to read: " 'The dearest wish that ever could be is to spend the summer of my thirteenth year with my father, who lives in California near the Pacific Ocean in a house made of mostly glass windows, especially on the side facing the ocean.' "

What a long sentence! I thought. *Why didn't Miss Wannamaker deduct points for that?*

I continued. " 'Leaving Dressel Hills, Colorado, behind will be a torturous thing for me, though. My best friend, Andie Martinez, and her family will go without me on their regular camping trip. And this year, an added feature to the normal adventure is a white-water raft trip down the mighty Arkansas River. I will sacrifice the time of my life in order to get to know the father who left me when I was just a kid.

" 'Then there is my little sister, Carrie, whom I must leave behind to face the trials of our mother's momentary fascination with a certain man. Her interest is such that she chooses to spend most of her time with him, much to the dismay of her household, namely her two daughters and one cool cat named Goofey.' "

Carrie interrupted. "Goofey doesn't care about anything, Holly. He just eats and sleeps. That's all."

She was right. The cat hadn't been affected by Mom's strange behavior in the least.

I turned the page. " 'There is another certain person who I will miss a lot. He is the kindest, smartest, coolest guy friend a girl could have. He has a photographic memory, so all the important things like my favorite cookie and soda pop are right there on the tip of his tongue. Nature and strange animals interest him. His love for God makes me want to pray more, the way he does. I can't reveal his name here, but the most fabulous thing that could happen, if I get my summer dream-come-true, is that he'll agree to do something very weird. This is it: When I leave Dressel Hills for the summer, this special person will promise to read the same books I read while I'm in California. It will be a token of our special friendship. Our reading list will be five books he picks and five I pick.' "

"Wow," said Carrie. "That's ten books."

"I know," I said, "but listen to what happens next: 'We'd make a reading schedule so that, even though we're hundreds of miles apart, we'd be thinking about the exact same things, precisely at the same time, and we'd be closer to each other for having made this pact.' "

Carrie had more ideas. "Would you seal it with a kiss behind the library?"

"No, silly." Little kids always seemed to bring up the kissing thing. "We're good friends," I explained. "Nothing more."

She giggled and snuggled up to me, anxious for more.

I kept reading. " 'But the very best and most secret summer fantasy is this: spending time getting to know my father. And hoping that when he gets to know me better, he'll love me as much as I remember loving him.' "

Carrie was stone still.

"Now you know why it's so important for me to go away." I tucked the English assignment away in my bottom dresser drawer.

Slowly, Carrie spoke, "I wish I could say the same thing about our daddy."

It was the first time she'd claimed him as ours. Hers.

"Someday you will. I'm sure of it," I said, leading her downstairs just as the timer buzzed for the pizza.

She pulled at my hand. "Want some advice?"

"Sure."

"Let Mom read your fantasy story."

Carrie was way off on that idea. Besides, Mom wouldn't appreciate what I'd written about *her*.

"You always let her read your stories and stuff," Carrie said.

Not always, I thought. There were secret lists and secret journals. Secret prayer lists and . . . secret *secrets*.

When Mr. Tate arrived for his date with Mom, he looked exhausted. Worried.

Mom came downstairs, wearing her light-blue shirtwaist dress. She looked pretty, but somewhat preoccupied. "We'll be attending a meeting at the hospital tonight," she informed me, "in case you need to call for any reason." Her words sounded stiff.

Carrie ran to hug her good-bye. I wanted to do the same. But as I crossed the room toward her, Mr. Tate said, "Holly, could you please watch Zachary while we're gone? It'll only be about two hours."

A totally outrageous request. He should've called hours ago! I wanted to say no, but Mom's eyes were squinting almost all the way shut. Something was wrong. I could feel it.

"Next time could you call me ahead of time, please?" I said

coldly. Inside I felt like screaming at him. How dare he take my mother and leave me with his spoiled, vomity kid!

Mr. Tate ignored my request, handing me a bottle of pills. "Zach will need one of these thirty minutes from now."

"Do they make him throw up?" Carrie asked as I squeezed the bottle in my hand.

Leave it to Carrie.

I fumed while Mr. Tate explained, "He's fairly nauseated all the time, but that can't be helped. Not immediately. We trust he's improving."

He turned and headed for the car, helping Zachary into the house. Sitting beside him on the sofa, Mr. Tate leaned over and kissed his son. Zachary reached his skinny arms up to his dad and hugged him limply.

"I'll be back soon, Zach," Mr. Tate said.

The boy held his thumbs up, just like Andie always did. Seeing him, Mom made some high-pitched sobbing sounds and rushed out the door.

Mr. Tate kept talking as though nothing had happened. "Zachary should be fine. Just keep him quiet, Holly. No excitement, please." He glanced out the window at Mom, who appeared to have lost it for some unknown reason.

"How am I supposed to do that when it's impossible to know what's going to happen next around here?" I said, stuffing the pills into my pocket.

Mr. Tate glared back at me. "Don't do this now," he said.

"Do what?" I said, my teeth clenched.

"You know what I mean," he said so sternly I was immediately convinced to cool it.

I hurried outside to Mom. "Are you okay?"

She dabbed at her eyes and shook her head.

"Mom?" I held her hand. "What's wrong?"

She could only cry.

Mr. Tate came then. He put his arm around her shoulder.

"The meeting is about Zachary," he said. "We hope and pray this medication will help him."

Carrie squeezed in between Mom and Mr. Tate, hugging them both.

Mr. Tate studied me with his beady eyes. "We're going to hear a specialist discuss Zachary's illness. We won't be late."

Zillions of questions zigzagged back and forth in my brain. When Mom and Mr. Tate turned to go, I wanted to shout them out, one by one. Most of all: *What is making Mom cry?*

Carrie waved as they backed out of the driveway. Then we hurried inside to find Zachary leaning against the green plaid throw pillows on the sofa, sound asleep.

"Are you gonna wake him up for his pill when it's time?" Carrie asked.

"Guess so. Must be pretty powerful stuff to make him so sick," I said, trying to read the label. "What's methotrexate?"

"Never heard of it," Carrie said. She raced to the stairs.

"Where are you going?" I called after her.

In a flash, she came downstairs with a huge book. "Here, Mommy reads out of this sometimes."

It was an important-looking medical book. "Where'd you get this?" I asked, touching the tan hardcover.

"Mommy had it in her room this morning. I heard her praying, so I sneaked into the hall to see. She was sitting on the bed, holding it."

I looked in the index under the *M*'s. There it was—methotrexate. A drug prescribed in the maintenance therapy of . . .

I held my breath. Zachary had cancer!

Chapter 10

Slowly, I closed the book and handed it to Carrie. "Put this back where you found it," I said.

"What's wrong?" Carrie asked.

"I'll tell you later." I hoped she wouldn't hassle me about it in front of Zach. He looked wiped out. I could tell by the way his arm was flung off to the side.

Gently untying his Nikes, I pulled them off. I was surprised by the lightness of his body as I lifted his legs onto the sofa. His red baseball cap slipped off to the side as he moved in his sleep. He was mostly bald underneath. No wonder he wore the cap everywhere.

All at once, I felt dreadfully wicked. Here was a very sick boy— not a spoiled brat—who hung all over his dad at mealtime. Who raced to the bathroom for vomiting sessions. Who'd lost all his hair to some powerful drug that was doing damage to his body while attempting to save his life. No wonder my mother sobbed when Zach gave his thumbs-up sign. No wonder!

"Stay here with Zach, will you?" I said to Carrie. Tears blinded my eyes. I ran upstairs to my room and threw myself on my knees. How could God forgive my selfishness?

I cried out for forgiveness.

"Have mercy on me, O God, according to your unfailing love;

according to your great compassion blot out my transgressions." I recited the first verse of Psalm 51 from memory. Mom had taught it to me when I first became a Christian.

Verse two was the part I *really* needed: "Wash away all my iniquity and cleanse me from my sin."

"Holly? You all right?" Carrie asked, coming into my room. She'd broken our rule about entering without knocking, but it didn't matter. Not today.

"I've been a real jerk about Zachary," I confessed. "But you, Carrie, you've been his friend." I reached up and hugged her there on the floor.

"I wanna be his best friend. But . . . what's wrong with him?" she asked.

B-E-E-P! the smoke detector wailed.

"Yikes, the pizza!" I yelled as I skipped down the steps two at a time. I grabbed two potholders and pulled the black pizza out of the hot oven.

"Carrie, get Zachary out of this smoke!" I shouted as I rushed the burnt mess out to the trash behind the house. Leaving the baking tray and potholders on top of the trash can, I raced back to the front of the house.

What a relief to see Zachary sitting with Carrie on the porch swing out front. He adjusted his baseball cap and grinned at me. *"Now* what's for supper?" he asked.

"I'll think of something. But first you need one of these," I said, pulling the pills out of my pocket.

Carrie ran to get a glass of water.

"Open all the kitchen windows," I called to her, propping the screen door open.

Here I was, alone with Mr. Tate's kid. He was pushing off the redwood porch with his toe, making the swing sway gently. He looked up at me and adjusted his cap.

"Uh, Zachary," I began. "I've treated you pretty lousy lately, and I'm sorry. You probably don't know it, but I think you're really brave." It felt good to apologize. I reached out my hand to him. "Friends?"

He nodded and smiled a toothless grin. His hand was much hotter than I expected.

"You're warm." I touched his forehead like Mom always did when I had a fever. My hand felt cool against his face. He *was* feverish.

"My neck hurts," he said.

"Where?" I was surprised to feel the swollen glands where he pointed. Really swollen. "How long has it hurt?" My heart pounded in my ears.

"Since this morning," he said, his face pink.

I helped him inside and told Carrie to bring the thermometer, *not* the glass of cold water.

"Coming," she called.

I felt numb. Not too numb to take care of Zach, though. I had lots to make up for.

Carrie brought the thermometer. Slipping it into his mouth, I hoped for the best. Temperatures that zoomed past 98.6 degrees always made me nervous.

We waited silently. The seconds crawled by until the thermometer finally beeped. I took it from Zach's mouth. One hundred two degrees! Acting calmly, I placed the thermometer on the coffee table.

Zachary looked up at me with his watery, bloodshot eyes. "It's high, isn't it?"

"You have a fever," I said, trying not to upset him. "And it's past time for this." I pulled the pill container out of my pocket.

Carrie hurried again to get a glass of water. "Here you go," she said, returning.

We hovered over this frail seven-year-old as if he were our own sick little brother. Zach popped his pill like a pro. Then he sipped water as we watched.

"I'm hungry," Carrie said.

I wondered if I shouldn't give Mom a quick call at the hospital. Checking my watch, I realized they'd been gone less than an hour.

Carrie went to the kitchen and pulled out sandwich fixings and a can of soup. But I didn't feel hungry. I helped Zach get settled on the couch in the living room again. His disease scared me silly. Aunt Marla had lost her fight with cancer last winter, and I'd used up a whole wad of tissues at her funeral. Now here was Zach with the same thing, and he was only seven years old.

The phone rang. I hurried to pick it up.

"Thank goodness it's you," I said quietly.

"What's wrong, honey?"

"It's Zach. He has a fever and his glands are swollen way up."

There was silence.

"Mom?"

"Just a minute, Holly." Her voice sounded muffled, like she was talking to someone in the background. At last, she said, "We'll be right home." Mom said good-bye and hung up quickly.

This was worse than I thought.

Carrie made Zach a sandwich, but after a few bites he lost interest. Looking up at me through drooping eyes, he said, "Talk to Jesus for me, Holly."

I knelt beside him at the couch and prayed. About his lumps, about his fever, and since I wasn't sure if he knew about the cancer, I said, "Lord, help the pill to work in all the right places."

Zach liked that. He smiled and faded off to sleep.

Dashing to my room, I took my secret prayer list out of hiding and curled up in my window seat. I wrote Zachary's name at the very top. *He* was first. Before Daddy and before my summer plans. Before Danny Myers and everything else on the list.

"I'm ashamed, Lord," I prayed. "I'm sorry for being so selfish. You know all about my summer and Daddy. If you want me to go, I know you'll work it out, in your way and in your time. It's up to you now. Amen."

Whew! I suddenly felt fabulous deep down—knowing that I was trusting God to handle things. Besides, there was plenty to do in Dressel Hills this summer. Like getting Zach well. And working on having a better attitude toward Mr. Tate.

Hearing the front door open, I raced downstairs to meet Mom

and Mr. Tate. They were leaning over Zach, who was still sound asleep on the living room couch. Mom whispered something to Zach's dad, handing him a pad of paper to write on. Mr. Tate stared blankly at it, then went to the phone.

"Will Zach be all right?" I asked Mom.

"He'll probably go back to the hospital," she explained, hugging me close. Then, "How high was his fever?"

"One hundred two degrees," I said.

"The doctor will want this information," she said, jotting it down on a piece of paper.

Carrie came into the living room just then, looking very worried. "When's my friend going to the hospital?"

Mom stared across the room at Mr. Tate. "Mike, uh, Mr. Tate will take him tonight as soon as he talks to the doctor on call."

"Tonight?" Carrie asked.

Mom nodded.

"Is he worse?" I asked, eager to tell Mom I knew about the cancer.

Mom led Carrie and me into the kitchen. "Zachary's in trouble," she said. "He has leukemia, and his immune system is very weak. He's picked up another flu bug, too, which is especially dangerous now."

"Why didn't you tell us this before?" I asked.

"We didn't want to frighten you. You had already lost your Aunt Marla to cancer and . . ." Her voice trailed off. I understood. She was afraid if we knew Zachary was dying, we might treat him differently. We might be afraid to get to know him. But now I wished I'd been told from the beginning.

I filled Mom's favorite mug with water and slid it into the microwave oven. Right about now she needed some peppermint tea to help her get through. It was obvious how much she cared for Zachary . . . and his father.

Mom motioned for me to sit down at the bar. "I've been so busy with Zachary these past weeks that I've neglected both of you," she said, looking at my sister and me. "Most of my so-called dates with Mike have been spent at his house tending to and comforting Zachary."

"Why you, Mom?" I asked.

"I've become very fond of Zach," she said, smoothing her hair back. "I want to make a difference in his life, if possible."

"Then it's not that you like Mr. Tate so much as a . . . a boyfriend?" I held my breath, hoping I was right.

"I didn't say that," Mom said softly.

Just then we heard Zach heading to the bathroom, moaning.

"Oh dear," Mom said, rushing out of the room.

I wanted to put my fingers in my ears to block out the sounds of his sickness. Poor kid. Having severe nausea was worse than almost anything. I remembered being sick last winter, and how I'd rather die than vomit. But Zach had to live with it all the time. I shivered, thinking about it.

Mr. Tate was off the phone now. He went upstairs to Zach in the bathroom.

Carrie and I sat like stiff soldiers in the kitchen. Her eyes began to fill with tears. "Is . . . is Zachary gonna die?" she asked.

"I don't know," I said softly. "I hope not."

After a while, the three of them came down. Mr. Tate carried Zach out to the car. Mom followed. Carrie and I stood on the porch, too scared to move.

Before they left, Mom came back and put her arms around us. "He'll spend the night at the hospital here, then they'll take him to the Denver Children's Hospital in the morning."

Dusk was falling fast. Twilight, Grandma Meredith called it. A faint smell of woodsmoke tinged the air. The mountains were dark against the red sky as twinkling lights showed up in one house, then another.

Looking at the lighted windows, I wondered how many other houses had sad, sick kids living in them. And how many of those kids and their parents knew God well enough to talk things over with Him.

Chapter 11

"Time for pj's," Mom said as Carrie and I came into the house arm in arm. "Meet me in my room in five minutes."

We raced to our rooms. Important stuff was going to be discussed tonight. I could feel it in the air. Slipping into my nightshirt, I wondered what Mom was going to tell us. I hoped it wasn't something more about Mr. Tate. I was doing my best to accept him, but I needed time to get used to the idea of Mom having a serious boyfriend.

I dashed to Mom's room, beating Carrie and claiming the spot on the bed nearest Mom.

Carrie dragged in her mermaid, the present from Mr. Tate. "Can we get Zach a stuffed Lightning McQueen to cheer him up?" she asked.

"Let's find out if he has one first," Mom said.

"He doesn't; I know," she insisted.

Mom had that faraway look in her eyes that means she's planning things a zillion miles an hour. "Hand me my address book," she said.

I reached for it on her nightstand.

She found the *M*'s and opened it, holding the place with her finger. "I want you girls to listen carefully," she said. "When I'm finished talking, then both of you will have a chance to ask questions."

Just as I had guessed, this *was* important.

"If things go as planned, Mike, uh, Mr. Tate, will accompany Zachary to Denver. He'll stay there with his son until he's much better and ready to come home."

Tears glistened in Mom's eyes. This wasn't easy for her.

She continued, "I'll call Grandma Meredith tonight to see if she can get a plane out tomorrow. If she can come stay with you girls, then I'll go to Denver for a week to be near Zachary."

Flipping through her address book, she located another phone number. "Maybe I can stay with my old friend from grad school. She and her husband live a few miles from the hospital."

For some strange reason, I remembered Mom's mug of tea still waiting for her in the kitchen. "Just a minute," I said, getting off the bed and heading downstairs.

I removed the cup from the microwave. Still hot. Dipping the tea bag into the water, I stirred in a teaspoon of honey. Just the way she liked it.

Gingerly, I stepped up the stairs, the mug brimming with peppermint tea. It was the least I could do for my mother.

Carrie looked like she'd been crying when I returned. I wished she wouldn't cry. All this was hard enough for Mom. "Do you have to go, Mommy?" Carrie asked.

Mom thanked me for the tea, then took a little sip. "I really don't *have* to," she said, sighing. "But I'd like to be there for Mike while Zachary is having treatment. And I hope my presence will help Zachary, too, in some way. He needs someone . . . a woman's touch."

She was probably thinking about him not having a mother, and wanting to fill that void. What she really meant to say was that he needed a *mother's* touch.

"Holly, how do you feel about my going?" She touched my hand.

"I'm glad Zachary will have you there," I said. "You have what he needs, Mom."

My tears welled up again, and Mom wiped them away. "Come here, you angels." She smothered us with hugs.

While Mom called her former college friend in Denver, Carrie and I sat on the bed, listening. Afterward, Mom let Carrie punch in Grandma's phone number. She talked for a while, then it was my turn.

"Haven't had a letter from you, Holly, for quite some time," Grandma said.

"Sorry, Grandma. I've been real busy. But school's out now, and I'll have more time to write."

"When are you coming to see us?" she asked.

"I don't know. Here's Mom." I handed the phone to her. It was time for Mom to tell Grandma about the plan.

Shortly, we heard Mom say that Grandma would be delighted to come and stay with her beautiful granddaughters. Then Mom was silent for a long time. Grandma must have something else on her mind.

In the middle of the silence, Mom pointed to the door, which meant Carrie and I should exit and give her some privacy. "Shut the door," she mouthed to us.

In the hallway, we stood, not breathing, trying to hear Mom's side of the conversation.

Nothing.

"What do you think's going on?" Carrie whispered.

"Let's wait in my room," I said. "See this?" I led her to my window seat—my heavy-duty thinking spot. "When life gets too hard to figure out, I sit here and talk to God. Sometimes I think first, then I pray. But telling Him everything is real important."

"Like what kind of things?" Carrie asked, squeezing in beside me on the window seat.

"It's different for everyone. Sometimes I pray about my school grades."

"Does that help you get *A*'s?"

"Praying *and* doing my homework does." I reached for a brush and began brushing, then braiding her hair. "But being close to God is the best part. I don't always ask for things. Sometimes I just like to share with Him. It's like talking to a good friend, the best friend in the whole world."

"Like you and Andie?" she said.

"Closer than that."

"My best friend is Zachary," she said. "Tonight he told me that people think he's dying, but he's going to fool them."

"I hope he does," I said, standing up. "I wonder if Mom's still on the phone." I brushed my own hair, getting it ready for a look-alike braid with Carrie.

"I'll go listen in the door crack." She grinned.

Carrie headed down the hallway. I couldn't help but peek around the corner and watch as she squatted near the door and put her ear to the crack. Her head bumped the door, making it squeak open. Carrie hurried back to me. "Mom said we should go to bed. She says we'll talk tomorrow."

"What do you think Grandma's telling Mom?" I asked without waiting for Carrie's reply. "Maybe catching up on family news?" I said, very curious at the long conversation. "Night, Carrie."

She scampered off to her room.

I turned the light off and slipped under the sheets, propping Bearie-O up close to me in the darkness.

What *was* going on? I hoped Mom and Grandma weren't talking about something concerning Grandpa's health. That's *all* we needed . . . more sick people in our lives.

Suddenly, I was hungry. Skipping supper was not my style. I went to search the kitchen for a snack. Peanut butter and crackers would do. And a glass of milk. There were celery and carrot sticks in the fridge, too. They'd be cold and crunchy. Perfect.

I turned the light off in the kitchen and sat at the bar, my eyes slowly getting used to the dim room. Goofey nuzzled his furry body against my bare legs. I reached down to pet his head. "You need some lovin'?" I asked.

He purred his answer.

"Come here, little one." I picked him up and put him on my lap. He curled into a ball, relishing the late-night attention. "Mommy's busy upstairs. You miss snuggling on her bed?"

Pur-r-r. Sure do, he seemed to say.

Curling up on Mom's bed was a treat. When I was sad or sick, that's where I wanted to be. One night I had slept with Mom all night. Carrie too. It was the night Daddy left.

The queen-size bed had been crowded. Carrie had insisted on bringing Goofey into the bed with all of us. I clung to Bearie-O all night, sobbing whenever I woke up. Mom got pushed to the edge when I had a bad dream, and Carrie's knees were in my back. So Mom and I ended up sleeping on the floor in sleeping bags. I remembered snuggling next to her as Goofey purred his kitty song above us in Mom's bed.

I was so hurt and confused. I loved Daddy and never thought anything could go wrong with his love for us.

Then, four whole years passed without seeing him. He didn't even write, other than sending birthday or Christmas cards. And not until the day before my thirteenth birthday—at Aunt Marla's funeral—did I see him again. He'd looked so handsome, too, wearing a navy blue suit. Saundra, his new wife, accompanied him as we rode together in the limo to the graveside service. Not exactly the perfect place for a girl to reunite and hang out with her long-lost dad.

Saundra had worn bright-red lipstick and gloves. Something about her glamorous ways must've made Carrie say she wasn't as sweet as Mom. But it's hard to beat a mother who's an angel. Not because she's perfect or prettier than other mothers—even though, well, she is—but because her beauty is *inside,* too. *No wonder Mr. Tate likes Mom so much.*

And Zachary? How could he resist her love?

Goofey jumped off my lap as Mom padded down the stairs in her slippers. Quickly, I flicked on the kitchen light. She didn't need to know I was sitting here in the dark, pondering my past. "Can't you sleep?" she asked, stroking my braid.

"Just a little hungry." I finished off the crackers and milk, hoping to hear about her long phone conversation.

Mom pulled out a barstool and sat. She lifted her hair off the back of her neck and held it there for a moment. "Holly-Heart, I have something to tell you. I'm sure you'll be very happy."

I leaned forward on my elbows. "What?"

She breathed deeply, like she wasn't certain how she should say it. Then the words spilled out. "I've decided to let you go to California to visit your father."

"Really?" *Unbelievable!*

"Yes," she said. "But there are some conditions."

I was all ears. I leaned forward, almost losing my balance.

"Grandma will arrive here tomorrow afternoon. Then, if it suits your father—she's phoning him now—she'll fly to California with you and Carrie on Monday and stay with you there for about two weeks."

Carrie is going, too!

"Oh thanks, Mom." I hugged her, feeling like a little kid inside. "Thank you for changing your mind."

"I knew how much you wanted to go. This just seemed to make sense, the timing . . . while I'm in Denver with Zachary."

There had to be more to this. "Did Grandma help you decide?" I asked.

Mom's laughter, warm and gentle, touched me. I was right; Grandma had lots to do with the decision. "You know me well, Holly-Heart. I feel much better about your going with Grandma there."

"And Carrie?"

"Yes, and Carrie," she said, with resolve. "You'll watch out for your little sister, won't you?"

"You know I will, Mom."

The phone rang.

She got up and went to the desk in the corner of the kitchen. "Hello?" Mom said, answering the phone. "Yes?"

I watched her face.

"That sounds good. Holly is thrilled. Yes . . . she's right here." She turned to me. "It's your father."

"Hi, Daddy," I said, not fully realizing all that had just happened.

"Looks like things are working out for you and Carrie to visit. We're looking forward to it."

"Me too." I tried to picture myself at his big beach house. "I can't wait."

"I feel the same way," he said. "And it'll be wonderful seeing Grandma again, too. Maybe we should fly Grandpa out and have a family reunion."

"Maybe Andie could come, too," I said, joking.

"Who's Andie?"

"Just kidding, Daddy. She's my best friend."

He chuckled. "You'll have to fill me in on all your friends."

I couldn't imagine him being interested in hearing about Andie or Danny Myers.

"This happened so fast," I said.

"It'll be great having you girls here. Your stepbrother is anxious to meet you both."

I'd completely forgotten about him. "How old is he?"

"Tyler's nine," he said. "He's already making plans to entertain you."

I couldn't say I was anxious to meet Saundra's son, especially if he was anything like her. Well, I'd just have to wait and see.

I said good-bye to Daddy, kissed Mom good-night, and pranced off to bed. I wouldn't get much sleep tonight, but who cared? I was going to California!

Chapter 12

The next morning I woke up early. Life was too exciting to stay in bed. This afternoon I was going to ride up Copper Mountain with Danny, and on Monday I was flying out to see my dad.

God had answered my prayer so fast, my head was spinning with the speediness of it, like getting a return email message from God. I couldn't wait to tell Danny about my latest miracle.

Sitting up in bed, I opened my devotional book. The Scripture was Psalm 18:30, "As for God, his way is perfect." No kidding! If I had tried to put the trip together this fast, well . . . it was obvious who was in charge here.

After breakfast, I phoned Andie. "Can you come right over?" I asked.

"Too early," she complained. "I'm sleeping in."

I assured her it was extremely important. "Besides," I said, "you have all summer to get caught up on sleep."

After I hung up, I loaded dirty clothes into the washing machine and cleaned up the kitchen while Mom and Carrie slept.

Boy, was Carrie's summer turning out radically different than she'd thought. Tagging along with me to California was the perfect answer to all her fears. Surf, sun, and Daddy awaited. Just two days away.

At last, Andie arrived, her dark curly hair still wet from her shower.

"What took so long?" I said, opening the door.

"Had to clean my room. Mom's in a spotless mood," she grumbled.

"Want to help me clean mine?" I laughed.

No way, her frown indicated.

"What did you drag me out of bed for?"

"I'll tell you. C'mon, let's take a walk." I didn't want Mom to hear Andie fussing about the latest turn of events.

"Where to?" she asked.

"The library."

"It's not open yet." She looked at her watch. "Too early for anyone sane to be out of bed on the first day of summer vacation."

"Guess Carrie and Mom are saner than both of us," I muttered as we left the house.

"You guys stay up late or something?"

"Yeah . . . some scary stuff happened with Zachary while I was sitting for him last night. He's real sick." I paused, then I said, "Because of that, I'm going to California in two days. My grandma's flying in this afternoon, and then she and Carrie and I are going to see my dad."

Andie stopped dead in her tracks. "Holly, are you crazy? What's the throw-uppy kid got to do with you going to California?" She stood in front of me with her hands on her hips, as if she dared me to take one more step.

"Mom wants to be near him while he's in the hospital in Denver, so Grandma's taking care of us, and . . . oh, Andie, I know it sounds complicated, but the way I see it . . . this is a miracle!"

"What're you talking about?"

It wouldn't be easy convincing her that God could use something as bad as Zach's illness and turn it around so I could go to California.

"It's like that verse in Romans," I explained. "All things *do* work together for good, because we love God."

At last, we proceeded down the sidewalk. Andie's fast pace told me she wasn't one bit happy with me. "I love God, too, Holly. What happens when *I* pray that you'll stay here this summer? That's for *my* good, like in the verse, right?"

She had a point.

"It's only for a couple weeks," I said meekly.

"Two weeks? Holly, that's forever!"

By the look on her face, this was going to be a problem between us, no matter how long or short my visit was.

"I'm going to California, and that's the end of it," I said.

"Whatever," she said angrily.

"Put yourself in my place for once."

"Right," she muttered.

Overhead, a jet left a vapor trail behind as it climbed up, up over the mountains, reminding me of the trip ahead and the short time I had to get ready.

I suggested we run back to my house without stepping on any cracks in the sidewalk. "Don't want to break your mother's back, do you?" I said, trying to chase away the dark mood that hung over Andie. Giggling, I pushed her onto some cracks.

Not so deep inside, we were still kids. Good thing Danny wasn't around to see us now. I doubted that the giggling and jumping would do much for his impression of me. Unless, of course, there was a logical reason for all the jumping.

Logical. That described Danny perfectly. Everything he did was carefully thought out. Even the way he expressed himself and the way he treated his friends. Just knowing I was one of his closest friends made me want to improve my posture—hold my head up, walk tall, throw my shoulders back a little more.

"You're really weird," Andie scoffed at the way I was walking. "What are you doing?"

"Oh, nothing." She didn't *always* have to know what I was thinking.

"Looks to me like you're developing a shape, Holly."

"You're kidding, right?"

"You should walk around like that all the time."

"Thanks, uh . . . I think." What had she noticed that I'd missed? Or was she being sarcastic?

"No kidding, Holly. You're starting to blossom. That's what my mother calls it. Who knows, in a couple months *it* could happen . . . you could become a woman."

I really and truly hoped so. I was tired of looking like the only praying mantis around. Guess seventh-grade girls think more about their bodies than they should. For sure more than eighth- and ninth-grade girls. *They've* already got their curves. But I figured if a girl like me could survive the seventh grade, where you feel all scrambled up, like in a giant mixing bowl, I could make it through till I truly "blossomed" and *it* happened.

"Look out," Andie said. "There are tons of cracks coming up."

We'd turned onto Downhill Court, my street. Part of the sidewalk was bricked, making it almost impossible to run and still miss the cracks. The street was still quiet, too early for activity. The laziness of summer had come.

♥ ♥ ♥

"I'd rather starve than eat *that* for breakfast," Andie told Carrie, who sat on the front-porch swing nibbling on a nectarine.

Carrie held up the rosy-colored fruit. "There's nothing wrong with fruit," she said. "Here, try a bite."

"Nope," Andie said, holding her stomach. "You didn't wipe off your spit."

"Don't be gross in front of my little sister," I warned.

"Give me a break, Holly." Andie plopped down on the swing beside Carrie.

"Okay, if you don't *break* the swing." I laughed.

Mom came outside, carrying a tray of toast and jelly, and some glasses filled with milk. "Anybody hungry?"

"I am," Carrie said, reaching for the tray.

"No thanks, I better go," said Andie, getting up from the swing, making it creak again. "Have to baby-sit my baby brothers while Mom runs errands. See you at Copper Mountain, Holly."

I nodded. "How much money do we need for the gondola ride?" I asked, forgetting what the youth pastor had told us last week.

"Not sure. I'll call you." Andie sauntered down the redwood steps and waved.

"Better get busy and start packing, Holly-Heart," Mom said. "If you don't start planning, you'll run out of time." She poured more milk for Carrie.

"I'll have my things packed in a flash," I said.

Carrie wiped her mouth, eyes wide. "Where's Holly going?"

It was then I realized Mom hadn't told Carrie about our exciting travel plans.

"To California," Mom said calmly. "And so are you."

"I am?" Carrie raised her eyebrows.

I hurried to sit on the swing with her, grabbing her hand. "It's going to be so fabulous, Carrie. We'll walk along the beach, shell hunting. Maybe you'll find some pretty ones to bring home. And . . ."

"Why are we going?" she asked.

Mom rehashed the whole amazing story. "It's a good time for both you girls to visit your father. Your grandma will fly out with you while I'm in Denver with Zachary at The Children's Hospital. Everything's set."

Carrie was quiet. I didn't know if she was too shocked to speak or just still too sleepy.

"Daddy has a stepson a little older than you, named Tyler. We'll both get to meet him for the first time," I said, hoping for a response.

Carrie stood up and placed her empty glass on the tray. "I'm not going," she said. "I'm staying home. What if Zach gets worse? I can't leave him behind. I won't." She reached for the screen door.

"Carrie, you *have* to go," I wailed.

"I'll handle this," Mom said, getting up and going inside after her.

Just great, I thought. *My sister's such a baby.* There was absolutely nothing she could do to help Zach by staying home. Nothing.

I sat there in the morning stillness, listening to the gentle humming sounds of insects as they sent secret messages back and forth. Leaning my head back, I could see the clouds playing follow-the-leader.

Slam went the screen door. I sat up.

There stood Mom, her arms crossed, wearing an exasperated frown. "Carrie simply does not want to go. She's upstairs crying about it, and I don't see the sense in forcing her."

I stuck my feet up under me on the porch swing. "That's weird. Yesterday she didn't want to stay behind with a bunch of sitters."

"There won't *be* any sitters around, with you and Grandma here until I return from Denver."

"Grandma? Me?" *What's happening?* I wondered.

"Holly, I'm sorry, but things have changed," she said abruptly. "The trip is off. I'm really very sorry."

"Why?" I cried. "Just because Carrie doesn't want to go? What about *me?*"

Mom pinched a dead leaf off the geranium plant.

"What about Daddy?" I continued. "He's expecting us."

"Your father will have to adjust his plans."

"Why can't I go alone? I'm thirteen. Why does everything have to change because of Carrie?"

"Holly, listen," Mom said. "Carrie's crying because she's afraid."

I sighed. "That's dumb. There's nothing to be afraid of. She's acting like a big baby, and I can't believe you're letting her."

Mom eased down into the porch chair. "There *are* things to be frightened of, and Carrie's not the only one who has fears. I struggle, too."

"Like what?" I didn't really care what, I just wanted to talk sense into Mom. And fast.

"Like losing you, Holly-Heart."

"How could that possibly happen?" I shot back. She was talking in riddles now.

Sighing, she stared down at her lap. "Maybe you'd end up wanting to live with your father."

I wanted to laugh. "That's the silliest thing I've heard. Why would I want to do that?"

She blew her nose. Now Mom was crying.

"If you want to know the truth, Mom, when it comes right down to it, there's only one thing that could make me want to leave Dressel Hills. And that's if you and Mr. Tate decided to get married." There, I'd said it. *My* greatest fear.

"What a terrible thing to say." She got up. "You have no right to threaten me with such a thing. Now, go to your room."

"I'd rather go to California!"

"That's out of the question now," she said.

The porch swing swayed as I gritted my teeth. So much for miracles and divine email messages.

Chapter 13

I was crushed. How could things be so perfect one minute and so messed up the next?

Lying on the porch swing, I stared up at the sky. Puffs of cotton dotted the blue. They seemed close enough to touch. Squinting one eye shut, I reached up, aiming for the smallest cloud in the bunch. My squinting squeezed out a tear. Then another. Soon, the cloud I reached for was a blurry blob. I dropped my arm and covered my face with it, letting out the sobs.

How could Mom do this to me?

And Daddy . . . When would I ever see him again? If not this summer, when? Once school started there would be no time. Eighth grade was much harder than seventh. Everyone said so.

The phone rang. I listened through the window, hoping it was Daddy or someone else talking sense to Mom besides me.

The screen door opened. "It's Andie, for you," Mom said, handing the phone out to me.

"Hello." I brushed my tears away.

"Well, don't *you* sound morbid," she said.

"Promise not to cheer if I tell you?"

"Maybe, maybe not," she said with a giggle.

"It's not funny, Andie. The trip's off."

"You're not going?" She was obviously happy.

"No." I explained my dilemma.

"Well, I called to find out what you're wearing to the sky ride," she said, ignoring my woes. "Don't forget, Danny'll be there."

"That's nice."

"Hey, I know you better than that," she said. "You really can't wait to see him, can you?"

Mom was giving me a signal.

"Gotta go now," I told her.

"Remember, wear pink," Andie said.

Mom stood by the kitchen door. She pulled her keys out of her purse. "I have to pick up some groceries for tonight." She looked at me searchingly. "I'll be back shortly."

I turned away. I didn't want to talk to her. She'd spoiled my summer dreams with her ridiculous fears. Now all I could look forward to was the gondola ride with Danny. If the Miller twins didn't get to him first.

♥ ♥ ♥

I'd seen crowded parking lots before, but this one was really hopping. Every teen in the church youth group, and all their friends, must've shown up to ride the gondolas up Copper Mountain.

I scanned the cars for Danny. Was he here yet?

Billy Hill was heading up the walkway leading to the ticket booth. I grabbed Andie's arm. "Look who's here," I whispered, popping a chunk of bubble gum into my mouth.

"Shh," Andie said. "Act cool."

"Wanna ride with me, girls?" It was Jared, sneaking up behind us. As usual.

"Guess again," Andie retorted, fluffing her curls. "Don't you have someone to hang out with?"

"Sure." He grabbed my arm playfully. "How 'bout you, Holly? You look lonely."

"Look again." I blew a bubble in his face.

"Thanks, think I will." Jared stepped back, playfully turning his head this way and that, as if admiring me.

"Oh, please," Andie groaned.

Just then I spotted Danny's auburn hair as he climbed out of the church van. I wondered if he was going to ride the gondola with our youth pastor. *Please come over and talk to me,* I thought, excitement bubbling up.

Andie and I purchased our tickets and stood looking up at the apparatus that held the gondolas on the cable line. Looked wobbly to me. The best thing about the ride, in my opinion, was that the cars were enclosed, with windows all around. Even though there was room enough for four, I secretly hoped Danny and I might have the chance to ride together. Just the two of us.

"Hey," Danny said to me, arriving in time for boarding.

"Hi, Danny." My smile was big. I could feel my face stretching . . . stretching.

"Step right this way," the man working the gondolas called. He pointed out where I should wait for the next car to come around. "Who's riding with this young lady?"

Danny stepped up. "I am." He grinned.

I caught my breath. What a smile he had. And the twinkle in his gray-green eyes did strange things to my pulse rate.

The worker steadied the gondola as it came around, and I stepped in. Danny climbed in and sat in the seat opposite me.

"Keep the window halfway down," the worker told us. "No roughhousing or leaning out the window. Don't throw objects out of the gondola. Okay, you're off." He slid the door shut, locking it behind us.

My hand clutched my purse. I wished for something to grab on to. No roughhousing . . . no problem! I wasn't exactly crazy about heights, and I was hoping our weight would evenly balance the car on the cables so it wouldn't swing in the slightest.

The car swung away from the wooden platform and out into the open air. I looked down at the parking lot, milling with people. But as we climbed higher, their faces faded, becoming small dots.

We passed over the tops of trees, blue-green pine and quaking aspen. The sun was shining, and a breeze swept through the window, smelling of damp earth and pine needles.

The gondola rumbled past the first set of terminals, shaking us. I shivered a little and looked over at Danny.

"First time on the sky ride?" he asked.

I nodded. "I rode one when I was little. Mom says Daddy took me for a ride on the Fourth of July, but I don't remember."

"You miss him, don't you?" His voice was gentle.

"More than ever."

"You seem a little sad today," he said.

I didn't want to spoil the gondola ride, but I *was* feeling lousy. And Danny had listened so well when I told him about my plans for California. So I shared everything that had happened in the last twenty-four hours—about Zachary and his cancer, our plans to go to California with Grandma, how Carrie had chickened out. "It seemed like God was working everything out," I said, "and then Carrie had to mess it up."

"Maybe God has a better plan," Danny said.

"But Mom's being totally unreasonable."

"Maybe she's worried. Mothers do that a lot, you know."

"No kidding," I said, recalling Mom's number-one reason for calling the whole thing off. Absurd!

The gondola began to sway. Not daring to peek down for a minute, I stared out my window at treetop level. Towering pines pointed to the blue sky, and Copper Mountain rose before us in all its splendor. Inside this tiny compartment, I felt uptight about being up as high as the birds, dangling precariously above jagged rocks and forested canyons.

"Nervous?" Danny asked.

"A little."

"It won't be much longer," he said, gazing out the window behind me.

Slowly, I turned to look. Approaching us, steadily, was a steep cliff. As we came closer, the cables veered up, up, up! Swallowing my bubble gum, I looked away from the terrain beneath us and back at Danny.

"We have to come back *down* that cliff, don't we?" I said.

He nodded. "But we could sing our favorite songs from choir tour to keep your mind occupied."

It was then that I realized Danny wanted to ride back down the mountain with me.

"If we sing in two-part harmony," he said, "it might be easy to forget the distance between us and the ground. We'll concentrate on the distance between our pitches." He laughed.

So we sang. And sang.

By the time the gondola reached the top and swung onto another wooden platform, I felt better. We climbed out carefully and took the steps from the platform down to the ground. Since we were among the first to arrive, we had a little time before the whole group gathered. A short talk was scheduled once Pastor Rob arrived, then a group hike, followed by the sky ride down.

A walkway made of wood chips led to five hiking trails, and a sign pointed the way to a nearby lookout site. "Let's wait over there for the others," Danny said, walking toward the lookout.

The lookout sat atop a large, flat rock, ringed with an iron fence. We stood at the fence and looked down. Far below, Dressel Hills snuggled in its peaceful, boring valley. Surrounded by shining mountains, the village seemed to taunt me. *You're stuck here for the summer. This is as far away as you'll ever get.*

The sound of laughter announced the arrival of the other kids. In a few minutes we were gathered around Pastor Rob as he shared his thoughts on the awesomeness of God's creation.

Afterward, Andie and I headed for the outhouses near the crest of the hill.

"How are you and Billy getting along?" I asked.

She tried to act sophisticated—not an easy task for Andie. "We rode up together. That's something, I guess."

I pinched my nose shut as we came within a few feet of the girls' outhouse. "Whew," I said. "It stinks."

Andie said she'd guard the door while I went inside. It was an old wooden outhouse, with a toilet lid built into a box. Flies buzzed around deep down inside the opening. Smelling the stench was enough to make me change my mind about using this facility.

"It's nasty in here," I called through the door. "I'm coming out." I pushed on the wooden door.

Stuck.

I pounded on the door. "Andie, get me out of here!"

"What's wrong?" she called.

"The door's jammed." I tried again. No luck.

The door jiggled a little. "I'm trying," Andie said outside.

More door jiggling and groaning.

"Guess you're trapped in there for the summer," Andie said. "I never would've picked *this* option, but it'll sure work to keep you in Dressel Hills."

"Stop it, Andrea Martinez," I hollered. "You know I'm not going anywhere this summer. Besides, the smell in here is making me sick."

"I'm doing my best to open the door," she called.

"Get some help if you can't do it yourself."

"I think I see Danny and Billy. They're waiting near the trailhead."

"Just please get somebody up here," I said, dying for a whiff of fresh mountain air.

"Wait here."

"Right, like I can actually leave," I muttered.

Stranded on the top of Copper Mountain, stuck in a stinky old outhouse was not my idea of fun. This had to go down in my journal as one of the most embarrassing moments of all time.

Fearful thoughts nagged at me. What if they couldn't get me out before dark? What if I had to spend the night up here . . . alone?

Then I heard them. Footsteps and voices. *Thank you, Lord.*

I peered through the splintery cracks in this wretched excuse for a rest room. Couldn't see a thing.

Don't freak out, I told myself, trying not to think about the insects and snakes and who knows what else lived in this miserable place.

Danny called to me, "Still in there, Holly?"

"Where else would I be?"

I heard laughter.

"There's only one *other* way out of there," Andie said.

More laughter. Was the whole youth group standing by the door?

"Get ready to pull . . . hard." Danny was in charge.

"Don't knock the old thing over," Andie said. "We want Holly out of there alive."

I heard a creepy sound over in the corner. But it was too dark to see. I covered my mouth. Should I scream? Andie would be yelling her head off if *she* were stuck in here. I knew that for sure.

Something tickled my head. Was it a black widow spider?

Remembering the giant June bug crawling around in my hair, I was too freaked to reach up and touch my own head. I froze.

Chapter 14

Just then the door of the outhouse flung open wide.

I squinted into the brightness. "Who's next?" I said, stepping out like my being cooped up in the smelliest, creepiest place in the world was a cakewalk. But I really wanted to reach up and kiss the sun.

Andie backed away. "I'll wait."

"Me too," said another girl. "Let's get outta here."

The line of waiting girls vanished rapidly.

When no one was looking, I grabbed Andie. "Look in my hair."

"What for?" she said.

"Is there a spider?"

She looked. "There's this." She held up a splinter of wood.

"I want it," I said, pushing it into my jeans pocket. "The perfect souvenir."

Pastor Rob called everyone to join him. "I'll blaze the trail," he said.

We started down a narrow, twisting path. Danny fell in step behind me. "That was some weird experience you had," he said.

"Nothing like that has ever happened to me." I could laugh

about it now that I could breathe the smell of pines and could turn to see Danny's smile.

The beauty of nature surrounded us as we walked. Trees seemed to sparkle with the sunlight, providing a shady retreat from the heat. Birds flew overhead, chirping and warbling, creating a picture-perfect setting for a walk with my youth-group friends.

But, sadly, the hike had to be cut short, because so many of us girls needed to use the rest rooms. None was brave enough to set foot in the only other option: the boys' outhouse.

Before too long, Danny and I were back on the gondola, heading down the mountain, skimming over the tops of trees. *Bumpity-lumpity-thump.* The gondola did its thing with the terminal overhead. Holding my breath for a while as we drifted down, I couldn't wait for the ride to end.

It was getting close to suppertime, and Grandma Meredith would be waiting at home, having arrived from the airport already, anxious to greet me. I wondered if she knew Mom was worried that I might want to live with Daddy. Was that something Mom would share with her former mother-in-law?

"You're too quiet," Danny said, his eyes searching mine.

"Just thinking."

"Feel like singing again?"

I didn't really, but Danny looked so eager.

"Remember our theme song for choir tour?"

"Sure—'Everybody Sing Praises to the Lord.' " The song was a favorite of mine. Danny's too. I sang as he harmonized with his clear tenor voice, almost forgetting how high we were off the ground. Almost forgetting about California until Danny mentioned it.

"I hope you won't take this wrong, Holly," he said. "I've been thinking a lot about your California trip."

"Really?" I was surprised.

"I agree with your mom. You shouldn't go." His face was serious.

"What do you mean?" I felt terribly hurt. "How could you say that?"

"You should obey your mother, regardless of your feelings, and stay home," he said.

Not only did he sound like a much older brother, but there was definitely a trace of snootiness in his voice.

"You have no right, Danny. Don't tell me what to do."

"Holly, please . . . don't be upset at me," he said. "This is just how I feel."

"Well, you're wrong, and so is my mom."

He looked a bit startled at my response. But I didn't care. Danny had no business interfering.

After the sky ride, I hurried over to Mrs. Martinez's car without saying good-bye to Danny. Andie was waiting inside. When we had pulled out of the parking lot and I was pretty sure Andie's mom wasn't listening, I poked Andie. "I have to talk to you. It's about Danny. He's a pain."

"Like how?"

"He said I shouldn't go to California."

Andie smiled slyly. "What's so wrong with that?"

"He has nothing to say about my life. Zero. It's not like he's my boyfriend or anything. Even if I were lots older and he and I were dating, well . . . I'd still do what is best for *me*."

She studied me for a second. Then she said, "But if you *were* going out with Danny, you'd be mad at him for being too possessive. Right? So it doesn't really matter, does it? You want everyone to see things your way or not at all."

"Whatever," I said, pulling on my hair stubbornly. We didn't talk for the rest of the short ride home.

I trudged up the steps and into my house. Grandma Meredith was waiting inside with open arms. "Hello, my dear girl," she said, reaching for me.

Tears spilled down my cheeks.

"Why, honey, whatever is wrong?" She hugged me close. "Come, Holly-Heart, it's time for us to catch up on some things." She led me downstairs to the family room, and once we were seated together on the couch, I poured out my frustrations.

"What do you think about praying for something you want really bad, Grandma, and it looks like the answer is yes? But then God doesn't let it happen like you thought. I was all set to go to California, nearly dying to go, and then Mom changed her mind." I paused to breathe. "All because Carrie didn't want to go, too."

Grandma's face was solemn. "Remember, dear, it's not easy for grown-ups to set their youngsters free, especially to parts unknown."

"Oh, Grandma, can't you get Mom to change her mind? Please?"

"Your mother is making the best decision she can, based on the circumstances."

"Yeah, right," I whispered. "Where is she now?"

"Upstairs, packing for Denver."

I didn't want to think about the Denver Children's Hospital and Zachary Tate's dire illness. I didn't want to think about anything except that my very special grandmother was here, her understanding nature shining through her eyes.

"We all long for that first taste of freedom, Holly-Heart," she continued. "But now you must think of your mother. She's thinking of *you*."

"Mom is letting Carrie's decision change everything. It's not fair."

"Well, it's not really your sister's fault, is it?"

I leaned against Grandma. "It's just that God was working everything out for me. So *now* where is He in all of this?"

"The Lord isn't to blame for things not turning out the way we want them to. There are things to be learned in this life."

I sighed. Deep down I knew she was right. God had helped us through tough times. And Mom was faithful about relying on Him when she made decisions. I could count on her no matter what.

She was my safe harbor in the hurricanes of life. No way could I disappoint her now.

"Maybe I was wrong . . . about Mom," I said at last.

Grandma leaned over and kissed my cheek. Then, smelling her delicious and famous beef and barley stew simmering, we both headed upstairs to the kitchen.

Carrie was still in the process of organizing her room when I knocked on her door. "Who is it?" she asked.

"Your fairy godmother, who else?"

"I don't want any wishes today," she said.

I laughed at her wit, waiting in the hall for an invitation to enter. "Well?"

"Well what?"

"May I please come in?" I asked.

"What's the magic word?"

"Aw, come on, Carrie, this is silly."

"The *magic* word," she insisted.

"How should I know? It changes every week."

"Exactly."

Hmm, now what could be on her mind?

"What about Zachary? Is that the magic word?" I asked.

"Nope."

"Summer vacation?"

"That's *two* words."

Exasperating little sister I have. "Ice cream?"

"You're not even close," her voice chimed through the door.

"I give up, then," I said.

"Holly, don't be mad." She opened the door. "*California*. The magic word's California, and you're going there all by yourself."

I sat on her bed. "That's not funny, Carrie. Don't you know how badly I wanted to go and you're—"

"I'm telling the truth. Mommy's on the phone with Daddy right now," she said, her eyes wide.

I didn't know whether to laugh or cry or dance for joy. So I did two out of three. "Give me your hands," I shouted, reaching for Carrie and swinging her around.

"What's going on in there?" Mom called from her room.

"Celebration." Oops, I let Carrie's revelation slip out.

"I couldn't help it, Mommy," Carrie said when Mom peeked around the corner. "I told Holly her good news."

Mom stepped back into the hallway, her eyes squinting. "You're happy, right?" she said to me.

I hugged her hard. "Oh, thank you, thank you, Mom. I love you so much," I cried.

After hugs and kisses all around, Mom sat in Carrie's bedroom. "Before you and I go off in different directions, Holly-Heart, let's talk. I'll be leaving for Denver tonight. Here's my friend's phone number in case you need to call me and can't through on my cell. Feel free to use it anytime and for any reason at all." She gave an index card to me. "Zachary has already begun treatment for septicemia."

"Sounds awful. What is it?" I asked.

"His immune system is so weak his body has trouble throwing off germs that cause minor sicknesses in healthy people, like colds and sore throats. It's a very serious thing for him to get a bug like this on top of trying to fight cancer."

"Does Zach know what's happening to him?"

"His father has explained enough to satisfy him without scaring him."

I pulled on my hair, twisting it around my finger. "Carrie says he's going to surprise everyone and live."

She smiled weakly. "I hope he continues to keep a positive attitude. That's very important."

"Mom?" I slid over beside her. "Do *you* think he'll make it?"

"I'm praying he will."

"Me too," I said, still wishing I'd known about Zach from the start.

"I have some last-minute packing to do," Mom said, getting up and heading back to her room.

I tucked my T-shirt into my jeans. Turning sideways, I stared at Carrie's mirror. Andie was right, I was beginning to develop a little. Had anyone else noticed?

I sneaked over to Mom's room. Coming up behind her, I gave her a bear hug. "I'm sorry," I said. "I was wrong about you, Mom. And selfish, too."

She turned around. "I love you, Holly-Heart. I'm sorry, too. This has been a difficult time for all of us."

I put my arm around her. "I resented Mr. Tate for taking you away from us. Then when you said Zach was the one taking up so much of your time, I understood better."

"I'm glad you do, honey." She stroked my hair.

Grandma and Carrie were standing in the doorway. Grandma's eyes shone with tears as she pulled Carrie close.

Mom closed her suitcase. "Well, dear ones, this is good-bye for a couple of weeks. I know you'll have a good time here with Grandma, Carrie. And, Holly, I hope you get to know your father better. Be sweet, okay?"

"I'll be just fine, you'll see," I said. "Thanks for letting me go, Mom. You won't be sorry."

The three of us followed her downstairs to the garage, watching as she got into the car and backed down the driveway.

I whispered, "I really love you, Mom," as she drove away.

It felt good knowing my mother trusted me with the visit to Daddy. If *she* thought I was grown-up enough, surely Danny would realize how mature I was, too. Now, if he would just stop trying to run my life.

Chapter 15

At church on Sunday, I told Andie and Danny my good news. "I'm leaving for California tomorrow."

Andie tossed her head back. "Go ahead, just leave me here alone. See if I care."

"I'll be back in two weeks, Andie. It's *not* the end of the world."

She pouted. "Maybe not for you."

I noticed that Danny's eyes had lost their twinkle. He didn't say anything, just stood there silently. When my grandmother called to me, I turned to go, leaving Andie and Danny standing there in the church foyer. Both of them looked rather forlorn.

That evening Daddy called one last time to make sure everything was set. "We're all excited about your visit," he said. "Tyler is helping Saundra get your room ready at the moment."

"I can't wait to see you again," I said.

"We'll have a great time together, Holly. I'm looking forward to your visit."

For the third night in a row, I had a lousy time falling asleep. But

I wasn't worried about being sleep deprived. *No problem,* I thought. *I'll get caught up on my rest sunbathing on Daddy's beach.*

♥ ♥ ♥

Monday morning, I got up extra early to shower and fix my hair. Just as I fluffed my hair for the final time, the phone rang.

It was Andie. I figured she'd call and apologize. Sooner or later.

"I hope you come back with a good tan," she said.

"Thanks. You're a true friend."

"Hey, guess what? You'll be back in plenty of time to go rafting with us," she said.

"Really?"

"Yep, Dad changed his vacation days just so you could come along with us," she said. "Isn't that cool?"

"It's fabulous. Tell him thanks."

She paused. "I'll really miss you, Holly."

"I'll write. I promise."

"Call me if you meet anyone fun, okay?" she said, laughing.

"I'll see you soon," I said. Then we hung up.

After a big breakfast of fruit, eggs, and homemade waffles, Grandma and Carrie helped me haul my luggage out to the car. I squirmed excitedly all the way to the airport. "Turn here," I told Grandma, pointing to the sign for arrivals.

"I'll drop you off here," she said, pulling up in front of our mini-airport. Quickly, she got out and opened the trunk while Carrie waited in the car. "Put your luggage on a cart, then get in line at the ticket counter while I park the car," she said. "Carrie and I will meet you there."

I hopped out and began to load my things onto a nearby cart, then wheeled it inside. For a small airport, the terminal was buzzing with people. I wondered where everyone else was headed this Memorial Day. California was *my* destination. I wanted to dance with delight all the way to the ticket counter.

"Holly," someone called to me out of the crowd.

Turning, I looked over my pile of luggage and spied Danny waving at me.

I was so surprised to see him. "What are you doing here?" I said.

"Thought I'd say good-bye. And . . . give you this." He offered me a square envelope.

"What is it?"

"Wait to open it on the plane," he said shyly.

I blushed. "Okay."

My heart did two-and-a-half flip-flops as I slipped the envelope into my overnight case. Danny helped push my luggage to the ticket counter. There, I filled out the address labels for each of my bags. Then we stood in awkward silence as the line inched forward.

"Traveling together?" the attendant asked when we arrived at the ticket counter.

Danny began to search for his "ticket," pulling the pocket linings out of his jeans. "Guess you'll have to go on without me, Miss Meredith," he said playfully.

I hammed it up. "Bummer. What a summer." I handed my ticket to the agent, who seemed concerned about Danny's lost ticket.

"Never mind, sir," Danny said. "I'll catch up with her later."

Danny helped me check the luggage. All but one piece—my overnight case. "I'll carry this on, thanks."

Danny glanced at my ticket. "Wow, you'll be in Denver at your connecting flight before I even reach home on my bike."

I stopped and looked at him. "You rode all the way out here on your bike?"

He nodded. "It was nothing, really."

"Thanks for coming," I said, still amazed.

"Good-bye, Holly." He turned to go before I could say more.

Good-bye, and thanks . . .

Grandma and Carrie returned just as he disappeared through the automatic doors. "I'm all set," I said. "I've got to head to gate four."

We walked toward the security checkpoint.

"Do you have something to read while you're on the plane?" Grandma asked.

I tapped the top of my overnight case. "In here."

Carrie asked, "Like what?"

"Something," I said secretively.

"Let me see," Carrie said, reaching for it.

"Not in your wildest dreams," I said, laughing.

"Holly, please?"

"Nope."

"I'll find your journal and read it while you're gone," she threatened.

"Do I look dumb enough to leave my secrets behind?"

"Aw, phooey," she whined. "You're taking all your journals with you?"

"No kidding. I'm smarter than you think."

"Well, you'd better get into line." Grandma motioned toward the metal detectors. "If you need help or get lost when you change planes in Denver, just ask a ticket agent," she advised. "Or check the monitors."

"I will, Grandma. Don't worry." I gave her a quick kiss. "Thanks for bringing me to the airport."

"Hurry home," Carrie said, standing on tiptoes to kiss me. "Don't talk to strangers."

"Okay . . . bye." I waved to them as I stepped into the short line. I was fabulously excited. And I couldn't wait to see what Danny had given me.

The minute I was settled in my seat on the plane, I reached for my overnight case. There was Danny's envelope. Carefully, I opened it.

I couldn't believe what I saw. A picture of me with a ghastly look on my face, my worst photograph ever.

Then I remembered. Looking closely, I saw the giant green June bug sitting in my hair. How long ago that seemed. Zillions of summer plans and dreams ago. And now some of the best ones were coming true.

Here I was on my way to visit my dad, and who but Danny Myers had come to see me off at the airport!

There was a note attached to the photo.

Dear Holly:

Jared willingly handed over this picture to me. It's for your eyes only. Now that it's in your possession, no one can blackmail you, can they?

I smiled and continued reading.

I can't believe I said what I did to you last Saturday at Cop-per Mountain. Yesterday too. I didn't mean it. What I really meant to say was I'll miss you, Holly, if you leave.

Always,
Danny

The small plane revved up its engines and began to back away from the terminal. Slowly, we taxied out. In a few minutes the plane sped down the long runway.

California, here I come!

I clasped Danny's note to my heart as the nose of the plane rose for lift-off.

HOLLY'S HEART

Sealed With a Kiss

To

Julie Marie,

my number one fad 'n' fashion expert,

and a "hearts-and-flowers" girl.

Chapter 1

"Holly!" called my best friend, Andrea Martinez. "Come up here."

"No way," I said. "I don't want to fall into the Arkansas River!"
I plunged my paddle into the frothing white water for stability,
holding it like the balancing pole of a high-wire acrobat.

"Aw, don't be such a scaredy," Andie hollered back. "Shooting the rapids up here is the only way to go!" She was sitting on
the bow of our raft, showing off for Billy Hill, who worked the
paddles with Danny Myers and Andie's dad. She put down her
paddle and held up her hands. "Look, no hands!" she squealed as
Billy grinned.

"You've gotta be crazy," I said, watching the boulders coming
up on the left.

Danny shook his head, obviously disgusted with her antics. He
relaxed his grip on the paddles as we floated into calmer water.

River rafting on the mighty Arkansas was the most excitement
I'd had all summer, not counting the weeks I'd spent with my dad
in California two months ago.

"Hold on now, Andie," her father warned. "The current's picking up." A river runner from back in his college days, Mr. Martinez
knew this river. But that was twenty years ago. Now he was our
paddle captain.

Brett, the *real* pro, our guide, sat next to Andie's dad. He was blond and tan, probably from a Colorado summer of river trips.

If Danny hadn't been paddling next to me in the raft, I might have been tempted to ask Brett for a crash course in white-water rafting. Not that Danny wasn't as good-looking. He was! He had thick, auburnish brown hair, and eyes a toss-up between gray and green, depending on the color of his shirt. But Brett wore a look of mature confidence.

Stealing another glance at him, I figured he was probably half-way through college—not exactly someone who would hang out with a bunch of eighth-graders like us in his free time.

Danny turned to see how I was doing on my first river ride. With Billy and Andie along, the adventure was twice as much fun. I still could hardly believe Andie and I had talked our parents into allowing Danny and Billy to come along.

Entering a wild stretch of river, the guys strained to control the paddles. I managed to steady mine. So far, it wasn't too hard, only because the real work was being accomplished by the others.

Andie took the big waves with ease as she rode up front, grinning from ear to ear. "C'mon, Holly," she called again. "You should try it up here. The view's great."

"No, thanks." A spray of water made me jump. "I'd like to live long enough to become a published writer."

Andie just laughed.

The rapids came every half mile or so, like clockwork. And on cue—in the middle of the churning white water—Andie hammed it up. Probably for Billy's sake and anyone else who might pay attention.

After the white water, we drifted downstream as gentle breezes cooled my sunburned face. Andie's mom chatted with Billy. Now and then she called up to Andie in front. "Hanging on, kiddo?"

Andie tightened her life vest at the waist. "I'm fine, Mom, see?"

Billy told Andie, "White-water rafting isn't dangerous unless you're careless." Pretending to be serious, he said, "So you'd better watch out." Then he laughed.

"This is only your first run down a river, Billy," Andie teased. "What are *you* talking about?"

Danny was more sincere. "There's a certain amount of respect you show a river as powerful as the Arkansas."

Andie rolled her eyes at that statement and continued to banter back and forth with Billy as we drifted lazily in the warm sunshine. Giant granite walls towered on either side of us, and huge boulders dotted the banks.

Andie's dad didn't seem worried about his daughter clowning around, so I tried to relax about it, talking quietly to Danny. Sounds carry on the river like over an amplifier. We could hear voices from another outfitter upstream, so I turned *my* volume down.

I liked Danny. Being here on a twelve-mile raft trip with him and the others in the middle of Browns Canyon, hours from home, was beyond cool. With Danny right in front of me, I felt safe, the way I'd felt when I visited Daddy in California. But as attentive as Danny was, I really didn't know how he felt about me.

Brett shouted back to us, "Hang on. Turbulent waters coming!"

Up ahead, I spotted some boulders in midstream. Excited, I asked, "Is this the Widowmaker?"

"The river map indicates it," Danny answered. With his photographic memory, he never forgot anything.

Peering around him, I could see sprays of white water about fifty yards ahead. My five-foot paddle suddenly felt heavy as I gripped it. The Widowmaker!

Water swirled around us like a milky-white hurricane. I felt dizzy staring into the frothing waters. I heard their roar as I paddled with decisive strokes. My adrenaline pumped as a giddy yet courageous feeling struck me.

As we dodged the boulders, I could see the cliffs getting closer.

I swallowed nervously, my arms aching as we fought to get

out of the current. The raft climbed a current, then fell, spraying us with icy water. Wiping my face with my arm, I paddled harder than ever.

Just when we cut into the water and were winning the race against the river's current, Andie lurched off balance. Her hands slipped away from the raft as she screamed. And then she flipped out of the raft into the swirling, icy waters.

"Andie . . . no!" I cried, lunging toward her, falling against Danny.

But she was gone. Lost in the rapids!

Chapter 2

Andie's dad instantly dove into the river. All of us watched in hor-ror as he tried to swim toward Andie, the current tossing him like a pebble.

Andie's mom was shouting, "Brett, please get them! Help them!"

His face tense, Brett steadied the paddles, fighting the current. He called to Andie's father, "Grab her and ride it out."

Mr. Martinez reached toward his daughter as another series of waves pushed Andie away, below the surface. My best friend in the whole world had disappeared from view.

Seconds passed as I held my breath. Still no Andie. *Let her be safe. Please, Lord, don't let her die!*

Another second or two ticked by. Then I saw her dark curly hair, and her arms smashing against the current.

"There she is!" I yelled as her father fired forward, grabbing her right arm.

The two of them bobbed in the current, narrowly missing the rocks. Soon the rapids became less violent, and Brett tossed out a long line with a throw bag at the end. Andie's dad seized the white bag at the end of the nylon rope.

My heart pounded a zillion miles an hour. Feeling helpless, I started to cry.

Danny touched my hand. "They're gonna make it, Holly," he said.

"Row to the right," Brett shouted to us. We paddled toward an eddy along the bank to keep from being swept farther downstream. Brett shortened the line, and the current made it taut. Straining through the bleak waters, grasping the line, Andie and her father inched closer . . . closer. Then they were close enough to reach out and grab the sides of the raft.

"I'm fr-freezing," Andie chattered as Billy pulled her on board. Her father slid into the raft, bringing gallons of the river with him.

"Let's paddle to shore," Brett ordered.

We made a quick landfall, and Brett began pulling a pile of wool blankets out of the narrow waterproof box secured to the bottom of the raft. "Hurry! Get her out of those wet clothes and wrap her in these." He handed the blankets to Andie's mom. "Every second counts. We must get her body temperature back to normal." Then he turned to Danny and Billy. "You guys scrounge up some dry firewood. I'll check on Mr. Martinez."

Brett, carrying a small paramedic's bag and a blanket, raced over to Andie's dad. He was sitting on the ground, vigorously rubbing his arms and legs.

I followed Andie and her mom a few yards away, where I held up one of the wool blankets for privacy. By now Andie was shivering so hard she could scarcely talk. Her mother pulled off the wet outer clothes. I was poised for action, with the wool blanket ready to wrap around Andie.

I noticed the strange look in her eyes, like she wasn't focusing. Her mom must've seen how scared I was. "This is hypothermia," she said calmly. But her hands shook as she helped Andie dry off. We wrapped another blanket around Andie's body and led her to a crackling fire, where Brett was already heating water for a hot drink.

Andie's dad was more alert and active than Andie, slapping his arms and moving his feet to get the circulation going. Maybe the weight of his body had given him some insulation against the icy water. But it was obvious they'd both had a thrashing.

Andie slumped to the ground near the fire, shivering. I stared at my friend, who looked like a half-drowned river rat, her lips colorless, her teeth chattering. She was almost too weak to sit up.

Hurrying to her side, I sat cross-legged on the ground. I leaned against her, rubbing her back to help the circulation. Her mom snuggled against her on the other side.

"You're going to be okay," I said, trying to convince myself as well as Andie.

She only nodded. It wasn't like her to be so quiet. She was usually a chatterbox. In fact, she'd talked me into being her best friend before I even had a chance to think about it! We'd laughed our way through grade school together, spent fabulous camping vacations together, and even survived seventh grade last school year. Together.

Andie was my complete opposite: the chattery, uninhibited half of us. Yet in spite of her feisty ways, Andie was my dearest friend. Seeing her nearly drown today had been the next-to-worst experience of my life. Mom and Daddy's divorce was the all-time worst, though.

I stared into the fire's tall blaze. Daddy had made a similar bonfire on the beach one night last June when I visited him. We'd talked about life and fear and other difficult things. Just the two of us.

Finally I got around to telling him about my faith in Christ. He didn't say much more after that. It was like my discussing it ruined the rest of the evening for him.

Just then Andie mumbled something, and her mom wrapped her arms around her shoulders.

Brett stirred powdered Jell-O into the hot water. "Here, this'll help warm her up." He handed the mug to Andie's mom, who held the mug to Andie's lips, helping her sip slowly.

I watched her face. She still seemed dazed. "Andie," I said, "your rescue has to be a sign from heaven."

"Heaven?" she whispered.

"God has something important for you to do here on earth." I'd always thought that way about successful rescue attempts. People didn't just get spared or get their lives back for no reason. At least not trivial ones. Surely God had Andie marked for some favored mission.

Billy burst into laughter. "Yeah, Andie, maybe you're supposed to try out for girls' volleyball after all."

I poked him in the ribs. "That's *not* what I meant."

Like some miracle, Andie snickered. "What Holly means is God has something more important planned for me than girls' volleyball," she said. "Besides, there's no way they'll want someone as short as I am on the team."

Brett flashed a smile our way. "Looks like she's coming around." He seemed relieved. So was I.

Danny slid a bit closer. "Why don't *you* try out for the team, Holly?"

I was dying to. "Perfect idea," I said. "Besides, I heard Miss Neff isn't coaching next year." The gym teacher with a knack for creating lousy nicknames had kept me from playing sports because of her nickname for me: *Holly-Bones*. Verbal disrespect toward slender humanity!

"Miss Neff is a great coach. Don't you like her?" Danny asked.

Andie cast a knowing smile. "Miss Neff has a bad habit of teasing skinny girls."

"So who's skinny?" Billy joked, looking around.

Danny ignored him. "Too bad you didn't try out in seventh grade, Holly. You could've easily made the team last year," he said. "It might be hard to get on the B team now, without that year of experience."

"But if I practice after school, won't that help?"

Danny nodded. "Let me know when you want to practice. I could coach you, too."

Andie raised her eyebrows. "Who *else* is getting tips from the pro?"

"Just Kayla Miller," he said. "You remember her, don't you? She hopes to make the team, too. She played back East at her school in Pennsylvania, before moving to Dressel Hills."

"What about her twin sister?" Billy asked. "Are you going to put *both* brunettes through their paces?"

"Last I heard, Jared Wilkins is helping Paula," Danny said.

Jared? Hearing his name still brought back sad memories. Guess a girl always remembers the first crush of her life.

Having both Danny *and* Jared spend time with the Miller twins made me nervous. Maybe Danny sensed my uneasiness, because at that moment he caught me by surprise. He turned toward me and touched my elbow. His gray-green eyes twinkled and my heart leaped up. Thoughts of Jared Wilkins floated far away.

I smiled back, feeling the warmth in my cheeks. Was Danny's offer to help me make the volleyball team the beginning of a closer friendship? Or was it just another one of his big-brother routines?

Chapter 3

My first volleyball practice session with Danny began two days after the raft trip. We started by working on my serve. A regulation-size net hung between two aspen trees in his backyard. After only two tries, I hit the ball over the net.

"You're a natural," Danny said. "Now let's try spiking the ball when the net's in your face."

We worked on techniques like how to get under the ball and how to spike. But just as Danny was about to demonstrate a new move, along came Billy Hill and half the church youth group. Well, actually it was only Andie, the Miller twins, and Jared Wilkins. Some private lesson this was turning out to be.

"Girls against the guys," called Andie.

Paula and Kayla Miller smiled, their perfect teeth glistening in the August sunshine.

"You're on," Jared said, spinning the volleyball on his pointer finger.

Danny's parents came outside and stood on the redwood deck. "Room for two more?" asked Danny's dad.

"C'mon down," said Billy, motioning to them.

The neighbors next door peered over the fence. Danny waved and *they* joined us, too.

Since the sides were uneven, Danny volunteered to referee. Paula Miller went over to play on the guys' side. She seemed flattered as Jared lifted the net when she ducked under. I wondered if she cared that Jared was the world's worst two-timer. Andie was watching Paula, too, as Jared turned on his charm. Too bad. Both Andie and I knew firsthand how it felt to be fooled by him.

Danny put his fingers between his teeth and whistled. "Ladies first," he said. Our side cheered its approval.

Andie served, and Billy bumped the ball back to our side. Kayla set me up, and I spiked it down right in front of Jared. He missed. Our first point.

"Check it out," called Andie. "Holly's volleys can't be beat." Everyone laughed except Paula's twin, Kayla, who seemed more interested in watching Danny. He seemed too busy keeping score to notice.

A few minutes later it was my serve. I glanced at Danny anxiously. He encouraged me with his grin and a gesture, a reminder to get down under the ball and follow through with the forearm motion he'd shown me today . . . before the crowd showed up.

I stepped back, took a deep breath, and served. The ball barely missed the net. Billy set it up for Danny's dad, who tapped it with his fingers. Jared came in for the kill.

I saw it coming and moved out of my position in the back row. Leaning down, I got under the ball. It shot high enough for Danny's mom to punch it over the net.

We volleyed back and forth three more times before Billy fumbled. Our score again!

For some reason, we were unbeatable. After winning two games in a row, we broke for a snack of chips, dip, and pop.

Danny invited me up to the patio, where he introduced me to his parents.

"We've seen you singing in the youth choir at church," his dad said. "It's nice to meet you finally."

Finally? What did that mean?

Danny's mom was pleasant. "Please come over any time, Holly," she said. Her smile reminded me of Danny's. "We love to entertain our son's friends."

"Thanks, Mrs. Myers," I said politely, hoping we could get better acquainted soon. There was so much I didn't know about Danny.

He carried the bowls of chips around the yard, stopping to talk to Kayla longer than any of the other girls. Her brunette hair was pulled to the back of her head in a ponytail and secured with a red beaded twist. Paula was sitting with Jared in the far corner of the yard, under a stand of aspen trees. She wore her hair the same as Kayla, only it was secured with an orange twist.

Just then Andie came running. She grabbed my arm and asked Danny's mom where the bathroom was.

"Through these doors—you'll see the powder room to the left of the kitchen," Mrs. Myers told her.

"Are you sick?" I asked Andie, locking the bathroom door behind us.

"No, but *you* might be when you hear this," she whispered. "Kayla likes Danny."

"I noticed," I said. "But worse—what if *he* likes *her,* too?"

"Danny's just exceptionally polite," Andie said. "That's all it is."

I noticed the thick, luxurious towels nearby. There was a mono-grammed *M* on each one.

"His parents must be rolling in it," I said.

Andie eyed the towels. "Give me a break. Nice towels don't mean anything."

Washing my hands in the cream-colored sink, I enjoyed the lilac scent of the reed diffuser on the counter. The bottle was especially elegant. "What if Kayla Miller and Danny have money in common?" I said. "What about that?"

"If you're going to freak out over something, just think about being stuck in eighth grade while Danny and Kayla trade notes in advanced math class, one grade higher."

I sighed. "You're right. They were in algebra together last semes-ter, when the Millers moved here in April. Yikes."

Andie picked up the pewter soap dish. "Now *this* looks expensive," she whispered. "Maybe you're right. Maybe Danny's folks are—"

"Who's in there?" cooed a female voice.

"Shouldn't you say 'knock, knock' first?" Andie asked.

"Okay. Knock, knock."

"Who's there?" we answered in unison.

"Justin."

"Justin who?" we asked, puzzled.

"Just in time for another game. Wanna play?"

I opened the door to see Kayla and Paula, the ponytailed wonders.

Andie giggled. "Hey, you're good," she said. "You fooled us. We thought there was only *one* of you talking."

Heading toward the sliding glass door leading to the patio, I lagged behind. The draperies in the family room coordinated perfectly with the sofa. Shelves filled with books covered the far wall. And was that a crystal chandelier over the dining room table? Money! They had it, all right.

We played volleyball until it got too dark to see, even with the impressive floodlights that came on automatically around the yard.

When it came time, Danny's father offered to drive Andie and me home. I jumped at the chance to ride in his new Lexus SUV. Unfortunately the Miller twins were also included in the invitation.

Paula and Kayla's house stood on the side of a hill in another classy part of town. As we turned into their steep driveway, Kayla asked Danny when they could get together to work on her serve. It wasn't what she said but *how* she said it that made me swallow to keep from choking. Talk about flirting. The girl had it down to an art form.

"What about tomorrow around three?" Danny's response was almost businesslike. But that was his way. He was probably totally in the dark about Kayla's cooing.

Tomorrow afternoon Danny and Kayla would practice volleyball techniques together. Unless I could spoil their plans somehow . . .

Danny's dad made small talk as he drove down the tree-lined streets toward Downhill Court. His sports utility vehicle was sleek and comfortable, and it made me think of one of my snail mail pen pals, Lucas Leigh. Recently, Lucas had written that he was car shopping. *I'm considering a Corvette, but there's nothing like a Porsche,* he'd written in his last letter.

I knew absolutely zip about sports cars, except that they were flashy and fast. As for me, this Lexus was cool potatoes!

When we arrived at my house, I thanked both Danny and his dad for a fabulous time. Then Andie and I scurried up the steps and into the house.

Goofey, my motley-colored cat, sat curled up under the card table. Mom and her date, Mr. Tate, were playing checkers in the living room.

"Hi, Mom," I said, kissing her cheek lightly.

Andie and I stood there for a moment, staring at the red kings invading Mom's territory. "Looks like you're surrounded," Andie said.

Mr. Tate looked up momentarily. "Holly," he said to me, "your mother saved leftovers for you and your friend."

"Thanks, Mom," I said softly. To *her*.

Mr. Tate continued to study me. "And," he said, pausing like what he was about to say was very important, "this is your night to clean up the kitchen."

Mom turned to me. "Because your sister's spending the night with Stephanie."

"Uncle Jack and my cousins arrived?" I said, thrilled to hear the news.

"Not Uncle Jack and the boys, just Stephanie," Mom explained. "She didn't want to go on a business trip with her dad, so she's staying at the Millers' house till Uncle Jack returns."

I glanced at Andie. "We were just at the Millers', dropping Paula and Kayla off."

"Well, that's where Stephanie's staying for now," Mom said, focusing on the game again.

"Why didn't *we* keep her?" I asked.

"Because I didn't want *you* to be stuck baby-sitting during your final days of summer vacation," Mom said. "Besides, Paula and Kayla baby-sat Stephie all the time when they lived in Pennsylvania."

The twins' father, Mr. Miller, had worked for the same company as Uncle Jack. After much persuading from the Millers, Uncle Jack decided to move to our ski village—Dressel Hills. His wife, my dad's only sister, Marla, died last February.

"When is Uncle Jack actually coming to town?" I asked.

"Last I heard, in a few weeks." Mom's checker was close to being snatched by Mr. Tate's king.

Mom's date stared at me. "You have kitchen duty, Holly," the not-so-great Mr. Tate said. A control freak, he was growing worse by the week.

In the kitchen, Andie and I loaded the dishwasher. "So . . . has you-know-who rearranged your life yet?" She was wise to keep her voice low.

I snickered. "That's just how he is. Could be that he's the take-charge type because of Zachary's cancer. Speaking of which . . ."

"E-ee-ow, zoom, crash!" Here came Zach. He'd grown a little over the summer, but for a seven-year-old, he was still very small.

"Hey, Zach. How're you doing?" I asked as he kaboomed and gazoomed his fighter plane in patterns around us.

"I'm remissed," he said.

"He's what?" Andie asked.

Zach jumped up and down, trying to get the word out. "I'm getting well. I'm remissed."

"That's great news," I said, giving him not-so-high fives all around the kitchen. "His cancer's in remission," I told Andie, who poured the powdered soap into the dishwasher.

"Let's celebrate," Zach said, opening the freezer and poking around, trying to find some strawberry ice cream.

"Hold on." I rushed back into the living room.

Mr. Tate looked up as I came in, the top of his bald head shiny with beads of perspiration. Seemed like he was playing checkers for keeps.

"That's fabulous news about Zachary," I said, thrilled.

"We're delighted, too." Mom clasped her hands together. "An answer to our prayers."

Mr. Tate's face broke into a rare smile. He reached for Mom's hand. "Now your mother and I can make the plans we had to put on hold for a few months."

Gulp!

Staring into this man's eyes, I was certain he wasn't the best replacement for Daddy. Could I live with him calling all the shots, stepping in all too eagerly as Mom's husband and my step . . . uh, father?

Zach was back in my face with a dipper for the ice cream.

"Is it okay with you?" I asked his dad.

Dramatically, Mr. Tate stretched his arm out to peer at his watch. "I believe it's too late for sweets," he announced.

"Aw, Dad," Zach whined.

Mom intervened. "But it's such a special time."

This was a mistake. By the look on Mr. Tate's face, Mom's pleading hadn't gone over too well. He simply shook his head with great finality.

Mom wilted.

Andie motioned to me from the doorway. *She* didn't think it was too late for sweets. And I wasn't about to ask Mr. Tate's permission, either.

I joined her in the kitchen, where I spotted today's stack of mail on the desk. Sorting through it, I discovered a letter addressed to Mom. On the envelope, our address, *207 Downhill Court, Dressel Hills, Colorado,* was followed by a large *U.S.A.*

"Who's this from?" I muttered, showing Andie the stamp.

She rotated the envelope, studying the postmark. "It's from Japan. Does your mom know anyone there?"

"Let me see that." I held it up to the light. "It's handwritten." My curiosity grew as I glanced toward the checker game in the living room.

I got Zach's attention. "Do you know when you and your dad are heading home tonight?" I asked.

"Nope," he said, carrying his jet planes and stuff down to the family room.

I whispered to Andie, "I hope they leave soon."

Sliding the mystery letter under the pile of mail, I dished up ice cream in record time. Andie and I smuggled our bowls upstairs. "Nothing like a huge bowl of strawberry ice cream shared with a best friend." I closed my bedroom door behind me.

Andie laughed. "Sounds like a verse on a greeting card."

"I'd rather write stories." I paused, thinking about that. "Or letters." Lucas Leigh flashed across my thoughts.

"Do you think your mom will let you read her letter?" Andie asked, taking a giant bite of ice cream.

"Mom tells me everything," I said.

"Everything?"

"Well, close," I said, spooning up a tiny bite and relishing the fruity flavor.

"Think she'll marry Mr. Tate?" At that Andie stuck her nose in the air, imitating the man's response to Zach's request for ice cream.

"Not if I can help it," I said with more confidence than ever. "Now, we need to devise a plan to ruin Kayla's volleyball lesson with Danny tomorrow."

Andie leaned back on her elbow on the floor. "Your little sister is staying with Stephanie over at the Millers', right?"

I nodded.

A gleam of mischief twinkled in her brown eyes. "Can you arrange for her to stay there all afternoon?"

"Easy," I said. Andie was on to something and it was perfect. "Let's call Jared and tell him Paula's coming over *here* tomorrow at three."

A silly grin played across her face. "Great idea!"

"Wait," I said, reaching for the phone and handing it to Andie. "What if he can't come?"

"There's no way Jared would miss out on some female attention."

"Andie, you're a genius!"

"Put that in writing, would you?" She dialed the numbers for Jared's house. If this little scheme worked, Kayla would have to take Stephie and Carrie along when she practiced volleyball with Danny because her sister, Paula, would be busy, over here visiting me. Until Jared showed up, that is.

Giggling, I waited. "This is the Plan of the Hour," I whispered.

Andie shushed me. "C'mon, Jared, answer the phone." A few more seconds ticked by, then she gave up. "I'll call later."

I went to my window seat, facing Andie, who'd flopped down on the floor. "How long do we wait before we phone Jared again?"

"Five minutes," she said. "Maybe he's in the shower. . . . Can a guy take one that fast?"

"Maybe," I said, reaching for Bearie-O, my favorite teddy bear, who was really Andie's. We'd traded best bears back in first grade, almost half a lifetime ago.

"Well, I can't shower in five minutes. My hair's so thick it takes that long just to get the shampoo rinsed out."

"I know what you mean." I draped my hair over my arm. "This takes half a day to dry."

"Ever wish you could whack it off?"

I stared down at the blond strands. "Not really. Why?"

"Just wondered," Andie said, watching the minute hand on her watch. "You've never really cut it your whole life."

"It's probably the best part of me," I said. "If only I had a perfect shape, like the Miller twins."

"Don't forget your personality. *You* have that. Besides, you're tall and slender and—"

"Make that *skinny* and underdeveloped," I interrupted. "People don't call me 'bones' for nothing."

"*People* don't. Miss Neff is just one person, and she probably calls you Holly-Bones because she thinks you can handle the teasing."

I sighed. "When school starts, I'll tell her I hate it. Then maybe she'll stop."

"You might not have a chance, you know. You're getting rounder—where it counts," she said in a silly voice. "Take it from your best friend, which is, by the way, another good thing you've got going for you."

I squeezed Bearie-O. "Why did Paula and Kayla Miller have to move here right when Danny and I were—"

"Holly!" Mom called from downstairs.

I took the steps down two at a time. "What is it, Mom?"

"That's what I'd like to know," she said, waving the mystery letter.

I scanned the living room for Mr. Tate. The house was empty. "Who's it from?"

"It's not signed," she said. "And no return address."

"What's it say?" By now Andie was at my side.

"It's very short, almost childish, but definitely humorous." Mom handed the letter to me.

I studied the handwriting on the envelope. The penmanship was scrawled. "Do you recognize the writing?"

Mom shook her head.

I opened the letter and read:

Dearest Susan,

I still remember the first time I saw you. It was a long time ago. I wish I could see you more often, the way it used to be. Please remember to laugh like in the old days. Okay?

Here's a joke to help you do that. Why doesn't a bald man need any keys? Because he has no locks. Ha, ha. (No offense.)

I miss you. I'll write again. Maybe sooner than you think!

I read it again silently.

"Strange, isn't it?" Mom said.

"Sure is," Andie said, surveying the envelope again.

"Do you know anyone in Japan?" I asked.

251

"Certainly not," she said. "And it says I've known this person for a long time."

"That's not all," Andie said. "The person writing the letter must know Mr. Tate." She giggled, and so did I.

Mom seemed to know what we were getting at. "He can't help it he's bald."

"But what person in Japan knows you're dating Mr. Tate?" I asked.

Mom motioned us into the kitchen. "Could there be another Susan Meredith?"

"No chance," I said. "This person even knows about your divorce. See, here it says, 'Please remember to laugh like in the old days.' " I shivered. "Ooh, it's almost spooky."

Andie had an idea. "If you really do get another letter soon, Holly and I will be glad to read that one and discuss it with you, too." Mischief glinted in her dark eyes.

"Thanks, I'll keep that in mind," Mom said, playing along. "You'll be my correspondence consultants." She looked at the clock above the refrigerator. "How late do you girls plan to be up?"

"Not too late," I said, leading Andie out of the room. "We have a couple more phone calls to make."

"Well, try to be extra quiet after ten. I'm getting up rather early tomorrow."

I stopped at the bottom of the stairs. "How come?"

"Mike and I are having breakfast downtown. We have some important things to discuss."

I frowned, glancing at Andie.

She mouthed the words silently, "Who's Mike?"

"Mr. Tate," I whispered, trudging up to my room, banging the door shut.

"What's wrong?" she asked, heading for the phone to call Jared.

"This could be the end of life as I know it." Mom and Mr. Tate were spending too much time together. I wished I had a Plan of the Hour to keep *them* apart!

Chapter 4

The next morning I tried to push Mr. Tate out of my mind by going over the scheme Andie and I had cooked up last night.

Everything was set to go for the Plan of the Hour. With Paula coming over here at three o'clock, Kayla would have to baby-sit Carrie and little Stephie, taking them with her to practice volleyball at Danny's. Jared had seemed more than willing to visit Paula . . . over here. The plan was worth celebrating with waffles for breakfast.

Andie talked me into letting her make waffles. She poured the batter with the finesse of an elephant. It oozed out the sides of the waffle iron, creating a cooked-on batter mess. Mega-waffles, that's what they were, equal to twice the size of Mom's. One and a half was all I could eat.

When the phone rang, I raced to get it, sticky fingers and all. The line was full of static, like it was a bad connection or . . . long distance.

"Hello?"

Silence.

"Hello?" I repeated.

"Is this Holly Meredith?" a male voice asked.

"Who's calling?"

"Did your mother receive a letter from Japan this week?" the voice persisted, ignoring my question.

"Yes, but she's busy now. May I take a message?" I asked. There was static on the line.

"Please tell her I miss her," he said, the static growing louder. The voice was muffled, yet familiar.

Then, *click*, he was gone.

I flew to the kitchen, licking the stickiness off my fingers. "Andie, guess what!"

She spun around. "Who was that?"

"Japan just called, I mean, *someone* from Japan called. I think it was Mom's secret admirer. Except there was something strange about his voice."

"What about it?"

"It sounded familiar."

"Really?" Andie asked excitedly. "Who?"

"I'm not sure," I said, clearing the table. "Probably just my imagination, but wait'll I tell Mom." Then I froze in my tracks. "Hold everything. Is this perfect timing or what!"

"What are you talking about?" Andie asked, still stuffing her mouth.

"This is exactly what I need to help get Mr. Tate out of my life."

Andie groaned. "Another plan? Is that what you're dreaming up?"

"Don't worry, I won't need your help for *this* one. It's perfect."

Andie looked relieved. She cut another bite of waffle.

"Now . . . first things first," I said. "Paula will be here at three. While she's here, you sneak over to Danny's. Remember to get a complete report of *everything*."

"Well, if I know your little sister, she'll have Danny wrapped around her finger. He'll be giving *her* volleyball pointers before the afternoon's over." Andie grinned.

"It's perfect." I could almost see little Carrie charming Danny. "She's something else, but then, so is our cousin Stephanie."

"How old is your oldest cousin?" Andie asked.

"Stan will be turning fifteen in September. When Uncle Jack gets settled and school starts, I'll introduce you to all of them."

It was obvious Andie liked the idea of meeting Stan, even though she and Billy Hill hung out a lot at youth group and school.

She carried her plate to the sink. "How are you going to entertain the well-heeled Miss Paula while you wait for Jared to show up today?"

"Play Scrabble."

"Think you can beat her?" Andie rinsed the syrup off her plate.

"No problem," I boasted.

"I hear she gets *A*'s in composition. Maybe you've met your match." Andie tossed her hair with a giggle and headed for the bathroom.

"Fabulous," I muttered, wishing it were Kayla I was playing instead of Paula. Beating Paula's twin in a game of words would make my day. No, it would make my school year, which was starting in a little over three weeks from now. Making every day count between now and the day after Labor Day—the first day of school—was urgent. If Kayla flirted her way between Danny and me, well, I wasn't sure if I could handle it. I hated the thought of anything—or anyone—hindering our friendship.

We spent the rest of the morning playing games and watching TV. At two-thirty, Andie left to catch the city bus to Danny's neighborhood across town. I set out the Scrabble board, Webster's Dictionary, and two glasses of root beer downstairs in the family room. Then I sang and danced around to Holy Voltage, my favorite Christian group, while I waited for Paula.

When the doorbell rang, I hurried to open it, expecting to see

Paula. Instead, our mail carrier stood there with a package for me to sign for, accompanied by a stack of letters.

The package, it turned out, was from Sears. I set it aside for Mom and flipped through the envelopes, finding a letter from Daddy, one from Grandma Meredith, and one from my pen pal, Lucas Wadsworth Leigh.

I traced the LWL stamped inside the fancy blue seal on the back of the envelope. Why was he writing again before I answered his letter? I tore open the envelope to find out.

> *Dear Holly:*
>
> *You may be surprised to receive this letter so soon after my most recent one. I'm writing about an idea I have for manuscript swapping. By that I mean, are you interested in reading and critiquing each other's stories? If you like this idea, please send one of your stories or essays along with your next letter, and I'll do the same.*
>
> *I found it interesting that you have collected the entire mystery series for children by my aunt, Marty Leigh. Not many women are so sentimental as to save their childhood books. I like that. Perhaps I can arrange to have her autograph them for you the next time she's in Colorado.*
>
> *I'll look forward to hearing from you. Happy writing!*
>
> *Lucas W. Leigh*
>
> *PS: Could you send a bibliography of your work, whether published or not?*

I pulled on my hair, twisting it hard. Lucas actually thought I was a grown woman with a beloved collection of children's books. *Probably he wouldn't write to me if he knew how old I really am.* But I didn't want to jeopardize my pen pal relationship with the nephew of one of my all-time favorite authors by revealing the truth now. I forced the guilt feelings away.

Checking my watch, I almost wished Paula wouldn't be arriving in a minute. I'd much rather work on my list for Lucas, proving what a mature person I really was. Then I remembered the reason I'd invited Paula over in the first place, and held my breath. My clever plan *had* to work!

By the time the doorbell rang again, I was a wreck. Paula was late, and I worried Jared would show up at the same time, making her very suspicious.

Quickly, I headed for the door, ready to welcome Paula Miller inside. But the words stuck in my throat as I opened the door. There, on either side of Paula, stood my little sister, Carrie, and my cousin Stephanie!

I stared at them in disbelief.

"Holly," Carrie sang, her hand on her hip, "aren't you going to let us in?"

"Uh, sorry," I said, stepping aside. Then, remembering my manners, I greeted Paula.

Carrie lugged her overnight gear inside, dumping it on the living room floor. Then she and Stephie disappeared upstairs.

Dumbfounded, I hustled Paula downstairs to the family room. I'd completely overlooked the chance of something like *this* happening. Why hadn't I realized Paula would bring the girls here with her, freeing Kayla up to meet with Danny? A best friend would do that. So would a twin sister.

"Want to play Scrabble?" I asked.

"I'd love to," she said, tucking her long hair behind her ears.

I began explaining the rules, going over every possible aspect of the game. "Any questions?" I asked.

"That was very good, Holly, but my sister and I play Scrabble all the time," she said, her voice sounding exactly like Kayla's.

I swallowed hard, embarrassed. Along with mismanaging the Plan of the Hour, I'd made a fool of myself, too.

But Paula let me off the hook by complimenting me on my hair. "It's so long and thick," she said. "I bet you can fix it a zillion different ways."

A *zillion*? That was *my* word.

I nodded, wondering what was happening at Danny's house

right now. Was Kayla smiling at him too much? Making him forget *our* friendship?

Uneasy about what I didn't know, I started the game. Paula knew Scrabble, all right. After three turns she was ahead by ten points. I was so caught up in the game, an hour passed like five minutes. At last, I'd met my match.

Upstairs, I heard Mom getting her peppermint tea ready. "Holly-Heart? You here?" she called.

"Downstairs," I said.

"It's raining so hard, the streets are flooded," she said. "That's why I'm late."

I'd hardly noticed the rain or that Mom was late getting home. This was the closest game I'd ever played. While I slid the tiles around on the rack, trying to make a word to outdo Paula, I suddenly remembered Andie.

Yikes! She was outdoors in this mess—sneaking around—spying at Danny's house. She was probably soaked to the skin by now. No good. Her ordeal in the Arkansas River last Tuesday had left her with a bad case of the sniffles.

"Excuse me a second, Paula," I said, leaving the Scrabble game. "I have to talk to my mom."

Mom was squeezing honey from the plastic bear when I raced into the kitchen. "It's an emergency," I began. "Andie's outside in the rain."

She looked at me funny. "Make sense, Holly. Why is Andie out in *this* weather?"

I pulled a stool away from the bar and plopped onto it. "This is terrible. Everything's wrong. *Everything!*"

"Why don't you start over, Holly-Heart . . . from the beginning."

I took a deep breath. It was no use. Besides, I could hear someone's footsteps on the front porch. I stood up to answer the door.

It was Jared Wilkins.

"Is Paula here?" he asked, his blue eyes eager to gaze on the brunette beauty, no doubt.

"In the family room. We were just playing Scrabble," I said, noticing his clothes were dry. "Did you get a ride?"

"Yeah, Danny's dad dropped me off."

"You were at Danny's?" I felt a tingle of hope.

"Just for a minute. Had to drop off a DVD I borrowed. That's when the rain started, so his dad offered me a ride over here. Weird, though, we saw Andie walking in the rain. She was drenched, so we picked her up and took her home."

I felt lousy about Andie but glad the rain cut Kayla's practice session with Danny short.

Jared asked, "What was Andie doing across town in the rain?"

I ignored his question. No need for him to know how badly my plan had flopped. "How's Danny doing?"

Jared grinned. "I'll give it to you straight. Kayla seemed pleased about the sudden change in weather when we left."

"What does *that* mean?" I tugged hard on my hair.

"Well, think how *you'd* feel," he taunted.

I shifted my gaze, staring at the overnight bag Carrie had left on the floor. It was none of Jared's business how I felt about Danny Myers.

"Why don't you go down and finish the Scrabble game with Paula?" I suggested, trying to hide my frustration.

Jared ran his fingers through his hair as he headed downstairs. I followed close behind, noticing how surprised Paula looked when she saw him.

"Do you mind if I leave you two alone for a sec?" I said, realizing how silly that probably sounded.

Jared jumped right on it. "Take your time."

I raced upstairs to the phone.

"Andie?" I said when she answered. "Are you okay?"

"Sort of." She sounded all stuffed up. "You won't like what I have to tell you."

"I already know," I said. "Jared's here."

She sneezed. "There's more. Kayla and Danny had a snack together at Danny's house. His mom served it to them in the breakfast nook."

"How do you know?"

"I stood under the trees in the neighbor's yard and watched through the windows." Andie coughed and blew her nose.

"Then what?"

"Danny's mom went out on the porch, tending her flowers, leaving Kayla alone with Danny for a while."

"Oh great." I could almost picture Kayla batting her brown eyes at Danny.

"I'm sorry, Holly. Looks like our plan fell through."

"No kidding," I whispered. "What a nightmare!"

Chapter 5

I turned a page in my diary and wrote.

> *Saturday, August 14. The Plan of the Hour failed . . . absolutely and totally failed, right down to the second it rained, forcing Danny and Kayla indoors. Some cozy setup for Miss Kayla Miller.*

It was nearly time for supper. Paula and Jared had just left, and I was pouring out my pent-up feelings of the day on lined paper. I felt sorry for girls who didn't write in journals. It was the best way to handle life sometimes. And what about people who didn't talk to God? How did *they* cope?

Sliding off my window seat, I sat cross-legged on the floor. Bearie-O fell forward, his droopy eyes looking sadder than ever. I smiled at him. "Hi-ya, Bearie-O. Are you feeling sad because I do?"

I moved his head to make him nod.

"You're the best bear a girl could own."

"You don't *own* him," Carrie said, startling me.

"What are you doing in my room?" I snapped.

She covered her mouth with her hands, but the giggles poured out. Then Stephanie stepped out from behind her.

"You! *Both* of you are in trouble," I shouted. "Why do you keep breaking the rules? You don't see me in *your* room, do you, Carrie?"

Stephanie disappeared quickly, leaving Carrie only half grinning in the fading light of evening.

"We heard you talking in the dark. It was Stephie's idea to sneak in. Honest, Holly."

"You're *older* than Stephie. Better spell out the rules of our house to her," I said, putting Bearie-O back on his shelf.

"It's dark in here." She flicked on the light switch. "Why are you sitting in the dark talking to your stuffed animals?"

"None of your business."

"Fine, don't tell me," she said. "But I've got a message for you from Mommy. She wants you to set the table. Mr. Tate and Zachary are coming for supper." Carrie left, closing the door behind her.

I stomped over to the light switch. Sitting in the dark was good for the soul sometimes. Maybe when Carrie grew up she'd understand.

Opening the bottom drawer of my dresser, I slid my journal into its hiding place. My notebook of secret prayers was underneath. So were copies of my letters to pen pals, including Lucas Wadsworth Leigh, all stored in an old legal file, a reject from the law firm where Mom was a paralegal. Another folder held *his* letters to me. Writing an answer to his last letter would be my first project tonight after supper.

This whole thing of "snail mail" pen pals had been Andie's idea. She was so bored last month, she challenged me to a contest. "Let's see who can get the most pen pals before school starts," she'd said. "And no fair getting extra money from parents for postage."

Andie was like that. Very bossy.

Not wanting to miss out on the fun, I had agreed. Soon *I* was ahead with six pen friends. Then she moved ahead, adding two girls from Panama. Quickly, I sent off for a girl in Rome. Tied!

Counting Lucas, I was actually winning. But for some reason, keeping this *male* pal a secret from Andie was important to me.

One week after Andie's challenge, I had discovered Lucas Leigh's name in the personal ads in a writer's magazine at the library.

Lucas Wadsworth Leigh, nephew to mystery writer Marty Leigh, is interested in corresponding with aspiring fiction writers, the ad read.

I couldn't resist. Marty Leigh was tops. I owned every book she'd ever written. If she was even remotely related to this Lucas person, well . . . I had to know more. So I'd sent my first letter off to Lucas W. Leigh.

Promptly, I received a letter back. A fancy seal was affixed to the back of the envelope with LWL on display in calligraphy, as if he were royalty or something. I'd learned Lucas was a junior in college—much older than I'd supposed. I realized then I'd never declared my own age of thirteen. What difference did age make in a writer, anyway? I'd told myself. Andie's daring nature was beginning to rub off on me.

"Holly!" called Carrie. "Mom's waiting."

I pushed my dresser drawer shut, wishing I could put it under lock and key. Especially with an immature younger sister and giggly cousin snooping around. "Coming, Mom," I called as I hurried downstairs.

Delicious aromas filled the kitchen. Mom had baked meat loaf with her yummy brown sugar and ketchup topping. And there were two yellow candles lying on the counter.

"What's the occasion?" I asked suspiciously.

Mom motioned for me to help. "Time to dish up."

"Celebrating Zachary's remission?" I asked.

"Good idea," she said, evading my question.

"Mom, you're not announcing something important, are you?" I held the forks in my right hand, suspended in time and space, waiting . . .

Please, dear God, don't let this be what I'm thinking.

I turned to face her, my heart beating wildly. Did I dare tell her what I thought of Mr. Tate becoming her husband?

The doorbell rang. "It's Mike and Zachary." Mom rushed to the door the way she once did when Daddy awaited her.

My heart sank. Was Mom in love?

I wanted to scatter the utensils around the dining room table. Instead I forced myself to fold the napkins neatly, placing *two* forks to the left of each plate.

"Hi, girls," Zach said, lugging a duffel bag full of toy planes and missiles and things. It was good to see him looking so cheerful. And healthy.

"Hungry?" I asked him.

He sniffed the air. "Smells good." He plopped down at the head of the table.

Mr. Tate carried a square white box. Zach pointed to it, acting excited about what was inside.

"What's in there?" Carrie asked, touching the lid.

"Uh, *that's* a surprise," Mr. Tate said, shooing her away.

I hoped it wasn't a wedding cake. The excitement in my mother's eyes worried me. She'd met Mr. Tate for breakfast early this morning. Had she gone and eloped?

With a grand wave of her hand, Mom announced, "Please be seated, everyone. Look for your name card beside each plate."

Name cards? This *was* special.

Zach found his place, next to Mom. Stephie was on the other side of her. Mr. Tate sat at the head of the table, the empty spot where Daddy used to sit years ago.

Mom carried the food to the table. Then Mr. Tate prayed without Mom asking, like he was in charge or something.

When the baked potatoes came around, I unwrapped the foil from mine, scrunching it into a ball. "Please pass the butter," I said.

I watched, almost jealously, as Mom worked first on Zach's potato, then Stephie's. She seemed so fond of Zach.

Mr. Tate waited for everyone to start eating before he tapped his fork lightly on his water glass. "I'd like to propose a toast."

Propose? Sounded scary.

He held up his glass. "Children, this is a toast to our new life together as a family. Susan, this is a toast to our new investment endeavor."

Mom looked scared, like something had just dawned on her. "Ah, wait a minute, Mike," she said. "I thought you were going to give me time to discuss this with the girls."

Mr. Tate lowered his glass. "You'd like their permission?" He looked at Carrie, then me. "Well, girls. What do you think?"

Carrie grinned. "When are you getting married?"

Mr. Tate's eyes shone. "Soon," he said, gazing at Mom.

Carrie smiled. "Goody. I'll have a brother," she said, pointing to Zach, who grabbed his throat, pretending to gag.

"Calm down, young man," Mr. Tate reprimanded him. "Your little friend is only being polite."

Now *I* felt like I might choke. Mr. Tate was much too serious. Couldn't he take a joke?

Mr. Tate turned and smiled at me. "How do you feel about this news, Holly, uh, Heart, is it?"

I coughed, despising him for putting me on the spot like this. Where were *his* manners?

"Excuse me, please," I said, leaving the table and rushing to the bathroom.

"Holly?" Mom called. "Are you all right, dear?"

All right was for kids with boring, uneventful lives. Kids with a dad who lived with them. Kids who didn't have to worry about possible stepfathers like Mr. Tate. Not kids like me.

I closed the door to the bathroom. Locked inside, I felt like I was drowning. Now I knew how Andie had felt with the mighty Arkansas River rushing around her. Pulling her into its powerful current. Grabbing her, thrusting her into its whirling waves, while she worked . . . pounding, thrashing . . . fighting to survive.

Exhausted, I sat on the edge of the tub. Why was *I* fighting so hard? This was *Mom's* choice. If Mr. Tate was right for her, why did I dislike him?

A light tapping came at the door. "Holly-Heart, it's me, Mom."

"I'm okay," I said, knowing full well that I preferred to stay in here, nursing my pain for the rest of my life.

"You don't sound okay," she said.

Mom was persistent—one of the many things I loved about her. She always knew when I needed to be alone, and when I needed her there, even the times I told her to leave me alone.

"Honey?" She was still waiting.

The tears came, so I couldn't answer. Besides, I didn't want to spoil her special night.

"Something must be very wrong," she said. "Are you sick?"

Oh yeah, I was sick, all right. Sick for all the years I'd missed Daddy. Sick that he left in the first place. Sick that he'd remarried. Sick that if Mr. Tate and Mom got together, Daddy would never be able to marry Mom again if he ever had the chance.

I ran the hot and cold water together. Fast. I blew my nose and muttered something about joining her for dessert.

"Are you sure, Holly?" She knew me well.

"Yes," I managed to say, turning the water off.

I heard her footsteps fade away as she went back downstairs. I wiped my face and stared at the washcloth. I stared at it. There were no *M*'s for Meredith on these towels like the *M*'s for Myers at Danny's house. The stuck-up Miller twins probably had mono-grammed *M*'s on *their* towels, too.

What if someone gave Mom a wedding gift of towels with *T* for Tate stitched on them? Instantly, I knew I would never, ever use those towels if we got any. *My* last name was Meredith, and nothing could change that.

Slowly, I took a deep breath and opened the bathroom door. One by one, I descended the stairs.

Everyone was almost finished eating. I sat down and picked at my meat loaf, feeling Carrie's eyes on me. My eyes were prob-ably red.

This minute I wished I were a little girl again, with Daddy sit-ting across from me at the head of the table.

Mom made small talk until I finally finished eating. Then Mr. Tate brought the white box over, setting it down in the middle of the table. I held my breath, certain there'd be a layer cake with white curlicues dancing around the edges and a miniature bride and groom smiling on the tip-top.

Slowly, he reached inside the box and lifted the plate up. "This," he said, "is a honeycomb."

I stared at the tiny cubicles of wax.

Mr. Tate cut a small portion off and gave it to Mom. One after another we were served the waxy stuff, heavy with honey.

Next came a demonstration. Mr. Tate picked up a bite-sized piece and began to chew it. "You work the honey out of the comb and spit out the wax."

"That's gross," said Carrie.

Zach was getting the hang of it, however. "Mmm, it's good."

Mom beamed down at Zach, putting her arm around him. "It's good for you," she said. Then, looking around the table, "It's good for *all* of us."

"Which brings me to some exciting news." Mr. Tate sat down and directed his gaze to me. "Your mother and I are planning to purchase some land north of here."

Mom nodded. "We spoke to a real-estate broker during breakfast this morning."

North of here? I swallowed hard. The *mountains* were north of here.

Mr. Tate continued, "This five-acre plot of land we're considering is a choice spot for a log home. And the perfect place for a bee farm, among other things."

Carrie's eyes widened. "Bees make honey. We're going to have bees?"

"Yes, we're going to become beekeepers and gather honey. And," he paused, breathing deeply, "get in touch with nature."

I stared at this man. Not only did he want to marry my mother, he wanted to ruin my life!

SEALED WITH A KISS

Chapter 6

I managed to speak at last, addressing only Mom. "Why do we have to move?"

"We don't *have* to, Holly," she said firmly. "But things are better in the country, uh, in the mountains. The air is cleaner and—"

Mr. Tate interrupted. "There are certain things you don't know, Holly. Your mother and I will discuss them with you in private." Here, he glanced at Zachary, who was picking the waxy honeycomb out of his teeth.

Anger boiled in me. Then Mom suggested Carrie and I clear the table.

Gladly. Anything to get away from this man. Mr. Tate was turning out to be someone great to hate.

"We'll have family devotions in one hour," he announced.

I looked at Carrie. "Family devotions?" I whispered.

"Yeah, isn't it cool? Zach's gonna be our brother."

Stunned at her response, I opened the dishwasher. Carrie, my own flesh and blood, was in favor of this nightmare.

I waited till Mr. Tate left the room. A sad lump stuck in my throat as Zach put his arm around *my* mother. Together, they headed downstairs to the family room.

I grabbed Carrie's arm. "Listen to me. This is serious."

"Ouch, you're hurting me," she wailed.

"I am not," I said, letting go.

"Holly, what's wrong with you?"

"I'm worried. Mom's going to marry Mr. Tate and move us out of town. We'll leave this house—Daddy's house—and live in some drafty log cabin where we won't even have our own bedrooms and we'll have to gather honey and berries for food like the pilgrims."

Carrie stared at me. "I'm telling. You're wrong . . . that's not what we're gonna do." And she raced downstairs, whining the whole time.

Betrayed. That's how I felt. I couldn't even share my greatest fears with my sister. She was off blabbing it to Mom and Mr. Tate this minute.

So what. Let her tell. And when I got in trouble for expressing my opinion, I'd announce that I was staying in Dressel Hills. Maybe Danny's rich parents would adopt me. Or there was always Andie. I rinsed and stacked the dishes, drawing the water for the pots and pans.

Just then Carrie came stomping up the steps. "They want to talk to you after the kitchen's clean, but before devotions." She seemed to enjoy ordering me around.

"You have an attitude problem, Carrie," I retorted. "Go play with Stephie."

"I can't. She's going back to the Millers' house tonight."

"Well, then, go do something else, unless you want to scrub these pans." I knew *that* would make her disappear. And I was right. She skipped out of the room.

Watching the minute hand on the clock above the fridge, I became more and more furious. Mom was supposed to be on *my* side. But it was obvious she was attached to Zachary. Sure, he was a motherless cancer patient, but now that he was in remission, couldn't she pay attention to her *own* kids for a change?

I tried to force the Tate-hate away by concentrating on the good things in my life, like Andie's surviving the icy Arkansas River, and how loyal she'd been, standing out in the rain for me. And school starting soon, with volleyball tryouts just around the corner.

And there was my literary pen pal, Lucas Wadsworth Leigh. What a cool name. He even sounded like an author, a best-selling one at that. I could hardly wait to write back to him. I had planned to tonight after supper, but that was before Mr. Tate ordered family devotions.

"Holly," Mom said, now in the kitchen.

Startled, I jumped. "Hew long have you been standing there?"

"Not long."

I rinsed off the meat loaf pan, wondering how long I'd scrubbed the same spot. "You wanted to talk to me?"

"*We* do," she said. "When you're finished."

"Mom?" I hesitated. "I don't want to live in the mountains. Can't we stay here?" I dried my hands.

"Mike and I have already made an offer on the property. It's truly beautiful up there, you'll see."

"I don't want to see. It's too far away. Besides, how will I get to school?"

"Those are things we'll discuss. Perhaps we can get a permit for you to continue at your school. It won't happen immediately. We'll have to build the house first, and winter's coming on soon."

Three cheers for winter. For *anything* that would slow down this ridiculous process.

"Let's talk downstairs," she said, putting her arm around me.

Mr. Tate was fooling with the sound system installed in our entertainment center. He pushed the Play button on the CD player. Holy Voltage interrupted the stillness. He jerked his bald head back, glaring at me. "What in the world is *that?*"

It was time to defend myself. "That's Christian rap. It's totally cool."

Mr. Tate frowned. "Cool? Let's have something soothing instead." He fumbled around with the system, obviously confused.

I waited, prolonging his frustration. The heavy rap beat made me want to dance across the room and turn up the volume so he could *really* get the message. It *was* a Christian group, after all.

A pleading look crossed his face. "Please turn it off, Holly."

In a flash, I pressed the correct button, wondering if this was how things would be when Mr. Tate was forever calling the shots.

He sat on the chair across from me. "There are some things you need to know about Zachary's remission, Holly," he began. "It is difficult for the doctors to project into the future. Of course, we're hoping for the best. But the best might only be a few years."

What does this have to do with anything? I wondered.

Mom continued, "We want to change our way of living, for Zach's sake. Perhaps prolong his life with the way we eat and things like that."

"The stress in the city alone can add to a person's susceptibility to disease," Mr. Tate stated.

Oh please, I thought. Dressel Hills was hardly a city. A ski village of ten thousand people wasn't stressful in the least.

"We'll have our own raw honey as well as plant herbs for teas," Mom said.

This didn't sound like the mother I knew and loved. The only herbs she cared about were in the tea bags she used to make peppermint tea every day after work. And honey . . . what was wrong with the stuff in our plastic bear?

"You're so quiet, Holly," Mom said.

I was thinking hard. "What about your long drive to work?" I asked.

"That's something else that must be considered," she said.

"Are you quitting?" I asked.

Mr. Tate responded with amazing speed. "Your mother has worked to support this family for a number of years. It's time for her to stay home and care for the family. Zach will continue to need attention as time goes on."

Funny, he mentioned only Zach.

"When will all this happen?" I asked, scared silly.

"It's likely that your mother and I will marry before the house is built. Perhaps before the holidays."

"Which holidays?" There were a string of them coming up.

"Maybe Christmas," Mom offered. "It will give us plenty of time to plan."

Mr. Tate leaned forward. The light bounced off his shiny head. At that moment I remembered the joke in Mom's mystery letter from Japan. Mr. Tate really *didn't* have any locks.

Here we sat in the family room, on the verge of altering our lives forever, while someone halfway around the world was reminding Mom to laugh like in the old days. And the phone call! How could I have forgotten to tell her?

Faster than lightning, I remembered my plan. Better than the Plan of the Hour, *this* one—the Plan to Save the Meredith Family—might just spare us from becoming Tate bait.

I summoned my courage with a deep breath. "Mom, I forgot to tell you about a long-distance phone call that came today."

She studied me. "Who called?"

"The man from Japan who sent you the letter."

Her eyes squinted. She glanced at Mr. Tate, who was suddenly all ears. A strange expression crossed her face. It seemed to relay a secret message for me only. Mom wanted me to drop the subject. Immediately. For some reason, she did not want Mike Tate to know about the letter.

Perfect! How could I resist a chance like this? By ignoring Mom's facial plea, maybe, just maybe, I'd set things in motion to win my family back. It was a risk worth taking.

I continued, "The caller asked if you'd received his letter."

"What's she talking about?" Mr. Tate asked. It was amazing how fast he played into my hands.

"Mom has a secret admirer," I announced. "He lives in Japan, but he speaks perfect English."

Mr. Tate chuckled a little. "A secret admirer, eh, Susan?" He got up and sauntered across the room to Mom, squatting down beside her chair. "What about this mystery man in your life?"

This was the first time in months I'd seen them this close. Usually it was *Zach* Mom was hugging.

I sneaked out of the room, confident I'd started something Mom couldn't finish . . . not without pulling Mr. Tate right into the middle of things.

Right where I wanted him.

Chapter 7

Dear Lucas, I began writing my letter in the privacy of my bedroom. *I am very much interested in exchanging stories.* I hoped this sounded grown-up enough to convince him to continue writing. Surprisingly, he hadn't pushed for personal info, including my age. Maybe my writing style had convinced him I was an adult. After all, I could write as well as any college student around.

I've enclosed a short story for you to critique, and I hope you'll do the same in your next letter. There. Now he would know I was sincerely interested in writing.

For fun, I chose "Love Times Two" as a sample of some of my best fiction. It had been an English assignment last school year. The main character in the story was really me, and the sister was really Andie. In the story we were both in love with the same guy. After she heard me read it, Andie had accused me of describing her "down to her toenails"—among other things. Still, it was a fabulous story.

The *A+* and the heading—*7th-grade English*—had to go, of course. A college guy wouldn't be caught dead writing to a thirteen-year-old.

Rewriting the story on Mom's computer, I found several things to revise. By the time it was done, I was prouder than ever.

Then I continued the letter. *Please tell me more about your aunt,*

Marty Leigh. I have admired her work for years and began collecting her books when I was only a child. It was true. Under twelve, you're a kid. I had read that somewhere. Besides, I'd received my first Marty Leigh mystery book on my eleventh birthday.

As for arranging to have her autograph my collection, well, it's not necessary. But thanks for the kind offer. That got me off the hook in case Lucas told his aunt about the "woman" in Dressel Hills who owned all her books. What a surprise it would be for her to discover me, a skinny little eighth-grader.

You'll find my list of works at the bottom of this page. The list would take a while to put together, so I set the letter aside.

Everything I'd written in my entire life was in the bottom dresser drawer, in a lavender file folder. There were essays and fantasies; secret prayer lists and secret journals; letters to pen pals and letters to imaginary people—famous and otherwise. There were also plans for surviving junior high, such as:

Plan A
Plan B (next best)
Plan C (if all else fails)

Next came the Loyalty Papers—guidelines for conducting a best friendship. Andie and I had written them in grade school. Only the copy remained. The original documents had been ripped to shreds after a fight Andie and I had last winter.

Poetry by the pages spilled out. And short stories—mysteries, romance, drama. Lucas had requested a list of my work, published or not. That included more than just fiction. So I set out to alphabetize my "work."

Halfway through, the phone rang. Mom called up the steps. "Holly, it's for you. Danny Myers is on the line."

Danny? Yes! I dashed to the phone in Mom's room. "Hey, Danny," I said.

"What are you doing?" he asked.

"Sorting through some of my old papers."

"Like what?"

"Oh, just some stories and poems and things I wrote."

"Sounds like fun. Maybe I could read them sometime." It sounded like he was asking.

"Sure, I'd like that," I said, wondering why he'd called.

"When do you want to practice for volleyball tryouts?"

I caught my breath. He still wanted to help me after spending a cozy rainy afternoon with stuck-up Kayla. "When's a good time for you?" I said, trying not to sound too anxious. Or surprised.

"I'm free next Saturday. Will that work for you?"

"Okay. Where?"

"Let's meet at school. The gymnasium will be open. It'll be good for you to practice where the tryouts are held," he suggested.

"Good idea," I said.

"See you Saturday around two o'clock."

I said thanks and good-bye and hung up. Immediately, I called Andie.

"Hello?" Mrs. Martinez answered.

"May I please speak to Andie?"

"She's not feeling well, Holly. Is there something you want me to tell her?"

"I hope she feels better soon," I said. "Tell her that."

"She'll be sorry she missed your call. Good-bye."

Poor Andie. Standing out in the rain this afternoon hadn't helped. And it was my fault.

The doorbell rang. It was probably Kayla and Paula's mom coming to pick up Stephanie. I went back to my résumé, Bearie-O keeping me company on the floor.

I figured the minute Mr. Tate and Zachary left to go home, Mom would approach me about my big mouth. Why should a silly letter from Japan cause a problem between Mom and me?

Japan. Hmm, might be an interesting place for me to have a pen pal. One who could read and write English, though. As far as I knew, Andie hadn't added any more pen pals. But there were only twenty-three days left before school started on September seventh.

"Who wants ice cream?" Carrie yelled from the kitchen at the top of her lungs.

"I do!" I left my project on the floor and zipped down the steps.

Carrie helped Mom dish up some chocolate ice cream. We sat at the bar as Mom looked at me, her eyes squinted half shut. Her eyes spelled trouble.

I blurted out, "I shouldn't have told Mr. Tate about the letter, I guess." I hoped to get this conversation over so I could finish my letter to Lucas.

"You guess?" Mom's eyes narrowed even more.

"I could tell you didn't want me to say anything about it. But why, Mom? What's the big deal?"

"*This* is the big deal. Mike has a tremendous amount of stress right now. With Zachary and other things."

"So he's too busy to have fun, is that what you're saying?"

Mom looked tired, confused. "Right now, Mike doesn't need to think there's someone else in my life."

"But there *is*," I said. "And it's not a mystery letter writer from Japan. It's Zachary. He's right in the middle of everything—the person you're always with when Mr. Tate's over here. I think he's a cute kid, too, but I wouldn't marry his dad just to give him a mother."

Mom stared at me for a moment, leaning on her elbows.

Carrie got up and stroked Mom's back. "Holly doesn't really mean it, Mommy. She's all mixed up."

We sat there without saying a word. At last I felt so uneasy I said, "The ice cream is melting."

Mom spooned up some of hers, glaring at me. "Lately, Holly, ever since your trip to see your father, I feel you've been trying to interfere in my life. I gave you a chance to exercise your independence this summer. Is this what I get in return?"

"That's not fair," I shot back. "And it's not just *your* life with Mr. Tate. It's ours, too."

"And Zach's," Carrie added, scampering out of the room.

"Now's not the time to discuss this," Mom said. "I have a very early day tomorrow."

"What, another romantic breakfast?" I scoffed.

"Holly, that's quite enough." She got up to rinse the empty ice-cream bowls.

I gritted my teeth. "I am not going to let you marry Mr. Tate just because you feel sorry for his kid."

She whirled around. "We have plans to buy property together. We signed a *contract*."

"Get your name off it. You're a paralegal; you know how to reverse legal documents."

"Holly, listen! I'm not interested in getting out of anything. Do you hear me? I am going to marry Mike Tate." Her face looked almost stern as her blue eyes squinted shut.

Tears spilled down my cheeks as I turned to run upstairs. Carrie was sneaking away from my room as I reached the top step. My important papers still lay on the floor. All but my journal. Carrie had broken our rule again. I wanted to scream at her as I searched for it.

I heard the bathtub water running. Jumping up, I dashed to the bathroom door. "You'll be sorry, Carrie Meredith," I shouted, pounding on the door. "Tell me where you put it. Now!" I kept pounding my fist on the door. "Did you hear me?"

Mom came upstairs. "Holly, what's going on?"

"Carrie's been in my room again. She stole my diary," I sobbed.

"I'll handle this," Mom said, leaning against the door. "Carrie, do you know anything about Holly's diary?"

"I didn't take it" came the tiny voice.

I shouted back, between tears, "Yes, you did. Or else you would've answered me before."

"I was scared of you before," Carrie said, opening the bathroom door a crack.

Mom turned, casting a disapproving look my way. "Holly, let it go for now. Okay?"

"But it's the most important thing I own," I cried. "I can't live without my journal."

I ran to my room, flinging myself across the bed. It seemed like the end of the world.

Chapter 8

I don't know how long I buried my face in the pillow. A good cry sometimes helps make things seem less disastrous. Still, I vowed I'd get my diary back, no matter what.

Anger for Mr. Tate simmered in me, too. I was determined to do whatever it took to save my family from him. It might be easier than I thought, especially since I was sure Mom wasn't in love with him. Downstairs, I had waited to hear her use love as a reason for marriage.

But she never had.

Wiping my tear-stained face, I knew she'd thank me someday for interfering.

Just then Mom peeked her head through the doorway. "Carrie has something to tell you, Holly-Heart."

Carrie crept around the door, shyly. "I'm sorry I snooped in your room, Holly, but I never touched your diary, honest." She disappeared before I could say a word.

I leaped off my bed and ran after her, into the hall. "Carrie, I'm sorry, too. I didn't mean to scare you. You know I'd never hurt you."

Her eyes grew big. "But you kept pounding on the door. I thought you were going to break it down."

"I was angry at you because you broke our rule."

"I won't do it again. I promise," she said.

Mom held the hair dryer, motioning to Carrie to finish drying her long hair.

"Good night, Carrie," I called after her. "I love you."

Back in my bedroom, I searched for my diary under an ocean of stories and paper on the floor. My back ached as I sorted through all the spiral notebooks in my drawer. And then there it was, in its usual place.

I hurried to tell Mom and Carrie. "It was right where I always keep it," I said.

Carrie got a mischievous look in her eyes. "Where . . . where? Just kidding," she said, laughing.

"Remember, you promised," I said, pointing my finger at her.

"I know," Carrie said as Mom braided her hair.

I put my hand in the small of my back as I headed to my room. The pain nagged at me. Maybe it came from leaning over so long, doing my résumé for Lucas Leigh.

I was too tired to finish alphabetizing my list of writings. There were more important things to do just now.

Reaching for my notebook full of secret prayer lists, I began writing a new page. Before I fell asleep tonight I would ask God to keep Mom from marrying Mr. Tate.

The next morning I dragged out of bed before anyone else. Even though I'd slept ten hours, I still felt groggy.

Smoothing the sheets, I noticed a spot.

Yes! My body clock hadn't stopped ticking after all. I'd become a young woman during the night.

High in my closet, there were personal supplies waiting for this moment. On my way to get them, I posed in front of the mirror. Andie was right, I *did* have more going for me than just my long hair. I was developing, too.

Wait, what was that on my chin? I leaned close to the mirror. A pimple had emerged overnight, too. Andie had warned me about such nasties.

I couldn't wait to tell her my big news.

Carrie was sound asleep when I peeked in her room, so I tiptoed to the kitchen. Some toast and a bowl of cereal was all I needed while I finished my résumé and letter to Lucas.

P.S. I think I know what you mean about cars and smooth riding, I wrote. *A friend of mine owns a new SUV, and it's very cool.*

I didn't know exactly how I would respond if he inquired about the car *I* drove. Maybe by that time, he'd be so impressed with my manuscripts, my age wouldn't matter. I could only hope so. Keeping part of the truth back was strange to me. It made me jittery.

I peeled a stamp off anyway and positioned it squarely in the corner of my envelope. Then I hid it upstairs in my bottom drawer.

I sat on my window seat by the open window, breathing in the early morning air. Mr. Tate's talk about fresh mountain air was pathetic. Fresh air was all around us, right here. There was no escaping it. And moving to a higher elevation wouldn't help Zachary. In the mountains it was harder to breathe; there was *less* oxygen. Zach was just a feeble excuse to move us away from Dressel Hills.

I showered and dressed for church, singing songs from last spring's choir tour, hoping to chase thoughts of Mr. Tate out of my mind. It was a day to celebrate my graduation from girlhood.

Using the hall phone, I dialed Andie. "Are you too sick to go to church?" I asked.

"I'm staying home," she said, coughing. "But you can come over this afternoon. Just don't catch what I have and miss out on your volleyball practice with Danny."

"How'd you know about *that*?" I asked.

"Paula Miller told me. She said Danny called her sister last night and mentioned it."

"He called Kayla? I wonder what about?" I asked.

"Probably something about volleyball tryouts. Who knows? Just don't freak. Danny likes *you* better, I guarantee it."

"Right," I mumbled into the phone.

"Remember, Billy and Danny are good friends, and Billy and I talk," Andie said.

"And exactly what are you holding out on me?" I asked.

She laughed in spite of her clogged nasal passages. "Wait and see."

"Speaking of waiting, *I* have major news," I said.

"Betcha not as big as my news."

"Bigger," I said. "But I can't tell you now."

"When?"

"Later."

"Aw, tell me real quick," she begged.

"Guess we're even." I giggled. "See you." I hung up the phone.

With a sudden burst of energy, I dashed to Carrie's room. She was in bed, still asleep, looking like the angel in the Christmas storybook Daddy had given us years ago. One arm was draped over the mermaid Mr. Tate had given her.

I wondered about our future—Carrie's and mine. Would Mom marry Mike Tate and become Zach's stepmother? Would I grow up to become Mrs. Danny Myers? Would there be a houseful of children? Maybe I'd be an author and keep my maiden name . . . or hyphenate it. Holly Meredith-Myers. Perfect. It even sounded famous. Our kids would travel with us as we went from one book signing to another. We'd hire a nanny or a tutor or a . . .

Carrie woke up just then, sitting up in bed. "Why are you staring at me?" she asked in her sleepy, little-girl voice.

"Oh, was I? Just daydreaming, I guess."

She rubbed her eyes. "What time is it?"

"Time to get dressed for Sunday school."

"Where's Mom?"

"At church . . . teacher's meeting."

"Can we have French toast?" she asked.

"I already ate, but I'll make you some."

"With Mr. Tate's honey?" She grinned.

I wondered why he was the first thing on her mind this morning. "Is there any honey left?" I asked.

"There better be," she said, jumping out of bed.

"Meet you downstairs in ten minutes," I said, heading for the stairs.

After a noon meal of pot roast and the works, I excused myself since it was Carrie's turn to do the dishes. Fifteen minutes later, I was standing at Andie's front door. Her curly-haired brothers toddled near Andie's mom as she welcomed me inside.

"Hi, Chris and Jon," I said, leaning over to hug the twins.

"Andie's upstairs," Mrs. Martinez said, adjusting Jon's blue suspenders. I took the steps two at a time.

"In here, Holly," Andie called to me from her room.

With the grace of a ballerina, I stepped into her bedroom. It was decorated in shades of pink. Streams of sunlight enhanced the colors as it poured into the window like a spotlight. Pausing there for a moment, I pulled my hair back dramatically, holding it up.

"*Now* what are you up to?" Andie said, laughing.

"Look closely. See anything different?" I posed this way and that, like a model.

Andie leaned on her arm, playing along. "Hmm, there's something new on your chin. Is that your first zit?"

I swung my hair around. "That doesn't count."

"Let your hair down and turn around," she said.

I did.

"Aagh!" she said, pretending to be shocked. "You've trimmed your hair."

I shook my head.

"Something *is* different," she said, scratching her head.

I stood up straighter. "Are you ready for this?" I said, prolonging the announcement.

"Out with it," she said.

"Feast your eyes on a full-fledged woman."

She let out a little squeal, jumped off her bed, and flung her arms around me. She nearly knocked over the floor lamp beside her beanbag.

Andie's mom walked past her room just then, carrying one of the twins. "Everything okay in there?" she called.

"The monthly miracle! It's finally happened to you," Andie said, her brown eyes sparkling.

"Shh! Don't tell the whole world," I said, enjoying Andie's definition—the monthly miracle. It had a unique twist to it.

"Now, what's this news Billy told you?" I asked, changing the subject and going to sit on the beanbag.

Andie threw herself on the bed and lay there with a silly grin on her round face. "Danny likes you. He thinks you're pretty special."

"Are you sure?"

"Billy said so." Andie propped herself up on one arm.

"Really?" I said, my heart in my throat. "What'll Kayla think when she finds out?"

"Just be ready for anything," Andie said, rolling over.

"I don't get it. I wouldn't try to break up a friendship *she* had with a church boy." I leaned forward.

Andie held up her hands. "Better stay away from me if you want to enjoy the last three weeks of summer vacation."

I pulled my T-shirt up over my nose. "How's that?"

Andie reached for a tissue, stuffing it up her left nostril. It hung down out of her nose while she sat there staring at me.

Finally I couldn't stand it any longer. "You're too much," I said, laughing hysterically.

"What a lousy way to spend the end of summer," she said, her voice more nasal sounding than before. "Hey, which reminds me, I just sent off for two more pen pals. And that makes *me* the winner of our contest."

"Not yet. There's still time," I insisted.

"Hey, we never planned the award for the winner. What should it be?" she asked.

"How about a year's worth of postage?"

"You must be running out of allowance money," she said, leaning against her hot-pink pillows.

"I can always baby-sit for Zach while Mr. Tate and Mom go house hunting."

"Sounds serious."

"Not for long." I was sure my Plan to Save the Meredith Family was the answer. Thank goodness for secret admirers and anonymous phone calls!

Chapter 9

Five days passed. It was Friday, August twentieth, the day before my practice session with Danny Myers.

I stared at my clothes closet. Time for new stuff. Mom and I had planned to go clothes shopping next week for school, but I needed something new . . . soon.

A knock came at my door. "Enter," I said, holding up two pairs of jeans.

Carrie held a stack of mail. "Looks like you got something from Lucas," she said.

"Who?"

"LWL." She grinned.

"Sit down," I said sternly, pointing her to sit on my window seat. "How do you know about him?"

"Uh, that night I sneaked in here, I read your letter from him."

I squinted my eyes, like Mom. "You better keep this quiet, you hear?"

"What's the big secret?" she asked.

"It's not a secret," I said. "Not really, it's . . ."

"You just said it was."

"Andie doesn't know about him yet, that's all."

Carrie stood up to leave. "Have fun reading your mail."

"Wait a minute. What's this?" I pulled out a letter addressed to Mom.

Carrie noticed the stamp first. "Hong Kong?"

"Hey, look. It's the same handwriting as the Japan letter."

"How can this guy be in so many places at once?" Carrie asked. "Did he sign his name this time?"

I held it up to the window. "Hard to tell. Guess we'll have to wait till Mom comes home."

"Mr. Tate's picking her up from work," Carrie said.

Perfect timing, I thought, snickering.

"I forgot to tell you that Stephanie wants to come stay over here next week," she said, going downstairs.

"Just please keep her out of my room," I hollered down.

On my window seat, I curled up, holding the letter from Lucas. The seal with the initials was a greenish color this time. Same postmark, though—Cincinnati, Ohio.

I read each word carefully. He liked my story, "Love Times Two," and complimented me on my story line. There was even a separate critique sheet with suggestions for characterization and setting. And he asked my permission to send it to his aunt, Marty Leigh. *I think this story has great possibilities,* he wrote.

Another surprise was he had just purchased a new Corvette. And . . . *gulp!* . . . he was requesting my picture. Could I please send one in my next letter?

Did I dare send a picture of myself? Maybe a head shot would make me look more grown-up.

Gathering up the mail, I carried it down to the kitchen, placing it on the desk in the corner. A brochure on log homes fell out of the pile. Peeking at it, I shivered as I thought of Mom and Mr. Tate's plans. Quickly, I placed the letter from Hong Kong on top of the stack.

Let's see how Mr. Tate reacts to this, I thought.

In the family room, in search of a picture for Lucas, I dug out our family photo albums from the large cupboard under the TV.

Beginning with last year's school picture, I studied one snapshot after another. There was one of me with my stepbrother, Tyler, on the beach beside the fabulous sand castle we'd made this summer. Another one at Andie's, goofing off in the big tree behind her house. So many to choose from, and none of them right. The words I chose to write on paper had convinced Lucas I was at least his age. But a visual image—that might bring a quick end to our literary correspondence. Unless . . .

A plan . . . to make me look older!

I closed the scrapbook and slid it back into its place in the cupboard. Heading upstairs, I had a fabulous idea. "We're going downtown, Carrie. Come ride bikes with me," I called.

"I'm reading." She was sitting at the kitchen bar with a handful of graham crackers. "Let me finish this chapter."

"Can't. Stores won't be open much longer."

Reluctantly, she closed the book and followed me to the garage, where we hopped on our bikes.

Leading the way, I pedaled down the bricked sidewalk, past the mailbox at the end of our block, through the tree-lined streets to Aspen Street, the main thoroughfare.

Turning left, we raced toward Center Square, a quaint area off the main drag where merchants sold their wares. The smell of warm cinnamon rolls lured me toward The World's Best Donut Shop. But Lottie's Boutique called silently from two blocks away.

"Where are we going?" Carrie asked, pedaling hard to catch up.

"You'll see." I glanced back at her. Carrie was out of breath trying to match my pace.

"Slow down, Holly," she begged.

"We don't have much time. Lottie's closes at five-thirty."

"I should've stayed home," she complained.

"Mom doesn't want you home alone yet. You're only eight. That's too young to baby-sit yourself."

"I'll be nine next month," she said.

I signaled for a right-hand turn. Carrie did, too.

"We're almost there," I called to her as we rode onto the wid-ened sidewalks of the county courthouse. Clusters of aspen trees grew along the street, framing the area.

"Look, there's Mommy and Mr. Tate," Carrie said, slowing her bike down.

I kept riding. "Where?"

"Coming out of the courthouse, over there."

I braked to slow down, catching a glimpse of them as they walked toward Mr. Tate's car.

"What're they doing?" Carrie asked, waving to them. But they couldn't see us here under the aspen trees. Just as well.

My heart pounded as I stared in disbelief. Couples often got married in front of a judge. Had they united in holy matrimony in some judge's deep, dark chamber?

I watched as Mr. Tate helped Mom into the car, a white enve-lope tucked under his arm. Oh no. Had he talked Mom into a quick wedding?

Still, they didn't exactly look like "Just Married" to me. They weren't even holding hands.

I felt like a spy, watching Mr. Tate walk around his car and get in on the driver's side. Inside, he leaned over and gave Mom a peck on the cheek. I could see her buckle her seat belt. If they *were* husband and wife, it didn't look like their marriage was off to a dazzling start. The kind Mom deserved. After all those lonely years without Daddy, working hard at the law firm, never even thinking of dating until a few months ago. Mom deserved a hearts-and-flowers kind of romance.

Wait. . . . Mom wasn't dressed like a bride! She wore a blue-and-white summer suit, her office clothes. No way would Mom get married in *that*.

I felt so confused, I almost turned around and rode home. But I had to check out the wigs at Lottie's Boutique. Lucas was going to have his picture of me, whether Mom had tied the knot with Mr. Tate or not.

Carrie and I rode side by side in silence. Past the Explore Bookstore. Past Footloose and Fancy Things.

"Stop!" I yelled, backing up.

Carrie hit her brakes. "What's wrong?" she asked.

"Nothing." I pushed the kickstand down. "Check out those shorts and tops to match. That's exactly what I need for tomorrow." I gazed at the cute pink outfit. "I *have* to see it up close. Stay here, Carrie, and watch our bikes," I said.

According to Andie, Danny really liked me. If that was true, I wanted to look extra special for him.

Skipping into the shop, I asked the sales clerk how much for the outfit in the window.

"It's on sale for $59.95," she said, pointing to the mannequin.

My heart sank. I had $75.50 in my savings account. How could I afford both the outfit *and* a wig?

"Thanks anyway," I said, turning to go. Now I had to choose between the new outfit for practicing volleyball with Danny Myers and a wig to make me look older for a photo to impress Lucas Leigh.

"Well, how much?" Carrie asked when I emerged from the shop.

"Too much," I said, getting back on my bike and pedaling fast.

We arrived in front of Lottie's Boutique with only ten minutes to closing.

"What are we doing *here?*" Carrie asked.

"Window shopping," I said, concentrating on the short brunette wig in the corner of the window.

"For wigs?"

"Uh-huh," I said, trying to imagine myself as a brunette.

"Who needs a dumb thing like that?"

Without thinking I said, "Mr. Tate."

Carrie giggled. "No, he doesn't. He'd look real funny with hair."

"It's a thought," I said, laughing.

Lottie's Boutique wasn't exactly hopping with customers. There was only one patron in the store, and she was trying on a blond wig. When she turned to admire it in the mirror, I recognized her. It was Danny's mom!

She recognized me, too. "Hi, Holly," she said, waving.

"Hello, Mrs. Myers," I said, eyeing the wig. "You look pretty as a blonde."

"Well, thank you." She beamed. "If I were twenty years younger, I'd buy a blond fall down to my waist, like *your* hair. Now, *that's* pretty."

I could feel my face growing warm. "Thanks."

"Danny says you hope to make the girls' volleyball team."

I nodded.

"He tells me you're a natural at sports."

"He does?" She was so easy to talk to. Like Danny.

"Yes, and he says you're a writer. Maybe you can tell me more about that tomorrow."

"Tomorrow?"

"Danny wants to bring you over for refreshments after you practice at the school. Is that okay with you?"

"That sounds nice," I said.

Nice? It was perfectly fabulous!

She studied the wig in the window. "Do you like this one?" she asked, coming near the showcase.

"It looks great on the model, but I doubt it's my style," I said.

"Well, you won't know unless you try it," she said, motioning for the sales clerk.

Before I knew it, I was wearing the wig. Mrs. Myers held up two mirrors behind my head. "Simply lovely," she said.

I moved my head around, examining all sides of the new me. "I, uh, I don't know. The color makes my face look pale."

"And older, too," the clerk said.

Mrs. Myers agreed. "You could get the same look with your *own* hair," she said. "A simple French twist is easy enough."

"Really?" I said. "It's easy?"

"If you'd like, I'll show you tomorrow," Mrs. Myers said.

In the mirrors, I saw Carrie standing behind me. She'd abandoned the bikes and followed me inside. Picking up a short, curly wig, she held it high. "Here," she said. "This one's perfect for Mr. Tate."

Danny's mom nodded, smiling. "I hear congratulations are in order for you girls."

Carrie piped up. "They are?"

"I saw your mother and Mike Tate at the courthouse this afternoon. They said they were picking up a marriage license."

Carrie pulled the wig on, her own long hair hanging down out of it. The news hadn't fazed her one bit.

For me, this bit of news meant hope. After all, a marriage license wasn't a marriage. Besides that, it was good only for thirty days.

Chapter 10

Mr. Tate was waiting as Carrie and I rode our bikes into the garage. "Your mother's ready to dish up supper," he said sternly, moving Carrie's bike away from Mom's car.

"It was Holly's idea to go downtown," Carrie volunteered.

Just great . . . blame me, I thought.

Mr. Tate stared, no . . . he actually glared at me. "Holly, you're in charge of things while your mother's at work. I'm quite sure you know when suppertime is around here." He checked his watch.

There was no use arguing. Obviously, the man couldn't remember having been a kid. Ever!

Yet he waited for my answer. Finally I said, "I'm sorry, it won't happen again."

"Well, I should hope not," he said. "As soon as your mother and I are married, she'll be here, *at home,* for you children. Now, before you do anything, you must apologize to her."

Must . . . should. This routine was too harsh. On top of that, Mr. Tate never cracked a smile. Was life so serious he couldn't enjoy living? And what was this about Mom quitting work? Wasn't that *her* decision?

Going inside, I washed up, thinking how to apologize to Mom.

A dark cloud hung over me at supper as Mr. Tate announced his wedding plans to my mother. Zach sat beside her while his father did all the talking. I noticed Mom's ring finger was still bare. No sparkling diamond.

After supper, when Mr. Tate went into the living room to read the paper, I told Mom I was sorry about being late.

"No problem," she said.

Surprised, I asked, "Did Mr. Tate talk to you about me being late for supper?"

"Not exactly," she said, helping Carrie clear the table. "But Mike's a stickler for promptness."

No kidding.

"Did you see the letter from Hong Kong?" I changed the subject. "Carrie and I are dying to know if it was signed." I put the leftovers away.

"No, as a matter of fact, it isn't," she said. "Which is strange."

I was more curious than ever, but I kept quiet.

"There's another joke in the letter," she said, looking for it on the desk nearby. "Here, listen to this. 'What did the worker bee say to the queen bee?' "

"I give up," I said. "What?"

Mom walked to the sink as she read, " 'Good day, your honeyness.' "

I laughed. "Why would someone write a joke about bees? Does this guy know you and Mr. Tate want to keep bees?"

"I have no idea," Mom said. "It's uncanny."

Carrie seemed to be enjoying this. "And so spooky," she said.

"And there's more," Mom continued. "The writer of the letter says not to worry. He wants to make sure there are many more happy times around here."

"What's *that* supposed to mean?" I asked, eager for another laugh about now.

"How would I know?" Mom said, a frown on her face.

Carrie wiped the table. "*I'll* be happy if Stephanie can come over all next week. Please, can she, Mommy?"

Mr. Tate appeared out of nowhere. "Don't beg your mother, Carrie. The question has already been settled."

This news brought a smile to Carrie's face. So Stephie must be coming to stay with us.

When I hung up the dish towel, I noticed Mom held the mysterious letter behind her back. "Time for family devotions," she announced.

Zach, Carrie, and I followed Mr. Tate downstairs to the family room, like mice following the Pied Piper. Mom came down a few minutes later and sat beside Zachary.

The Scripture was from the first chapter of Romans, about encouraging each other in the faith. I listened as Mr. Tate read the devotional book. The story was almost humorous, especially because *he* was the person reading it.

The story was about a boy who complained and criticized his best friend, hoping to get him to do things his way: "Give your friend ten compliments for each negative thing you say to him," the boy's mother suggested. Sadly enough, he couldn't think of that many good things.

My mind wandered, creating an instant list of negative things about Mr. Tate. Could I come up with ten *compliments* for him?

Mr. Tate wrapped things up with a long prayer. He prayed for every missionary I'd ever heard of, and some I hadn't. I really wanted him to pray and ask if God's blessing was on his and Mom's wedding plans. Seemed to me the blessing was definitely missing.

After the prayer Carrie and Zach sat at the computer and played one of our family computer games. I ran upstairs, heading for my room. On the way, I spied Mom's letter from Hong Kong sticking out of the phone book on the kitchen desk. That's when my idea struck.

Disregarding Mom's plea to keep the letter a secret, I went back to the family room and waved the letter in Carrie's face. "Look,

Mom opened her letter from Hong Kong," I said, hoping to attract Mr. Tate's attention.

Mom's eyes widened. She leaned forward on the sectional.

Carrie wore a glazed expression as she maneuvered the buttons on the game pad. "Move! You're messing me up," she said.

Even though Carrie wasn't interested, Mr. Tate watched my every move. *Perfect.* This charade wasn't for Carrie's benefit anyhow.

"C'mon, Carrie," I begged, standing between her and the screen. "You *have* to read this letter from Mom's secret admirer."

She pressed the Pause button. "Did he sign it this time?" she asked.

"No, but the letter is handwritten, and he seems to think he can make Mom smile again."

Mr. Tate stood up abruptly. "Let me see that letter," he demanded, his hand outstretched.

I glanced at Mom, who was by now in third-degree agony. Her eyes warned me severely, but I ignored them. Instead I looked Mr. Tate square in the face. "Better ask Mom about it first," I said, playacting for all it was worth.

Mr. Tate looked ridiculous standing in the middle of the family room with his hand reaching out for the letter.

"Mom?" I said, enjoying this repeat performance.

She kicked off her shoes. "Mike, it's nothing, really. Most likely some practical joke. That's all."

I tossed the letter to Mom. She could decide what to do now that Mr. Tate knew a second letter had arrived.

Mission accomplished!

"I think you'd better go to your room, Holly," Mr. Tate ordered.

Mom looked surprised. "Why, Mike? What's the problem?"

He cleared his throat. "You and I need to . . . uh, discuss some things, I believe. Privately." The man was a drill sergeant.

"I'll go," I said. "Gladly."

Tingling with victory, I headed for my room. Now to make my list of ten Tate things, minus the compliments, of course.

I wrote:

Mr. Tate is:
1. *Bossy*
2. *Unreasonable*
3. *Too strict*
4. *Bald*
5. *Too serious*
6. *Too old (for Mom)*
7. *Unromantic*
8. *Stingy (not even a diamond chip for a ring!)*
9. *Strange (honeycombs for dessert? Give me a break!)*
10. *Pushy*

With a flick of my wrist, I folded the list and hid it in my bottom drawer. There. I felt better with that out of my system.

Now for something *really* interesting. I found Lucas's last letter and reread it. His idea about showing my short story to his aunt thrilled me. If the best mystery writer in the world thought I had promise as a writer, I'd definitely believe it.

Getting off the floor, I posed for the mirror. I swept my hair up, away from my face, like Danny's mother had suggested.

She was absolutely right. I *did* look older with my long hair up. Forget the wig. I would spend my money on the snappy shorts outfit. First thing tomorrow. That is, if Mom let me. No way would she stand for ignoring her wishes about the latest mystery letter. The worst thing she could possibly do was ground me tomorrow. Poor timing on my part. If I didn't show up at the school gym by two o'clock tomorrow, Danny and I could be history!

Early the next morning, my alarm jangled me awake. I stumbled out of bed and hurried to the shower, anxious for my afternoon practice session with Danny. But first—this morning sometime—I planned to stop at Footloose and Fancy Things and buy the cute outfit in the window.

Pulling on some jeans and a T-shirt, I stumbled back to my room. There sat Mom on my bed. Her eyes were sleepy, but not squinty. "You're up early, Holly."

"I'm going downtown," I said, hoping she'd skip the questions.

"Shopping?"

"Just a little."

"That's something you and I need to do before school starts. Can we set aside some time, just the two of us?"

I liked what I was hearing, but I was puzzled with this no-lecture routine. "Cool," I said, towel-drying my hair.

"Honey," she said slowly. "Who do *you* think is sending those letters to me?"

I perched on my window seat, thinking. "Are you saying you *don't* think it's a practical joke? You only said that to make Mr. Tate think . . ."

"Please don't bring Mike into this," she said, her eyes narrowing into a squint.

"I don't get it, Mom. Why's he so touchy? It's just a letter. Besides, you're not *really* engaged, are you?" I stared at her ring finger.

She touched my comforter lightly, tracing the stitching. "We had a slight disagreement last night," she said softly.

Yes, the beginning of the end! I thought.

"Are you okay, Mom? Did he say something to hurt you?"

"I'm not in the mood to talk about this," she said, getting up. "But I do love you, Holly-Heart. It's been so long since we've had a talk." She looked gloomy now.

"Are you sad about Mr. Tate?" I asked.

"I'm not sad at all. Just missing the way things used to be before . . ."

"Please don't marry him!" I blurted out. "He's not right for us. I know it."

"I have to think things through," she said. "He and I are going to talk on Tuesday night. Will you watch Carrie and Stephie for a few hours then?"

"Sure, Mom," I said, even though I didn't want to make it easy for her to see Mr. Tate again.

"Thanks, sweetie."

"Love you, Mom." I fluffed my hair to dry it.

"Need a ride downtown?" she asked.

I grinned. "Sure, but I have to make a quick stop at the bank as soon as it opens. There's a really cute outfit at Footloose and Fancy Things. You won't believe how cool it is."

Mom's eyes twinkled. "Danny Myers must be someone extra special. When do I get to meet your friend?"

"You did, sort of. Last year at choir auditions, remember?"

She paused to think. "Is he tall with auburn hair?"

"And an amazing memory. Danny remembers everything—even my favorite soda. You should hear him quote entire chapters from the Bible. And he prays over his meals. Even at school."

"This boy sounds too good to be true," she said with a sad little smile. She headed toward her room.

I prayed silently that someone like Danny would sneak into Mom's life. The anonymous letter writer was right. Mom *did* need to laugh again.

By the time we finished eating breakfast, it was time to leave for the bank. Carrie and I climbed into the car, and I thought how fabulous it was being with Mom again, without Mr. Tate hovering endlessly.

Mom and Carrie stayed in the car while I ran into the bank and withdrew sixty-five dollars from my account. I figured with tax, I'd need extra for the outfit.

Soon enough I was carrying the two-piece outfit to the car, swinging the bag as I bounced down the steps. I showed it off to Carrie and Mom as we rode home.

"It's definitely your color," Mom said with an approving glance. "I hope you tried it on."

"Don't worry. I've had enough outfits that were too loose around my waist not to remember."

Carrie piped up, "You don't look *that* skinny anymore, Holly."

Mom shot me a knowing look. "You're filling out, all right. And it's all happened this summer."

"Maybe my sister will get fat," Carrie said, giggling.

Mom turned into the driveway. "That'll be the day," she said, turning off the ignition.

I spied the mail truck coming. Carrie saw it, too. "Beat you to the mailbox," I challenged her, running toward it.

I won. Reaching for the mail, I immediately saw a letter addressed to Mom. It was postmarked Hawaii. I studied the envelope. "Hey, check this out." I showed the letter to Carrie. "There's no return address."

"Is it from the same guy?" she asked, peering at the handwriting.

"How can it be? It's Hawaii. Besides, the handwriting is different." I hurried up the steps and into the house.

Carrie ran ahead of me into the kitchen. "Holly's got the mail," she called to Mom.

"Thanks," Mom said, spying the letter. "Hmm, who's this from?" Quickly, she tore open the envelope.

I leaned against Mom, following along as she read silently.

Dear Susan,

Need another laugh? Here's a silly riddle to brighten your day: "What did the queen bee say to the baby bee?

"Bee-hive yourself!"

I simply couldn't resist this bee joke. It's so dumb, it's funny. Can't quite imagine you getting close to a beehive, let alone gathering the honey.

With sweet thoughts of you,
Your Secret Admirer

"This is nuts," Carrie said. "Who *is* this guy going around the world, writing letters to our mom?"

"He certainly knows a lot about me," Mom said, sitting at the bar and reading the letter again.

I grabbed her arm. "Isn't this exciting?"

"Either exciting or a sick joke," she said.

"Any idea who's writing to you?" I said.

"Didn't I ask *you* the same question just this morning?" She planted her elbows on the bar.

Pulling out a stool, I hoisted myself up. "You don't think *I* put someone up to this, do you?"

Mom tapped her pink fingernails on the counter top. "This is just so . . . bizarre."

"And mysterious," Carrie chimed in.

"And now *two* different styles of handwriting," Mom said, frowning.

"How could someone possibly know all this stuff about us, er . . . you?" I asked, feeling uneasy, like someone might be spying on us.

"I don't know, but I'd like to find out." A hint of a smile crossed her face. "You are not to mention *this* letter to Mike, uh, Mr. Tate," she said. "Do you understand, girls?"

"Yes," I said.

"Promise?"

I looked into her blue eyes. "I promise."

She pulled Carrie over next to her. "And you?"

"I promise," Carrie said solemnly.

"I mean it." She shook her finger at us.

The tone of her voice and her eyes indicated she meant business like never before. However, there was one minor detail Mom had overlooked. Stephanie was coming over tomorrow night. What if *she* happened to spill the beans to Mr. Tate on Tuesday when he came to pick up Mom?

The more I thought about my nosy little cousin hanging out at our house, the better I liked it. The setup was fabulous.

Mom fixed cheeseburgers for lunch. I ate hurriedly, then excused myself. There were many advantages to not having Mr. Tate around. *He* wouldn't approve of eating and running. Mom was cool. She didn't mind as long as I didn't rush though supper, our special family time.

"Spaghetti tonight," she called as I took the steps two at a time.

In my room, I brushed back my hair, pulling it into a single ponytail. Next came the new shorts outfit. A perfect fit! I squirted on some light perfume, glad my cheeks were still rosy-tan from the summer.

"Not too bad, Holly-Bones," I whispered as I smiled into the mirror. I was ready to meet Danny Myers.

Chapter 11

Giddy with excitement, I imagined how the volleyball practice session with Danny might turn out. I sped up my pace, hurrying down the street to the school.

As usual, Danny was prompt. He met me at the gym, wearing green gym shorts and a white T-shirt. The contrast of white against his face made him look tanner than usual. "Hey! Ready to warm up?"

"Okay, let's go," I said, following him around the gym. A believer in limbering up the muscles before working out, Danny put me through my paces, showing me how to stretch out properly so I wouldn't strain anything.

Next he had me practice serving techniques—how to put a spin on a fast serve. We bumped the ball, spiked the ball, and set it up. But I could think of only one thing: When would Danny reveal his feelings for me? I couldn't get Andie's comment out of my mind.

Thirsty from running around, I stopped at the drinking fountain. Danny came over and got a drink, too. But he remained silent about anything but volleyball.

Over an hour later, Danny stopped bouncing the ball and held it. "I think that's enough for today." He flashed me a grin. "You're great, Holly. I hope you'll make the team."

"Thanks." Still panting from the exercise, I wiped my face.

"Want to drop by my house for a snack?" he asked. "My mom's expecting you."

"Okay." I could only hope his mom hadn't said anything about seeing me at the wig shop yesterday.

Danny and I began walking the long trek to his house. He lived at least a mile from the school. Now maybe we'd have time to talk for a change. Really talk.

"My mom baked your favorite cake." His eyes twinkled.

"How'd she know?"

"*I* remembered," he said.

My heart pumped ninety miles an hour. "Oh yeah, I should've *remembered* you would remember." With that we burst into laughter. Danny's gray-green eyes danced in the afternoon light.

We walked in silence for another half block. *What is he waiting for? What if Andie's wrong?* I thought.

At last I broke the silence. "Do you really think I have a chance of making the team?"

"We'll keep working at it," he said. The way he said *we'll* made my heart skip a beat. That is until he suggested that maybe Kayla Miller could be of some assistance, too.

"I'm fine with *you,*" I said, hoping he'd take the hint.

Instead he asked about my short stories. An awkward change of topics.

"Oh, I love to write mysteries. But they're not so easy," I replied. "You have to know the ending so you can work the plot backward."

"That's good. I'll remember that," he said, smiling.

Good for you, I thought, totally confused.

Danny's mom had ice-cold lemonade and angel food cake

waiting in the breakfast nook for us when we arrived. What an inviting sight after the long walk in the hot sun.

"Did you have a good time?" she asked, pouring lemonade.

Danny nodded, smiling. "Holly's something else. You should see her catch on . . . and fast."

Mrs. Myers sat at the table with us. She opened her address book and found the *M*'s. "What's your street address, Holly?"

I must've looked puzzled at first.

"I like to keep a record of addresses of Danny's friends—you know, for party invitations, things like that," she said.

"It's 207 Downhill Court," I replied quickly, observing the graceful motion of her hand. "You write something like my aunt Marla. She had the most beautiful handwriting ever."

"Mom's been writing like that all her life," Danny joked.

"I'm not kidding, Danny. Look at it . . . her handwriting's beautiful. Those perfectly formed loops on her *L*'s and the *T*'s are crossed slightly above the center of the line. Wow."

"Which tells something about Mom's personality," Danny said. "If I remember correctly, the loops mean she has confidence and self-discipline, which is true."

I looked at him curiously. "Do you know about handwriting analysis?"

"Sure . . . there's a book on handwriting at the library. I read it a couple of years ago. Let me think a minute." He stared into space a second. I could almost hear his brain sorting through one memory bank after another. "Yes, there it is."

"Where?" I said, looking around the breakfast nook.

His mom chuckled along with me. "Danny's amazing," she said, excusing herself while I waited for the final "read out" from my friend's wonder-brain.

At last he snapped his fingers. "I've got it! The book I read is called *Handwriting: A Key to the Real You*."

Faster than a speeding microchip, I thought of Mom's mysterious letters. The handwriting had changed, though. The first two letters had definitely been scrawled. Today's letter was more refined, almost stylish. Had the letters been written by two different men?

"Danny." I turned to him suddenly, filling him in on the strange letters Mom was getting in the mail. "Want to help me solve an international mystery?"

"What are the clues?"

"I'll make a list for you," I said.

Eagerly, Danny went to the kitchen counter, pulling out scraps of paper from the top drawer. "Here's some paper." He brought the tablet to me and scooted it across the table.

I began to outline everything I could remember about the letters and their content, showing Danny when I finished. "There. Any ideas how to tell who's writing anonymous letters to my mom?"

"We could check out the handwriting book at the library," he said. "We'll study the penmanship on the envelope and in the letters to see what personality type we're dealing with. It should eventually lead you to your mystery man."

"That's logical," I said.

Logic . . . Danny's strongest point.

Mrs. Myers peeked around the corner. "Holly? Any time you're ready for your new hairdo, let me know."

"I almost forgot," I said, studying the list of clues once more.

Danny looked startled. "You're not going to cut her hair, are you, Mom?" he asked, concern in his voice.

"Never," she said, waving her well-manicured hand.

Danny seemed to admire my hair with a fleeting glance.

Hmm, maybe Danny wasn't all logic after all. . . .

"Why is my mom changing your hair?" he asked pointedly.

"I want a new look, and your mom's the pro," I said, deciding to conceal the real reason.

Danny said no more about my new do, gathering up the notes I'd written.

His mom directed me to the powder room off the kitchen. In the mirror, I observed her every move as she wrapped my hair into a smooth French twist, securing it with thin hairpins.

Stepping back when she was finished, I stared at the young woman in the mirror. "It's so . . . well, grown-up!"

"It certainly is. And quite becoming, too," she said.

I touched my hair lightly. "Do you mind if I wear it this way home? I'll return the pins."

"Go ahead, have fun with it. And forget the pins. They're yours to keep."

"Thanks, Mrs. Myers," I said, feeling shy.

"Call me Ruthanne," she said with a broad smile.

I nodded, feeling uneasy about addressing a grown-up that way. She pointed me in the direction of the family room, where Danny sat waiting with his back to us.

I stepped into the hall, inching my way toward him. I called, "Guess who?"

He turned slowly, tilting his head.

I stood very still. "It's the new me. Like it?"

He blinked his eyes. "You look eighteen, at least."

"Really? *That* old?"

"It's incredible, Holly."

I couldn't let on how pleased I was with his opinion of my appearance. "Guess I'd better head home," I said, noticing the clock on the mantel. It was nearly five o'clock.

Danny seemed confused. "You're going out in public like that?"

"Why not?"

"It, uh . . . it's not you," he stuttered.

"Well, yes, it *is* me," I said, beginning to feel frustrated. Was he ever going to talk to me about, well, whatever Andie thought he had on his mind?

"We can ride home on the bus, okay?" Danny suggested.

"Sure," I said.

I thanked Mrs. Myers repeatedly for the new hairdo and refreshments. Then the shyest, most logical guy in Dressel Hills and the amazing new Holly Meredith walked together to the city bus stop.

♥ ♥ ♥

Downtown, sitting side by side in the bus waiting for the light to change, I noticed a photo booth in the drugstore window across the street. "Let's get off here," I said, pulling the cord overhead.

"Where are you going?" he asked, catching up with me.

I held my hands up to protect my hairdo from the evening breeze. "I want to take a picture of my new look," I said, depositing the coins in the slot outside the mini photo booth.

Parting the purple curtain, I sat down and posed. First, two serious shots, then two smiley ones. Still seeing spots, I stepped out of my private photo shoot feeling like a movie actress. I waited for the pictures to develop, frustrated by Danny's restlessness.

"They'll be ready in a second," I said, thinking about Lucas and hoping one of these was good enough to send off to him. If I mailed it before six o'clock tonight, he'd have my picture by next Tuesday.

All four poses turned out great. I was delighted. Only *one* pose was suitable for Lucas Leigh, however. I could hardly believe it was me. And neither could Danny.

"It's a sophisticated side of you I've never seen before," he said.

"And might never see again," I teased.

"May I have one of those?" he asked, studying the pictures.

"Sure. Which one?"

He pointed to the very one I planned to send to Lucas.

Chapter 12

I stalled about the photos, talking Danny into letting me show them to Mom first. Then we caught the bus again, riding it to Downhill Court.

"See you in church tomorrow?" Danny asked as the bus stopped to let off passengers one block before my street.

"Sure," I said. "And thanks for your help at the gym today."

The bus jolted to a stop at the corner of Aspen and Downhill Court. "You'll make the team if you keep practicing," he said as we hopped off.

"Hope so." We crossed the street, the sun beginning to drop behind the mountains.

"I'll call you, Holly." He walked me to the door.

"Okay."

He opened the door for me. "Maybe my parents could invite you and your mom and sister over sometime . . . to get better acquainted. Since we go to the same church, you know."

"Really?" I said, wondering what Mom would think. But then it wasn't like Danny and I were dating or anything. He hadn't even said he liked me yet.

"Well, I'll see you tomorrow, Holly-Heart."

I blushed. "That's my mom's nickname for me."

"Mind if *I* call you that?"

"Better ask Mom," I teased.

"Okay." He waved as he turned to leave.

I dashed into the house, conscious of simmering spaghetti sauce. The aroma filled the house.

Upstairs, I yanked the bottom drawer of my bureau open, finding my letter to Lucas. I searched for an envelope and a scissors to cut the best picture off the strip of four. Carefully examining the pose one last time, I slipped it into the envelope.

"I need a stamp quick," I called to Mom as I raced downstairs.

"Kitchen desk drawer, top right," she said, stirring the sauce, her back to me.

I snatched up a self-stick stamp and plopped it on the envelope. "I'll be right back." I glanced at the clock. Ten minutes till six o'clock!

"Holly," Mom called to me when I was halfway out the back door. "Andie has been trying to reach you all afternoon. I said you'd call her the minute you got home."

"Can't *this* minute," I shouted back. "I have to catch the last mail pickup." With that I rushed down the back steps, my tennies flying over the bricked sidewalk to the mailbox on the corner.

Just ahead of me, I could see the mail truck making its turn onto my street. I ran faster. The key dangled on the postman's chain as he reached to unlock the mail receptacle. Out of breath, I sprinted toward him.

"Looks like you're just in time, missy." He reached for my letter.

"Wait a sec," I said, checking to see if everything was in place.

"Take your time." He scooped up a pile of mail and headed for the postal truck.

Then I did a strange thing. I held the envelope close to my heart and made a wish. . . . And I whispered, "Please, make this wish come true."

Slam-a-clump! The mail truck door shut. The uniformed postal worker climbed behind the steering wheel.

"Here's my letter," I said, slipping it into his hand.

With a wave, he was off.

I stood there a moment, watching as the truck made its way down the tree-lined street, wondering what had come over me. Making wishes was for blowing out candles on your birthday. Not for mailing letters to pen pals!

Turning, I plodded back toward the house. When I strolled in the back door, Mom mentioned that Andie had called again. Inquisitive Andie. She would want to hear how things went with Danny, of course.

Well, there was nothing to tell. Except he *did* call me *Holly-Heart* and asked for my picture! And he said he'd see me tomorrow at church . . . *and* there was the possible invitation to his house. Replaying the events of the day, I realized there might be some good stuff to share with my best friend. Just nothing earthshaking.

My thoughts strayed to Lucas. Now, *there* was someone who wasn't afraid to speak his mind. Sensitive too. But then, writers were like that.

For a guy who lived across town, Danny sometimes seemed so out of reach, even though I was pretty sure he liked me. Standing in the kitchen, I was completely confused.

"Wash up for supper, girls," Mom said. Looking at me for the first time, she did a double take. "What happened to your hair?"

I grinned at her. "It's the new me." I turned around, showing off. "Like it?"

The phone rang.

Mom waved her hand. "It's probably Andie again. Let it ring till after supper."

Hearing the phone *ring-ring*ing and ignoring it was like Mom stashing strawberry ice cream in a padlocked freezer and throwing away the key. Pure torture.

After supper, I deserted the kitchen to call Andie back. Taking the phone downstairs into my "office," I sat on the lid of the toilet seat and phoned Andie.

She answered the phone like this: "Okay, let's have it. Everything from the very first second."

"Well, hello to you, too," I said, laughing.

"I'm waiting" came her no-nonsense reply.

"Okay," I said. "Danny met me at the school gym, wearing green shorts and a T-shirt. There was a pocket on the left side of the shirt with blue stitching and—"

"Holly, get real. Who cares about topstitching? Get to the good stuff."

"Like what?"

"C'mon. When did he tell you, well, you know?"

"Nothing like that happened," I said. "You must be dreaming. Danny never even mentioned it."

"He didn't? But Billy said—"

"Look, Andie, I'm not interested in your secondhand information. Danny can talk to me if he has something to say. I don't want to hear things passed from Billy to you . . . to me."

"Hey, don't get huffy," she said. "I just thought—"

"Yeah, well, you *thought* wrong."

"It's not my fault," she insisted. "Billy told me exactly what Danny told him."

"I hear you, but I'm not playing Whisper Down the Lane, either. Besides, I have other things to talk about."

Andie was silent, but only for a half second. "Like what?"

"Like my pen pal, Lucas Leigh. He's the famous Marty Leigh's nephew. We've been writing for a while now."

"Really? Marty Leigh's nephew? How come *I* wasn't informed of this sooner?"

"I don't know why. Maybe just for the fun of it."

"Or maybe," she added, "to win our pen pal contest by cheating. You're supposed to report all pen pals by Labor Day, the day before school starts. That's only two weeks away."

"Well, I'm reporting *now*. It's not Labor Day yet, is it?"

"I'm still winning," she bragged. "I got two more names from the Philippines just today."

"Okay, let's just say you won," I said. "I don't care about this stupid contest anymore. It's more fun having just a couple of dependable pen pals, and one to exchange manuscripts with."

"What?" she gasped.

"You heard me. Lucas and I are critiquing each other's writing. It's very exciting."

"Sounds boring, if you ask me."

"Boring to someone who doesn't write stories or keep a journal."

"You don't know if I write in one or not," she shot back. "Maybe I do, maybe I don't. You'd better watch out, Holly, I could drop this news about Lucas Leigh to Billy and he might—"

"Sounds like blackmail to me," I said. "We're best friends, remember?"

"Whatever," she said snidely. "This conversation's going nowhere."

"You got *that* right. Call me when you're thinking clearly. Goodbye." I hung up.

In church the next day, Mom sat with Carrie and me, minus Mr. Tate. *He* sat three rows ahead of us with Zachary, who kept waving his Sunday school paper back at Mom.

Across the aisle, Billy Hill was sitting with Andie and her family. She gloated about it when I caught her gaze. Danny was sandwiched in between his own parents, like it was the safest place to be with Kayla Miller sitting directly behind him. And Paula Miller was perched beside Jared Wilkins, who wore a satisfied grin.

After church, Danny motioned to me. I told Mom I'd meet her at the car.

"Don't be long," she said, turning to round up Carrie.

I hurried over to see Danny. Kayla waited in the side aisle, probably hoping to talk to him, too.

"Hey, Holly," he said. "Your hair looks much better today."

"Thanks," I said, touching it.

"Will you be home this afternoon?" he asked.

"Sure."

"Great. I'll give you a call, and maybe we can go to the library to look for that handwriting book. Okay with you?"

My heart pounded. "Good idea," I said brightly, hoping to discourage Kayla, who was still hanging around.

"What did your mom think of the pictures?" he asked.

"Pictures? Oh, those," I said, remembering fast. "Haven't had a chance to show them yet. But Mom really liked my hair up."

His parents waved to him from the back of the church.

"I think my dad's anxious for dinner," he said. "I'll call you around three o'clock."

"Okay. Bye," I said, waving triumphantly to Kayla, who spun away when she heard Danny say he planned to call me later.

On my way out, I noticed Mr. Tate. He nodded, and I smiled without speaking. Seeing him again made me realize how much better off we were without him hanging around.

Back at home, we savored Mom's famous roast and onions, potatoes, and carrots dinner. She sang church songs while carrying serving dishes into the dining room.

Then, after stuffing ourselves, I spooned up the leftovers into plastic containers, thinking of Mom. She seemed much happier again. Back to normal. When Mr. Tate did his "helicopter-hover," she seemed tense. Insecure Mr. Tate had a way of cluttering up the atmosphere.

Wiping the crumbs off the place mats, I struggled with the idea of Mom seeing him again this coming Tuesday night to work things out between them. I wondered how Mr. Tate would react to another letter from Mom's secret admirer. Of course, I wouldn't think of disobeying her *this* time, but as soon as my cousin Stephanie arrived tonight, I'd see about putting her up to something. Anything!

The doorbell rang and I ran to get it.

What was *this*? Through the screen door, I stared down at Zachary Tate. Then I noticed Mr. Tate parking his car in our driveway.

"Hi, Holly," Zach said. "My dad wants to see your mom."

"Oh," I said. "Does *she* know about this?"

Mom strolled into the living room. "Open the door, please, Holly-Heart." When she saw Zach, she bent down and held her arms wide.

He ran to her, snuggling against her. "Oh, I've missed my handsome boy," she said.

Mr. Tate was all smiles as he landed his helicopter presence in our living room. "And we've missed you, too," he said, gazing at Mom.

Zach looked up longingly at Mom. Man, it was disgusting. And just when I thought things were falling apart with these people. Guess absence does make strange things happen.

"Zach wants to stay here and play with Carrie. Okay with you, Holly?" Mr. Tate asked.

"Actually, I have plans this afternoon. I mean, I can't baby-sit for you today." I looked at Mom for moral support.

"We wouldn't have to be gone long," Mr. Tate said to Mom. "Wouldn't you like to go for coffee somewhere, Susan?"

"Perhaps for an hour or so." She turned to me. "It won't be baby-sitting for you, not if Zach and Carrie play together. Maybe they could ride bikes while you read or whatever. Isn't Zach's bike still out in the garage?"

The helicopter blades hummed loudly as Mr. Tate landed on Mom's suggestion. "Splendid idea. Yes, by all means, go outdoors with the children, Holly. Get them in shape for roughing it in the mountains." At that he winked at Mom.

I breathed deeply and then said again, "I'm sorry, Mr. Tate, I have plans to go to the library. You should call ahead if you want me to watch Zach. You'll have to take him and Carrie along with you if you want to go to coffee." It felt good finally standing up to Mr. Michael Tate.

Mom looked at me, surprised.

Surprised? Wait a minute, I thought she'd be furious!

Encouraged, I dug my heels in for the fight.

Mr. Tate revved his motor and nearly lifted off the floor with his hovering. "I'm not asking you, Holly, I'm *telling* you. Zachary will stay here with you and Carrie. Now, do as your mother said and get the bikes out of the garage."

I hurried to my mother's side. "Mom," I said, "do I have to change my library plans with Danny?"

She looked at Mr. Tate. "I'm really sorry about this, Mike. Holly does have some plans with a friend of hers. And I think she's right, you should call ahead. As for today, I believe I'll be staying home with my daughters."

Now it was Mr. Tate's turn to look shocked. "Don't let Holly run your life, Susan," he retorted. "If she were my daughter I'd—"

"Well, she's *not* your daughter, Mike. Not now or ever. And if you don't mind, I have some important business to take care of." Hastily, she showed the bewildered-looking man to the front door.

Zachary started to cry.

Oh great, I thought. Just when Mom was doing so well and telling it like it is, Zach—the real focus of her affection—was going to get emotional and spoil everything!

"Come here, darling," Mom said, reaching for him. She knelt on the floor and cuddled him. "You're okay. That's right," she said, stroking his hair, rocking back and forth.

"As you know, Zachary is easily upset," Mr. Tate said accusingly. "He'll be fine when we're back home. Come along, Zachary."

"I want to stay here," the boy whined, clinging to Mom. "I want Susan to be my mommy."

Talk about manipulation. Here was a seven-year-old pro.

"I know, I know," said Mom in hushed tones. "We'll have to see about that later."

"I'll call you, Susan," Mr. Tate said, leading Zach out the door.

"No, I'll call *you,*" Mom said with determination.

I wanted to cheer as the Tates backed out of the driveway. Inside, a strong feeling told me Mom and Mr. Tate were through. Finished!

Chapter 13

Deliberately, Mom turned and marched into the kitchen. I wanted to cheer her actions, but I bit my tongue.

At exactly three o'clock the phone rang. It was Danny.

"Hi, Holly-Heart," he said.

I laughed softly. "Did you ask my mom if you could call me that?"

"Is she there?" he asked seriously.

"Danny, how can you be so gullible? Of course you don't have to ask her permission."

"I was just joking," he said, but I wondered if he was saying that to cover up. "I called the library about the handwriting book. It's on reserve in your name. We can pick it up today if you'd like."

"Perfect. Now all I have to do is find Mom's letters so we can compare the handwriting." I walked downstairs with the phone, hoping for some privacy. Carrie was reading on the sofa, so I ducked into the bathroom. "My mom doesn't know anything about what we're up to," I said, lowering my voice. "We have to keep this mystery-solving stuff a secret, okay?"

"That's cool," he said. "But will you be in trouble if she finds out?"

"You know what? I think she'd really like to know who's sending the anonymous letters. And, get this, the last one was signed, 'With sweet thoughts of you.' Isn't that romantic?" I almost forgot I was talking to a boy!

"Wouldn't it be even more romantic if she knew who was writing to her?" he said.

"That's what I'm hoping to figure out. With your help, of course."

Danny was quiet for a moment, then he said, "Holly, are you hoping your mom's secret admirer might qualify for a stepdad?"

"Not exactly. But if Mom's going to have a boyfriend, er, *man* friend, it would be nice if he's someone *I* like, too. And so far, the mystery letter writer beats the competition to pieces."

"Even better than that nice man with the sick boy?"

"Well, between you and me, Mr. Tate's not so nice. And his son isn't so sick anymore. It's too bad about Zach, though. He would have been a nice stepson for Mom."

"Really?" He seemed surprised.

"Yeah, Mom got attached to him. It all started last spring when she signed up to teach Zach's Sunday school class, then found out he had cancer. This summer he's been around here a lot. Besides, Mom has a soft place in her heart for kids. If she and Daddy had stayed married, there'd probably be a bunch of us by now."

"It's hard for me to imagine brothers and sisters running around everywhere," he said. "Being the only child isn't that bad."

I could tell he wasn't ready for sweet talk on the phone. And that was fine with me. After all, for two members of the opposite sex, Danny and I were nearly as close as best friends could be—minus the boy-girl stuff.

There was a click, signaling another call.

"Uh, Danny, can you hold a sec?"

"No problem."

I answered the incoming call. "Hello?"

"This must be one of my favorite nieces," said a deep voice.

"Uncle Jack, hi!" I said, excited to hear from him.

"Has Stephanie arrived there yet?" he asked.

"She's coming tonight for supper. You could probably still catch her at the Millers' house."

"Thanks."

"When are *you* coming back to Dressel Hills?" I asked.

"Next week sometime. The boys and I are doing some sight-seeing here in Seattle today before my business meetings start up again."

"Wow, it'll be cool having you and my cousins living so close to us."

"Cool, indeed," he said, chuckling. "See you soon, Holly, dear."

I switched back to the other line. "Danny, are you still there?"

"Uh-huh." He seemed distracted. "I'm making loops."

"You're what?"

"Perfecting my handwriting. Trying to imitate my mother's flaw-less penmanship."

I filled him in on the other phone call. "That was my uncle Jack calling long distance."

"Isn't he the husband of your favorite aunt? The one who died last year?" asked Danny.

"You remembered?" I was sincerely impressed.

"Of course," Danny said softly. "And I was sorry to hear about it."

"You know, I still miss Aunt Marla. Next to Mom she was the sweetest person I've ever known. She used to wear her hair up sometimes, too," I said. "Oh, tell your mother I really like how she fixed my hair."

"Well, it wasn't *my* favorite," he said. "But come over any time. My mom likes girls, probably because she doesn't have any."

"Maybe she'll have a daughter-in-law someday," I said.

That topic must've made him nervous. He changed the subject instantly. "Can you meet me at the library in thirty minutes?"

"Sure, I'll be there."

"Good-bye, Holly-Heart." The way he said my nickname sent a tingle down my spine.

"Bye," I said.

Carrie was still curled up on the sofa, reading. I darted past her, heading upstairs. On the living room couch, Mom lay sound asleep. I crept over to snoop at a piece of paper lying on her lap.

It was a copy of the contract on the mountain property. Leaning closer, I scanned some of the first paragraphs. Wow, it looked like she *was* getting out of the deal with Mr. Tate. She'd marked out words and initialed everything. More than ever I hoped their short-lived romance was over.

Turning toward the kitchen, I went in search of Mom's secret-admirer letters. The last I'd seen them, they were in the kitchen on the desk. I poked through the bills, separating them from a pile of coupons. I looked under the phone book. No letters.

The next most logical place to look was probably Mom's bedroom. Logical. Wait—was I beginning to think like Danny?

Tiptoeing upstairs to her bedroom, I sneaked across the floor. I spied something colorful sticking out of her Bible on the lamp table beside her bed—the foreign stamps on the envelopes.

"This is not really stealing, Lord," I said as I whisked the letters away to my room. "I'm doing this with Mom's best interest in mind, but I'm sure you already know that, right?"

Curling my legs under me, I snuggled against Bearie-O on my window seat. I'd almost forgotten to thank the Lord for answering my prayer about Mr. Tate and Mom.

Impulsively, I hopped off the seat and rushed to open the bottom dresser drawer. Reaching for my secret prayer list, I found the page with my number-one most urgent request: *Please keep Mom and Mr. Tate from ending up together.* I added the date of the answered prayer: *Sunday, August 22.*

ONLY GOD COULD DO THIS! I wrote in giant letters.

Chapter 14

The public library was nearly empty when I arrived. Danny—
punctual as always—waved to me from a table near the reference
section.

"Hey, Holly. Check this out." He pointed to a page in the
handwriting book.

Sitting down, I saw a lineup of famous signatures from George
Washington to John Kennedy. And . . . Winston Churchill, Laura
Ingalls Wilder, and Billy Graham.

I pulled Mom's letters out of my backpack. "Here's the first
one . . . from Japan." I showed him the second letter. "This one
has a Hong Kong postmark and stamp, with the same handwriting. Then a third letter came from Hawaii. The writing is different,
don't you think?"

He agreed with me, then opened the handwriting book to
chapter two. "Let's take a look at the slant of the letters. It says
here that if the writing leans to the right, the writer has a strong
urge to communicate. In other words, your mom's mystery man
is talkative."

We compared the two different handwritings.

"What do you think?" I reached for my tablet.

"We need a list of characteristics for the writer of the first two letters and a separate list for the latest letter writer," Danny said.

"I can do that." I marked my headings on the lined paper. *Writer 1* for the two letters from Asia and *Writer 2* for the letter from Hawaii.

An hour later, the great list maker had two lists—with Danny's help, of course.

WRITER 1	WRITER 2
Left-handed	Communicative
Immature	Fun-loving
Imaginative	Practical joker
Determined	Confident
Brave	Family pride
Arrogant	Intelligent
Sloppy	Trustworthy
Athletic	Athletic
	Business-minded
	Religious
	Romantically inclined

"Hey, I think I like writer number two," I said, studying the two lists. "He's cool."

"Stepfather material?" Danny joked.

"Puh-leez!" I said it too loudly. The librarian raised her dark eyebrows and stared at us like a bull ready to charge.

Just then, out of the shelves behind us, came a mysterious-sounding voice. "Better keep it down over there, or you might end up with the boogeyman's signature."

Startled, I whirled around, catching a glimpse of Jared Wilkins' brown hair. I'd know him anywhere.

"Who was that?" Danny asked, looking around.

"Just your imagination," I said, laughing.

Now the librarian really did look ready to charge. In fact, she stood up and leaned against her desk.

"We're going to get kicked out of this place. That's never happened to me before," Danny said, a worried look on his face.

"Shh," I said, my finger on my lips.

"Can we please not get thrown out?" he whispered.

"Relax. Don't worry so much. Here," I said, shoving a blank piece of paper under his nose. "Write your first, middle, and last name."

Danny frowned. "What for?"

"For me to figure *you* out, that's what."

"Oh, *I* get it. You think now that you've seen one book on the subject, you're a pro at graphology."

"Hey, that's good," I said. "Let your emotions come out sometimes. It's not good to hold them in so much. Gives people ulcers."

"I already have one," he said so straight-faced I believed him.

"I'm sorry. I didn't know." Once again, I spotted Jared sneaking around behind the shelves, holding his hand over his mouth to cover his laughter. While Danny studied our list, I shook my head at Jared. It was a warning for him to get lost. Fast!

I should've known he would ignore my signal. Here he came, wearing jeans and jacket to match, rolled up at the sleeves.

"Hello, Holly Meredith," he crooned, soft enough to keep us from getting booted out.

Danny looked up. "Doing research today?"

Jared grinned at me. "You might say that."

I couldn't help it; I blushed.

Danny sat up straight in his chair. "Ready for track season?" he asked.

"Always," Jared said, flexing his arm muscles. "Well, it looks like you two have some work to finish. Catch you later." He swaggered past the librarian, who seemed to be holding back her urge to charge us . . . and not for overdue books, either.

"Let's review all the angles," Danny said, "and take a look at the content of the letters."

I pushed Jared Wilkins out of my mind as we reviewed the silly riddles about the bald man without any locks, the "your honeyness" queen bee, and the beehive.

"It appears someone knows your mother was dating that Tate fellow and hoped to divert her attention," Danny said.

"Makes sense."

"Here's something." He pointed at the first letters. "It looks like a young person started writing the letters and then someone with 'family pride'—that could be a father or an older friend—took over the writing."

"According to our lists, these two writers have something in common. Athletic ability," I said, rechecking.

"Now think, Holly. Who do you know that's left-handed, has a great imagination, isn't afraid to take risks, and plays sports?"

I kept staring at the list. "And he must have a messy room and think he's hot stuff."

Danny leaned closer, elbows on the table, resting his chin on his fists.

"Only one person fits that description," I said after a long moment. "My cousin Stan."

"Who?"

"My fourteen-year-old schizoid cousin. Uncle Jack's son."

"Are you sure?" Danny asked, his eyes searching mine.

"I'm positive."

Just then I noticed Kayla Miller crouching down, pretending to look at the bottom shelf in one of the reference sections. No way did I want her in on this secret mission. Quickly, I gathered up our notes. "I need some fresh air," I said.

Danny followed, checking out the handwriting book, asking for my card as we arrived at the bullpen, er, check-out desk.

"Keep those lists handy," he said as we headed into the bright Colorado sun.

It was fabulously hot for late August. As we passed the city park, near the library, I noticed the sky was cloudless. Families were gathered for picnics under stately cottonwood trees, enjoying the last days before school doors opened.

My mind zoomed back to my oldest cousin. Why would Stan write those stupid letters to Mom? And what was he doing in Japan? I knew he had gone along on a business trip with Uncle Jack, but I'd never heard they were going overseas. And what older buddy did he know in Hawaii who could have been bribed to write the latest letter?

I studied the list for writer number two as we strolled through the grounds near the courtyard. "This writer is talkative, has a great sense of humor, would write an anonymous letter as a joke, and takes pride in his family," I said, thinking out loud.

Danny continued, "And he must have kids, or else he's proud of his own parents."

"Good point." I sat on the concrete strip that ran along the front of the county courthouse grounds.

"If he's religious, that might mean he's a Christian," Danny remarked. "*That's* good."

"And he has a good head for business. But best of all he's romantic," I said loudly, hoping the notion might rub off on Danny.

"Any idea who that might be?" Danny asked.

"Let me see the book again."

"Here." Danny held the book for me.

It fell open to the chapter on famous people. My eyes almost popped out. There was the name of the famed mystery writer, Leigh, written with an ornate flourish.

"Let me see that," I said, almost pulling the book out of Danny's hand. I held it close, studying the slant, the loops, the beginning and ending strokes. "This is so cool—Marty Leigh's handwriting."

"Who's Marty Leigh?" Danny asked.

"You don't *know*?"

He leaned back on the cement wall, crossing his arms in front of him. "Should I?"

"She's the greatest mystery writer of our time," I said proudly. But I didn't say that I was pen pals with her nephew.

"*She?* So Marty must be a woman."

"And what a writer she is." I didn't like the way Danny was looking at me. Like he doubted my opinion.

"Guess I'm not much into novels," he said.

"If you don't like fiction, what's left?" I studied him incredulously.

"For me it's science and nature books, mostly."

"I like nature, too. But I also *love* fiction."

"Nonfiction broadens the mind. You should try it more often. It's true, you know. Fiction is merely someone's imagination running wild."

I wasn't sure where he was going with this. "I thought you were interested in my fiction . . . *my* imagination running wild," I reminded him.

"Sure, I'll read your stories sometime. Right now we have a mystery to solve."

"I'm not sure if *we* do or not," I said, feeling hurt.

"What's wrong, Holly?"

"There's only one mystery, and I'm looking at him," I said, dashing off down the sidewalk, my tablet and book under my arm, my backpack slung over one shoulder.

"Holly!" he called after me.

Danny had to know what I meant. Billy and Andie and everyone in Dressel Hills seemed to. I had every right to be upset.

I walked faster. "I know *exactly* who wrote the letter from Hawaii," I said. "I have to get home and tell my mom. See ya."

Then I took off running, leaving Danny-cold-fish-Myers behind without a clue.

Chapter 15

I ran all the way home. Past the village ski shops and down the narrow street of my childhood. Away from Danny.

Carrie and Stephanie were sitting on the front-porch swing sipping lemonade. Their soft giggles mingled with the creaks of the swing. When I reached them I was out of breath, but I couldn't wait another second to ask Stephie the question burning inside me. "Did . . . your brothers . . . go to Japan?"

"Yes," she said.

"And . . . Hong Kong?"

"Yes," she repeated.

"What about Hawaii?" I asked, catching my breath.

"Last week," she said sheepishly.

"The night you were here for supper, right?"

Stephie nodded, her chin-length hair bouncing.

"The night Mr. Tate announced his plans to marry Mom?"

"Uh . . . yeah," she said, her brown eyes growing wide.

"You talked to your father on the phone long-distance that night when you went back to the Millers' house, didn't you?"

Her lower lip trembled. "Uh-huh," she said in a squeaky get-set-for-tears voice.

I picked Stephie up off the porch swing, twirling her around and around, squealing, "Yes!"

We fell into a heap on the redwood floor of the porch, nearly knocking over the pots of Chinese-red geraniums. Mom poked her face out the door, obviously puzzled.

"Perfect," I said when I saw her. "You're just the person we need to talk to."

"Before you do, have you seen those silly letters anywhere?" she asked, holding the screen door open a few inches.

"Oh, those." I reached for my backpack. It had landed topsy-turvy under the porch swing. "Here." I handed them to her.

Her eyes narrowed. "Holly Meredith . . ."

"Before you get upset, Mom, I have some news that'll make your hair stand up and boogie."

Carrie and Stephie giggled, even though I was certain Stephie knew what I was about to announce.

"Here, Mom, you need to sit down first," I said, taking her arm and guiding her to a chair like she was a helpless invalid. I stood back and made a pretend drum roll in midair. "Are you ready for this?"

"Tell us!" Carrie shrieked.

"This announcement is all about true love," I said. "For . . . I am quite certain that Uncle Jack's in love with you, Mom."

Stephie and Carrie began jumping up and down, giggling.

"Please, girls," Mom said, insisting they sit down. "Now, Holly, what on earth are you saying?"

I began to unravel the tale of two letter writers. "One was a teenage boy who got the ball rolling as a practical joke with two anonymous letters to you, after overhearing a description of Mr. Tate's lack of hair."

"Bald Tate," said Stephie, no doubt repeating the term she'd used to her brother Stan on a long-distance phone call.

Mom looked completely lost. "Will you please slow down, Holly?"

"Okay," I said. "But think about it . . . remember the long-distance call I told you about? It must've been Stan disguising his voice, pretending to check up on the letter he'd mailed from Japan."

Mom leaned forward, listening more carefully.

"And after *that* phone call came the third letter, surprising us with new handwriting. . . . A different person. Another writer!"

"We *know* all this," Mom said, pushing a strand of blond hair away from her face.

"Yes, well, Stephie ate supper with us the night Mr. Tate told us his plan to move us to the mountains and start a bee farm," I said, eyeing Stephie. "Later that night, she talked to her father in Hawaii."

Mom looked disturbed. She started to speak. "Oh, Holly—"

"There's more," I interrupted. "The best part is this. What Stan started as a joke turned out to be a way for Uncle Jack to take up where Stan left off, with his beehive joke . . . and the 'sweet thoughts of you' sign-off. Stephie, tell my mom I'm not making this up."

"Well?" Mom said, leaning over to look into the freckled face of her sneaky little niece. "Did you play spy-kid at our house?"

"I leaked the info," she said in a tiny voice.

"You told your daddy about my plans with Mr. Tate?" Mom asked.

"Daddy said to tell him if you were dating anyone. *And* if you were happy. That's when I told him about the marriage license and the log cabin. And . . . you know, stuff like that."

"Why do you think your daddy wanted to know about these things?" Mom asked, holding the lemonade glass without drinking.

"Because nobody, except Carrie, was very happy about Mr. Tate. Especially you, Auntie Susan."

I watched Mom's expression. "Don't you see, Mom?" I said. "All of us knew it but you."

"Well," Mom said. "No sense fussing over the past."

"I agree," I said, tickling Stephie. "What else is Uncle Jack planning?"

"More secrets," Stephie said, giggling so hard she fell over.

I started to say, "Fab—"

"—ulous," Carrie finished for me. "Just fabulous!"

"Isn't this the most amazing and romantic thing?" I said.

"Don't jump to conclusions," Mom said, pouring lemonade for me. "It's just three silly letters."

"That's what *you* think," Stephie said and started giggling again. Her chestnut hair flew around her little head as she danced around the porch, almost bumping Mom's geraniums.

It was obvious Stephie knew more than she was telling. Much more! What *was* Uncle Jack up to . . . really?

Chapter 16

Wed, *August 25,* I wrote in my journal.

> *My life isn't even half as exciting as Mom's! On Sunday we*
> *found out that Uncle Jack is her secret admirer, and I just*
> *learned that she and Mr. Tate ended things over the phone.*
> *Yes! That's all great, but it's been three long days since*
> *Danny and I had our dumb fight. Should I call him or wait*
> *for him to make the next move?*

Closing my journal, I sat at my desk and stared out the window. Waiting for Danny could take forever . . . it could be Christmas before we got things worked out. *Worked out?* We weren't even really clicking.

Besides that, there was Kayla Miller—forever smiling at Danny, always sneaking around corners.

I sighed, slumping down on my window seat. Bearie-O flopped against me. Compared to Mom's relationships, my friendship with Danny was a joke.

Another letter showed up in the mailbox today . . . for *her*! Postmarked Seattle. I tried holding it up to the light in my room, but it was no use. I couldn't see through the envelope.

"I know who it's from," Stephie said, sneaking into my bedroom and coming up behind me. "It's from my daddy!"

"Someone should teach you some manners," I said, hiding the letter behind my back. "Still spying, I see."

She rolled her eyes and zipped her lips shut, throwing away the "key."

When Mom arrived home, she snatched up the letter and disappeared into her bedroom like a squirrel hoarding a precious acorn. I wasn't surprised later when she said—with a twinkle in her eyes—that I would not be reading *this* one.

On Friday a dozen pink roses arrived for Mom before she got home from work. I sneaked a look at the card. It said: *From your not-so-secret admirer.* Now, here was a guy Danny Myers could take lessons from.

Then, to top things off, Uncle Jack called after supper.

"What's up?" I asked as Mom hung up the phone.

"Uncle Jack and the boys are back in town. He invited me to spend tomorrow evening with him," she said, acting like it was no big deal.

"And?"

"He said to dress very casually."

"Where's he taking you?"

"He was very secretive about it," Mom said, seeming to enjoy the mystery aspect most of all.

"So how casual is *very casual?*" I asked.

"I guess I'll have to investigate my wardrobe." She gave me a hug before dashing up the stairs.

"But this is your first date with Uncle Jack," I called to her. "Shouldn't you wear something wonderful?"

She shrugged it off. "Oh, you know your uncle," she said offhandedly. But her smile gave her away.

I took the phone downstairs to my "office" and called Andie. "Mr. Tate and Mom really are through, just like I thought," I said. "It's so cool, and now my uncle's taking her out."

"You're kidding. Your *uncle* and your mom on a date? How weird is that?"

"They're *not* related," I said. "Not by blood, anyway."

"He was married to your dad's sister, right?"

"Uh-huh. Aunt Marla died six months ago."

"Speaking of guys and girls, how are things between you and Danny?" she asked.

"Not so good," I said. "Last Sunday, he started putting down the kind of books I like. I got fed up and told him off."

"You did? Whoa, Holly, that's not a good way to win friends and influence people."

"No kidding." I was beginning to feel sorry about the blowup.

"So what else is new?" she asked.

"Well, Lucas owes me a letter. I should be getting a story to review from him soon." I didn't tell her about the picture I'd sent with my gloriously grown-up hairstyle.

"Better hope Danny doesn't find out about Lucas," she warned.

"Oh, Lucas is no competition in that department—the guy's a junior in college, for goodness' sake."

"That old!" she said. "You never told me that. Are you really sure it's smart to be writing to a guy so much older than you?"

"We're just critiquing each other's work, Andie. It's no big deal. Anyway," I said, "would you miss out on a chance to find out more about your favorite author?"

There was a pause. "Maybe not," Andie said. "Well, gotta run. Bye."

When I hung up, I heard giggling just outside my "office" door. I sneaked over, listening, then opened the door quickly. Carrie and Stephie ran screaming in opposite directions.

"What's with you two?" I demanded.

Carrie played the innocent while Stephie kept laughing, crouching behind the sectional.

"Don't you know it's rude to eavesdrop?" I said. "This better never happen again."

"Or what?" Carrie asked, eyes shining.

"Yeah." Stephie peeked over the sofa. "Or what?"

"That's it . . . I'm telling Mom," I said, stomping up the steps.

When I found her, Mom was in her room, staring blankly into her closet. Nope, she wasn't in the mood for tattling. "Solve things with your sister and cousin the best you can," she advised.

"But, Mom," I whined.

"This is Stephie's last night here," she said. "Can you endure the kid stuff till tomorrow at noon when Uncle Jack comes to pick her up?"

"Only if you can keep her and Carrie out of my life between now and then," I said, frustrated.

"Uh-huh," she muttered.

I could see she was too preoccupied with picking out just the right *very casual* outfit for her date with Uncle Jack.

Clumping off to my room, I complained to my journal instead.

When the mail arrived the next day, I hit the jackpot. Three letters! One from my pen pal in Italy, one from Daddy in California, and one from Lucas Leigh. I sat on the porch and tore open Lucas's letter, reading it first.

> *Dear Holly,*
>
> *Thanks for your recent letter and picture. I hope you don't mind that I passed your story on to my aunt, Marty Leigh. She has some comments to make about it, and she'd like to make them in person. She's scheduled to go on a book tour to promote her hot new kids' series, and—believe it or not—we'll be in Dressel Hills at the Explore Bookstore on Labor Day. Would you like to meet us there around 12:30 for lunch? If I don't hear differently from you, I'll assume it's a go.*
>
> *My aunt wants to discuss with you the possibility of including "Love Times Two" in the first issue of a new teen magazine she is starting, called* Sealed With a Kiss. *Interested?*
>
> *Looking forward to meeting you, Holly!*
>
> *Lucas W. Leigh*
>
> *PS: I've enclosed a photo of myself you may keep.*

I stared at the picture. Lucas Wadsworth Leigh was the best-looking college guy I'd seen in my entire life. Could it be he wanted to take me to lunch nine days from now . . . right here in Dressel Hills? And what was this about maybe becoming published?

My heart pounded as I scooped up the other letters and dashed inside the house to the phone. I punched Andie's number.

Br-ring! Please be awake, Andie. I need you!

Br-ring! It rang again.

"Hello?" Thank goodness she answered.

"Andie," I said. "I'm desperate for your expert help. Can you come right over?"

"What's going on?" she asked. "Is this about Danny?"

"Worse, er, better—oh, just get over here. I'll tell you then." We hung up.

On the way to my room, I brushed past Stephie and Carrie sitting on the stairs. "Watch it," Carrie said.

"Yeah," Stephie said, carrying her overnight bag down to the living room.

Good, I thought. *Stephie's leaving. One less snoop around here.*

Carefully closing my door, I wished there was a lock on it for private occasions. That wasn't all I wished. I wished I'd told the truth. I'd led Lucas to think I was much older.

I sat very still on my window seat, contemplating my dilemma. A very famous author wanted to talk about publishing me in her new teen mag. Would she still want my story when she found out I was only thirteen and a half?

Leaning over, I brushed my long hair down, hoping to put it up the way Danny's mom had a week ago. Getting my hair into a French twist was the least of my worries. What kind of clothes should I wear to meet none other than Marty Leigh and her nephew—my own pen pal?

I tore through my closet and found absolutely nothing.

Chapter 17

"You told him *what?*" Andie said, plopping herself cross-legged on the floor in my bedroom.

"It's not *what* I said. Just what I *didn't* say," I moaned, sticking my head out my bedroom door and scanning the hall for kid-sized snoopers.

"You've gotta be warped right down to your split ends, Holly Meredith."

I leaped onto my bed. Andie just sat there on the floor, her eyes boring a hole in me. She was right. There was no easy way out of *this* mess.

"C'mon, Holly. You know you have to tell Lucas the truth."

"You sound like *me* talking to *you*," I said, sorting through his letters for the zillionth time. I found the first letter Lucas W. Leigh had ever written to me. His penmanship was nearly as good as Danny's mother's.

Andie crawled over to the bed. "What're you doing?"

"Analyzing his handwriting."

"What for?"

"To see if he's accepting and . . ." I hesitated.

"And what?"

I sighed. "Forgiving."

Andie held Bearie-O close to her. "What's the big deal? Give the guy a call and tell him the truth. If he's as smooth as you think, he'll laugh it off. If not, forget it."

"That's easy for you to say." I rolled over and propped myself up on my elbows. I told her about his aunt's interest in my writing. "Think about it—Marty Leigh has plans for my story, 'Love Times Two.' "

"You mean *our* story," Andie said. "Remember, it's about me, too."

I ignored her. "I made a wish, Andie. And it's starting to come true."

Her eyes bugged wide. "What wish?"

"It probably sounds stupid, but I made a wish on the last letter I sent Lucas," I said, remembering the magical moment.

"What sort of wish?"

I took a deep breath, eyeing my friend. "Don't laugh, please?"

"I promise."

"The wish was about writing to Lucas, hoping it might lead me to the truth about my stories. If I have any writing talent."

"So you've been using him because of his author-aunt," she stated flatly.

"It's just that if I could somehow know I had true writing talent, I'd work day and night to write as well as Marty Leigh."

"That I'd like to see. Holly the Sleepless Author," she said, making fun.

"Anyway, if I blow things now and tell the truth about my age, maybe he and his aunt won't—"

"Won't want to bother with a kid writer," she interrupted me.

"Right. So . . . I have a plan. Will you help me?"

"Help you continue this charade?" She was twisting a dainty curl around her finger.

"I just want to try to look as old as I did in the picture."

"*What* picture?"

"The photo booth snapshot I had taken after Danny's mom did my hair last Saturday," I explained.

Andie frowned. "This just gets worse and worse." She sighed. "Why don't you just call Mrs. Myers? I'll bet she'd be happy to help you look exactly the same way again."

That *wasn't* funny. "Don't you dare breathe a word of this to her or to—"

"I know, I know . . . to precious Danny," she said.

"Promise?"

"Maybe, maybe not."

"Andie! I won't introduce you to my cousin," I bribed her.

"Hmm. Sure wouldn't want to miss out on meeting Stan," Andie said, scratching her head. "All right, worry-bean, you win."

I smiled. "Here's the plan. Can you get your hands on some mascara and eyeliner?"

"Mom's got tons of it," she said.

"Perfect. Make sure you get it over here by ten o'clock on Labor Day morning."

"Why so early? That's the last day to sleep in before school starts."

"C'mon, Andie, cooperate with me. You have all next week to sleep in."

"Yeah, yeah," she said, getting up to leave. "See you in church tomorrow." She turned around and giggled at me. "Can't believe you got yourself into such a mess, Holly. This takes the cake."

"Get outta here," I said, tossing a heart-shaped pillow at her.

She caught the pillow and threw it back. "What I wouldn't give to tell Danny Myers about all this."

I leaped off the bed. "Andie, you promised!"

"Oh yeah, almost forgot."

I opened my bottom dresser drawer and ripped a page out of my journal. "Here," I said, shoving the paper under her nose. "Write your name."

"What for?" Her eyes were wide.

"Just do it."

She scribbled *Andrea Martinez* with a pen from my dresser.

"Thanks," I called after her as she dashed down the stairs.

"Happy analyzing," she yelled back.

I stared at the paper. Not a single *A* in her name was closed at the top!

I froze. If the handwriting book was correct, Andie's open *A*'s meant she could *not* keep a secret. Not at all.

♥ ♥ ♥

Uncle Jack showed up after lunch to pick up Stephie. His handsome face looked tan from his time in Hawaii, and his wavy brown hair had blond streaks from the sun.

"Daddy!" Stephanie called to him, running to the door.

"Hi, shortie," he said, gathering her up for a big bear hug. He leaned over and wrapped his arm around Carrie, too. Then he spotted me, hanging back close to the stairs. "Whatcha hiding over there for, Holly?"

He came over and gave me a big squeeze. How good he smelled—fresh, like summer wind.

"Take a look at this young lady," he said. "Boys must be calling 207 Downhill Court day and night."

I brushed my hair away from my shoulder. "Thanks," I said, blushing, as always.

Carrie jumped on his back, pulling the collar of his shirt. He grabbed her and swung her around. She squealed. "Where are you taking Mommy?"

Uncle Jack lowered his voice mysteriously. "It's a very special secret surprise."

"I wanna come, too," Carrie said.

"Me too. Me too," Stephie squealed.

"Well," Uncle Jack said, pulling his pretend beard, "if we take you along, what about Holly?"

"And Stan and Phil and Mark," shouted Carrie.

By now the girls had wrestled Uncle Jack to the floor. Mom appeared from the kitchen just as Stephie sat on his back. Carrie messed up his hair, giggling hysterically. It was good to see *hair* again.

Mom smiled, wiping her hands on a towel.

"Hello, Susan," Uncle Jack said, sitting up and pulling Stephie onto his lap while Carrie hung on his neck.

"Hi," Mom said, almost shyly. "Looks like you've met our welcoming committee."

"And some welcome it was," he said, tickling Carrie and Stephie again.

"We're going on a date with you, Mommy," Carrie announced, trying to pull Uncle Jack's Reeboks off.

"There's room for everyone," Uncle Jack said, looking at Mom. "But only if it's okay with my date." There was an irresistible twinkle in his voice.

"Sounds like fun," Mom said, laughing.

Uncle Jack jumped off the floor, bringing the girls up with him. "Okay, then, we'll see you ladies at five-thirty."

"Give us a hint where we're going," Carrie begged.

"Only one," he said, pulling a piece of straw out of his shirt pocket and slipping it into his mouth. "What political office does a horse run for?" he asked, with the straw dangling off his lips.

"What's 'political'?" Carrie asked.

"I'll tell you later," Uncle Jack said, poking her ribs.

I stood close to Mom. "What political office *does* a horse run for?" I asked.

"Mare," Uncle Jack said, straight-faced.

For some reason, the joke struck me funny. I laughed till the tears came to my eyes.

"I don't get it. What's the hint?" asked Carrie.

"The joke's the clue," Uncle Jack said, kissing her forehead. "Think about it."

"Don't worry, Carrie. *I* don't get it, either," Stephie said, heading toward the door with her dad. Mom and I followed behind them.

"Jump in the van," Uncle Jack told Stephie, taking the straw out of his mouth and shoving it into his blue jeans.

Carrie hurried off to see our boy cousins while Mom and I stood on the porch, waving to them in the van. Stan sat smugly in the front passenger seat, trying to look cool. Phil and Mark hung halfway out the windows.

Mom quietly thanked Uncle Jack for the roses.

"My pleasure," he said, giving her a peck on the cheek, the way he used to when all of us visited Uncle Jack and Aunt Marla back east.

He kissed me, too. "Wear your rattiest jeans tonight," he said with a wink.

Carrie raced back to the porch as the sleek gray van pulled out of the driveway and disappeared down our street.

I turned to Mom. "Where do *you* think we're going?"

"Think about it," she said, playing Uncle Jack's game.

"You *know*, don't you?" I said, glad to see the stress gone from her eyes.

"It'll be a date to remember," she said.

I ran upstairs to add important info to my journal, starting with Lucas and ending with Uncle Jack.

Soon it was time to get ready for the "family" date. It felt weird and good at the same time. Then I remembered it was just last week that *Danny* had suggested Mom and Carrie and I come to his house for dinner sometime. Like that would ever happen.

Carrie ran past my room shouting, "Look, there are horses in our street!"

I gave my hair a final brushing and flew down the steps to see.

A hay wagon, pulled by two horses, waited like Cinderella's pumpkin coach. Stan, Phil, and Mark sat in the back, chewing long pieces of straw. Uncle Jack jumped down off the wagon, heading for the house.

"Mom!" I called upstairs. "You're never gonna believe this."

"Believe what?" She appeared at the head of the stairs, a sweater draped over her shoulders.

I stared at her. "Mom, you look so young tonight."

"Why, thank you, Holly-Heart. I *feel* young," she said, fluffing her hair in the mirror just as the doorbell rang.

Funny, I thought. *Mom and I should trade places on Labor Day when Lucas Leigh comes to town.*

Mom went to the door and opened it. There stood Uncle Jack, grinning. "Are m' ladies ready?" he asked, tipping his straw hat.

"Certainly," Mom replied, taking his arm. They walked down the sidewalk, very dignified.

Carrie, my cousins, and I burst into loud giggles. *What a change from Mr. Tate,* I thought as I clambered aboard the wagon. *Thank you, Lord!*

Chapter 18

Exactly one week later Uncle Jack took all of us out on a "date" again. Guess we made a good impression the first time. Anyway, it was fun having so many relatives around—even if it meant squeezing all of us into a single raft on the wild Arkansas River.

That night I wrote in my journal about riding the rapids with Uncle Jack and our cousins. No one fell overboard this time, but we *did* get soaked. Best of all, I couldn't remember seeing Mom laugh so much.

Counting the hours till I met Lucas face-to-face took most of my energy, as well as my thoughts. Andie and I did a practice run on my makeup and hair after church on Sunday. It was amazing the difference a little—*a lot*—of makeup could make. To complete the look, I found the perfect tailored suit at a secondhand shop.

But on the day of Lucas's visit, Andie showed up ten minutes late. She had me totally freaked by the time she arrived.

"Hey, it's Labor Day," she said. "What do you expect? My mom had me hand washing and waxing the floors."

"Right," I said. "Somehow I can't picture it. But nice try anyway."

"Hold still," she insisted, carefully outlining my eyes with dark liner.

At last, I was ready.

"Now what?" Andie stepped back, admiring her handiwork.

"Let's role-play till it's time for me to leave," I said.

"Huh?" Andie stared wide-eyed at me.

"You be Lucas, and I'll be me."

"You're crazy."

"Not really. It helps to plan what I'll say."

"You mean you don't know?" Andie said.

"I have a plan."

"Oh great," she muttered. "Another plan."

The phone rang. "For you, Holly," Mom called to me.

I whispered to Andie, "Check to see if my mom's downstairs."

She crept out into the hallway and peered down the staircase. "All clear."

I dashed to the hall phone, keeping my face toward the wall. "Hello?"

"Hi, Holly." It was Danny.

"Oh, hi," I said softly, hoping Mom would stay downstairs.

"I've missed you," he said.

"You have?" I said, wondering why he hadn't called for two whole weeks.

"Yeah," he said. "I know it's been a long time since we researched the handwriting book at the library, but . . ."

"Look, Danny," I said, checking my watch, "I'm really sorry, but I can't talk now. I'm kinda in a hurry. Can we talk later?"

"Please listen. I'll make it short."

"Okay."

"I've been thinking," he said. "About us, er . . . you and me, you know."

"Uh-huh?" I heard footsteps on the stairs. My heart pounded. No way could I let Mom see me this way.

"Holly," Danny said, taking a deep breath. "Would you consider being my girlfriend?"

I saw the top of Mom's head out of the corner of my eye. She was coming upstairs fast.

"Uh, sorry, Danny, I'll have to talk to you later. Bye!" I left the phone dangling as I dashed to my bedroom and slammed the door. Hiding in the closet, I told Andie, "If Mom wants me, I'm unavailable."

"Are you crazy?" she said through the crack in the closet door. "What's going on?"

Just then . . . *knock, knock.*

"Holly, come hang up this phone, please," Mom said.

I heard Andie open my bedroom door. "I'll do it," she said, closing the door safely behind her.

Inside the dark closet, I suddenly felt disloyal to Danny in my globbed-on getup, preparing for a lunch with Lucas Leigh. All summer I'd waited for this moment—for Danny to ask this question—and now I couldn't even give him an answer! All because of the game I was playing with Lucas. And with myself.

Once Andie was absolutely sure Mom was out of sight, I stuffed all my Leigh mysteries in an overnight case and sneaked down the stairs and out the back door.

Andie walked me to Aspen Street, where we said good-bye. She wished me luck with Lucas and made me promise to tell her every thrilling detail.

Downtown, the souvenir shops bustled with end-of-summer tourists. I caught my reflection in the donut-shop window as I made my way to the Explore Bookstore. Pushing my shoulders back, I snickered at the shapely look I'd achieved with a wad of tissues stuffed in all the right places. No question, I appeared older than thirteen.

As I waited for the light to change, I heard Jared Wilkins' voice behind me. "Holly, is that you?"

I kept facing forward as I heard him running to catch up with me. I ignored the traffic light, hoping to lose Jared in the shuffle of cars and people.

"Wait, Holly! Watch out!" he shouted.

A car swerved. I kept running, raising my left hand to protect my perfect French twist. Only half a block more to the bookstore.

Just then, I felt a hand on my shoulder. Jared whirled me around. "You could've gotten yourself killed back there."

"What do you want?" I said, anger and embarrassment boiling up inside me.

He stepped back, a perplexed look on his handsome face. "Well, well, what is *this?*"

"None of your business, that's what. Now, leave me alone."

"You look absolutely dazzling, Miss Meredith," he said, his eyes focusing on my hair. "I've never seen you look so, uh . . ."

"Grown-up?" I said.

He snapped his fingers. "That's it! You look much older. But why?"

"Please excuse me," I said, pushing past him.

"Going my way?" he asked.

"I hope not," I said, cringing inside. Jared would blow my cover for sure. It would serve me right for thinking I could pull off such deception.

"Man, Holly, you're acting so strange."

I looked at my watch. *Five minutes to go.* "Will you *please* get lost?" I asked, my voice shaking.

"Hey, don't cry," he said, backing away. "If it means that much to you, I'm outta here. See you at school tomorrow."

I stood there close to tears as Jared turned and walked away. He was right—I *was* acting strange. So strange I hardly recognized myself.

Dreadful apprehension—and a bit of determination—flared up inside me as I headed for the bookstore.

The place hummed with people, overflowing with quiet conversation and occasional laughter. Ferns and ivy hung in potted baskets from the ceiling. Bamboo chairs were scattered around for book-inspecting by prospective buyers.

Then I saw him . . . Lucas Leigh. My summer pen pal was unmistakeable.

Quickly, I hid in the corner, behind one of the high-backed bamboo chairs. There, I was able to observe him privately. Wearing navy blue dress pants and a light blue dress shirt, he seemed older than his picture. And attentive to each of the fans waiting in line.

I felt really ridiculous hiding in this outrageous getup. Pulling a tiny mirror from my purse, I checked my makeup. The new Holly smiled back at me, French twist and all. Thoughts of honesty crept into my mind, spoiling the moment. I felt jittery. Even sinful.

I glanced at the wide table where Lucas stood beside a stack of Marty Leigh's most recent book. My favorite author wore a bright green two-piece dress with pearl earrings. She was signing a book for an obvious fan. The girl watched her, apparently awestruck.

Feeling as shy as the girl looked, I drew a deep breath and stood up. It was now or never.

Chapter 19

I tried to move but stood frozen behind the chair. Then something inside me popped loose. The truth! It was time to let it emerge. I began pulling the pins out of my French twist on the way to the ladies' room. Inside, I searched for a brush in my purse and some tissues to wipe off the eye makeup.

"Please, Lord, forgive me," I whispered as I shook my hair free. Frantically, I washed away the heavy makeup. Next I pulled out the tissue wads, revealing my own true shape, such as it was.

Stepping back, I admired the real Holly Meredith in the mirror. Perfect.

Then, taking a deep breath, I left the rest room and marched toward Lucas Leigh and the book-signing event. I waited in line like the others, and when it was my turn at the book table, I said, "Hello, Lucas. I'm Holly Meredith."

He looked a bit surprised but shook my hand and introduced me to his aunt. "Marty, this is Holly, the writer of 'Love Times Two.' "

"So very pleased to meet you, Holly," she said, smiling broadly.

My heart pounding, I shook hands with Marty Leigh.

Lucas seemed confused. "I hardly recognized you, Holly. You looked much older in your picture," he said. "I thought—"

"I'm sorry," I confessed. "I must tell both of you the truth about myself. I'm really only thirteen and a half. I shouldn't have misled you. I guess I wanted to impress you."

Miss Leigh smiled warmly. "Holly, dear, you don't have to impress me. I'm already impressed with you."

"You are?" I felt self-conscious with Lucas staring at me.

"Oh yes," she said. "You have a marvelous talent, my dear. And thirteen or thirty, I plan to help you get published." She touched her single strand of pearls.

Lucas nodded, smiling. "I hope you can join us for lunch, Holly."

"I'd like that," I said, surprised at his kindhearted reaction to the real me. The line of people was growing longer behind me. I reached for my overnight case, filled with many Leigh mysteries. "I'd be honored if you'd sign these," I said.

She wrote her name in each novel, just as it had appeared in the handwriting book Danny and I discovered at the library. When she finished, I thanked her generously. Then Lucas escorted me upstairs to the coffee shop while my favorite author of all time continued to sign books and greet her adoring fans.

"My aunt will join us soon," Lucas said, leading me to a table near the windows. "How's this?"

"Fine, thanks," I said as he pulled out the chair for me.

"You certainly don't write like a thirteen-year-old," he said, handing the menu to me. "Your story was better than most of the stories my college classmates write."

"Thanks." I blushed, which was probably a good thing, after scrubbing all that makeup off. About now, I could use a little color on my face.

"It's true," he said, reading the menu. "Please, order whatever you'd like."

"How about a cheeseburger with everything on it?"

"Just what my younger sister usually orders."

"Really? You never mentioned her in your letters," I said, realizing how dumb my comment was, especially since a considerable amount of info had been missing from *my* letters, as well.

"How old is she?" I asked.

"Almost thirteen, and she loves to write. Especially letters."

"Think she'd want a pen pal?"

"Good idea," he said, smiling.

Soon Marty Leigh joined us, presenting a copy of her latest book to me. She ordered ginger ale for us, then proposed a toast. "Here's to *Sealed With a Kiss*." She raised her glass. "To the first issue."

In great detail, she explained her plan to include my short story in the November issue of the magazine.

"Are you willing to do some rewriting?" she asked.

"Whatever it takes." I felt giddy.

"That's the spirit," she said, taking another sip. "What do you think of the magazine title?"

"It's perfect," I said, pushing my hair back and letting it hang down behind my chair. I felt so good about going through with the truth. Maybe I'd write a book about this crazy day. Someday. For now, I'd have to record every amazing facet in my journal.

That evening, I told Mom all about my thrilling day, especially the part about the new magazine.

"*Sealed With a Kiss* will be out in three months," I told her. "I can't wait to see my story in print."

"Our Holly-Heart is going to be a published writer," she said, reaching for my hands and dancing around the kitchen with me.

"How much money will you get for it?" Carrie asked.

"Wait and see." I laughed as Goofey arched his kitty back and meowed under the desk.

When all the hoopla died down, I excused myself and slipped off to my bedroom. What an incredible day this had been. In more ways than one!

Perched on my beloved window seat, I listened to my heart. And I wrote my answer to Danny Myers' important question.

HOLLY'S HEART

The Trouble With Weddings

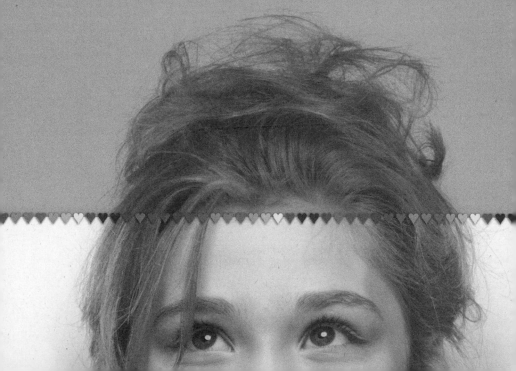

To

Aleta Hirschberg,

my sweet Auntie 'Leta,

whose mother-heart

has touched hundreds

of Kansas schoolchildren

. . . and me.

THE TROUBLE WITH WEDDINGS

Chapter 1

A bad case of curiosity caused me to tiptoe down the hall to Mom's bedroom. Holding my breath, I listened for the slightest sound of early morning activity. No way would Mom allow my snooping. Not in a zillion years.

My fingers touched the cool doorknob as I glanced over my shoulder, ears straining. All clear. Slowly the door glided open, and I crept into her rose-colored room, neat as always.

Scanning the room, I spotted Mom's latest greeting card from Uncle Jack. The pretty card stood on the antique pine dresser beside the lamp. I reached for it, a twinge of guilt tickling my conscience.

Pink rosebuds danced around the edges of the romantic card. Dying of curiosity, I turned to the inside. Just as I thought. The note at the bottom confirmed my suspicions. I read the words *I'm counting the hours till I see you again, Susan. Love, Jack.* A red ink heart twinkled up at me. Uncle Jack was no artist, but the happy face in the middle said it all: Jack Patterson was in love with my mom!

Creak! The steps! My heart pounded as I put the card down near the ceramic lamp. I crept to the door and peeked through the crack. Mom had reached the top step and was making the turn into the hallway leading to her room.

Yikes!

I stepped backward, away from the door, darting here and there searching for a hiding place. But where to hide? In a flash I scampered into Mom's walk-in closet. I spied her huge clothes hamper. *She'll never find me here,* I thought.

Then, slithering inside, I yanked the dirty clothes out from under me and covered myself with them as I waited, listening.

"Holly-Heart! Time to get up for school," Mom called at my door, halfway down the hall. Lucky for me I'd left my bedroom door shut. Even if I didn't answer, she wouldn't call me again, at least not for a while.

I could hear her soft footsteps on the carpet as she approached her room. Inside, she hummed, swooshing the curtains aside. *She's in some fabulous mood today,* I thought, secretly congratulating myself on finding the perfect hiding place.

One of Mom's pet peeves was nosy people. She wouldn't be singing now if she discovered me snooping. I could almost see her, wearing one of her many wool skirts with a sweater or blouse to match, her shoulder-length blond hair swept up or back, away from her face. She was probably settling down for her devotions about now. I could almost hear the pages of her Bible turning as she found the verses for the day.

Mom loved her morning quiet time. It felt good to know she took time to spend with God before going to work at the law firm where she was a paralegal. It hadn't always been that way, though. But now all of us were Christians. All except Daddy . . . and his new wife.

Good thing there were tiny slats in the side of the hamper, or I'd be suffocating by now. My legs were scrunched. How much longer? Sooner or later Mom would be wondering why I wasn't up and in the shower.

Br-r-ing! I jumped as Mom answered the phone. Lifting the

lid, I eavesdropped. Mom would freak out for sure if she knew I was here.

"Good morning, Jack," Mom cooed.

In spite of the pain of being hampered in like this, I grinned. Things were perfect. Mom was dating my favorite living relative. His former wife, my aunt Marla, had been Daddy's sister. *She* used to be my all-time favorite relative, but she'd died of cancer last February, three days before my thirteenth birthday. It was a nightmare for all of us . . . as bad as when Daddy divorced Mom.

Last month Uncle Jack surprised us when he moved his consulting business from Pennsylvania to Dressel Hills, our ski resort town in the middle of the Colorado Rockies. Best of all, Stan, Phil, Mark, and little Stephie—our cousins—were only a few blocks away. And Mom was happier than ever. Well, at least as happy as when Daddy lived here.

"Tonight?" I heard Mom say. "I'll ask Holly first, but I'm sure she won't mind."

Mind what? I closed the hamper lid silently. My knees were frozen now, my neck stiff. If I didn't get out of here soon, I'd be late for school. I could almost see the principal shaking his head in disgust. No way would he buy the trapped-in-the-hamper story.

"Holly!" Now my little sister, Carrie, was calling me. "Wake up," she said, pounding on my bedroom door.

I gasped. This had to be the dumbest thing I've ever done.

"Mommy, Holly's still asleep," she said, coming so close I could hear her shrieking Mom's name inches from me.

"Just a minute, Carrie," Mom said. "I'm on the phone."

"But I can't find Goofey anywhere," she whined like a typical eight-year-old. "He's *nowhere.*"

"I'm sure he's around somewhere," Mom said.

Carrie stomped down the hall calling, "Here kitty, kitty."

Scr-i-tch, scr-a-tch! Something was clawing the outside of the hamper. "Meow!" It was Goofey. He must have followed me in here. My heart sank. *I'm doomed,* I thought, crouching down even farther and covering myself with soiled laundry.

I heard Mom place the phone in its cradle. "Carrie, dear," she said as she headed toward the walk-in closet . . . and me. "I think Goofey's in here, in my closet." She opened the door.

I held my breath. *I'll never snoop again, Lord. I promise. Just please get me out of this mess!*

Scr-a-a-tch! Goofey was pawing harder at the hamper.

"There's nothing to eat in there," Mom was telling our cat. Her knees cracked as she bent down to pick him up. "Here, I'll show you," she said, lifting the hamper lid.

That's when my heart stopped beating. . . .

THE TROUBLE WITH WEDDINGS

Chapter 2

"That's strange," Mom said. "I was sure I did my laundry yester-day."

A tiny stream of air escaped my lips as I exhaled inside the hamper, preparing for the wrath of Mom.

She continued. "See, Goofey? It's nothing but a pile of dirty clothes." Goofey meowed again. Then . . . *bam!* Mom let the lid drop. "C'mon, let's get you some breakfast." Her footsteps grew muffled as she reached the carpeted steps leading downstairs.

"Close call," I whispered as I pulled myself out of the hamper like a butterfly struggling from its cocoon. Free at last, I flung the dirty clothes out of my way, limping out of Mom's closet and past her dresser. I blew a kiss at Uncle Jack's card. "It's all your fault," I whispered, grinning as I headed for my room.

I found my journal in the bottom drawer of my dresser. I scribbled *Wednesday, September 22: I knew it! Uncle Jack's in love with Mom. More later.*

I glanced at my watch. It was late. If I skipped shaving my legs, I could shower and be ready for breakfast in ten minutes. But . . . yikes! Tryouts for girl's volleyball were after school today. I *had* to shave. Danny Myers would be there cheering for me. How could I impress my best guy friend and Miss Tucker, the new coach, with cactus legs?

In the shower, an idea struck. I would shave during lunch, in the girls' locker room. Perfect! After drying off, I tossed a disposable razor onto the back of the toilet. I grinned at the mirror as I brushed my teeth. If this morning's narrow escape was an indication of my luck today, I could hardly wait for tryouts.

At breakfast Mom asked if I would baby-sit for Carrie, Stephie, Mark, and Phil that evening. "Uncle Jack and I are going out."

"Why can't Stan at least stay home with the boys?" I asked, gobbling down some cold cereal.

"Uncle Jack didn't offer to have Stan sit with Phil and Mark." She wiped the counter. "Stan must have other plans."

"Okay—this time." I gulped down my orange juice. "Isn't this your second date *alone* with my uncle this week?" I teased her.

Carrie piped up. "Uncle Jack used to let us all come along. Not anymore." She giggled.

I waved a napkin at my sister. "That was then, this is now."

"Right," Mom said, wringing out the dishcloth. There was a twinkle in her eyes and a spring in her step.

That's when I noticed the run in Mom's nylons. "You'll have to change your hose," I said, pointing to it.

She stared at her leg in horror, then dashed upstairs. "We're running really late, girls," she called to Carrie and me. "I'd better drive you to school."

I swallowed the last of my orange juice and raced to my room to grab my books.

"Girls," Mom called from her room. "Who's been in my clothes hamper?"

I froze.

"Not me," Carrie said.

"It's a mess in here," Mom insisted. "Holly?"

I stretched my aching legs, remembering my hiding place. A high price to pay for snooping, especially on the day of volleyball tryouts. "It's really late, Mom. We *have* to go," I said, ignoring her question and heading downstairs.

"I'm coming," Mom said. "Can't figure out what happened to that enormous pile of dirty clothes in my hamper." She pressed the garage door opener. "It's the strangest thing," she muttered.

Settling into the backseat, I breathed a thank-you heavenward. No more snooping for me—a promise I intended to keep.

I slipped into eighth-grade science class unnoticed, claiming the nearest desk in the back of the room. My stomach rumbled as I glanced at the clock. Could I last till lunch?

I spotted Andie. She was wearing jeans and a purple shirt under her new jean jacket. Did she have her usual package of peanut butter sandwich crackers stashed nearby? I sure could use a nibble right about now.

Coughing, I hoped to get my best friend's attention. But she didn't turn around. So I wrote a note to her, folded it, and passed it to the boy in front of me. He tapped Andie's shoulder—how obvious can you get? Andie turned around at the exact moment the teacher did.

Mr. Ross stepped to the front of his desk, adjusting his glasses. "Miss Martinez, please step forward."

Andie blushed deeply. Before getting up, she stuffed the note into her sock.

"What is the rule in my class concerning note passing?" Mr. Ross asked, sliding his glasses up again. I could see smudges on them as he stepped closer.

Andie cleared her throat. "It's not allowed, sir."

"And did you receive a note?"

"Yes, Mr. Ross."

"You broke the rule, then?"

She nodded.

Mr. Ross looked past Andie at me. "Who else is involved?"

I couldn't let Andie take the blame. Standing up, I confessed, "I am, sir."

"Both of you will see me during your lunch break." At that, he turned and headed back to the board to write the day's assignment.

Lunch? How would I have time to shave my legs *and* show up for Mr. Ross's lecture? Besides, a girl could starve to death by then.

♥ ♥ ♥

After class, Danny Myers was waiting by the door. Almost fifteen, he was taller than most guys in ninth grade. Logical and *very* spiritual, Danny possessed a unique quality that calmed me down. It was one of the coolest things about him. That and his amazing memory. His only flaw: Danny was a bit controlling sometimes—and preachy. I found that out last summer when we had an argument about my going to visit Daddy in California.

"Hey, Holly." Danny reached for my books. "Walk you to your locker?"

I smiled. "I'd like to *hide* in my locker." I began to tell him about passing the note to Andie in science, but he assured me that Mr. Ross wouldn't make me miss lunch.

"I hope not, 'cause I'm starved."

He reached into his pocket. "Here, try these."

"Almonds?" I tore the tiny package open.

"They're quick energy, and good for you, too."

"Thanks." I smiled up at my health-nut friend. "Once again, you saved my life."

"My pleasure," he said, running his free hand through his auburn hair. "I'll walk you to your next class."

"Perfect," I said, spotting Kayla Miller posing beside her locker with that flirtatious grin of hers. It made me mad. Not her grin as much as her unmistakable crush on Danny.

♥ ♥ ♥

The almonds helped me make it till lunch break. By 11:45, I was more worried about shaving my legs than anything else. Mr. Ross was sure to lecture away our entire lunch hour.

Andie waited outside the science room door. "Ready for this?" she asked.

"Sorry I got you stuck in the middle."

"Don't worry. If we're polite, he'll let us off."

"You're sure?"

"Just watch." She opened the door and sauntered in.

Mr. Ross sat at his desk. He slid his smudged glasses up his nose as we came in. "Please be seated." He gestured to the front row of desks.

Andie sat quietly, folding her hands on the desk. I mimicked her.

"Very well, girls. Let's chat."

He's going to drag this out forever, I thought as I tried to match Andie by faking an interested expression.

"Are the rules of this classroom clear to you both?"

Andie nodded. So did I.

"Do you understand there must be consequences for misdeeds?"

"Yes, sir," said Andie. Ditto for me.

"Very well. You will both write a five-hundred-word essay on the importance of following rules. In short, on responsibility."

No problem, I thought almost gleefully. A writing assignment— the least terrible punishment of all time.

I stole a glance at Andie. Poor thing. For her this was worse than being grounded. She despised essays or anything resembling them.

"Mr. Ross, may I say something?" Andie asked.

"You may."

"The note I received from Holly Meredith wasn't willfully breaking the rule."

Mr. Ross raised his bushy eyebrows. "Oh? How is that?"

"The note was important. About matters of life and death."

"Life and death, indeed." He stood up, stuffing his hands into his pockets and frowning. "Please explain."

"Well, sir, Holly didn't get enough to eat this morning at breakfast. She just wanted to borrow a few morsels."

"Morsels?"

Was he falling for her story? I looked at my watch. *C'mon, Andie, hurry it up.*

"Are you saying your friend here is malnourished?"

"Well, she *is* quite thin, as you can see," she said, pouring it on thicker than ever.

Mr. Ross focused a concerned look on me. "We do have a social worker in the building three days a week. If you aren't getting enough nourishment at home, Holly, there are some avenues that can be considered."

Oh great, Andie, I thought. *Get me reported to Social Services, why don't you?*

I said, "Thanks, but that's not necessary."

Andie continued, "Excuse me. I really must get my friend to the cafeteria now."

I wanted to strangle her.

"By all means," Mr. Ross said. "And girls . . . the assignment for tomorrow . . ."

He's going to cancel it, I thought.

" . . . is due bright and early," he said with an air of finality.

Out in the hall, Andie groaned, "An essay! Look what you've done, Holly."

"*I* did? *You* made it sound like my mom neglects to feed me."

"Sorry about that," she said as we rushed to lunch.

"You oughta be," I said, dashing through the line in the cafeteria, grabbing a sandwich.

"What's your hurry?" she asked, catching up with me.

"Have to shave my legs," I whispered, finding a table.

She rolled her eyes. "Please, I'm eating."

I giggled. "Hurry. You can cover for me in the girls' locker room."

"For what?"

"For snoopers while I take my jeans off and shave my legs in the sink."

"How bad are they?" She leaned over and slid my sock down.

"Get outta here." I playfully pushed her away.

"Why should I cover for you when you got me in trouble with Mr. Ross?" she said, reaching for her chili dog.

"Best friends do things like that for each other," I said, clearing off my tray. "So . . . are you coming?"

"I can't eat that fast. I'll catch up with you in a second."

Racing to the girls' locker room, I glanced at my watch. Seven minutes to shave Sherwood Forest before Miss Wannamaker's composition class. I searched my backpack for the disposable Bic razor. But it was nowhere to be found!

Chapter 3

I made a mad dash around the locker room, jiggling one locker latch after another, searching for an open one . . . with a razor.

"Are you nuts?" Andie appeared by my side, hands on her hips.

"Frantic," I cried. "I forgot my Bic."

"Is *that* all?" She went to her locker, swirled her combination lock, and produced a precious blade. "Here."

"Thanks." I hugged her, then raced to the sink. "You're the world's best friend."

"Now that I saved your skin . . ."

"And that's no lie," I said, slipping out of my jeans.

"Don't you think you owe *me* something?" she said.

I swooshed warm water and soap over my bare leg. "Is this a hint?" I laughed. " 'Cause if it is, I already know what you're up to."

"That's good, because there's no way on earth I'm gonna write that essay for Mr. Ross."

By the look on her face, I knew she was serious. "It wouldn't be honest if I wrote it." I skimmed the blade over my leg.

"Come on, Holly, this is not for a grade. It's a punishment."

I grabbed a towel out of my locker. "Still, it'll have your name on it, right?"

"None other than. Look, I'm going to be late for class," she said, a little huffy. "See you at tryouts."

"Thanks again," I said, waving the shaver as she disappeared through the door.

♥ ♥ ♥

After school I hurried to the gym. A line of girls was already ahead of me. Most of them had played volleyball last year in seventh grade. Danny had warned me that the competition would be stiff, but now it hit me hard. My throat turned as dry as cotton, so I darted to the drinking fountain.

Kayla Miller was there, too, getting a drink. Her twin sister, Paula, stood in the line waiting for tryouts. "I think I'm going to throw up," Kayla said, holding her stomach and looking pale.

"What's wrong?" I asked, convinced she *could* be sick by the expression on her face.

"Just nervous, I guess," she said. "I have to make this team."

"You made the team back East, didn't you?" Paula and Kayla's family had moved here from Pennsylvania last spring.

She nodded, her ponytail bobbing up and down.

"Then you shouldn't have anything to worry about."

She smiled faintly. "Hope so."

"Well, I've gotta run." I sprinted to the locker room, where I pulled on green shorts and a white top. Last year these shorts had haunted me with their ridiculously wide legs. Now, as I viewed them in the mirror, they almost fit. At last my scrawny legs were acquiring a shape. At long last.

The new coach, Miss Tucker, stood in the middle of the gym floor, blowing her whistle. I ran my hand over my right leg. Smooth. Andie had saved the day. She showed up just then with Danny Myers and Billy Hill. Billy was as cool as a guy gets. He'd helped me play a trick on Andie at my birthday party last February. Now he was her closest guy friend and one of Danny's best friends. I waved them over to my side of the gym.

Danny lit up when he saw me. "How's the competition?" He leaned against the wall beside me.

"Like you said, lots of it."

"But *you're* ready, Holly." He flashed a smile at me. He was right. I was ready and had been for weeks. All those summer practice sessions with Danny had paid off.

Kayla Miller was called first. I watched her serve like a pro. I swallowed hard, nervous, as she did her thing on the court. And *she'd* felt like throwing up?

Danny must've sensed my insecurity because he turned to me and whispered, "Never forget, you're an amazing athlete. You really are, Holly."

Jared Wilkins wandered over. Something about the bounce in his step—and his crazy, fun-loving ways—still appealed to me even though I hung out mostly with Danny now. I wished my heart would stop beating so wildly every time my first crush showed up.

"Hey, Holly. Good luck out there." Jared's blue eyes twinkled another message, too. I wasn't sure what.

"Thanks," I said, looking up at Danny's face, wondering if he'd noticed Jared's subtle flirting.

"Excuse me a second," Danny said, heading for the rest room.

Instantly, Jared came over and took Danny's place beside me. "You're a hard one to track down these days," he said.

I wasn't sure what that meant. But then Jared wasn't the easiest guy in the world to figure out. It was one of the things I liked about him. I pushed a stray strand of hair back into my braid. "I've been right here in the gym ever since school got out today."

"I don't see you around much anymore." He leaned closer to me.

"Well . . ." I blushed. "Danny's been helping me get ready for the tryouts, if that's what you mean."

He arched his eyebrows. "Hanging out with Danny?"

"Well, I guess you could say that. Ever since September sixth at 7:15 P.M.," I announced, remembering when I'd answered Danny's very special question in a letter.

"Really? That long?"

Danny was back, and he slipped in between Jared and me. "Wait'll you see Holly do her stuff out on the court," he bragged to Jared.

Jared nodded, then he winked when Danny looked the other way. I blushed again. A girl doesn't easily forget someone like Jared even if he had turned out to be a rotten flirt.

The whistle blew, its shrill sound echoing off the walls. "Holly Meredith," called the coach.

I sucked air in too fast and almost choked.

"Remember Philippians 4:13, Holly. You can do everything through Him who gives you strength," Danny reminded me.

I smiled and headed toward middle court.

Andie shot me her famous thumbs-up. "Go for it, girl."

No matter what, I promised myself I'd keep my cool. And I did. Setting up, spiking, bumping the ball—I was wired for this moment. Next I showed off my serve. After three good ones in a row, Miss Tucker asked me to put a spin on the next serve. And I did it!

Thank goodness Danny had insisted I drill this. I could hear his voice above the crowd. "Yes! Keep it up, Holly!"

Coach Tucker pulled me over after the rotation and patted me on the back. "Meredith, you're really good." She lowered her voice. "Be ready to show up for practice tomorrow . . . three o'clock sharp." I wanted to hug her, but thanked her instead. It sounded like I'd made the team.

Miss Tucker blew her whistle. "Stan!" she called to him across the gym. "Cover for me just a second."

A tall blond boy emerged from the crowd—my cousin! "Good show, cuz," Stan said, shuffling the pages on his clipboard. "A little rough around the edges, but not bad."

I leaned over and pulled up my socks. "What're *you* doing here?"

"Didn't you hear? I'm the student manager for the girls' B team."

"Just great," I muttered as I walked off the court, away from him.

Andie yelled to me from the sidelines. "Holly, you were amazing!"

Danny, standing beside her, beamed his approval.

"Coach hinted that I made the team," I said. Excited, my friends gathered around. Andie did a little jig before she hugged me, and Billy gave me a high-five. Jared congratulated me next, but his smile faded a bit when Danny moved in beside me. Was he jealous?

After everyone left, Danny went to get his jacket on the bleachers. "I'll call you tonight," he said, heading for the door.

"Okay. Thanks again for your help."

Danny nodded, turning around. Then he stared at me. Well, not really stared, just looked terribly pleased.

My heart skipped a beat as he waved good-bye.

Chapter 4

"Wow, Holly," Andie said, swinging her backpack as we walked to the locker room. "You were hot chocolate today."

"Thanks," I whispered to my toes.

"Hey, what's wrong?" she said, pulling on my sleeve.

"My *cousin*. He's the student manager for girls' volleyball."

Andie stopped cold in her tracks. She put her hands on her chubby hips. "That guy's your *cousin*?"

"Uh-huh. That's Stan Patterson."

"Why didn't you tell me? He's drop-dead gorgeous."

"He's my cousin, silly."

"So? You *have* to introduce me."

"I do not." I opened my gym locker.

"Ho-l-ly," she whined. "I've seen him around school but didn't know he was related to you."

"Well, he is." I pushed my hair over my ears.

Andie continued. "You promised you'd introduce me to him even before your uncle Jack moved here. Remember last summer?"

"Faintly."

"Hurry and get dressed before he leaves," she begged.

"Have to shower first."

"Just shower at home."

"No," I said stubbornly.

Then I saw that familiar glint in her eyes. She twisted a curl around her finger. Look out . . . trouble.

"Have *I* got an idea for you," she began. "An even trade. You introduce me to your cousin, and I'll forget about the five-hundred-word essay for Mr. Ross."

"You'd do that? Write your *own* essay just to meet my schizoid cousin?"

She was laughing. "Yep, you heard it here."

The essay punishment was, after all, my fault. "Okay." I gave in. "It's a deal. But I've got the best end of it." I ran off to the showers, which were mostly occupied. I managed to find a private stall. Soon I was back, dressing and brushing my hair.

Andie gathered up my dirty clothes and rolled them into the wet towel. She stuffed them into my gym bag. "Would you hurry?"

"Relax, will ya?" I fastened a clip in my damp hair and headed out the door with Andie leading the way.

Back in the gym, Stan and Miss Tucker stood on the sidelines, comparing notes.

I sized up the situation. "Doesn't look like a good time for personal introductions."

"We'll wait," she said, locking her stance like a stubborn mule.

Almost on cue, Stan glanced up, motioning to me.

I nodded to Andie. "Now's your chance."

"Gotcha." She followed me onto the gym floor, our tennies squeaking as we went.

I introduced Andie to Stan. "I don't think you've met my best friend, Andrea Martinez."

"Hi, Andrea," he said. "Are you in eighth with Holly?"

She nodded, speechless.

"Andie, this is Stan, my cousin."

She snapped to it. "I've seen you with Billy Hill and Jared

Wilkins. We all go to the same youth group at church. Maybe you could come with Holly sometime."

Stan smiled. I could tell he was studying her, but only casually. No way would he be interested in *my* best friend. Besides, Mom had said there was a girl back East he was writing to. "Maybe sometime," he said.

Just then, Andie's mother showed up pushing a double stroller. She paused in the doorway with Andie's two-year-old twin brothers.

Stan turned. Before we could say a word, he had darted across the gym to see the toddlers.

"What's he doing?" Andie asked, surprised.

"Stan's a sucker for little kids."

"Really?"

"Not babies, little kids," I said as Stan knelt down to talk to Chris and Jon.

"Hi, Mom," Andie said as we followed Stan over. "Whatcha doin' here?"

"It was so nice out," she said. "Thought we'd soak up some of the September sunshine."

Chris bounced up and down. "An-dee-dee," he said, pointing his chubby little finger at his sister.

"He's desperate to get out," Mrs. Martinez said.

Andie unbuckled him, took his hand, and walked him around the gym.

Stan, in turn, unbuckled Jon and lifted him up into the air, pushing his brown curly head high into the basketball net. Jon giggled and squealed for more. "Here you go," he said, showing Jon a basketball, saying the word over and over, letting him try to hold it. Andie couldn't take her eyes off Stan, and neither could little Jon.

"It's getting late," Andie's mother said. "We'd better start home."

Andie helped put the twins' sweaters on before we headed for the door.

"Nice meeting you, Stan," Andie said.

"Same here," he said, waving to the toddlers.

Outside, the autumn air was turning brisk. It was like that in the mountains. Summer was over almost before it got started in Dressel Hills, Colorado.

"I think I'm in love," Andie said on our way down the hill toward the city bus stop. Her mother pushed the stroller ahead of us.

"Good grief. Don't be so dramatic. And have you forgotten Billy? He's nuts about you."

"Whatever," she said. "Call me after supper. I've got an essay to write." The bus pulled up to the corner, half a block away. She ran to catch up with her mother and brothers.

The bus was filling up fast. "Better hurry," I called, strolling past the Soda Straw, a fifties-style diner with a soda fountain and every flavor of ice cream in the world. Today it was hopping with kids, most of them fresh from volleyball tryouts.

Kayla Miller dashed out the door, her ponytail bobbing up and down. "Holly, wait up," she called to me.

I waited on the sidewalk for her to catch up. Her grin was gone. In its place were accusing eyes. "I saw what happened at the gym right before you and Andie left."

Puzzled, I made a face. "*What* happened?"

"Stan, uh, your cousin. You were talking to him."

Now I was really confused. "Maybe you'd better spell it out, Kayla."

"You introduced him to Andie, didn't you?" Her eyes squinted partway shut, the way my mom's eyes do when she's upset.

"Yeah, so?"

She looked away. "You don't know this, but I've liked Stan for as long as I can remember. Before we moved here, he and I went to different schools, but we always talked after church."

I listened, still wondering what she wanted from me.

She continued. "Then Mrs. Patterson died and Stan's dad started attending another church. Anyway, I didn't get to see Stan much after that. Now . . . here we are in the same junior high, and he doesn't even seem to know I exist."

I scratched my head. "Why are you telling *me?*"

"You're his cousin, Holly. Couldn't you set me up with him?"

First Andie, now Kayla. "I really don't know what you see in him. Besides, my best friend is bugging me to—"

"You're helping *her,* aren't you?" she interrupted.

I nodded.

"Please, just help me get to know Stan better."

"But he *knows* you already, doesn't he?" I said, totally confused.

"C'mon, Holly," she said. "Please?"

I burst into a panic attack. "This is too weird. My cousin moves to town, and everyone's all mushy over him."

"Because he's so cute," she crooned.

"Cuter than Danny?" *Oops.* I caught myself too late.

"Danny Myers?" she said. "He's okay, I guess, but . . ."

"Then, are you saying you don't like Danny?" I couldn't believe I was asking this.

"What makes you think that?" She played with her ponytail.

I breathed deeply. "Remember last summer? You practically begged Danny to help you with your serves. You flirted all over the place, even at the library."

"But don't you see? It was all about getting close to Stan. I was sure he'd be involved with the girls' volleyball team this year. That's why I wanted to make the team so bad. Danny's just a friend."

"Really?" I didn't buy it for one second.

"So, will you?" she asked again, tears glistening in her eyes.

This girl's either completely lost it over Stan, or she's the best actress around. I opened my mouth to speak.

"Holly," Andie called to me, running across the street toward us.

"What's up?" I said, surprised to see her.

"The bus was too full for all of us, so I let Mom and the twins go ahead. I'll catch the next one." She glanced at Kayla Miller. "Am I interrupting something?"

"Not really," Kayla said, wiping her eyes. Then looking me square in the face, she said, "Call me with your answer tonight." And she dashed into the Soda Straw.

"What was *that* about?" Andie's dark eyes demanded an answer.

How could I tell my best friend that the girl I suspected of chasing the guy I liked was really more interested in Andie's latest crush?

"Please, Holly," she called after me as I turned to go. "Talk to me."

"Later." I looked back at her, forcing a smile.

Under my breath, I said, "*Much* later," as I trudged toward home.

THE TROUBLE WITH WEDDINGS

Chapter 5

I kicked every little stone along the sidewalk as I walked. There was no big rush to get home. At the beginning of the school year, Mom had said since Carrie was turning nine in a month I could take my time getting home. Besides, I was an eighth-grade student, which meant more freedom.

So I took my time fuming over my stupid cousin Stan. I was freaked out at the sudden interest the female population of Dressel Hills Junior High was showing in him. Andie, Kayla . . . and who knows who else? I didn't dare tell him. He already had a mammoth ego.

Downhill Court—my street—came into view as I turned away from the ski shops downtown. Dressel Hills was a blaze of gold, the only fall color we had here in the Rocky Mountains. Back in Pennsylvania, trees turned every imaginable hue. Here, people drove for miles to see the shimmering yellow of the quaking aspen trees nestled against the backdrop of dark evergreens.

When I got home, Mom was in the kitchen putting a casserole into the oven. "How were tryouts?" she asked.

"You'll never guess in a zillion years." I leaned my books against the sink, trying not to grin.

She tossed the potholders aside and hugged me. "You made the team!"

"I still can't believe it."

"*I* can—after all the hours of practicing over at Danny's. How is he, anyway?"

"He's really cool, Mom. He treats me great."

Mom's eyes squinted half shut. "What's that supposed to mean?"

"You know. He's the coolest boyfriend ever."

She looked like she was gonna drop her teeth. "You're dating him?"

"Of course not. Didn't I explain all that? Danny knows I can't date till I'm fifteen—and even then only in a group setting. He just calls me his girlfriend because he likes me, and I like him. All we do is hang out at school and at youth group—you know, like good friends."

Mom set the oven timer. "Just so your friendship doesn't become too exclusive. Do we understand each other?"

I nodded that I did. "You don't have to worry about me, Mom." Then I remembered Mom's upcoming date with Uncle Jack. "When's your date picking you up?" I asked, moving my books to the long bar in the middle of the kitchen.

"Six o'clock. That's why I made chicken casserole. You'll be feeding the whole crew, minus Stan. Think you can handle things?"

"No problem. Except I do have lots of homework tonight." I was thinking of the essay on responsibility I had to hand in to Mr. Ross first thing tomorrow.

"I'm sure Uncle Jack will make it worth your while. He pays by the kid per hour," Mom reminded me.

I hoped my uncle would continue to date Mom. It was good for business. And by her smiles . . . good for Mom, too.

"By the way, Holly, I'm planning a surprise birthday party for Carrie—a week from this Saturday." Mom followed me upstairs to my room. Goofey padded up behind me.

"Who did you invite?" I plopped down on my four-poster bed and snuggled with the cat.

Mom closed the door, then sat on my lavender window seat. "I've invited Stephanie, Mark, and Phil, of course, and Carrie's new friend, Brittany Lloyd, from school."

"What about Zachary Tate? I know Carrie would love to see him again." I stroked Goofey's neck, and his purring rose to a rumble. I wanted to hear what Mom would say about her former boyfriend's kid coming to the party.

She breathed deeply, slowly exhaling. "I don't think it would be wise. Zachary had a rough time when his dad and I stopped seeing each other. I wouldn't want to tamper with his feelings now for anything in the world."

I leaned back on the bed. "I never see Mr. Tate or Zachary at church anymore."

"I think they must attend a different church," Mom said. "I really do miss having Zachary in my Sunday school class."

I bet she did. Mom had a strong maternal instinct I liked to call a mother heart. If she and Daddy had stayed married, there'd probably be a bunch of us kids by now.

"What do you think about Carrie's surprise party?" Mom asked. "Counting Carrie, there'll be five kids."

"Sounds perfect for a nine-year-old." I pulled out my assignment notebook. "I won't be able to help you with the party much. There's an ice-cream social at the Soda Straw with Pastor Rob and the youth group. Okay with you?"

"Uncle Jack will be here to help." Suspicious-looking twinkles gleamed from her eyes as she mentioned his name.

I grinned. "You really like my uncle, I see."

"Is it obvious?" Mom said, fooling with her hair.

"Does Uncle Jack know you're in love with him?" *The question I've been dying to ask.*

A smile danced across her cheeks. "Who wants to know?"

"Mom . . . tell me!" I jumped off the bed and raced to the

door, blocking her exit with my body. "You're stuck here till you tell me."

Mom giggled like a schoolgirl. "I better let you get to homework before the troops arrive." She reached out and touched my hair. "I really appreciate you, Holly. You're so responsible. I know I can always count on you."

"No fair changing the subject." I moved aside to let her pass. She closed the door, leaving me alone with my pen poised to write an essay titled, "The R-Word: Responsibility."

I wanted to laugh out loud. Mom was right. Usually I *was* oozing with responsibility. But note-passing in science had been a big mistake. I wouldn't let Mr. Ross know that I secretly enjoyed having an excuse to write an essay. Writing was my life. Books too. I mean, if I was going to be stuck on a deserted island, I would definitely take stacks of them, along with notebooks and sharpened pencils.

♥ ♥ ♥

By the time Uncle Jack and the cousins showed up, I'd finished my rough draft, fifty words over the five-hundred-word limit. *Good . . . room to revise,* I thought as I raced downstairs.

In the living room, Stephie was riding piggyback on her dad. He wore tan dress pants and a herringbone sports coat. Mark reached up and tried to pull Stephie's hair. When he saw me, Uncle Jack put Stephie down and straightened his striped tie. "The line forms to the right," he said, turning to look outside.

"What line?" asked Stephie.

He leaned closer to the picture window, pushing the curtains aside. "Guys are flocking to Holly's house. Look, can't you see them?"

Stephie ran over for a peek. I sneaked up behind him and tickled his ribs.

"Oh-ho, there," he said, whirling around. "Asking for a tickle session, are you?"

Stephie hollered, "You'll lose, Holly. You will!"

I backed away, smiling. "No thanks, I'll pass."

"Chicken!" Phil shouted, pulling on my arm. "Here, Holly, I'll tell you where he's ticklish."

Uncle Jack pulled out his wallet. "Looks like you're in for a busy evening. Here's payment in advance."

Forty bucks!

"Uh, that's too much," I said, staring at the money.

Uncle Jack acted surprised. "Four kids for four hours? Sounds just right to me."

Goofey wandered into the living room, and Uncle Jack started sneezing. "Stupid allergies," he muttered, taking out a handkerchief to blow his nose. I stuffed the money into my jeans before he could change his mind.

After supper I had all baby-sitting details under control. Carrie and Stephie were playing upstairs, and Mark and Phil were glazed over in front of the TV. I was cleaning the kitchen when the phone rang.

"Hello?" I answered it.

"Is Phil Patterson there?" a tiny voice asked.

"Uh, yes, he is. Who's calling?"

"He knows who it is," *she* said.

I hurried downstairs to the family room. "Someone wants to talk to you." I handed the phone to ten-year-old Phil.

"Hello?" he said. Silence. Then he yelled, "Aa-agh! Get back, it's Elaine Thomas!" He tossed the phone to me.

I stared at Phil while his eyes did a roller-coaster number. Mark lay on the floor, laughing hysterically as I quickly pushed the off button.

"What's wrong with Elaine Thomas?" I asked. "She sounded okay to me."

"She's a toidi!" yelled Phil.

"Yeah," shouted Mark.

"Toidi—toidi—toidi—toidi," chanted the boys.

"Sounds like I should flush your mouths out," I said, watching as Phil and his younger brother acted weird. "Okay, okay. What's a toidi?" I asked.

"Idiot spelled backward," said Phil, cackling.

Never ask, I thought. *Never ask.* I headed back to the kitchen. How did Uncle Jack put up with all this grade-school nonsense? Aunt Marla was in heaven, but her kids needed her down here—learning about "toidi" and other major stuff. I missed her.

Swishing the kitchen counter clean, I wondered how Daddy's sister would feel if she knew Uncle Jack was dating my mother. Two times in one week!

Chapter 6

The next morning I beat Andie to Mr. Ross's classroom. "Good morning," I said, standing beside his long desk. "Here's my essay."

Mr. Ross pushed his drooping glasses up his shiny nose.

Without saying a word, he read the entire essay as I stood like a statue, waiting. Slowly, he placed the paper on his desk and removed his glasses. "This essay is unusually well written, Miss Meredith."

"Thank you," I said.

"I hope you are taking one of Miss Wannamaker's creative writing classes this semester. She impresses me as a teacher who might assist a talented young person such as yourself."

I nodded. "Yes, I enjoy her classes very much."

"Very well," he said, putting his glasses back on. "Have you had breakfast today?"

"Yes, sir," I said. "I had a fabulous breakfast." Then I added, "My mom's a great cook," in case he had any more notions of contacting a social worker.

Andie arrived, bringing the bustling sounds of the congested hallway in with her. She flashed a smile when she saw me and headed for Mr. Ross. He adjusted his tie, the same boring one he'd worn the whole first month of school.

Andie didn't wait for Mr. Ross to read her essay; she laid it on his desk and left. "What's your rush?" I asked as she zipped past me.

"Gotta do a little spying. On Stan."

"What'll Billy say if he finds out?"

She stopped in the middle of the hall. "Will he even notice?"

"Are you kidding?" I pulled her away from the crush of the crowd. "Billy really likes you, Andie."

"Not half as much as I like Stan."

I wanted to slap some sense into her. "You're wacko if you hurt Billy's feelings for a schizoid."

"What's *that* mean?" she asked, leaning against the wall.

"Schizoid?" I laughed. "You know, split personality. Sometimes cool, sometimes a total jerk."

"No way, not Stan. He's so together." She cracked her gum.

"Oh please," I said. "I oughta know, don't you think? The guy's a jerk."

"He can't be *that* bad."

"You'll see."

"Worse than Jared?"

"Almost."

"I don't believe you," she said and scurried off.

I trotted down the hall. Then I spotted the number-one jerk of all time—Jared Wilkins—waiting at my locker.

"What do *you* want?" I said, reaching for my combination.

"Nothin' much." He shrugged his shoulders.

"Then what are you doing here?"

"Just wondering what you're doing."

"What's it look like?" I stared at him, annoyed.

"You seem upset. Everything okay?"

"Till *you* showed up, everything was perfect."

"Holly, listen, I'm not here to cause trouble for you and Danny. It's my own fault the two of you are so, well . . . happy together." His dancing blue eyes looked surprisingly serious for a change. "I miss you, Holly-Heart."

I could hardly find the numbers on my combination lock. *Where is Danny, anyway?* If he was here, like he always was before school, this conversation wouldn't be happening. I looked up to tell Jared to get lost, but he was gone.

♥ ♥ ♥

At lunch Danny was waiting for me inside the cafeteria doors. "Ready for volleyball practice?"

"I can hardly wait." I grabbed a tray and got in line. "What's for hot lunch?"

"Some pasta dish." He reached for a tray.

"I'm starved." I saw Mr. Ross peek into the cafeteria. "Guess I better not say that too loud. Mr. Ross might have me hauled off to a foster home."

"That's not funny," Danny said as we moved through the cafeteria line. He reached for a tuna sandwich and an apple. Healthy foods.

"What did you mean about a foster home?" Danny asked, frowning at my choice of pasta and soda.

"Just forget it." I walked to a table and sat down.

Danny set his tray down beside me. "Is something wrong?" he whispered.

"Not really," I said, but it wasn't true. I could still hear Jared's words from this morning. *"I miss you, Holly-Heart."* And he'd said it so seriously. Not playfully like always before.

"You're upset," Danny said before we bowed our heads and he prayed over our lunches. I said amen at the end.

Salting my pasta, I asked where he was this morning before school. "You always show up at my locker first thing."

"You shouldn't salt your food before tasting it," he said, criticizing me instead of listening to what I said.

"Where *were* you?" I repeated.

"Billy and I shot baskets over at the gym." He bit into his tuna sandwich, lettuce and all.

"Andie's making a big mistake if she chooses to like another guy more than Billy. He's so good to her." I twirled noodles around my fork.

Danny looked surprised. "This is news. Is Andie thinking about someone other than Billy?"

"Yeah," I grumbled. "Didn't I tell you? She's got her eyes on my cousin Stan, but he couldn't care less. He has a girlfriend back East. Besides that, Stan's nothing like he used to be. Maybe it's Aunt Marla's death, I don't know. But he's turned into a splitzo schizoid."

"A what?"

"A split personality."

"Hey, nobody's perfect," Danny said, chuckling.

His attitude was starting to bug me. I would have thought he'd stick up for Billy—and for me!

"Whose side are you on, anyway?" I said.

Danny frowned. "What's this *side* stuff? Holly, are you feeling okay?"

I spun around. "Can we just not talk about Stan anymore?"

Danny raised his eyebrows. "If he's the reason you're upset, why don't you talk to him about it? Proverbs says, 'An offended brother is more unyielding than a fortified city—' "

"Stan's *not* my brother." I jumped to my feet. "And why do you have to preach to me? I'm a Christian just like you. First you lecture me about what I eat, and now you tell me what to do with Stan. It's starting to bug me."

Danny stretched his hand toward me. "I didn't intend to hurt you. I only want to help."

I waved him away. "That's not how it sounds. You're trying to run my life." Turning away, I hurried to the girls' rest room. There, I scowled at the mirror, then fished for the brush in my backpack. I started rearranging my hair, beginning with the part. I cringed with every stroke of the brush. How dare Danny Myers treat me like I was a spiritual baby. I bet *he* didn't have a secret prayer list or write in the margins of his devotional. Just because we were hanging out together didn't give him the right to act like this.

I marched off to my composition class in a huff.

Jared was waiting by the door as I hurried to snag my favorite seat . . . beside the window. He followed me into Miss Wannamaker's room. "May I sit here?" he asked, pointing to the desk beside mine. He actually waited until I nodded before sitting down.

"Thanks," he said, like it was a great privilege. His eyes lit up like, uh . . . kind of like Mom's had yesterday when we talked about Uncle Jack.

I swallowed hard. Could Jared Wilkins really and truly care for me? I pushed the ridiculous thought from my mind as I reached for my three-ring binder.

"Dear class," Miss Wannamaker said as if beginning a letter. It was her way every day. "Today we shall discuss the proper outlining procedure for research papers."

I found the yellow tab marking the "Comp I" section in my binder and set out to take the best notes ever. After her lecture, Miss W gave us twenty minutes to begin the assignment—an eight-hundred-word essay or short story about any aspect of a metamorphosis, human or otherwise. It was due in two weeks.

First I looked up *metamorphosis* in *Webster's Dictionary*. It meant "A complete change of a substance, structure, or shape."

Hmm, what to write about? Staring out the window, I watched as golden aspen leaves shimmered in the autumn breeze. A transformation of color. My eyes wandered to the top of Copper Mountain. Years before, men had sliced a path through the tree-covered slopes, transforming the mountain into a skier's paradise. Nope, I wouldn't write a nature essay. Not this time.

I let my eyes wander slightly to my left. There sat Jared, his pen racing across the blank page. *What if?* I thought. What if I let my imagination run wild? What if I transformed Jared Wilkins into a polite, trustworthy, *true* friend? A magical metamorphosis, but on paper only.

Delighted with my idea, I set to work, using Jared's name just to help me relate more closely to the final fictitious character. I would change all names to fictitious ones later, of course.

Finishing the first paragraph, I set my pen down and sneaked a glance at Jared. I grinned at the thought of transforming him. The idea excited me more than I cared to admit.

THE TROUBLE WITH WEDDINGS

Chapter 7

One week later—two days before Carrie's birthday party—I arrived at school a bit late. Andie stood waiting for me in the main hall, near the front doors. "Where've you been?" she said, biting her nails. "I thought you were sick or something. I even looked in your locker and—"

"You opened my locker?" I said, moving through the crowd of kids in the hall, hoping she hadn't snooped *too* much.

"I oughta know your combination by now, don't you think?" She stayed close to the wall to avoid mad scramblers headed for lockers, homerooms, you name it.

"Have you opened my locker before?" I asked, feeling uneasy, wondering if she'd discovered my writing assignment. It was nearly finished, and no way did I want *anyone* but Miss Wannamaker to see the finished product.

She looked at me, surprised. "Well, we *are* best friends."

"I know, Andie. It's no big deal," I said, playing it down in case she picked up on my concern and suspected something. Still, I dashed to my locker, which was hanging open. "Andie, you left my locker open!"

"I did?"

"You just said you opened it." I hoped she was the *only* one snooping around. There was top-secret stuff in there.

"Sorry," Andie said. "Guess I was just in a hurry to find you."

I shook my head, fuming at her. "There's no excuse for irresponsibility," I muttered, reaching for my three-ring binder. I flipped it open to the yellow tab marked "Comp I" and noticed two pages were out of order. Maybe I had mixed them up myself. I grabbed my science book and closed my locker. "Why were you looking for me before?"

"I wanted to ask you something about Stan," she said, starry-eyed.

I should've known. Between Andie and Kayla, I almost wished Uncle Jack and my cousins had stayed in Pennsylvania. Well, not really—then Mom wouldn't be having fun going on dates with Uncle Jack . . . and I wouldn't be ready for a new tax bracket, thanks to all the baby-sitting money I was hauling in.

"Just tell me one thing," Andie continued. "Is Stan going to the ice-cream social on Saturday?" She grabbed my arm. "Because if he is, I need a new outfit."

"You do not," I said. "Besides, he doesn't even know about it. Uncle Jack's been trying out different churches since they moved here."

"Can't *you* invite him?" she pleaded.

"I could, but I won't." I headed for science class and opened the door to the stairwell. There stood Kayla. "Hey," I said, brushing past her on my way to first period. She'd been driving me crazy, too, with her phone calls every single night of my life since our chat in front of the Soda Straw last week.

"Wait . . . Holly!" Kayla called, running up the stairs after me. "Will you give this to Stan for me?" She held out an envelope, sealed and addressed with his name.

"Why me?" I stared at it. A hint of sweet perfume rose out of the paper.

Andie pushed past me, scowling at Kayla. "Leave Stan alone!" Andie said.

Kayla's note to Stan fell to the steps.

"Excuse me!" I said, scurrying up the steps, leaving Andie and Kayla alone with their common misery.

After school—volleyball! Danny met me as usual. I was hesitant to see him. The past week had been very up and down between us. If it wasn't his health kick, it was his concern over my relationship with Stan. Then there was the constant quoting from Scripture. Our friendship was in trouble, and nothing I could say seemed to make a difference. He was even opposed to my reading so many mysteries. *Might not be good for you, all that detective stuff,* he'd said at lunch yesterday.

More than ever, I wondered what I'd seen in him in the first place. "How's the team?" he asked, interrupting my thoughts.

"The team's fine. But Stan's still a pain." I nodded my head toward my cousin, who was writing on his clipboard like some hot shot.

"Why? What's up with him?" Danny asked.

"Just watch," I said, hurrying to take my spot on the court. As I rushed across the court, I nearly plowed into Jared, who had appeared out of nowhere.

The volleyball game began. Our first serve flew over the net. It came back high and short, so I spiked the ball, giving us a point.

Later, when I was up to serve, Stan blew his whistle at me. "Watch your right leg, Holly," he yelled.

I looked down and discovered I was nowhere near the boundary line. Taking a tiny step backward, I served.

Net ball. It was Stan's fault for picking on me. A few minutes later he blew his whistle at me again. "Carrying!" he shouted. He pointed at the other side. "Your serve."

I turned to Miss Tucker, who sat on the bench. "Coach?"

She nodded her head, agreeing with Stan.

Just then Paula Miller, Kayla's twin, showed up. She sat down on the front row of the bleachers, her eyes glued to Jared, who was standing on the opposite side of the gym.

Kayla served next. We volleyed back and forth three times before I set it up for Amy-Liz, who spiked it over. When it came back low, I stretched to reach under the ball but fell out of bounds trying.

Stan blew his whistle while I lay sprawled on the floor. I wanted to wrap his precious whistle around his neck.

Danny came over. "You okay?"

"See what I mean?" I whispered to him, getting up.

"It *does* seem like he's singling you out."

"It's not fair. Stan's picking on me for no reason."

Folding his arms, Danny said, " 'Be at peace with each other,' Mark 9:50 says."

I glared at him. He was preaching again, and it bugged me worse than ever.

Jared wandered over, eyeing Stan. "What's he think he's doing?"

I shrugged, feeling strange about all this attention.

Stan blew his whistle again. "Take your position, Holly," he called.

"You better quit picking on me," I said right in his face.

Kayla pointed to the spot next to her. "Play here, Holly. Please?"

"Oh no, you don't. If you want info about Stan, ask him yourself."

"Hol-ly," she whined.

I moved to another spot, away from the schizoid-crazy female. Danny sat on the sidelines, watching Stan like a hawk. Jared sat high in the bleachers, cheering every shot I made. Kayla kept looking at me, even though I tried my best to ignore her. And Paula? She looked like a droopy-eyed cocker spaniel because of Jared.

At last, practice was over. Kayla sauntered over to Danny, probably as an excuse to get close to Stan. But Danny ignored her, peering over Stan's shoulder, studying his clipboard. I should've been thrilled to have a guy looking out for me like that, but the real excitement was coming from high in the bleachers. I could feel Jared's eyes on me, even though I refused to satisfy him with a glance.

I dashed to the locker room, hoping to escape a lecture from Stan . . . and to get away from Danny, who seemed to have a Bible verse for everything lately. Taking my time, I dragged out my shower and hid in the locker room until I was sure Stan and Danny were gone.

Sneaking past the doors leading to the gym, I headed for the hall to my locker. The door creaked open, and I heard my name. It was Stan. The whistle still hung from his neck as he called to me.

"What do you want?" I growled.

"Look," he said, catching up with me. "I don't know what's bugging you, cuz, but—"

"Me? Why don't you get rid of that stupid whistle for starters!"

He laughed. "You think you're so hot, Holly, but you're not as good as you think you are."

"I'd play better if you weren't breathing down my neck every second." I flung my hair off my shoulder.

"Blame it on me, if you want. I'm just doing what I do best."

"Right. Making a jerk of yourself, bossing people around."

"So *that's* it. You can't handle your cousin calling the shots." He put his hand on his hip.

I clenched my fist. "This was *my* school first."

"Well, it's my school now." His lips curled into a sickening smile.

"You really have an attitude problem," I said, tapping my toe as hard as I could.

He laughed under his breath. "So . . . we're stuck in the same school. What's the big deal?"

"Yeah," I mumbled, looking away. "Stuck, all right."

"Listen, Holly." He sounded serious. "I don't like this thing between my dad and your mom any more than you do."

I couldn't believe my ears.

"You're way off base. Their dating has nothing to do with us."
I stared him down.

"Well, Danny thinks so."

I was shocked.

"He thinks you're mad at me because my dad's dating your
mom."

"Well, he's wrong," I said, turning to go. "I like the idea of your
dad taking Mom out. She's having fun for a change. And Danny
has no right to stick his nose in our family." I shifted my gym bag
to my right shoulder.

"Whatever." Stan shoved open the gym door with a mighty
push as he left.

So much for confiding in Danny. Be at peace with each other,
huh? *Well, Danny better learn to practice what he preaches instead
of stirring up trouble.*

I dashed down the hall, opened my locker, and buried my
head inside. It was a mess in there. Usually my things were super
organized, but my volleyball schedule was making neatness impossible. I pulled everything out of my locker and sat on the floor,
sorting . . . and letting the anger pour out.

Soon I heard footsteps. I spun around, expecting to see Stan
again.

But this time it was Jared.

"Need some help?" he asked.

"What are you doing here?" I flipped through my assignment
book.

"Waiting to see you." His smooth voice reminded me of last
year when I first met him.

I avoided his eyes. "Danny might not—"

"Danny left about thirty minutes ago."

I was curious. "Did he say anything before he left?"

"Only that you needed space to work things out with your
cousin." He came over and leaned against Andie's locker.

"There he goes second-guessing me again. Some nerve after he
interferes with my family." I made a pile of papers on the floor.

Jared picked up my books. "Wish I could help."

"It's no use," I said, organizing everything inside my locker. "I have to work this out myself."

"Okay, but remember—I'm here if you need me."

I wanted to cover my ears and run away. "Please, not now, Jared. Don't do this, okay?"

"Just tell me one thing, Holly, and I'll leave," he said, his face looking truly serious. "If I can prove I've changed, will you give me a second chance?" He stood tall, almost stiff . . . waiting.

Words escaped me as I stared in disbelief at Jared.

He turned to go. "Think about it, Holly. Maybe I'll see you at the Soda Straw on Saturday."

I could only nod as he turned and walked away. Strange. This was the very thing I'd dreamed up for my creative writing assignment. But was it actually possible for a boy like Jared to change? And how would Danny feel if I ended our special friendship for Jared, my first crush?

Chapter 8

At home, Carrie's announcement took my mind off things. "There's a huge envelope in the mail for you," she said the minute I stepped in the door.

"There is?" I followed her to the kitchen. On the desk was a pile of letters waiting to be opened. I picked up a manila envelope, eyeing the return address. Yes! Just what I'd been waiting for.

Reaching for a sharp knife from the wooden wall rack, I carefully sliced it open. Inside, a typewritten letter was attached to my first soon-to-be published story, "Love Times Two."

"What is it?" Carrie asked, leaning on my arm.

"It's from Marty Leigh, the editor of *Sealed With a Kiss,* a new teen magazine."

"Can I see it?"

"Let me read it first." I held the embossed stationery, reading every word before handing it to Carrie. Enclosed was a copy of my story with red markings in the margin. I scanned the manuscript. Marty Leigh had written suggestions for revisions. And if I worked hard, I could whip my story into shape for the very first issue.

"Wow! Fifty bucks. You're gonna be rich," Carrie said, reading the letter.

"That's not rich. I make almost that much in one evening

baby-sitting for you and our cousins." I slid the letter and story back into the envelope. "Where's Mom?"

"Buying stuff for my birthday. What are *you* getting me with all your money?"

"It's a secret." I scampered off to my room, carrying the phone with me.

Carrie bounded up the steps after me. "Can't you give me one little hint?"

"I haven't bought your gift yet," I answered absently, pulling my journal out of its usual place.

"Phooey," Carrie said, trudging out of my room and back downstairs.

I closed my bedroom door, got settled on my window seat, and began writing.

Thursday, September 30: The best thing about today came in the mail. I might become published this year. The worst thing that happened was my fight with Stan after volleyball practice. He's turning into an impossible snob. I can't begin to imagine what Andie or Kayla sees in him. Maybe it's his good looks, but blue-eyed blonds are a dime a dozen around here.

Jared's acting strange. Not his usual flirty-strange. Something's different. He wants a second chance, but I don't think I can trust him again. And then there's Danny—he's getting more and more preachy every day. Besides, he said stuff to Stan about Mom and Uncle Jack dating that really got me wound up. Sometimes I think we were better off just friends.

The doorbell rang.

I called down to Carrie. "Look out the window before you answer it."

"It's Andie. Should I let her in?"

"Of course, silly." I sat on the top step, waiting for my best friend.

She wore dark blue jeans and a hooded sweat shirt. "Hey, what's up?" she asked, taking the steps two at a time.

"You'll never believe it," I said, leading the way to my room.

"Try me." She closed the door behind us.

I poured out my woes, first about Stan, then about Jared. Andie's eyes grew wider with each new detail. "I can't believe Stan would treat you that way," she said finally. "He's just so . . . so wonderful."

"Well, it's true." I leaned against the pillows piled up on my bed.

"Jared's another story. You can't trust him, Holly, not for a single minute. In fact, I guarantee he's the same smooth-talker he ever was."

"But what if for some reason he really wants to change?"

Andie looked shocked. "You've really lost it, Holly."

Our eyes locked for an instant, then I turned away.

She touched my arm. "I think I know what your real problem is," she said more softly. "You never quit liking Jared."

"Maybe . . . I don't know."

"Well, he hurt you once; he'll do it again." She slid over beside me. "Besides, what would make him want to change?"

I toyed with telling her about my story featuring the transformation of Jared Wilkins, only not using his actual name. But she'd never let me live it down.

"You're better off liking Danny," she said. "Even though he's downright pompous sometimes. Just because he remembers Bible verses is no excuse for using them on his friends. He told me the other day that I should read Proverbs 21:23. When I went home and looked it up, I nearly choked."

"Why?"

"Are you ready for this? 'He who guards his mouth and his tongue keeps himself from calamity.' Hey, he could've just come out and said I talk too much."

I giggled.

"One thing, though, now I'll probably never forget that verse. So I guess in some ways Danny's not so bad."

"Maybe, but he and I got along lots better before he started bossing me around. It's maddening." I scooted off the bed, picking up my binder off the floor.

"*Now* what are you doing?" Andie asked.

"If you promise not to try to change my mind, I'll let you in on a secret."

She pulled up her socks. "I knew it. I just knew those little wheels were turnin' inside that brain of yours. Holly Meredith, you're up to no good."

"Here's my plan. Since Jared seems positively sincere about wanting me back—even said he'd prove that he's changed—I've come up with the perfect plan."

Andie leaned forward, all ears. "Like what?"

"A test."

"What kind of test?"

"A test designed to analyze his behavior." I flipped through the binder to locate my outline. "Here, check this out."

"Whoa, Holly, you're not kidding, are you? That's one hefty checklist. He'll never make it, you know."

"There's more. I want you to help me."

"Me? How?"

"By being your charming self. You know, smile at him, ask him to sit with you at youth meetings, call him. Stuff like that."

"He'll think you put me up to it, Holly. It'll never work."

"Maybe it will, maybe it won't. But it's worth a try. Please, Andie?"

She twisted a curl around her finger. "If I *do* cooperate with your little scheme, what will you do for me?"

I leaped to my closet. "Choose anything you see. You can wear anything in my closet for as long as you want."

"Good try, Holly, but you've overlooked one tiny detail."

"Oh?" I said, playing innocent.

"You're a size three and I'm a size, uh . . . bigger."

"Well, then, what about jewelry, books, teddy bears?"

"We *already* traded our favorite bears, remember?" she said, still playing my game.

"So." I turned to the mirror. "What is it you want?" I brushed my hair, knowing exactly what she'd say.

"Stan, your cousin. Can you deliver him to me?"

"You want him baked, boiled, or fried?" I faced her. "After everything you know about my cousin, you're still nuts over him?"

"What about you and Jared? I think I see a parallel. And you can't say one word about it, because in my opinion, you're doing worse. Much worse."

She had a point. I knew Stan was wrong for her, and she felt the same about Jared. I sighed. "Who knows if I can talk Stan into anything right now. We're not exactly on the best terms."

Andie leaped off my bed. "I've got it. Invite him to the ice-cream social. Tell him you want to introduce him to all the kids at your church. When it comes to tables, make sure Stan sits across from you and Danny. Then leave the rest to me. Okay?"

No way would Stan attend a social with *my* church group.

Andie smiled up into my face. "You don't want to be stuck with Danny all year, now, do you?"

I pulled on my braid. It wouldn't be easy getting Stan to show up on Saturday, but in order to get Andie's help with observing Jared, I had to. "Okay, it's a deal," I said. "Here, let's sign a secret pact." I reached for my journal, found today's entry, and neatly printed the plan.

At the bottom of the page, Andie scribbled her name and the date. I wrote my name in my best cursive, under hers.

It was done. We had a pact.

Chapter 9

The minute Andie disappeared, I phoned Stan. "Patterson Consulting." It was Uncle Jack.

"Hi, it's Holly. Is Stan home?"

"Hi, kiddo. Let's see if I can scrounge him up for you."

Uncle Jack was like that. Upbeat and . . . awfully cool. I couldn't remember ever seeing him grump around. Even when Aunt Marla died, he had been sad, not crabby.

Soon he was back on the line. "Stan says he's busy. I tried to hog-tie him and drag him over here, but I couldn't hold him down long enough to get him tied up to haul."

I laughed. "So, what you're really saying is Stan refuses to talk to me?"

"Don't take it seriously, cutie. Your oldest cousin is in a blue funk."

"Blue funk?"

"Ever been there?" he asked with a chuckle.

"He's like . . . depressed, is that it?"

"Come to think of it, depressed is a step up from blue funk."

I remembered the dumb stuff Stan and I had said to each other after school. "I guess I can't blame him. His bad mood may be partly my fault."

"Well, is there a message I can zap him with . . . from you, I mean?"

"Tell him my church youth group is having an ice-cream social at the Soda Straw this Saturday at two-thirty. And . . . I'm inviting him."

"Sounds delicious," Uncle Jack said. "Anyone else Stan might know?"

"Lots of girls." I laughed.

"I'll tell him. That oughta make some points."

"Thanks," I said, feeling weird about Uncle Jack being in the middle of my plan.

"The social may be just what Stan needs," admitted my uncle.

I had no idea what Uncle Jack meant, and I sure wasn't going to push for more information. We said good-bye and hung up.

After school on Friday there was a long volleyball practice beginning with three laps around the gym. Miss Tucker—not Stan—called the shots today, carrying the clipboard around, smoothing her short dark hair, blowing the whistle. Stan kept score while Kayla flashed her sugar-wide smile at him every few minutes. So disgusting.

Stan looked positively bummed out, like he'd lost his best friend or something. After practice he called me over to the bench. "What's this about Saturday?"

"Just an ice-cream bash with a bunch of kids," I said coolly, secretly hoping he was interested.

"Yeah?" He thought for a moment, then looked up at me. He wore a kind, almost pained expression. "Sure, I'll be there."

What could be wrong? I had more sense than to ask. Didn't want to spoil this breakthrough.

"Okay, see ya." I hurried to the locker room, changed clothes without showering, and raced home to phone Andie.

Saturday was Carrie's birthday. Uncle Jack showed up before she finished breakfast. He winked at me as he and Stephanie escorted the birthday girl out of the house.

As soon as they backed out of the driveway, Mom scurried around, opening kitchen cupboards, pulling out party supplies. "Want to help me decorate the dining room?" she asked.

"Perfect." I reached for the pink-colored rolls of crepe paper lined up on the kitchen bar. Decorating for parties was one of my favorite things. I wanted to transform our dining room into a magical maze of pink clouds whispering against the ceiling-sky. Balloons would shimmy beneath the crepe paper canopy and dance to the birthday song.

I slid a chair close to the corner and went to work. "Wish I could see Carrie's face when she gets home."

"She'll be very surprised," Mom said from the kitchen.

I twisted and looped until the dining room seemed to disappear. In its place was a merry party land fit for a nine-year-old princess. Taking a giant breath, I began blowing up balloons.

Mom came in just then, gazing in awe at my creation. "It's wonderful, Holly. You've outdone yourself."

My cheeks burned from balloon blowing, and I stopped to catch my breath. "I could use Stan's help right now. He's the best balloon blower-upper I know."

Mom straightened the tablecloth. "He may not be the best help now. His girlfriend back East just broke up with him."

No wonder he looked so depressed yesterday. But what fabulous timing. Andie would be delirious with this news. "That's too bad," I said, feeling a tiny bit sorry for my schizoid cousin.

"Maybe you could introduce him to some of the girls in your youth group." Mom had a twinkle in her eye. "It would be nice if Stan had a church home, uh, with us, you know."

I clued in to what she was getting at. "And wouldn't it be nice if Uncle Jack went to the same church as we do, too?"

She blushed and headed into the kitchen to bake Carrie's birthday cake.

♥ ♥ ♥

By two-thirty the Soda Straw was packed with ice-cream fanatics. Danny, prompt as usual, waved to me from the booth in the corner. I slid into the seat across from him. He looked puzzled, probably about the seating arrangement I'd chosen.

I picked up a menu and explained. "We need to save space for my cousin Stan. He's coming to eat ice cream with us."

"Okay with me," Danny said. "You and Stan must've patched things up."

"Not really. I'm just trying to befriend the new kid on the block."

Kayla and Paula arrived wearing look-alike dresses. Carrot-orange . . . like two-legged vegetables. Even the identical ponytails, pulled carelessly to the back of their heads, stuck out like the tassels on homegrown carrots. Next came Amy-Liz with her friends Shauna and Joy. Billy Hill and Jared arrived together, followed by Stan and a bunch of others.

Where was Andie?

I excused myself and rushed over to Stan. In order to keep my part of the pact, I had to get Stan to sit with Danny and me at our booth.

"Wanna sit with Danny and me?" I asked.

Stan nodded as we passed a table of girls, including Kayla, who suddenly looked more like a smiley pumpkin than a boring carrot with her sugar-sweet grin.

Jared merely smiled as we swept past him. In a strange sort of way, I missed his winks.

When we got settled in at our table, the waitress came around and we ordered. A strawberry sundae with three scoops of ice cream for me, a root beer float for Danny, and for Stan, who sat across the table from us, a banana split.

Danny and Stan began talking immediately, discussing favorite sports figures. "Want to borrow my book on Tony Dungy?" Danny asked him.

"Sure," Stan said. "Thanks."

It wasn't long, and the waitress brought our desserts. I glanced at my watch. Two-forty-five. What was taking Andie so long?

Dipping into the giant sundae in front of me, I fumed. This wasn't like Andie. Where *was* she?

I spooned up my ice cream, instantly retreating into strawberry heaven. "There's nothing like strawberry ice cream," I said as Danny stared.

"You're going to eat *all* that?" he said.

I snickered. "Watch me."

Stan leaned forward on his elbows. "You haven't seen nothin' yet. Holly devours ice cream like it's rare and endangered."

Danny kept staring. "Won't you get sick?" he asked. "Shouldn't you go easy?"

I didn't like the tone of his voice. Why couldn't he mind his own business?

Pastor Rob wandered over. "Hey," he said, shaking hands with Stan. "Are you a friend of Holly's?"

"We're cousins," Stan said, introducing himself. "I just moved to town."

I noticed Kayla creeping up behind our youth pastor. She'd locked her cat eyes on Stan, watching his every move.

Ding-a-ding-a-ling.

Andie came in the door just then, pushing a double-wide twin stroller. All heads turned as my best friend made her grand entrance with her baby brothers dressed in matching Winnie the Pooh outfits.

"Holly . . . hey," she said, heading over to our table. She parked the stroller in the aisle, and girls came from all directions. They even stumbled over each other to get to adorable Jon and Chris. "Help yourself," she said, handing Jon to Shauna.

Chris whimpered when he spied my sundae. "Here, you go to Auntie Holly," Andie said, picking him up and planting him on my lap.

Chris clapped as I gave him a taste of my ice cream.

"Now, there's a smart kid," Stan said with a grin.

But Danny looked worried. "Can he eat sweets at his age?"

"Lighten up," I whispered. "Two-year-olds can eat most anything."

Shauna quickly returned little Jon to Andie. Jon must've seen me feeding Chris, because he let out a wail. "It's okay, buddy, you can share some of mine," Andie told him. Then she began to work her magic on Stan. She rocked Jon from side to side, standing beside our table, talking baby talk to her brothers, chatting with Stan and Danny and me. I almost asked her to sit with us but remembered she wanted to handle things *her* way.

The waitress checked on our table, her order pad poised. "Any other orders here?" she asked.

"Yes, please." Andie leaned over with Jon in her arms and reached for the menu on the table. "Can you hold him a sec?" she asked Stan.

"Fork him over." Stan slid over against the wall to let Andie into the booth beside him.

Amazing, I thought, pushing the gooshy remains of my sundae aside.

"Anything else?" the waitress asked.

"May I please have an order of fries?" I asked.

Danny stared at me as the waitress nodded and cleared away my ice-cream dish.

"Like I said," Stan said. "You haven't seen nothin' yet!" While my cousin held little Jon, the toddler pulled on the pocket of his shirt with sloppy wet fingers. But it didn't seem to faze Stan at all.

"You're really good with kids," Andie said.

Stan nodded and smiled, then made funny faces to make Jon laugh.

Kayla swaggered over to our table. "Looks like you could use some help here." She reached for Chris, who was bouncing and chattering on my lap. Then she stood there with him, smiling at Stan, who was too busy with Jon to notice. Soon she left, taking chubby Chris back to her table, where her sister and three other girls were sitting.

When the waitress returned with my fries, I salted them and poured ketchup off to the side.

Danny cleared his throat. "Any idea what Proverbs 23:20-21 says?"

"Let me guess. Something about eating too much?" I smiled when Andie raised her eyebrows.

"Go ahead, tell her," Stan said, egging him on. "Let her have it."

Danny began to recite, " 'Do not join those who drink too much wine or gorge themselves on meat, for drunkards and gluttons become poor, and drowsiness clothes them in rags.' "

Andie clapped. I boiled. This wasn't funny.

The other kids were settled at tables all around the restaurant, oblivious to what was happening. Slowly, I turned to face Danny. "Do you have any idea how high and mighty your remarks are?"

"They're God's words, not mine," Danny said solemnly, still scowling at my French fries.

"Okay, then, what about *this* verse? First Corinthians 10:31: 'So whether you eat or drink or whatever you do, do it all for the glory of God.' "

"Bravo!" Andie said.

I glared at her. "Stay out of this."

Her eyes widened as I took another bite.

Stan, embarrassed, excused himself, sliding out of the booth with little Jon. Andie moved out to make room for him. She shot me a weird look and helped Stan buckle Jon into the stroller.

"I need some fresh air," Stan said, heading away from us, stroller and all.

"Just great, Danny," I said. "Look what you've done. My cousin shows up for the first time for our youth group, and you go and scare him off."

"Doesn't look like he's too scared to me."

I turned to see Stan and Andie settling in at a quiet corner booth across the room. Looked like Andie was doing just fine without me. Mr. Macho Man pushed the stroller back and forth with his foot, while Andie chattered away.

Talk about split personality. Maybe now Andie would see Stan for who he was. How could a guy sneer at his cousin and carry on with two-year-olds all in the same day?

Disgusted, I turned my attention back to my French fries. "Well, never mind about Stan and Andie," I told Danny. "*We* aren't getting along. Not even close!"

"We aren't?" Danny pushed his glass away and leaned on his elbow, frowning. "You're upset again, is that it?"

"Look, do I have to spell this out for you?" I stood up.

He leaned back against the red vinyl seat, folding his arms. *Oh fabulous,* I thought. *He has to think this one through.*

I couldn't see myself hanging around for one of his profound responses. I grabbed my jacket and purse. "Bye, Danny," I said, heading for the door.

Under my breath, I said, "Good-bye forever."

Chapter 10

I stomped down the sidewalk and headed across the street toward the park, inhaling the brisk mountain air. Telling Danny off wasn't as hard as I'd thought it would be. In fact, I hadn't even planned on doing it—it just happened! And I didn't feel one bit sorry.

When I spotted the swing sets in the park, I began to run. I needed to put some distance between me and bossy Danny Myers.

The park was buzzing with the sounds of little kids. Some were hanging upside down on the monkey bars, others were swinging higher than high, and three girls sat digging in the sandbox. Finding my favorite wooden bench near a clump of aspen trees, I sat down to think. Thinking didn't always solve everything, but it helped. Not as much as praying, though.

The sun felt warm on my back, so I unzipped my jacket. Leaning back, I observed a giant cloud formation. A two-headed monster with floppy ears and a bushy mustache grinned down at me. Slowly . . . slowly, his grin faded and a triple-decker strawberry sundae took its place.

Ice cream!

I sat up thinking of the ice cream and French fries I'd ordered. Then I snickered. Danny had been stuck with the bill, and it served him right for hounding me about my food cravings. Somehow, hard as I tried, I couldn't picture *Jared* acting that way.

Shoving thoughts of Danny out of my mind, I pulled a small tablet out of my purse and began writing my list from memory.

Jared must observe all of the following until Thanksgiving Day.
> *1. No flirting.*
> *2. No talking to girls.*
> *3. Must not accept phone calls from girls.*
> *4. Must not accept letters, notes, or cards from girls.*
> *5. Must not . . .*

I felt someone watching me. Looking up, I jumped. It was none other than Jared Wilkins. He was gazing at me intently, holding my container of French fries. "Still hungry?" he asked.

I reached for it, smiling. "Thanks."

"No problem." He was still standing behind me, his brown hair picking up highlights from the sun.

"Did you see what happened with Danny and me back there?" I popped a French fry into my mouth.

"It was pretty obvious, don't you think?"

"How'd you know I'd be here?" I asked.

"I pay close attention to details." He winked. Then he grabbed my tablet off the bench.

"Jared . . . no!" I leaped up, reaching for my tablet. "That's private!"

But he twisted away, and before I could stop him, he'd opened it.

"Some list you've got going," he said, smiling.

"That's none of your business," I insisted.

"Does this mean I get the second chance we talked about?" he asked, holding the tablet high over his head.

"*We* didn't talk about any such thing."

"Oh, you're right. It was my idea." He handed the tablet back to me, leaning on the bench. "But you won't be sorry if you do."

"I haven't promised anything." I stepped back, secretly admiring him.

"But you are thinking about it, aren't you?" He was pushing the second-chance idea hard. But why?

"Just look at the list again." I opened the tablet and handed it to him. "I made it impossible, as you can see."

"Whatever it takes," he said, scanning the page, then shifting his gaze to me. A smile crept across his handsome face.

"What's this *really* about, Jared?" I set my fries aside. "Why do you want to prove you're not a flirt anymore?"

"You want the truth?"

I nodded, waiting for his answer.

His eyes grew sober. "There's only one reason." He took a deep breath. "I *miss* you, Holly. I want us to get along much better than before."

My heart beat wildly. What was a girl to do? The best-looking guy in the entire universe had just declared his feelings. And I came *that* close to believing him!

I mustered up enough courage to spell out my plan. "Okay, here's the deal," I said, taking the tablet back. "I make a list of do's and don'ts . . ."

I needed a name for my outrageous plan—fast. So I chose the same name I'd used in my story. "Uh, we'll call it the Scrutiny Test to Analyze Nascence. You sign on the dotted line, and I watch and wait."

"Nascence?" he said, coming around and sitting in the grass in front of me. "*That's* a word?"

"Nascence is birth or growth . . . maturity. Like when a Christian reads the Bible and talks to God every day. Change happens—like a metamorphosis."

"Sounds like Danny-speak," he said.

I gasped. "Oh no. Really?"

He shook his head. "Just kidding." Then he said, "Where do you get these words, anyway, Holly?"

"I read a lot. Sometimes even the dictionary."

"The dictionary?" His eyes grew wide.

"Well, just when I'm bored."

Stretching his arms over his head, he studied me. At least he wasn't laughing. Not yet. "And what if I pass this Scrutiny Test to Analyze the Nascence of Jared Wilkins. What then?"

"What do you mean?" I said, knowing exactly what he was getting at.

"Will you be my girlfriend then?"

I laughed. "There's *no way* you'll pass."

He leaned forward, looking more thoughtful than ever. "But what if I do?"

"I can't promise anything." It sounded heartless, but this boy had a reputation for flirting that didn't quit. No way would it disappear in two months . . . or at all.

He reached over and picked up the French fry dish. "Guess I better return this to the Soda Straw." Standing up, he brushed the grass from his faded jeans. "So when do we start this test of yours?"

"Tomorrow." I stood up quickly. "And to keep it secret, let's use the code word STAN—for Scrutiny Test to Analyze Nascence— get it? It'll be perfect at school. Kids will think we're talking about my cousin."

I thought it might even drive Stan Patterson crazy if he overheard us talking about STAN. Who knows, it might irritate that stupid whistle off his neck. It was the perfect code word. I was a genius, after all!

"Whatever the writer says," Jared replied.

"I'll get to work on it." Then I remembered the rewrite on "Love Times Two." "Wait. I can't have STAN ready by tomorrow."

"Why not?" He looked positively crushed as he fell into step with me, heading for the street.

I told him about the new teen magazine *Sealed With a Kiss*. "The first issue comes out next month. Short stories for girls only."

"Who's the editor?"

"Marty Leigh, the best mystery writer of all time."

"I've heard of her. Where's her magazine published?"

I told him, wondering why he was so interested.

"I have to read your story when it comes out," he said. "Now, how soon can we start STAN?"

"Monday," I said. "That'll give me the rest of the weekend to plan it."

We were coming up on the Soda Straw. I hung back when Paula and Kayla—the orange-dress wonders—slinked down the steps waiting for Amy-Liz and her friends. Then I spotted Danny and Billy leaving the restaurant together.

"Guess you'd better go in without me," I said.

"Yeah, I see what you mean," Jared said, slowing his pace.

"Besides," I added, "this could be your last chance to flirt before STAN starts."

Jared smiled the dearest smile ever. "Test or no test, those days are over now, Holly. You'll see."

I couldn't believe my ears. His words sounded like something straight out of my story assignment for Miss W's composition class!

My heart sank as Jared ran across the street to the Soda Straw. I missed him already. Too bad. There was no chance this side of the continental divide that the two-timer could ever *truly* reform deep down.

I ran to catch the city bus, slipping into a seat on the side facing the Soda Straw—hoping for one last glance of Jared.

He dashed up the walkway and toward the door without so much as a fleeting look at Paula Miller or any of the other girls. Amazing. But was this too good to be true?

Chapter 11

I hopped off the bus a block away from Explore Bookstore. Carrie's birthday party was probably going strong about now. I could almost hear the kids singing "Happy Birthday."

Soft music greeted me as I opened the door to my favorite bookstore. Busy as usual. I headed to the stationery section. A diary was the perfect birthday gift for my sister. Now that she was nine, she could start to record the events of her life.

An array of diaries and journals of all styles, colors, and sizes were lined up on the shelf. Clothbound ones with pink polka-dot hearts and others wearing funky leopard print. There were five-year diaries with teeny-tiny locks and keys no bigger than a fat toothpick, and flowery ones with famous sayings inside. I stepped closer, opening the one with the tiny lock and key.

Behind me, I heard familiar voices. Turning, I noticed the Miller twins coming into the store. They saw me, too. I waved but secretly wished they'd leave me alone.

My wish didn't work. Here they came, all smiles—those sugary ones. Kayla spoke first. "Hey, Holly. Buying a diary?"

"For my little sister," I said, half ignoring her.

"I need to talk to you." She moved closer. "Is Stan interested in Andie?"

I shrugged. "Don't know."

"They sat together at the Soda Straw, playing with Andie's baby brothers for the longest time," she said, prying for answers.

"I honestly don't know, Kayla," I said, inspecting a red five-year diary.

Paula spoke up. "What about Danny Myers?"

"What about him?" I kept my eyes on the row of journals.

"Are you still together?"

"What do *you* think?" I turned to see two sets of made-up brown eyes. Exactly alike.

"Andie said you and Danny had a fight," Paula continued. "And you called it quits, and Jared ran off after you."

"People come and people go," I said flippantly. *How nosy can you get?*

It was Kayla's turn. "Paula likes Jared, you know." She glanced at her twin, smiling.

"Really?" I said coolly, wondering why Paula couldn't speak for herself. It made me feel weird seeing her all batty-eyed over Jared while I planned a scrutiny test to prove he was still a jerk.

Wait a minute! A brilliant idea struck just then. Paula Miller could be prime Jared-bait. She was the perfect person to assist me with the STAN test.

"Jared's lonely these days. Maybe you could help cheer him up, Paula," I said.

She perked up her ears. "What do you mean?"

"He's gotten some lousy press from the girls in this town. A rumor's been going around about him being a smooth-talker, or . . . something like that."

Paula's eyes lit up. "Yeah, I know. Last spring when we first came to Dressel Hills, Andie warned us about him. She said he was rotten." She batted her mascara-laden lashes. "But he seems nice enough to me."

"Why don't you give him a call sometime soon?" I picked up the pink polka-dot diary.

"Are you and Jared friends?" Paula asked.

"Sure. We go back to seventh grade." I pulled out a scrap of paper and wrote down his phone number. "Here, call him tonight."

Her eyes sparkled, and the famous smile emerged. "Thanks, I will."

I ought to be the one thanking her! I thought, giddy all over.

Then Kayla stepped forward like she wanted to corner me. "What about Stan? Can you find out if he likes Andie?"

"Me?" I said, taking a step backward.

"You're his cousin. Please?" She was whining again. This was too much. Were my eyes playing tricks on me or what? The orange dresses were closing in—making me dizzy.

"All right, all right," I said, inching back. "I'll find out for you, Kayla, but right now I have to pick out a birthday present. See you two later." I charged between them, heading for the cash register with the five-year diary and the polka-dot heart diary in my hand.

"Two diaries today?" the cashier asked.

"Yes, please," I said. "One's for my little sis, and one's for my little STAN."

She rang up the bill, looking positively puzzled.

Back home, I helped Mom clean up Carrie's party mess. Actually, Uncle Jack had done most of it. Carrie wanted the streamers to stay up over the weekend, and Mom didn't mind.

"Happy birthday," I said, giving Carrie the bookstore bag.

"*Another* present?" Stephie glared at Carrie. "She's so lucky."

Uncle Jack stroked Stephie's curls. "It's her birthday, honey."

Carrie peeked inside the plastic bag. "*Two* diaries?"

"The fat one with the lock and key is for you," I said, pulling the polka-dot heart one out.

"Thanks, Holly." She played with the little key dangling from a red string.

"It's time you start writing down your secrets," I suggested.

Mom and Uncle Jack went to sit in the living room, holding hands as they sat on the sofa. I could hear computer game music floating up from the family room. "Phil and Mark must be downstairs," I said.

Uncle Jack nodded as I came into the room. "They're turning into game wizards." He chuckled his soft, comfortable laugh.

Carrie and Stephie knelt in the middle of the living room floor, checking out the diary's lock and key. Then Carrie eyed the diary in my hand. "Who's that one for?"

I flopped down on a corner of the sofa. "Oh, this is just for a little project of mine."

Carrie looked at me funny. "A secret project?"

"Well, sorta."

"You have too many secrets, Holly-Heart."

"But secrets are such fun," Mom said. Uncle Jack put his arm around her, and she snuggled next to him.

It was then I noticed the gold heart locket around Mom's neck. "Is *this* a secret?" I leaned over to touch it.

Mom looked at Uncle Jack, and a silly smile crept across her face. "It's our anniversary. Five weeks ago we had our first date."

Uncle Jack nodded, winking at me.

Counting weeks? This was serious!

"What's for supper?" I asked, unzipping my jacket and hanging it in the closet.

"How's Guiseppe's sound?" said Uncle Jack.

"Fabulous." I shut the closet door. "How soon?"

"Around six-thirty," Mom said.

"Perfect." There was plenty of time to work on the rewrite of my story for *Sealed With a Kiss*.

"How was the ice-cream social?" Mom asked.

"Okay, I guess."

"Just okay?" Mom quizzed me.

I wasn't going to recap the private—and disgusting—details of the Soda Straw scene. Not now.

"Did Stan show up?" Uncle Jack asked.

"Yeah, and he actually helped Andie baby-sit her brothers."
Mom's eyebrows arched. "Andie took Chris and Jon along?"
"She had her reasons."
"That seems odd," Mom said.

It was odd only if you didn't know how Andie's mind worked. She was a master manipulator, and right now she would do most anything to get Stan's attention.

Uncle Jack smiled knowingly as I headed for the stairs. He could explain Andie's reasoning to Mom.

In my room, I sat curled up on my window seat. Goofey came and snuggled with me. Mom had stuck him away in my room during Carrie's party. That way Uncle Jack's allergies wouldn't act up so much.

I began work on my rewrite of "Love Times Two." Marty Leigh was not only a terrific mystery writer, she was also a wonderful editor. The *only* editor I knew. Still, I was impressed with her suggestions for making my story better.

The doorbell rang, and I heard Stan's voice as he came in. Soon, loud shrieks floated up from the family room in the lower level. Phil and Mark were probably protesting having to switch off the computer game so Stan could watch sports on ESPN. That's how seniority worked around here. Stan, being the oldest, had final say. Just like with Carrie and me. Thank goodness my cousins only came over here a couple of times each week.

At Guiseppe's, all of us started out on our best behavior. Phil and Mark sat on either side of Stan. Uncle Jack sat next to Mom, and Stephie squeezed in on the other side. Carrie and I waited as the waitress moved another table over, making room for us.

After we ordered, I studied Stephie's face. She looked like a seven-year-old version of Aunt Marla. Having your mother die had to be the worst thing in the world. Worse than divorce. I couldn't imagine growing up without Mom. She was fabulous.

The waitress brought our soda around. "Special night?" she

asked, smiling at Mom and Uncle Jack, who looked positively in love.

Uncle Jack pointed to Carrie. "This young lady is celebrating her birthday."

"Well, happy birthday, missy. Let's see what we can do about that," the waitress said, scurrying off.

Eight-year-old Mark blew bubbles in his soda.

"Cut it out, fish lips," Stan said, frowning.

"Leave me alone," Mark shot back.

"*That* can be arranged," Stan said, acting sophisticated as he turned to eye two cute girls at another table.

Phil dumped red pepper flakes into his hand, then licked them off his palm.

"Ew!" I said. "How can you eat that stuff?"

"It's good," replied the ten-year-old with the iron tongue.

"Let me try," Mark said, reaching for the shaker.

"Let's try our manners on for size tonight," Uncle Jack said, taking the shaker away and casting a disapproving glance at the boys. "Remember, we're out with the ladies."

Mom giggled, leaning against him.

Oh puh-leeze, I thought. This was getting out of hand. Mom was acting like a schoolgirl.

Halfway through pizza munching, the manager and all the waitresses gathered at our table. Our waitress asked Carrie her name, then the group clicked their fingers six times before singing their birthday song. Carrie soaked up the attention. Stephie looked a little jealous as she leaned on Uncle Jack's arm.

Later, after the birthday hoopla had died down, Stan raised the red flag at our table. Before you could count to ten, our waitress appeared to refill his soda glass.

Carrie gasped. "Oh no, that reminds me. . . ." She stared at the flag. "I forgot about my Columbus report."

"When's it due?" I asked.

"Tuesday. I'll never get it done in time." She touched the flag at our table. "This reminded me."

Mom looked confused. "Why the flag?"

"When Columbus got to San Salvador, he put a flag in the ground to . . ."

" . . . stake his claim for Spain," I finished. "You have nothing to worry about, Carrie. I remember all that stuff from grade school. I'll help you with your report."

"Goodie!" she said, and with that, reached for another slice of pizza.

A very loud *bu-u-rp* came from Phil's direction. He burst into hysterical laughter. So did Mark.

"Philip Patterson," Uncle Jack said sternly. We all stared, embarrassed. "What do you say for yourself?"

Phil turned redder than the little flag. "Excuse me, please," he mumbled.

I wanted to hide under the table. These boys needed a mother . . . like now. Then it dawned on me: *My* mother was the only candidate. I shuddered. It was fine for her to have fun on dates with Uncle Jack, but all of a sudden I realized we were sitting at Guiseppe's eating pizza like a regular family. And *certain* members of the family were behaving badly.

I glared at Phil and little Mark. And at Stan, who sat between them doing absolutely nothing but stuff his face with pizza. Carrie's birthday had turned into a horrible event. Was this a sneak preview of coming attractions?

Chapter 12

Later that night, I helped Carrie with her Columbus project. Thank goodness we had encyclopedia software for the computer. This way we could get the actual dates and details an eighth grader forgets after five years. Even after Carrie finished with her information, I continued to sit at the computer and read.

"Thanks for helping me," Carrie said, then left my room.

"Be sure to write your best," I called after her.

"Do I *have* to?"

"You want a good grade, don't you?" I closed my bedroom door and opened the bottom drawer of my dresser. The new pink polka-dotted journal was waiting to be filled with do's and don'ts for Jared. I reached for it, anxious to launch STAN.

An hour later the phone rang.

"It's for you, Holly," Carrie called to me.

I raced to the hall phone. "Hello?"

"Hi, Holly. It's Paula Miller."

"Hey."

"Something very weird just happened," she said.

I couldn't imagine what she was talking about. "What?"

"I called Jared, you know, like you told me to."

"Uh-huh."

"He said he couldn't talk to me and please not to call back."
She sighed. "It was just horrible."

I was stunned. "Maybe he was sick or something."

"Well, he seemed all right at the ice-cream social."

"You're right, he did," I said.

"What do you think's going on?" she asked breathlessly.

I didn't dare tell her. "Look, Paula, maybe he was just busy
or something. Why don't you try talking to him at church tomorrow?"

"Okay. Good idea," she said. "Bye."

I hung up, mystified . . . still trying to comprehend Paula's
words. Jared refused her phone call? This was unheard of. Besides,
STAN hadn't officially started yet!

On Sunday, Uncle Jack picked us up for church in his SUV. I
slid across the soft middle seat between Carrie and Stephie. The
boys sat in the back.

Mom looked radiant as we rode to our church. Uncle Jack's eyes
twinkled with the usual mischief as he stopped at the first traffic
light. But when I caught him watching Mom, I saw more than the
playful sparkle in his eyes. This was serious.

Mark hollered from the backseat, right in my ear. "Tomorrow's
Columbus Day!"

"No school," announced Carrie.

"Do you have off work?" I asked Mom.

"We all do, don't we, Jack?" she said, nodding her head.

"Hey, that's right, we do," he said. "Let's do something extra
special together."

"Like what?" Carrie asked.

"Like sleep in," hooted Stan from the back.

"Boring," Phil said.

"Yeah," said Mark. "Let's go hiking instead."

"Good idea, isn't it, dear?" Uncle Jack said, turning to look at Mom.

"We could pack our lunch and take it up Copper Mountain," Mom said.

"On the gondola," Uncle Jack said.

Not that. I just barely survived the sky ride last summer. Besides, those were the days when Danny and I were good friends. I didn't want to relive that particular time in my life. Remembering would make me feel lousy about storming out of the Soda Straw last weekend. True, Danny had annoyed me with his never-ending preaching, but was that a good reason for me to freak out and totally demolish our friendship?

"I'd rather not go on the gondola again," I told Mom.

"Aw, don't be scared," little Stephie said, holding my hand. "I'll ride with you."

Stan snickered behind me, and I whirled around.

"Keep quiet!" I snapped at him.

"What's the matter, you a scaredy-cat?" he taunted.

"I've been on the sky ride twice now," I said, remembering my father had said I'd gone with him when I was little.

"Well then, third time's a charm," Stan sneered.

I wanted to close his mouth permanently. Too late—the church was in sight. Uncle Jack pulled into the parking lot next to Andie's family's car. Mrs. Martinez was getting one of the twins out of his car seat. Chris, I thought it was.

Next thing I knew, Stan had hopped out of the van and was helping with little Chris. Talk about a splitzo schizoid. Stan was a prime example of it. If only Andie could see his nasty sneers and hear his snide remarks. But all she knew of him was *this* side of him—the Stan-to-the-rescue side.

Andie did some fast-talking and got her dad's permission to sit with Stan in church—with all nine of us in the same pew. I was closely observing Andie and Stan when a terrible thought hit me. What if someday she ended up married to Stanley Patterson? She'd be my cousin! The cousin part was fine; it was the wife-of-Stan part that worried me.

Soft organ music filled the church as people filed in. Across the aisle, Kayla Miller sat with her twin sister. *Someone ought to give her a crash course in being subtle,* I thought as she proceeded to gawk at Stan and Andie.

Jared and his parents came in together. He looked straight ahead as he passed the Miller twins. Poor Paula. She was going to have a tough time talking to him today. I, however, was very impressed.

Breathing deeply, I reached for the hymnal. Mom looked absolutely angelic sitting next to Uncle Jack on the far end of the pew. Was she ready to give up being single for this man? I wondered if Daddy had any idea Mom was dating again. And not only dating again, but dating Uncle Jack—his former brother-in-law.

When the sermon began, I had a hard time paying attention. Zillions of someday thoughts raced through my mind. My cousin with my best friend? Unthinkable! My uncle with my mom? Positively weird! My first crush, Jared Wilkins, with *me*? Impossible!

When church was over, the only thing I could remember was the pastor's text from Mark 9:50—"Be at peace with each other." It just so happened to be one of the verses Danny had used to try to get me to patch things up with my cousin Stan two weeks ago. Was God trying to tell me something?

The next day, Columbus Day, Uncle Jack took everyone to Copper Mountain. Everyone except Stan, who decided to stay home and sleep in . . . and me. Mom let me skip the gondola ride and go shopping with Andie instead. I'd saved up over $170 worth of baby-sitting money and wanted to get a jump-start on Christmas shopping.

Andie and I hit every Columbus Day sale imaginable. Even the donut shop had a two-for-one special. By late afternoon we were exhausted. Lugging our purchases, we hopped off the bus near my house. That's when I saw a white flag stuck in our front yard.

Andie spied it, too. "What's that for?" she asked.

"Beats me." I squinted to see as we came closer.

A slight breeze made it ripple as Andie ran onto the lawn, stretching the homemade banner out. "What's 'J. P.'s claim' mean?"

"Must be one of Uncle Jack's tricks," I said, wondering what he was up to. "Let's go inside and find out."

Everyone was downstairs in the family room, watching a video in the dark. "Come look," Mom said, motioning Andie and me over to the sectional. "This is Copper Mountain in the fall." The aspens were like gold against the dark evergreens.

Stephie bounced up and down. "Watch this," she said. "Here's what you missed today, Holly-Heart."

I watched as Stephie hurried into the gondola with Carrie.

"Uncle Jack took this from inside our gondola," Mom said, narrating. "Here's where Stephie and Carrie wave and giggle back at us."

I watched as the cable went over the first set of terminals, making the car sway high over the treetops. The girls' expressions changed quickly at that point.

"That's the part I hate most," I whispered to Andie.

"That?" Andie laughed. "The swinging and swaying's the best part of the ride for me. The wilder, the better."

The camera shifted to another gondola, behind the cameraman. There sat Mark and Phil clowning around, making faces as Uncle Jack used his zoom lens to get a close-up of the younger boys.

"Is Stan here?" Andie whispered.

I shrugged. "He's probably still at home."

When the video was finished, Uncle Jack rewound it. Then the doorbell rang, and Carrie and Stephie ran to get it. Mom kept telling us over and over how beautiful the autumn was in the high country. Every time she said it, it was like she wanted to say something else. Something more important than the seasons changing. Her face glowed with excitement as she turned the lights on.

Just then Carrie and Stephie came racing back downstairs.

"Who was at the door?" Mom asked, leaning her head against the sectional.

"Our neighbor," said Carrie. "He wants to know what the flag's all about in our yard."

"Oh yeah," I said. "Andie and I saw it, too."

"Uncle Jack put it there," Carrie declared. "Just like Columbus."

"What for?" I asked.

Uncle Jack walked across the room and grabbed a pool stick from the rack on the wall. "I'm staking my claim on Susan Meredith and her family." He stood in the middle of the family room with the pool stick in his right fist.

Stan wandered down the steps just then. "What's going on?" He stared at his father.

"Welcome, son," said Uncle Jack in a deeper voice than usual. "You are about to witness a significant moment."

Stan sat down in the chair across from me. What crazy antic did Uncle Jack have up his sleeve today? Slouching there in his chair, Stan looked disinterested.

Uncle Jack cleared his throat. "Just as Christopher Columbus staked his claim on the newly discovered land, bringing gifts to the natives, I, Jack Patterson, do press my flag into the soil of Susan Meredith's heart."

Mom applauded the silly speech. Was this for real?

Then Uncle Jack pulled a square box from his shirt. "And now . . . a gift for the number-one native."

Mom giggled as he approached her, kneeling at her side. "She already said she'd be my wife," he told all of us. "So this will make our engagement official."

Stephie and Carrie squeezed in to see. I was sure he was giving Mom a ring, but then, you never know with Uncle Jack.

Mom opened the velvety lid. "Jack," she whispered, "it's beautiful!"

I slid over next to her, curious. It *was* beautiful. More than that, it was expensive. I could tell by the size of the diamond.

Uncle Jack took Mom's left hand in his and gently slipped the ring onto her fourth finger. He got up off his knees and playfully pulled Mom to her feet. "Ta-da!" he said with a grand flourish, spinning her around. "Susan, we shall wed and live happily ever after."

Andie started clapping, and the rest of us joined in. "I've never been to a proposal of marriage," she said.

"Me neither," I said, laughing.

Carrie and Stephie joined hands with the engaged couple, and Mark and Phil ran around outside the circle, trying to tickle their father. Andie and I joined in the fun, making a circle of our own. Then my uncle reached over and gave me a bear hug, the kind that used to come frequently, before Daddy left. Mom held me close, too.

At last we sat down, deciding whether to celebrate by cooking cheeseburgers at home or by letting the Golden Arches do it. When I turned to look for Stan, he'd disappeared.

THE TROUBLE WITH WEDDINGS

Chapter 13

The next day after volleyball practice, I rushed home to record the day's events in my STAN journal.

> *Week One, Day One: It's totally shocking—Jared's ignoring every girl in school! Even Paula Miller. I know because she came crying to me about it. Again! He's being a real jerk in a new and improved sort of way. Amazing.*
>
> *And . . . it was so weird the way he couldn't wait to meet me at the library first thing this morning. I mean, he actually seemed eager to read the requirements of STAN and get on with signing the agreement. He's actually following through with this!*

♥ ♥ ♥

After supper, Kayla called with more questions about my cousin. "Holly," she pleaded, "will you *please* find out what's going on between Andie and Stan?"

"I'll see what I can do."

"You said that before, but you didn't call me back."

"I've been busy," I said, frustrated with her demands.

"Too busy to talk to your best friend . . . then call me right back?"

I sighed. "Like I said, I'll see what I can find out."

Hanging up, I wondered about Andie. Maybe I *should* give her a call. Nah, she'd just want to yak endlessly about Stan. On the other hand, I needed to talk to her about Jared and the secret pact she'd signed promising to help with my STAN plan.

Andie answered on the first ring.

"I didn't see you much today," I began. "Just thought I'd call and check on things."

"Things are so cool," she said. "Stan and I are talking a lot. It's like a dream come true."

"That's nice," I mumbled, even though it wasn't nice at all. She was too far gone over Stan to see the light now.

"And I have you to thank, Holly."

"Speaking of which," I said, "remember our pact?"

"Sure do, and have *I* got a scheme for you."

"Like what?"

"Tomorrow I'm mailing a letter to Jared inviting him to the Harvest Festival," she said.

"That's almost a month away, but sure, go for it."

"Hmm, whoever heard of refusing your own mail," she said, laughing, probably thinking that Jared would be very tempted to open anything from a girl.

"If you put your return address on it, he'll know it's from you. So that won't work."

"I'm one step ahead of you. No return address—how's that?"

"Oh, I get it. When he opens the letter, he'll *have* to read it, and then we'll know he failed STAN."

"What's Stan got to do with Jared?" she asked.

Yikes! The code word just slipped out. "Uh, what did I just say?" I pretended not to know.

"You said something about failing Stan," she said. "Please, don't get *him* involved in this, Holly, or I'm out."

"Don't worry, my cousin's not involved." Suddenly, I remembered

Kayla's plea for information. "Uh, by the way, do you think Stan likes you?"

"Hope so. Why?"

"Just curious."

"Hey, just think, if Stan and I get married someday, I'd not only be your best friend but your cousin. Is that cool or what?"

"Where do you come up with these ideas?" I asked, as if the thought had never crossed my mind.

"Never mind, I can tell you're not in the mood."

"Whatever."

"Want me to spy on Jared tomorrow?" she asked.

"Sure, just don't talk about it at school. Call me after volleyball, okay?"

"I'll *be* at volleyball practice tomorrow. Stan asked me to wait around for him."

I still couldn't picture Andie and my cousin together. "Okay, see you then." I hung up.

The Scrutiny Test Analyzing Nascence took most of my energy at school the next day. If I wasn't spying on Jared—checking to see if he was either failing STAN by talking to or looking at girls—I was enduring Paula's nonstop complaining about the sudden change in him.

"It's just not like Jared," she whined.

"He *does* seem different, doesn't he?" I said.

Even Billy Hill noticed. "Something's up with Jared," I overheard him say to Amy-Liz on the way to math. "He's acting strange."

By the end of the week, the whole school was buzzing with rumors about Jared Wilkins. One rumor had him suffering side effects from some medication he was on for a rare disease.

He was waiting at my locker Friday after school. "Hey, Holly-Heart."

It was the first I'd seen him smile all week. "This is pure torture, isn't it?" I said.

"You'd be surprised." He grinned. "I've never had so much fun getting slammed with rumors and jokes and other nonsense."

"Want to call the whole thing off?"

"No chance," he said.

His response made me terribly nervous. I mean, what if he *did* pass the test?

Danny walked past my locker just then. I turned away, trying to avoid him. "I've got to do something about Danny," I muttered into my locker, feeling a little twinge of sadness for the way things had ended between us.

"Like what?" Jared asked.

"I don't know. He looks so depressed. Maybe I should talk to him. I mean, we were such good friends before. . . ."

"Has he called you?"

I shook my head. "I walked out on *him.*"

"You two could talk things out and still be . . . uh, friends, couldn't you?"

Was Jared for real? I expected him to say something else. Something like, "Forget Danny, you've got me." But he hadn't. Instead, he handed me an envelope.

"Oh, before I forget," he said, "could you give this to Andie for me? I recognized her handwriting."

I stared at the letter addressed to Jared. Turning it over, I saw the address written in Andie's best cursive. This was the letter she'd sent to test him. Part of the STAN plan I'd concocted.

"You're right. It's Andie's writing."

The envelope was unopened!

Chapter 14

Tuesday after lunch, I stopped off at my locker with Andie. A note stuck out of one of the vents at the top.

Andie leaned close to see. "Who's it from?" she asked.

The note turned out to be from Danny, asking when we could talk. "This is just great," I said, refolding it.

"What's wrong?"

"Danny, that's what." I opened my locker and peered at the mirror attached to the door. "I'm a jerk," I said, fluffing my hair with my fingers. "Danny wasn't so bad."

"Hey, do you like being preached at, and I mean constantly?" She banged her locker shut. "Remember how controlling he was? Think it over, Holly. You're better off without him."

"Maybe," I said, heading for fifth period. But I wasn't absolutely sure. It was crazy, but I still liked Danny. Or maybe it was admiration. I mean, how many walking memory chips does a girl get to meet in one lifetime?

♥ ♥ ♥

After school Danny was waiting near the doors to the gym as I hurried in for volleyball practice.

"Hey," he said softly. "Get my note?"

I nodded.

"When can we talk?"

"What about?" I asked.

His eyes were sober. "You and me."

"Uh, I've got volleyball now," I said. "Miss Tucker makes us run extra laps if we're late."

"Later then?"

"I can't hang around after school today. Mom and I are going shopping for her wedding next month."

"Your mother's getting remarried?" He seemed to brighten. "When?"

"Thanksgiving Day," I said. "And we're all dressing like pilgrims." We laughed at my dumb joke.

"Can I call you later tonight?" His eyes had sort of a pleading quality.

"Sure," I said. Just then Stan rushed past us, his whistle hanging from his neck. He shot me a strange look. "Talk to you later, Danny," I said, dashing off to the girls' locker room. Changing clothes at record speed, I made it back upstairs before Stan's whistle blew, signaling the start of practice.

Stan scowled, not only at me, but at all the girls. Good. At last even Kayla was seeing his grumpy side. If only Andie were here.

Halfway through practice, Jared showed up. He sat in his usual place, high in the bleachers. This STAN thing was getting out of hand. Boys were starting to ridicule him. Certain girls were avoiding him; others were vying for his attention more than ever. Like Paula Miller, for instance.

After practice I waited for him at the bottom of the bleachers. "Hi," I said, feeling a bit sorry for him.

His smile warmed my heart. "Hey, Holly, you're looking really good out there."

"Thanks."

"So how am I doing?" His eyes searched mine.

"I, uh, don't know about this STAN thing anymore," I said.

"What do you mean?" He followed me across the gym. "I

agreed to it, remember? So what's the problem? I'm doing what you wanted."

I stopped to look at him. *Really* look at him. "It's all wrong, Jared. Every single part of it."

"How's it wrong?"

"Because STAN is turning you into a . . . a . . ."

Thwe-e-ep! It was Stan's whistle.

I spun around. "Now what do you want?" I said.

"Lay off, Holly." Stan stood at the volleyball net, clipboard in hand, and glared at me.

I looked first at Jared, then my cousin. "Huh? I don't get it."

Stan folded his arms. "Keep me out of whatever it is you're talking about."

I couldn't help but giggle. "It's nothing about *you*," I said, trying to force a straight face.

Jared grinned, too. "Yeah, it's nothing, man."

I eyed my cousin, holding his precious clipboard. Driving him crazy with STAN was perfect genius. He'd never believe we weren't talking about him—never in a zillion years!

He was glaring at me now. "And stop telling everyone about the wedding, too."

"What's eating you?" I said.

"You know what. There shouldn't be a wedding at all."

"You're pathetic," I said as he sauntered back to the bench and sat down.

"What's buggin' him?" Jared said.

"He's a pain, that's what."

Jared stuffed his hands into his pockets. "Maybe both of you should back off . . . give each other a break."

I stared at him. He was starting to sound like Danny, telling me what to do. "You're doing it, too, Jared," I said.

He looked confused. "What? What did I say?"

Thoughts of STAN whirled in my head. Jared's personality was changing—for the worse. The fun-loving Jared had disappeared, and in his place was . . . what?

I sighed. "Maybe this scrutiny test was a big mistake. I mean, you're *so* different. Nothing like you used to be. I think STAN's turning you into someone . . . uh, someone *awful*. Let's just forget the whole thing." I turned and headed for the girls' locker room.

"Holly, wait!"

I turned around. "Not now, Jared. It's over." And this time I ran all the way down the steps to the locker room, leaving Jared standing in the middle of the gym floor.

It felt good getting away from him . . . *and* Stan. In the shower, I let the water beat on my back for the longest time.

Mom pulled up in front of the school. "Hi, Holly-Heart, ready to shop till we drop?"

"I'm ready, sure. Can't wait," I said, settling into the front seat. "We don't have much time before the wedding, you know." I pulled a piece of paper from my backpack.

Mom glanced over. "What's that?"

"We have to be organized about this if you're going to have a perfect wedding." I held my list up.

She smiled. "I should've known."

"First we need invitations, and they must be mailed this week."

Mom looked horrified. "This week?"

"Yep. Six weeks in advance of the special day. That's *this* week." I opened my backpack, scrounging for a pencil. "Another big item is flowers, you know. And a photographer. We must have pictures, lots of them. And . . . food. What would a Thanksgiving Day wedding be like without food? How do turkey hors d'oeuvres sound?"

"Slow down, Holly," Mom said, finding a parking space in front of Footloose and Fancy Things. "Aren't we getting ahead of ourselves? My wedding day is important, but it's not the first time, you know. Second weddings shouldn't be too showy."

"Says who? You've waited a long time for the right guy to show up. And if Daddy had been thinking straight, he'd have come to his senses and married you again instead of—"

"Holly, please. Let's not get into that."

"Do you agree with me—this wedding *has* to be special?"

She nodded. "Special, just not too fancy."

"Where's *your* list?" I asked just as Mom got out of the car to feed the meter.

"Relax—please? My list is right here," she said, pointing to her head as we made our way into my favorite shop.

Footloose and Fancy Things was the most exclusive shop in Dressel Hills. The cushy decor and soft music reminded me of a big-city department store. There were mirrors everywhere, and luxurious chairs to relax in while waiting for someone to come out of the plush dressing rooms and model an outfit. That someone happened to be my mom. She deserved the best fashion critic there was—me.

Modeling an off-white dress with a gentle brocade bodice and sleeves, Mom stood before me, smiling. "This is ecru," she said. "It's appropriate for a second-time bride."

"Why not a white gown?" I argued. "And shouldn't it be longer? You know, with a train?"

Mom rolled her eyes. "Darling, maybe we should talk." She sat down, sinking deep into the soft armchair beside me. "I said before, second weddings usually aren't too showy." It was almost a whisper. "I haven't changed my mind about that."

"But you didn't have a big wedding with Daddy; why not throw a big bash with Uncle Jack?" I insisted.

"Did it ever occur to you that Uncle Jack might want to have a say in the planning? This is his wedding, too."

"Okay, we'll let Uncle Jack decide a few things," I said.

Mom looked at me sideways. "Maybe you're getting too caught up in this," she muttered, hoisting herself out of the chair.

As soon as she disappeared into the dressing room, I dashed to the bridal section. That's when I spotted the perfect dress for a bride. I couldn't wait to show Mom.

When she came out to model another dress—a pale green just-below-the-knee-length thing with ripples for a hem—I took her arm and escorted her to the dazzling white dress with a chapel-length train fit for a queen.

"Now *this* is you." I stepped back, admiring the enchanting dress. "Please, Mom. Just try it on."

Mom smiled. "It's lovely, dear, but it's *not* me."

"Mo-o-m," I whined.

"I'll make you a deal," she said, lowering her voice. "I'll choose *my* wedding dress, and you choose yours. Okay?"

"That's not funny," I said. Then a fabulous idea popped into my head. "What if I choose the dresses for Carrie, Stephie, and me to wear for the wedding party. What do you think?"

"Sure, that's okay with me, Holly-Heart." She stroked my hair.

Things were looking up. Mom would say almost anything now to get me off her bridal train, er, out of her hair. So while she went off to try on another nonbridal look, I browsed through the Juniors section of the dress shop.

The trouble with weddings is, by the time you're old enough to have one, you're too old to know what's cool and what's not. With that thought, I reached for the gorgeous hot-pink dress with beaded silver accents that was calling out to me. The fabric shimmered all the way down to the striking beaded hem. I was holding in my hands the perfect choice for the coolest junior bridesmaids' dresses in Dressel Hills, Colorado. Wouldn't Mom be thrilled?

Chapter 15

I waited with Mom as the cashier rang up her boring cream-colored dress. "I found the perfect dress in Juniors," I told her. "You have to see it, Mom. We could order three of them exactly alike for Carrie, Stephie, and me."

Her fingers were busy touching the brocade bodice of her wedding dress. Her mind was apparently a zillion miles away. "That's nice," she said, handing a credit card to the clerk.

Just then Andie's mother showed up. "Shopping for your wedding, I see." She eyed Mom's purchase. "Your dress is lovely."

Lovely? She hadn't called it *fabulous* or *beautiful*. So I was right. The dress was definitely average—ho-hum. I couldn't stand by and let Mom's wedding day be average. It had to be extra special . . . even memorable. And I would see to it.

Mom showed off her dress, chattering with Mrs. Martinez. Then she signed the credit card purchase slip.

"Excuse me, Mom," I said, interrupting her. "Can you come look at the dress I found in Juniors real quick before they close?"

But Mom was caught up with Andie's mom and, of course, wedding talk. "Here, honey, go ahead and order the dresses if you'd like to," she said offhandedly. "I'll be across the street at the florist. Meet me there." Then she handed her credit card to me.

Well, I instantly tore off in the direction of the glitzy hot-pink and silver dress. Just the thing to add pizzazz to a wedding that, so far, seemed to be headed in the direction of Dullsville.

Quickly, I found the dress on the rack again. My size. On the shelves against the wall, I discovered a pair of shoes to match, along with beaded hair accessories. I placed the order for two more dresses—in Carrie's and Stephanie's sizes—and hurried out of the store. I was glad the white plastic completely concealed the flashy dress I'd just purchased.

When we arrived home, I would surprise Mom and model it. She'd be so impressed with my choice. After all, weddings ought to be an occasion for celebration. Especially at Thanksgiving.

Back at home, Uncle Jack greeted us at the front door. His hair was messed up, probably from being playfully attacked by the kids. Stan was at the library doing homework again. He'd been hiding out there a lot lately. Maybe he thought if he hid from reality it would go away.

"Whatcha got there, Holly?" Uncle Jack asked, trying to peek under the plastic.

Mom intercepted. "No sneaking peeks. First look is on our wedding day."

"That goes for the *bride's* dress," he teased. "Not for the daughter-of-the-bride's dress." He planted a kiss on my cheek.

"It's our *new* tradition, right, Mom?"

Mom looked puzzled. "Traditions are repeated customs. I don't know about Jack, but I intend this to be *my* last wedding." Uncle Jack burst into laughter and kissed Mom. And not on the cheek, either.

With that, I dashed upstairs to hang up the dress. But my eye caught something taped to my bedroom door. Stopping to look more closely, I discovered a list of phone calls. Danny's name was listed, followed by his phone number.

Uncle Jack called up from downstairs. "Holly, did you find your phone messages?"

I leaned over the banister. "Thanks, Uncle Jack."

"Looks to me like you need a private secretary," he teased.

Inside my bedroom, I carefully removed the plastic. Then I closed the door and slipped on the most fabulous bridesmaid dress ever.

Standing in front of the mirror, I posed like a model. Swinging my hair up off my shoulders, I held it there, admiring the color and style of the dress.

Suddenly I remembered last Easter. Carrie had found the most incredible dress, a silk one, complete with a silvery embroidered hem. But the colors weren't right for Mom. And she absolutely refused to buy the *hot-pink* Easter dress. Carrie had complained and whined and nearly threw a fit, but none of that changed Mom's mind.

I stared at the mirror, twirling myself around. I was determined to wear this dress to Mom's wedding even though it had exactly the same colors as the dress that got away . . . from Carrie, anyway.

First look on the wedding day . . . Mom had told that to Uncle Jack.

Well, that goes for this dress, too, I thought, giggling. What a sensible idea. One that would spare me from having to return three perfectly gorgeous dresses. Even if Mom didn't like it, everyone else would love the brilliant pink color and shimmering silver beading. I was so sure.

Pulling the plastic over the hanger, I hung my bridesmaid gown toward the back of the closet. With zillions of wedding plans on her mind, maybe Mom would forget about this purchase. I could only hope so.

It was time to return some phone calls, starting with Andie. I hurried to the hall phone.

"What's up?" I said when she answered.

"Not much. Where've you been?"

"I went shopping with Mom to pick out her bride's dress today . . . uh, sorta. She didn't like the one that looked like a *real* bride, so we compromised. She got the dress she liked, and I picked out dresses for the girls in the family."

"Matching dresses?"

"Uh-huh. The clerk said they're one of a kind, the only dresses like them in Dressel Hills."

"That's cool, I guess." She sounded glum.

"What's wrong?"

"Stan. He's weird."

I wasn't too surprised. Especially after what had happened today after school. "I warned you. My cousin can be positively maddening sometimes."

"Well, he's mad, at least. At his dad for getting married again." She paused. I could hear her take a breath. "And at *you,* Holly."

"At me? Again?"

"He said you're spreading stuff around about him."

I sat on the floor in the hallway. "Well, let him whine all he wants. The fact is, Jared and I were *not* talking about him, and that's the truth."

"Jared? How's he fit into all this?"

"It's nothing, really."

"You just lost me," she said. "But speaking of Jared, I ran into him after school at the Soda Straw. Amy-Liz and I popped in for sodas, and there he was. Holly, he looked really awful. Like someone just died."

"Really?" I felt guilty.

"Yeah, he looked miserable, so I went over to talk to him, and he wouldn't even look at me. Then I got a bright idea. I bribed Amy-Liz to go and flirt with him. And she did. But he kept his face down the whole time. Then he said the weirdest thing, without looking up."

"Like what?"

"He said, 'Take your flirting somewhere else. I can't talk to you now.' Can you believe it? You and your test have turned Jared into some kind of *weirdo*."

"How do *you* know what he said to Amy-Liz?"

"I have proof."

I wasn't sure what she was getting at. "Huh?"

"Proof," she said again. "Will you be home tonight?"

"Sure, why?"

"I'll be right over," she said, hanging up without even a good-bye.

Now what? I hung up the phone. Just as I did, it rang. "Got it," I called to Mom. "Hello?"

"Well, hi there, Holly." It was Daddy, calling from California. "How's everything going?"

"Fine, thanks. How are you?"

"We're fine here." It bugged me when he said *we.* "How's school?"

"Okay. Except for Stan."

"What do you mean?" he asked.

"He's causing trouble for me at school."

"Your *cousin* Stan?"

"Uh-huh."

"That's hard to picture. He's always been one of the best kids around."

"Well, he's changed."

"I wonder . . . could it have something to do with his dad getting married again?"

I held my breath. How'd Daddy know? "Um, maybe" was all I could say.

"I think I understand your cousin's motivation. Stan's probably worried about having two more sisters in his family." Dad chuckled.

"Did Grandma Meredith tell you the news about the wedding?"

"Yes, and she seems quite happy about your mother getting remarried." He paused. "I've been wondering, Holly, how do *you* feel about Uncle Jack becoming your stepdad?"

I tried to swallow the rising lump in my throat. I opened my mouth, but nothing came out. *I mustn't cry,* I thought. *Daddy will get the wrong idea.*

"Holly, are you there?"

I coughed. "I'm okay." But my eyes were clouding over with tears. "You know, Daddy, Uncle Jack will always be an uncle to

439

me. Just because he's marrying Mom doesn't mean he'll take your place. No one could ever do that." Just saying that made me feel better.

"I didn't intend to upset you, honey. Are you sure you're all right?"

"Uncle Jack's lots of fun. Mom's in love, and everything's fine." I wondered if Daddy believed me, the way my voice sounded so quivery.

"You're crying, honey, aren't you?"

"Not because I'm sad, Daddy. Honest."

"Well," he said, "I'm happy for your mother. And Uncle Jack, too. He's getting a terrific wife."

I couldn't believe he'd say that. Why hadn't *he* stayed married to Mom instead of leaving us and messing up our lives? I didn't say what was on my mind, of course, just asked him if he wanted to talk to Carrie. When he said that he did, I ran to find her.

Carrie shyly took the receiver. She and Daddy still hadn't talked much since he'd reentered our lives last winter. Meanwhile, I sat on my window seat thinking about Daddy's question. What made him think Uncle Jack could replace him, now or ever? I squeezed Bearie-O hard. It was then I realized Daddy might've been upset with the news of Mom's wedding. It must be lousy finding out your wife is marrying another man. Even though she's not your wife anymore.

Just then a knock came at my door. "Holly, are you in there?" It was Andie.

I leaped off my window seat and met her. "Wow, that was fast."

She pulled an MP3 player out of her backpack.

"What's that for?" I asked.

"The proof I told you about. Just listen."

She pressed the play button. "Take your flirting somewhere else." The voice was unmistakably Jared's. "I can't talk to you now," he was saying.

I stared at the recorder, astonished. "Play it back," I told Andie.

Once again, we listened to Jared's startling response.

"Well, this doesn't sound like the Jared we once knew," Andie remarked.

I nodded, stunned. "When did all this happen?"

"An hour after volleyball practice. Stan and I were studying at the library, then he took the bus home. I met up with Amy-Liz at the Soda Straw, which is where we ran into Jared."

Curling up on my bed, I asked, "Does Jared know Amy-Liz was taping him?"

"No. I hid this in her bag. Clever, don't you think?"

I inspected Andie's detective equipment. The microphone was so tiny. "Very cool."

She returned the MP3 player to its case. Then she sat on the floor, leaning her head on my bed.

"Looks like *I'm* keeping my end of our secret pact."

I stared at the canopy overhead. "Well, to be honest, there's no need for it now," I told her.

Andie leaned up on her elbows, staring at me with her brown saucer eyes. "Why not?"

I was close to telling her that I'd called off Jared's test, but the phone rang. "Hold on. I'll be right back." I darted to the hall phone.

"Hello?" I said.

"Hey, Holly. It's Jared."

I wondered why *he* was calling. "What's up?" I asked.

"I've been thinking."

"Yeah?"

"I wondered if you could clear up something for me."

I sneaked down the hall to see if Andie was overhearing my end of the conversation. "Like what?"

"Like the reason you're so mad at me for following all the rules on your list. It has to mean only one thing."

"What?" I waited.

He took a deep breath. "Like maybe you never wanted me to pass STAN in the first place."

"Do you really think that?" I was starting to feel jittery.

"It's this feeling I have, Holly. Like maybe you only agreed to STAN for the fun of it." He paused. "Well, am I right?"

"Of course not, Jared. I didn't dream up something just to waste your time and mine. But actually, I think we should just forget about STAN. It was a dumb idea." I switched the phone to my right ear. "Look, I have a friend over right now. Can we talk later? Bye." I whirled around to hang up the phone, only to meet Andie's scowl.

"What do you mean, 'forget about Stan'?" she said, eyes accusing me. "This must be what Stan was talking about today." She grabbed my arm and pulled me into my bedroom, pointing to my window seat. "Have a seat, girl. It's time we talked."

"There's nothing to talk about, Andie. Honest."

Now her hands were on her hips. "I *heard* what you said."

"What you *thought* you heard was nothing about Stan."

"I heard you say his name to Jared." Her eyes were boring a hole into me.

"You were hearing things." I crossed my legs under me.

"Are you calling me a liar?"

I sighed. This was hopeless. "You're mixed up, Andie. Just forget it. Please?"

"I'm going to get to the bottom of this, and you can't stop me." She reached for her MP3 recorder and stuffed it into her backpack.

"Where are you going?" I asked, bounding off the window seat and following her into the hallway.

"Over to Jared's house. He's going to talk to me whether he likes it or not." With that, she slammed my own bedroom door in my face.

I felt like I'd been punched in the stomach by my best friend.

Chapter 16

At school the next day another note was attached to my locker. *Danny doesn't quit,* I thought as I read the note. Mom's wedding was more than a month away, and Danny was asking me to let him come to the wedding "as a good friend."

I hadn't the slightest clue how to respond to Danny's strange request. I was beginning to feel maxed out with stress. So I stuffed the note in my jeans pocket and headed off to homeroom, hoping things might calm down sometime soon.

In my composition class, Jared passed me a note. He asked me the exact same thing Danny had! I wondered what would happen if I personally invited *both* guys?

Funny, for a girl who'd hardly been noticed by boys last year, I had come a long way. I grinned to myself. If Danny knew what I was thinking, he'd be quoting Proverbs and the verse about pride going before destruction. Yeah, he would.

At lunch, I sat at a cafeteria table alone. Danny was nowhere to be seen. But Jared was. He came right over and sat down. He started in without even saying hey or anything. "It's okay with me, Holly, if you want to officially call off the scrutiny test. But at least give me credit for one thing."

"Like what?" I bit into my chicken salad sandwich.

"At least say I passed STAN."

He had a good point. "You *are* amazing, Jared. How'd you change yourself like this?"

"I wanted to convince you that I wasn't a jerk by following your plan. And you're right, Holly—the test *was* stupid. But stupid or not, I agreed to it and so did you. So I've decided to keep my part of the deal until Thanksgiving."

He wasn't kidding. I could tell by the serious look in his eyes.

"Well, if *you* want to, fine. But count me out."

"Whoa, wait a minute. You agreed to this thing, too." He looked a little peeved.

I picked at the chips on my plate, not saying anything.

Jared snapped his fingers. "I've got it! Maybe *you* could become a scrutiny test victim. I'll create a test to analyze perfection . . . in Holly Meredith. What do you say?"

I felt ridiculous. And Jared was right; I wasn't perfect. I just liked to pretend I was. "Go ahead," I said. "Make your list. What do I have to do?"

He opened his spiral notebook. "Number one," he said as he wrote it, " 'Love the Lord with all your heart.' " He flashed his wonderful smile at me.

I giggled.

He started to write again. "Number two. 'Love your neighbor as yourself.' "

I could see what he was getting at. I'd treated some of my "neighbors" pretty lousy. Including my cousin Stan.

Clicking his pen, Jared ripped the paper out and handed it to me. "That's all, Holly. That's my list."

"Are you sure you and Danny haven't traded personalities?" I reached for my milk and took a sip. "You're starting to get awfully testy."

He grinned. "Danny and I have more than one thing in common now." And then he did it—he winked at me!

I leaned forward. "Hey, I think you're back . . . the real Jared. You're really in there somewhere, aren't you?"

He tilted back in his chair. "What can I say, Holly-Heart?"

I liked him better already. Maybe I *would* ask him to come to the wedding as my guest after all.

Stan came through the line and headed for our table. "Hey, Holly," he called to me, sitting down without an invitation. "I don't know what's going on between you and Andie, but she's sorta freaked out. Can you straighten this mess out with her?" He wasn't asking. This was a command.

Jared looked at me, then tapped the paper I held in my hand, reminding me of his list. *Love your neighbor as yourself.* The words rang in my ears.

I sighed, then smiled. "I'll see what I can do."

Stan looked shocked. "You will?"

"Uh-huh." I smiled at him for a change.

His eyes softened for a second. "Thanks, cuz."

Well, it sure wasn't easy taking orders from an older cousin, especially one with a major attitude problem. But Jared let me know I'd done the right thing when he winked at me again. I felt absolutely fabulous.

Just then Paula and Kayla wandered over. "This looks like the place to be," Kayla cooed, eyeing Stan.

Paula, in turn, looked over at Jared. "No one's having half as much fun as you three," she said.

"Have a seat," I said as Jared slid over next to me, making room for Paula. Lots of room.

Kayla sat across from us, beside Stan.

Jared turned his attention back to me. "When's that story of yours coming out, Holly?" he asked.

"Next month," I said, pushing my hair back.

"I'm going to read it, you know," he said.

"Okay," I said, gathering up my trash. I could see by the desperate look in Paula's eyes that she was dying for a chance to talk to Jared alone. So I excused myself and left.

When I got to my locker, there was Andie, pacing. She grabbed my arm as usual. "Talk to me, Holly, 'cause Jared won't."

"You really went over there last night?"

"Only for about five seconds or so." She opened her locker.

"That's weird."

"Jared refused to see me. His mother said so."

"Sounds like he's sticking to his end of the deal."

"So are you gonna tell me why you're spreading stuff around about your own cousin? It's making me mad."

"I can only tell you one thing," I said. "I was *not* talking about my cousin to Jared yesterday. It's the honest truth, and if you can't trust your best friend, then go ahead and think what you want."

She stared at me, her dark eyes beginning to squint like Mom's when she's upset. "You better not be lying."

"I'm telling the truth."

"Then why did I hear you saying Stan's name on the phone with Jared yesterday?"

I could see she wasn't going to let this drop. "Promise you'll keep a secret?"

"I promise." Andie waited, seemingly breathless for my response.

"STAN is a code word, an abbreviation for Scrutiny Test to Analyze Nascence."

"Huh?" Andie looked bewildered.

"It's a long story."

"Why do you need a code word?" she asked.

"That way no one will know what Jared and I are discussing."

"Oh, I get it. Duh! People will think you're talking about your cousin. Nothing more."

I nodded. "Right."

"Makes sense."

"Remember, Andie, not one word to Stan about this."

Later, when Jared and Stan hurried past our lockers, they were grinning at us as they headed to their own lockers—minus the Miller twins. I watched as Jared moved down the hall, away from us.

Andie poked me. "Daydreamer, wake up. You still like Jared, I see. It's all over your face."

I shrugged my shoulders.

"I bet you end up hanging out with him when your silly scrutiny test is all over."

"Can't decide." I reached back and touched my long hair. "Besides, there's something even more important than Jared right now."

Andie was all ears. "Who? Someone new?"

"It's my cousin, silly. I want to make sure things improve between us before the wedding. We're going to be living in the same house together real soon."

"So have you planned the perfect wedding for your mother?" She pulled out her books for the next period.

"It's not easy planning weddings. Especially because my mom wants to keep things simple."

"Who's going to be in the wedding party?" she asked, stacking up her books.

"Mom's friend from work is the matron of honor. Stan's the best man. And all six of us kids will stand at the altar with them. That's Uncle Jack's idea."

"Who's giving your mom away?"

"Nobody."

"Isn't that just too weird?"

"She's old enough to give herself away, don't you think?"

"Hmm, I guess," she said. "Am I invited?"

"Of course, silly. *Everyone's* invited."

"Really? Like who?"

"Well . . . the Miller twins and their parents since they knew Uncle Jack back East, and pretty much everyone from our church, which means Danny and Jared and—"

Andie looked shocked. "*Both* of them?"

"Yeah," I said, laughing. "They don't know it yet, though. And they've both asked me if they can come."

Andie smirked. "Well, let's hear it for Miss Popularity."

I mumbled, "Yeah, yeah."

Danny showed up just then and asked if he could walk me to fifth period.

"Sure," I said, and he reached for my books. It almost felt like the old days, before our friendship derailed.

He said, "I called you yesterday, but you were gone. Did you get my message?"

"Yeah, and I started to call you back, but something came up."

"Can we talk now?"

I nodded. "Got your note."

"Okay with you?"

"It's not a good idea," I said.

"Why not?" He stopped dead in his tracks in the middle of the busy hallway.

"Because weddings are, you know, places to hang out with . . . uh . . . *everyone*."

"Oh, I get it," he said, opening the classroom door for me. "You have other plans, like maybe with Jared, right?"

He was partly right. But I didn't want to hurt his feelings more than I already had. "I do accept your offer of friendship, Danny. Let's be good friends again like we were before."

A broad grin stretched across his face. "Sure, Holly. That'd be great."

As Danny turned to leave, heading off for his class, Jared walked past. Directly in front of Jared stood Paula, Amy-Liz, and Shauna, making a human blockade, trying to force him to look at them. He grinned at *me*, refusing to even glance at the girls blocking his way.

Giggling, I turned and hurried to find a seat in math.

Jared was perfectly amazing. If he really wanted to continue STAN till Thanksgiving, it was okay with me. Let him make a spectacle of himself.

At the moment it was hard to focus on what the teacher was saying. I could still see Jared winking at me during lunch, and I was secretly relieved. The *real* Jared—yet new and improved—was back.

Chapter 17

That night Uncle Jack arrived with all four cousins. He made pop-corn—enough for a houseful of snack-crazy children and two lovey-dovey adults. Everyone sat around the family room while Mom and Uncle Jack chose their wedding music from a CD of the Brooklyn Tabernacle Choir. For a minute, I thought the walls were going to cave in, especially when Uncle Jack turned up the volume on "To God Be the Glory."

Who could sit still with the sounds of the upbeat choir vibrating through the house? Phil sat on a blue beanbag, moving his head to the beat. "Sounds like this might be a cool wedding after all," he said.

"You can say that again," Uncle Jack said, giving Mom a squeeze.

I thought of the pizzazzy dresses I'd ordered yesterday. If Mom and Uncle Jack's recessional was to be soul music, why couldn't I wear a celebration color like hot pink?

Stan clicked his fingers to the beat while his brothers threw popcorn at each other's mouths. It felt good having Stan around for a change. He was actually behaving himself. Well, sorta. He was still tormenting our cat, Goofey. "This cat's gotta go," he said, picking up my beloved fur ball. "Dad's allergic to him. And . . . besides that, he's ugly."

I crawled over the floor and rescued Goofey from Stan, cuddling him like a baby. "We named him Goofey because he's not a regular-looking cat. He's goofy looking."

Stan laughed. "No kidding."

Uncle Jack sneezed three times, then dug into his pants pocket, searching for his allergy pill. Finding it, he popped the pill into his mouth and swallowed without water.

Carrie stared at him, wide-eyed. "How'd you *do* that?"

Mark laughed out loud. "Ever hear of spit?"

"Eew, sick," Carrie said.

"Yeah, sick," Stephie echoed.

"That's nothin'," Phil spoke up. "Watch this." He started to pull his eyelid up.

"Never mind, son," Uncle Jack said, sparing us from Phil's eyeball trick.

Long after they'd left for home, Mom knocked on my bedroom door. "Holly, can you model your dress for me now?"

I came to my door. "Uh, what about tomorrow? Is that okay with you?" I said, hoping she wouldn't push the issue. Maybe she'd forget by then. Tomorrow she had appointments with the caterer and the organist.

"Sure, that's fine, Holly-Heart. Sweet dreams." She kissed my forehead.

"You too, Mom." She headed down the hall to tuck Carrie in. *Phew—close call!*

Grabbing my nightshirt and robe, I headed for the shower, where I could do some fast thinking about stalling tactics . . . just in case.

The caterer appointment took longer than Mom planned on

Thursday, so she put off meeting with the organist till Friday. By then she'd completely forgotten about seeing my dress. It was a good thing, too. Carrie's and Stephie's dresses were ready to be picked up at Footloose and Fancy Things, on special order from Denver. Now, how to keep them hidden till the day of the wedding?

A whirlwind of days spun past as Thanksgiving approached. I decided to tell Jared that he was welcome to come to Mom's wedding, but that I'd be focused on family that day. And the bride-to-be? Well, Mom was a giddy but happy woman. Uncle Jack, of course, was his comfortable, take-things-in-stride self.

Grandpa and Grandma Meredith arrived two days before the wedding. They didn't seem to mind camping out in the family room, where the sectional pulled out to a queen-sized bed. Gifts were piled up everywhere, with more on the way, I was sure. Congratulatory cards and notes were arriving in the mail every day, most of them containing money. My darling mother was getting married to Uncle Jack, and everything seemed to be going along at a near-perfect pace.

Stephie and the boys moved their stuff into our house on the day before the wedding. Uncle Jack and his kids had been renting a large town home a few blocks away. But now they were coming to live with us.

The trouble with weddings is when your mom marries a man with four kids, reality whacks you on the head sooner or later. For me, the reality whack came when I lost my privacy.

Mom showed up in my room for a heart-to-heart chat. "Carrie and Stephie will have to share your room with you, dear," she began, almost apologetically.

I felt betrayed. "Oh, Mom, no . . . please, no!"

"The boys will bunk in Carrie's old room, just for a while."

"What do you mean?"

She sat on the bed beside me. "I know you won't like this, Holly, but we're thinking of moving to a bigger house eventually. Maybe building a home."

"What's wrong with *this* house?" I sank back against a mountain of pillows and glared at the ceiling. Feelings of panic swept over me.

"We haven't decided anything yet, dear." Mom leaned back on the bed, close to me. "Please, don't worry, Holly-Heart. Now's a happy time. Okay?"

Carrie and Stephie came into my room without knocking, dumping a pile of clothes and stuffed animals on my window seat. "There, that's a good place for now," Carrie said.

Then Stephie turned to me, holding something behind her back. "I, uh, snooped in your drawer, Holly," she said, looking terribly guilty. "And I found this." She held out the polka-dot heart journal with the weekly record of STAN in it.

"You little sneak!"

"I . . . I'm sorry, Holly. When I found it, I thought it belonged to my brother. But then I gave it to him and—"

"You showed this to *Stan*?" I flew off the bed.

She stepped back, away from me. "He said it wasn't his, that I should give it back to you."

"Mom?" I pleaded. "Do something, please?"

Mom stood up slowly. "Girls, I'd like both of you to meet me in the kitchen."

"Okay, Aunt Susan," Stephie said. She left the room with Carrie, the pair of them giggling as they ran down the steps.

I turned to Mom. "There's no way your sleeping arrangement will work. I refuse to tolerate Stephie's snooping." Tears began to fill my eyes, but angrily I brushed them away.

"Let's not worry about who's going to sleep where just now," Mom said. "The wedding comes first. We'll work out the plans for the new house soon enough." She left the room, a spring in her step.

Let's not worry . . .

That was easy for *her* to say. My father had built this house. It was the only house I'd ever known. Everything I loved was here. I scuffed my feet against the rug as I headed for my window seat. Nearly sacred, this spot had served as my private corner of the world. Secret lists were written here. And stories and journal entries. Letters to pen pals and notes to friends . . . and zillions of prayers had been prayed here, too. Tons of them had already been answered.

I sat down in my favorite place, fighting the urge to shove Stephanie's pile of clothes off onto the floor. But in the corner, crumpled up, was the dress she'd worn to her mother's funeral, nine months before. I remembered Stephie's swollen eyes, her tear-stained face. Remorse swept over me. *Now's a lousy time to be angry with her,* I thought as I very carefully folded up Stephie's clothes.

Thanksgiving Day came early at the soon-to-be Meredith and Patterson household. Mom drove to the church to meet with her matron of honor. The florist and caterer would be waiting there for Mom's last-minute instructions.

I was responsible for getting Carrie ready. Stephie too. Uncle Jack dropped her off early. The girls couldn't wait to put on their fancy dresses.

"Look," Carrie said, all smiles when she first saw the junior bridesmaids' dresses. "It's the same colors as the Easter dress from last year, isn't it? The one Mommy didn't like."

"Stand still," I said, zipping her up. "We have to be ready soon. Uncle Jack's picking us up in forty minutes."

Stephie ran down the steps in her satin dress. "Here, kitty, kitty," she called.

"Goofey's down here," Grandpa called up from the kitchen.

I was puzzled. "Why's she looking for Goofey?" I asked Carrie.

"Because Uncle Jack said he could be in the wedding." She ran downstairs after her cousin.

Our ugly cat in the wedding? Who ever heard of such a thing? Besides, Uncle Jack was allergic to Goofey.

I turned my attention back to my long French braid, smoothing the hair on top of my head with my freshly manicured fingers. That done, I posed for the mirror. "Absolutely smashing," I said.

Downstairs, Grandma's eyebrows arched dramatically when she saw us in our matching dresses. "Your mother's taste in clothing seems to have changed recently," Grandma said.

"Aw, Grandma. Don't you like our dresses?" Carrie asked. Spinning around, she made the skirt swirl.

Just then Stephie came into the living room carrying Goofey. She held him tightly in spite of his fussing while Carrie snapped the leash on him.

"You're not *really* taking this cat to Mom's wedding, are you?" I said.

"Don't worry so much, Holly. It'll be okay," Carrie said.

"Yeah." Stephie nodded. "Daddy says the whole family has to be in the wedding. Right, Carrie?"

"Just ask Uncle Jack if you don't believe us," Carrie said, showing off in front of Grandpa and Grandma.

With Goofey on a leash, we climbed into Uncle Jack's van and sped off. There was still a slight chance that Mom's wedding ceremony could turn out to be absolutely perfect. I thought of hiding our cat in one of the Sunday school storage cupboards.

At the church, Mom was hidden away upstairs in the bridal chamber, getting dressed in her ecru-colored dress. Carrie, Stephie, and I waited in the usher's room just off the foyer area. Grandma stayed with us, too, humming as she waited.

How can I get Goofey out of here? I wondered. I *had* to make sure the wedding went off without our cat spoiling everything.

Picking him up, I headed for the door. "Goofey's got some dirt on his whiskers," I told Grandma, who was frowning now.

"You'd better stay here," she said. "Time's getting short. Goofey looks fine to me."

My heart sank as I stood there holding him. I stared at the gold, orange, and red floral ring around his neck, a mixture of wildflowers in rich fall hues. "Where'd he get this fancy collar, anyway?" I asked.

Stephie came over to pet him. "His collar matches the wedding flowers," she said. "That's where."

Fall wildflowers? Aargh! I stared at the three of us in our hot-pink and silver beaded dresses. They hardly fit with the harvest bouquet theme. Mom would have a fit for sure.

"Three minutes and counting," Stan said, poking his head into the room, handing over our wildflower nosegays. "Man, do *they* clash." He frowned and shook his head as he closed the door.

I swallowed hard. This was supposed to be Mom's special day. A day to remember. *She'll remember, all right.* I looked at my watch. Time to line up.

In the hallway, I noticed Billy Hill, dressed up as never before. I'd invited everyone from the church youth group, but I was surprised to see him here, especially since he'd been avoiding Andie and me ever since he learned of her interest in Stan. He smiled as I walked past him toward the foyer of the church.

Mom stood nearby, just outside the double doors leading to the sanctuary. She held a bouquet of miniature sunflowers, and there was a matching floral bouquet near the altar.

She let out a tiny high-pitched squeak, seeing our dresses for the first time. Her hand flew to her mouth as she stared at us in horror.

The matron of honor, wearing honey gold, attempted to stifle a giggle. So did Carrie. Soon, Mom was holding her sides, laughing. It was a good thing the organ swelled to a loud crescendo right then. That was our cue.

I made my way down the aisle between the pews decorated with wildflowers displaying the brilliant shades of autumn. I was next. I thought of tossing away my clashing flowers, but I definitely needed something to hold on to as I walked down the aisle.

A gentle wave of snickers crisscrossed the church as guests viewed the peculiar color combination. I cringed. This was all my fault. So much for the perfect wedding.

Halfway down the aisle, I winced. There sat Kayla Miller, wearing a dress exactly like mine! Exclusive, one of a kind deal? Yeah, right. I held my breath to keep from crying.

On the bride's side of the church sat Danny with his parents. He was more than handsome in his brown dress pants and tan dress shirt. When he smiled, I knew we were still friends in spite of everything.

Two rows ahead of Danny sat Jared with Paula Miller. He looked amazing in a dark suit. But *she* was wearing *another* dress just like mine. My legs felt rubbery as I made my way to the front of the church.

This was outrageous. I wanted to hide under the altar. Instead, I took my place beside a large floral bouquet, turning to face the crowd.

Out there, in a sea of faces, Paula was grinning up at Jared. And what was he doing? Smiling right back at her. It was the last day of the scrutiny test, and he'd completely blown it.

Chapter 18

In a total state of panic, I watched Carrie walk down the aisle. Behind her came little Stephie, with Goofey on a leash. A not-so-soft stream of laughter rippled through the crowd as they crept to the altar.

At last all eyes were on my mother as the organ swelled with the familiar wedding hymn. She wore the sweetest smile in the world, and I saw Uncle Jack's gaze meet hers, never once taking his eyes off the radiant bride. Stan, the best man, and Phil and Mark stood at rapt attention.

"Dearly beloved," the minister began as Mom took Uncle Jack's arm at the altar.

A quick glance at Goofey made me shudder. He was curled up on the groom's shiny black shoes. Uncle Jack pinched his nose closed with his right hand, stifling a sneeze. He searched first one pocket then another for a handkerchief.

Oh great, I thought, *he's forgotten to take his allergy pills.*

Mom looked concerned, but Uncle Jack blew his nose and smiled. The ceremony continued.

Mark stood quieter than I'd ever seen him. Then I noticed he'd locked his knees. Mom had warned all of us at rehearsal, "Keep your knees slightly bent during the ceremony. Don't forget."

It was obvious Mark had forgotten.

While the vocalist sang "The Lord's Prayer," Mom and Uncle Jack bowed their heads, holding hands. Seeing them together like this gave me a warm feeling inside, even in spite of the clashing dresses and fall bouquets . . . and the cat's presence at the wedding altar. And in spite of Jared sitting with Paula.

Just as the vocalist finished his last, long amen, Mark silently slumped to the platform. He must've blacked out. Mom gasped, and in a second, Stan scooped him up and carried him out. Uncle Jack remained calm and reassured Mom with a playful wink.

What else can go wrong? I swallowed hard, wishing this wedding were over.

The most solemn moment of the ceremony was about to begin— the repeating of the vows. Uncle Jack blew his nose for the second time.

When the minister asked, "Do you, Jack Patterson, take Susan Meredith to be your lawfully wedded wife?" Uncle Jack opened his mouth to say "I do," but "Ah-ah, I, uh, *ah-choo!*" came out.

The guests applauded. The perfect wedding was turning into a three-ring circus.

Three rings are better than none, I thought as the latest problem presented itself. Stan was outside with Mark, and he had the ring!

"What token of love do you wish to present to your bride?" the minister asked.

Uncle Jack reached into his coat pocket. Then both pants pockets. I saw the twinkle in his eye. Was he trying to fool the audience? He shrugged his shoulders . . . no ring. Then, ever so slowly, he reached up behind Mom's ear and with a grand flourish produced a cereal-box ring.

The guests burst into applause again. Things quieted down soon enough while Uncle Jack placed the fake ring on Mom's finger, slightly above her elegant diamond.

They kissed longer than ever before. Finally the minister presented them as Mr. and Mrs. Jack and Susan Patterson. The soulful strains of the recessional began.

Goofey refused to be led on his leash, so I handed my bouquet to Phil and reached down and carried the cat down what seemed to be the longest church aisle in history. The minute my feet touched the foyer, I raced to the ladies' room. Goofey hid under a chair in the waiting area of the posh rest room. "That's where you belong," I whispered to him.

Andie showed up in a flash. "That was the coolest wedding," she announced.

I stared at her in disbelief. "How can you say that?"

"Because it was."

Kayla Miller came in, minus her usual grin, and glared at my dress. "My sister and I were told by the store manager that these were the only dresses like this in Denver."

"Denver? You drove all the way *there*?" I said.

She nodded.

"No wonder," I muttered, pulling on my braid.

"Hey, don't let it bug you," Andie said. "You're so lucky, Holly. Your uncle Jack is one of the sweetest guys around."

Kayla agreed. "Did you see how he pulled that crazy ring out of her mom's ear?"

That's all they could talk about—the wacky wedding. I slipped out of the rest room when they weren't looking. The stress was making me hungry. Besides, I had to know what Jared was doing showing up with Paula Miller on his final day of the scrutiny test.

Heading for the reception hall, I hoped to sneak a snack. Mr. Ross, my science teacher, was working in the kitchen. Then Miss Wannamaker, my creative writing teacher, came around the corner, carrying punch glasses. Was this for real?

"Oh, hello there, Miss Holly," Mr. Ross said, spying me. "What can I do for you, young lady?"

"Oh, nothing," I said, sitting down, feeling dizzy.

"Look. She's exhausted," Miss W said, bringing a tray of hors d'oeuvres around.

"Did you have a good breakfast today?" Mr. Ross asked.

I remembered vaguely some juice and toast early this morning. I nodded. Didn't want him to think I'd been neglected. Not on Mom's wedding day, for pete's sake.

Looking up at Mr. Ross, I noticed his hot-pink tie. Something was up! Mr. Ross owned only one tie that I knew of: The one he wore every single day of his life. Then I noticed his smudgy glasses were missing. He was wearing contacts, too. I looked from Mr. Ross to Miss W. They were smiling at each other, oblivious to me. So *that* was it. Mr. Ross was in love.

I took a bite of a cracker.

Behind me, I heard someone say my name. When I turned, I saw that it was Jared.

"Hey," he said, sitting beside me. "Some wedding."

"Yeah," I whispered.

"I hope ours is half as much fun." He winked at me.

I blushed. "You can't be serious."

"We have more in common than I thought." He pulled the first issue of *Sealed With a Kiss* out of his pocket. "You are *some* writer, Holly."

"Where'd you get this?" I asked, puzzled about the magazine.

He flipped through and located my story without saying a word. There it was, in print: "Love Times Two."

"Wow, I'm published." My name was just under the title in medium-sized letters. I read halfway through before stopping.

"How's it feel?" he asked.

"Fabulous."

"Are you ready for this?" He turned the page.

I studied the two-page spread. It was a story called "Love Minus One." The author's name was Janeen Williams. I'd never heard of her.

"How do you like my new pen name?" he said with a grin.

I looked at him, frowning. "You've got to be kidding. Did you really write this?"

"I wouldn't lie to you."

"Jared, you're crazy."

He was still smiling. "Let's collaborate."

"On a story?" I looked into his mischievous face.

"You figure it out," he said as the rest of the wedding party made its appearance.

"Not till you explain some things first."

"Such as?" he said.

"Why was Paula sitting with you during the wedding?"

"Oh that." He scratched his head. "It was Paula's idea. She came in and sat down. When I started to get up and leave, my dad gave me the evil eye . . . and you know the rest."

Silly me, I believed him. "Well, as far as I'm concerned, Jared, you've passed STAN with flying colors. Whenever you want to start acting like your former self *all* the time—"

"If you don't mind, I think I'll carry on as is," he interrupted me, straightening his tie.

I gasped. "What did you just say, Jared?"

He stared blankly, trying to act innocent.

"Jared, what you just said . . . that was a direct quote from my story on metamorphosis for Miss Wannamaker's class."

He looked sheepish. "Uh, yeah, I guess it was."

"What's going on?" I demanded.

He began to tell about the day he'd snooped in my locker. "I noticed your locker door hanging open—and your essay was right there. That's when I got the idea to change myself. Exactly the way you wrote it in your assignment."

"Which explains why the pages were out of order. You rat!" Andie was right about one thing. I *had* created a monster. "Jared," I stated simply, "STAN's over now. You can cut the serious routine any time. Please?"

"Okay, Holly-Heart, how's this?" he said, offering his arm.

"Much better," I whispered, slipping my hand through the bend in his elbow as he escorted me to the receiving line. Then, with a wink, he stepped back into the crowd. I could only hope the scrutiny test monster was gone forever.

I took my place in the family lineup for the formal wedding photographs. Uncle Jack held the bride's hand as the camera clicked. I'd never seen such love sparkles in Mom's eyes. Perfect or not, this *was* a day to remember.

I smiled for the camera, but deep inside I worried, just a little, about having to share my room with two young snoopers, and about trying to survive with three *boys* living in my house.

That's the trouble with weddings. You don't know exactly how things are going to work out, but you hope—with all your heart—that it's very close to *and they all lived happily ever after.*

HOLLY'S HEART

California Crazy

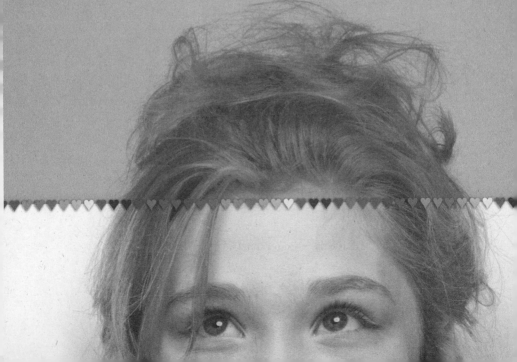

To

Lori Walburg VandenBosch,

my very first editor

and dear friend.

CALIFORNIA CRAZY

Chapter 1

Happily ever after? Right! I thought as I locked the upstairs bathroom door. Two weeks ago, Mom had married Uncle Jack, and our perfectly peaceful surroundings changed overnight. Now my boy cousins—Stan, Phil, and Mark—were brousins, as in cousins-turned-stepbrothers. What a shock adding three boys to an all-girl household! To top it off, their seven-year-old sister, Stephie, was a spoiled brat and the biggest little snoop around.

I stared at the bathroom mirror, furiously brushing my hair. Our house on Downhill Court—the house Daddy had built—was now crawling with people. Stan, fifteen, had claimed the queen-sized sofa bed in the family room. Phil, ten, and Mark, eight, had invaded Carrie's bedroom, forcing me to share my room with two super snoopers: Carrie, nine, and Stephie, also known as the "baby" of our newly blended family.

Mom and Uncle Jack were the only ones who didn't seem to mind the crowded conditions. In the time it took for them to say "I do," my life had been altered forever!

"Holly!" Carrie pounded on the bathroom door. "Hurry up!"

"Hey, I just got in here," I yelled through the door.

"Did not," she called back. "You've been hogging the bathroom all morning."

Hmm, I thought. *Carrie's acting more like Stephie every day. Annoying!*

I sighed and ignored the banging. Not only was the house overrun with zillions of people, my bedroom was now cluttered with personal belongings times three! And to top it off, my window seat was practically defunct—at least for quiet times and journal writing. Its latest function was to serve as Stephie's bed. Pillows, stuffed animals, and blankets were piled up in both corners of my beloved spot. Carrie's bed was a fold-up cot, stashed in a corner of the room during the daytime.

Staring back at the mirror, I longed for the quiet days, before Jack Patterson and company moved to Dressel Hills, Colorado, our fabulous ski village in the heart of the Rockies.

"Holly!" Carrie shouted. "Mom wants you downstairs right now!"

"Nice try," I hollered back. "Mom's out Christmas shopping with Uncle Jack." They were also buying groceries. Saturdays were grocery-buying days. Now that Mom was remarried, there was a man instead of me to lug the groceries to the car—one of the real advantages of having a stepdad.

"I just saw Mommy," Carrie insisted.

"Yeah," I muttered, "in your dreams."

"Holly!" Stephie joined the campaign. "If you don't come out now, I'll wet my pants!"

"*That's* an interesting approach," I said, laughing but feeling slightly guilty. "Why don't you use the bathroom downstairs?"

Stephie turned up the whine. "Stan's combing his hair in there."

"Yeah," Carrie blurted. "And he said if we didn't disappear, he'd turn us into cat food."

"Sisters . . . brothers," I whispered. "What a perfect nightmare."

"Go back downstairs and bug Stan some more," I suggested, posing in the mirror as I pulled my long blond hair away from my face. "Maybe he's finished primping by now."

"But what about the cat food?" Stephie asked.

I sighed, exasperated. "Look, Christmas is coming soon, and Santa doesn't bring toys to kids who bug their big sisters."

That got them. Quickly the girls scampered down the stairs.

"Good riddance," I whispered, reaching for my toothbrush. I remembered the fabulous bedroom that had been exclusively mine before the Patterson takeover. My private dresser drawer, the bottom one where I kept my writing, had to go. Mom insisted it be cleaned out to make room for Carrie's clothes. So . . . good-bye to my secret storage of journals, short stories, and pen pal letters. Now my writing notebooks were boxed up and stored under my canopy bed, the safest place I could find. For now.

The day after Mom's wedding, I had purchased a diary that locked. It was the only possible way to maintain my secrecy. I'd hidden the key in this bathroom, safely tucked away under a flower arrangement on top of the white cabinet above the toilet. Who would think of looking up there for a diary key?

I glanced at the cabinet on the wall. *The super snoopers will never find it,* I thought, feeling smug. But, of course, it wouldn't hurt to double-check. Standing on tiptoes in my new brown suede boots, I positioned my feet on the toilet lid. It wiggled under my feet, so I lifted the lid and seat for a sturdier base. Couldn't afford to crack the seat and get stuck paying for it now that my savings were totally wiped out. But, glancing down at the cool boots, I didn't mind the depleted funds. They were worth every penny I'd spent.

Bam! Something outside bashed against the bathroom door. I flinched. "Is that you, Carrie?"

"If you don't want to be responsible for this door getting knocked down, you'd better open it now!" my sister shouted.

"Just hold on," I said, steadying myself. "Give me two seconds."

"Okay," she said, "I'm counting. One one-thousand, two one-thousand. Time's up!"

I thought the door would cave in from the pounding, and

then, miraculously, the doorbell rang. Carrie scrambled downstairs. Good, privacy at last!

I reached for the top of the cabinet and grabbed Mom's fancy new Christmas arrangement. One little peek underneath would assure me of the diary key's safety. I stood on tiptoes, stretching, reaching . . .

And then it happened—my right foot slipped. I grabbed for the wall, anything, to stop my fall, but I was well on my way into the toilet. Well, not all of me, just my foot. I squealed as the cold water sloshed up over my socks and halfway up my leg. The icy cold water was bad enough, but . . . Yikes, my expensive boot!

I stared at the brown suede boot, now soaked with toilet water. So much for the totally cool look. Then I tried to pull my foot out.

It was stuck.

"Help!" I screamed, ready to yell that I was caught in the toilet, but that sounded really dumb. Instead, I stared, horrified, at the curvy narrow part of the toilet where the sole of the boot was trapped. I shuddered, wishing I'd worn my bedroom slippers instead. Wiggling my toes, I tried to free my foot from the toilet's grasp, but it was no use.

Mom and Uncle Jack were gone from the house. Stan was primping in the bathroom off the family room, two levels below. Phil and Mark were playing at a friend's house—which meant Carrie and Stephie were my only hope.

I took a deep breath and called for them. "Carrie! Stephie! The bathroom's free!" There, that should get an immediate response.

Leaning my head toward the door, I listened. I balanced myself with my left foot and held on to the sink with my left hand. "Carrie!" I called again.

Nothing. The house was perfectly still. Funny, when you *wanted* someone around, this place was as dead as dried-up pine needles.

"Anybody home?" I shouted at the top of my lungs.

My shouting was met with silence. What could I do? How long

before someone would need to use this bathroom? For the first time in my life, I wished we were a one-bathroom house.

Staring down at my cold, soggy foot, I resisted the momentary urge to reach into the water and unzip my boot. *Nah,* I thought. I wiggled my foot again. Even with my boot unzipped, I was sure I couldn't get my foot out of the toilet.

Br-r-ring—the phone! My heart sank as I checked my watch. One thirty-three. It was probably Jared Wilkins, the coolest guy in Dressel Hills Junior High.

The church youth group Christmas party was only two weeks away. Was Jared calling to talk about that? I was dying to know. Of course, it's a little tricky to answer the hall phone when you're locked in the bathroom with your foot stuck in the toilet.

The phone continued to ring as I waited, helplessly, counting the rings.

Chapter 2

It was quite obvious to me now: I was totally alone in the house. Under any other circumstance, I would have been thrilled.

Eight . . . nine . . . ten . . . eleven rings. The phone stopped on the twelfth ring. *Just perfect,* I thought, disgusted with myself. *If only I'd closed the toilet lid before I crawled up here!*

If onlys always got me in trouble. I could easily get carried away with them. For example: *If only* Daddy's sister, Aunt Marla, hadn't died of cancer last year, leaving Uncle Jack sad and alone with four kids to raise. *If only* Daddy hadn't divorced Mom and moved to California. *If only* I'd hidden my diary key in a better place!

A giant cramp was beginning to zap my foot, creeping up my leg. Probably from the weird position I was standing in. Wait a minute! Why *was* I standing?

I decided to do myself a favor and sit down. It wasn't easy perched on the edge of the toilet seat. Pulling a towel off the rack, I rolled it up to make a softer, higher seat. It wasn't exactly comfortable, but it beat doing standing isometrics.

I was determined to look on the bright side of things. Let's see . . . something to be thankful for. I stared down into the toilet. Thank goodness, it was flushed!

Leaning my left arm against the sink, I was able to rest my

head. Then I noticed the dripping faucet. I studied the situation, counting the seconds between drips. Every nine seconds a sizable droplet of water escaped from the faucet and fell into the sink. How many drops of water were lost each minute?

Hmm, I thought. *Sixty seconds in an hour. Nine into sixty is . . .*

"Got it!" I said out loud. "This faucet leaks 6.6 drops per minute." Wow! That was 396 drops per hour. What a waste.

Trickling water droplets tend to make people thirsty, so I reached for the paper cup holder beside the mirror.

"Holly!" a deep voice called from downstairs. "Are you up there?" It was Stan, the top-dog brousin in the Patterson-Meredith household.

"Help!" I yelled with all my might. "I'm stuck, er, locked in the bathroom."

I heard footsteps, welcoming them as my heart pounded.

"You're what?" Stan asked.

"I'm locked in the bathroom," I replied, standing up.

Oops! The towel slid into the toilet.

"Well, why don't you just turn the lock?" he said.

I shifted my balance. "I, uh, can't."

"Really?" Suspicion oozed from his vocal cords.

I waited, hoping he wouldn't leave me stranded. "It's kinda hard to explain. Uh, my foot's stuck!"

He chuckled. "What do you mean?"

I sighed. "If I tell you, promise you won't laugh?"

"Hey, this sounds good."

"Stan, do you *promise?*"

"Hey, whatever."

I hated it when he said *whatever* that way. It bugged me more than anything. My foot was killing me and so was my leg. "Promise me!" I demanded.

"What was the question again?"

"Stan!" Tears dripped off my face and onto the floor.

"Hey, calm down in there," he said. His voice grew suddenly gentle. "Are you hurt?"

"Not really hurt as in cut, slashed, or beaten. But bruised, now that's a major possibility," I answered.

Stan cleared his throat. "Where's your foot stuck, Holly?"

"In the toilet," I blurted.

Silence, total silence. And then I heard it, faintly at first—a ripple of laughter coming from the other side of the door.

"Stan, you promised!" I yelled, massaging the muscles in my thigh.

"Did not," he said, laughing harder than before.

"Look, I wouldn't be laughing if you were in this situation," I shouted over his cackling. But deep inside I knew I would be howling, too.

Finally he tried the door. "It's locked, all right. Now what do you want me to do?"

"Open the door, for starters," I demanded. "Take the door off the hinges if you have to." I hoped he'd move quickly. I was starting to feel a sharp pain in my foot as more strange muscle spasms fluttered up my leg.

"Good idea," he said. "I'll be right back."

Minutes ticked away like the slow drips emerging from the faucet. Three hundred ninety-six times, twenty-four hours a day. I wasn't even close to figuring the multiplication when I heard Stan's footsteps on the stairs.

Bang-a-whack! It sounded like he was really hammering the hinges. "I'll have you outta there in a jiffy, little sister," he said in the worst John Wayne imitation of all time.

"Please hurry," I whispered prayerfully.

Br-r-ing! The phone rang again.

"Don't answer it," I shouted to Stan. "Get the door off first."

I could hear him grunting. Taking doors off hinges must be lots harder than it looks when they do it in the movies. The phone kept ringing. Was it Jared? Right now, I didn't care who was calling.

Six rings later, Stan heaved the door up and off the doorframe.

He propped it against the banister in the hall and raced to the phone.

"Stan!" I turned on the whine the way Stephie does. "Come back."

I could hear Stan's voice just around the corner in the hallway. He was talking politely for a change. Then he said, "Please wait a second."

Suddenly he appeared, his head peeking into the bathroom. He gasped dramatically when he spied my foot in the toilet. "Man, you're not kidding," he said. Then he held up the portable phone. "It's your father. Long distance."

"I can't talk now," I snapped.

Stan shook his head. "I don't think that'll fly. He's leaving for an appointment in a few minutes. Says he wants to bounce an idea off you before he leaves the house."

"Fabulous," I whispered, accepting the phone from Stan.

"Hi, Holly-Heart," Daddy said, using the nickname Mom gave me because I was born on Valentine's Day.

"Hey. What's up?"

"It just occurred to me that you and Carrie have a long vacation from school coming up soon. I wanted to invite both of you here for Christmas." He exhaled into the phone. "What do you think?"

Think? How could I think with stabbing pain running up and down my leg? "Uh, Daddy, let me think about it and call you later. Okay?" I hoped he wouldn't misunderstand my abrupt response.

"That's fine, honey. Call me after seven tonight, your time. I believe I've caught you at a busy time."

Busy I could handle. Stuck in the toilet was a different matter. "I'll call you later, Daddy," I said, wincing as I handed the phone back to Stan.

"Looks like you're hurt," Stan said. "Let's get you outta there."

I tried to jerk my numb foot out of the toilet, but nothing happened. I wanted to scream. Maybe they'd have to amputate. Or maybe I'd have to walk around with a toilet attached to my foot for the rest of my life. I guess there could be worse things. Maybe I could launch a sweeping fashion trend in Dressel Hills. Who needs elevator shoes when you can wear a toilet?

Stan looked at me funny. "Holly, you're not paying attention to anything I just said."

"I'm trying to divert my mind away from the pain."

"Can you wiggle your toes?" he asked.

"A little."

"Good." He leaned over and looked into the toilet. "What is that towel doing in there?"

"Keeping my foot company. What do you think?" And then an idea struck. "Quick, go get some dish detergent."

He stared at me. "What for?"

"Just get it," I said. There was no feeling left in my right foot. If the soap trick didn't work, maybe the paramedics would have to break the toilet with the Jaws of Life!

Chapter 3

Stan returned with a bottle of lemon Joy in his hand.

I grabbed it from him and began to squeeze it upside down into the toilet. "Now, swish the soap around with your hands," I suggested.

He backed away. "You've gotta be kidding."

"We need lots of suds," I said seriously. "That's how Andie got a cheap ring off her finger once. The soap will make the toilet slippery. Trust me."

Stan opened the cabinet under the sink. He pulled out a toilet brush. "Here, try this."

First I used the end of the brush to dip the wet towel out of the toilet. With a fling, I tossed it into the bathtub. Then I stirred the brush around, faster and faster till it resembled a white tornado.

Like some miracle, the soap trick worked. Slowly I eased my foot out of the tight opening. I wanted to dance for joy, but my foot was too sore. So I simply flushed the toilet.

Stan sat on the edge of the bathtub beside me as I unzipped my soaked boot. "I need an honest answer from you," he said, grinning from ear to ear.

"Ask me anything." I felt mighty giddy.

He scratched his blond head. "How did your foot land in the toilet, anyhow?"

I wasn't about to reveal the reason for my afternoon's adventure. Not in a zillion years! "My lips are sealed," I said, patting his arm. "But thanks for the rescue, brousin."

"No problem. Glad it was a success, little sister." There it was again, Stan's lousy John Wayne imitation. But it didn't matter; it was fabulous having this conversation with my new stepbrother—the first decent one since the Patterson takeover.

Stan got up to leave. Suddenly he stopped and stared down at me. "Uh, Holly, are you really okay?"

"I think so, why?"

A very serious expression spread across his face. "You look a little *flushed,* that's all."

"Why, you!" I screamed and tried to stand up. When I did, I lost my balance and toppled into the tub onto the wet towel. I decided right then and there I'd never, ever wear perfumed toilet water, no matter *who* gave it to me.

While Stan put the door back on its hinges, I soaked my aching foot in the tub with Epsom salts and warm water. As for the boot, it was hopeless. If I worked at it, I might have enough baby-sitting money saved up to buy another pair in a couple of months.

Then I remembered Daddy's long-distance phone call. Maybe the California Santa could bring me an exact duplicate on December twenty-fifth. I decided to call him back after supper. I wasn't exactly sure how Mom would take it, but I knew it would be fun to spend the holidays in a sunny beach setting.

Drying my foot with a clean towel, I thought about the advantages of wave surfing at Christmas as opposed to what we usually did at home—snow skiing. Surfing in December would make great headlines for my diary.

Oh yeah . . . the diary key, the reason for my slide into the toilet. Glancing up at the cabinet above the toilet, I grinned. Perfect hiding place—even I couldn't get to it.

When I was finished drying my foot, I closed the toilet lid.

Gingerly, I stepped up and planted my feet firmly on top. Reaching up, I lifted the Christmas arrangement and felt for the diary key underneath it. I leaned up on my tiptoes, my left foot—still wearing the dry boot—supporting me as I groped for the key. If only I could see what I was doing.

Inch by inch, my right hand covered the entire area while my left hand held the arrangement. Where *was* it? I felt around again. And again. It was useless. The key to my life's secrets had vanished!

I replaced the flower arrangement and did a one-footed hop off the toilet seat. I couldn't decide which was worse, being stuck in the toilet or losing the key. The whole thing was a nightmare—the absolute worst.

Back in my room, I spotted a note stuck to my mirror. In Carrie's handwriting it said, *I found your diary key in the bathroom yesterday. Here it is.* A tiny silver key was taped to the paper.

Wait till I get my hands on her, I thought, ripping the key off the paper and dropping it into my pocket. Boiling with anger, I opened the closet door and reached for my bathrobe.

Back in the bathroom, I turned the shower on full blast. I was certain that Carrie had helped herself to the pages of my diary. It wasn't the first time and probably wouldn't be the last. Not unless I came up with a better hiding place.

Soaping up, I envisioned the packing process for my trip to California. Along with clothes—and as many mystery novels as I could squeeze in—I would take a locked overnight case full of diaries, past and present. It was the perfect hiding place; in fact, it might be the only answer to my super-snooper problem at the moment. Why wait till California when a crawl space could serve the same purpose? Carrie and Stephie would never think to look under the steps for diaries—stashed away in a suitcase.

I couldn't wait to investigate the storage space under the family room steps. What genius!

After dressing, I went to my room to dry my hair. When someone knocked on the door, I switched the hair dryer off, ready to do battle for a little privacy. "If it's Carrie or Stephie, stay out," I called.

It was Stan. "Hey, you sound tough."

I opened the door to see him grinning in the hallway. "Jared awaits," he said, handing the portable phone to me.

I closed the door and snuggled into my four-poster bed. "Hi, Jared," I said into the phone.

"How's Holly-Heart?"

Jared's smooth approach always took me off guard. I giggled a little.

"Will you be at church tomorrow?"

I ran my fingers through my still-damp hair. "We're going to early service," I told him.

"That's cool—one less hour till I see you."

I laughed. Jared was pouring on the charm. Again. He'd already won me over last month by passing my scrutiny test—after Danny Myers and I decided to be just friends.

"Talk normal, okay?" I said. Really, sometimes Jared was too much! "So what are you doing?" I asked, propping my sore foot on a throw pillow.

"Been thinking about Miss W's latest writing assignment. How about you?"

"The research part is fun," I said. "I'm doing my paper on the Sally Lightfoot crab. What're you doing?"

Jared paused. I heard him flipping pages. "Ready for this?"

I sighed. *What is he up to now?*

"Ever hear of the Goliath beetle of Nyassaland, Africa?" he asked seriously.

I couldn't help it; I laughed. Hard.

"What's so funny?" he said. "Don't you like my choice of insect?"

"It's fine," I said. "It's just, uh, I don't know . . ."

"What?"

"It sounds biblical, I guess."

"That's why I picked it," Jared insisted. "If there's a beetle called Goliath, where's that put David?"

I giggled so hard, I snorted. "You're crazy."

"Well, then, I think we're a perfect pair," he said.

I blushed. It was amazing, this transformation that had taken place in the past few months. Jared was totally different. He never flirted with other girls anymore.

"Holly? You still with me?" he asked. It was a double meaning.

Shyly I mumbled something about having to clean my room. I knew Mom and Uncle Jack wouldn't want me to get carried away with talking to Jared. It would seem too exclusive.

"I'll see you at church," he said. "Bye."

I said, "Good-bye, Jared," like the whole world awaited my phone farewell. It felt good to have a guy friend who really listened to me for a change. And I couldn't imagine a more thoughtful guy than Jared.

Chapter 4

I began cleaning my third of the room. It was hopelessly messy with Stephie's stuffed animals strewn everywhere and Carrie's dirty clothes in a pile the size of Mount Everest. Well, almost. I stripped my bed and stuffed the sheets into a pillow slip. Then I heard Carrie and Stephie come in the front door downstairs.

Snatching the diary key out of my jeans pocket, I dashed down the steps, taking two at a time, even though my right foot still hurt a little from the toilet adventure.

I cornered the culprits in the living room. "You two better think long and hard about this," I said, waving the key in their faces. "This is off limits to you, and you know it."

Stephie's eyes grew wide. "I didn't do it," she shrieked. "I'm too short to reach that high."

Now I knew it was Stephie who'd spied on me. "You just gave yourself away, little rascal," I said.

Then, turning to Carrie, I confronted her. "Stephie spies and you do the dirty work, is that it?"

Carrie stared at me in silence.

"You never used to do this stuff before Stephie moved in," I persisted. "Are you gonna let a seven-year-old control your brain?"

Carrie put her hands on her hips. "I don't have to listen to you, meanie," she said haughtily.

I flipped my damp hair over my shoulder and sat down. "Just wait'll Mom hears about your snooping. Now, sit down!"

Stephie folded her arms stubbornly. "Don't tell us what to do."

Still standing in the middle of the living room, Carrie snorted at me. Stephie mimicked Carrie's hands-on-hips routine.

I wanted to strangle them both, but fortunately Mom and Uncle Jack arrived. They looked tired from shopping. Uncle Jack smoothed his wind-blown hair, then helped Mom out of her coat and hung it in the closet.

"Mommy . . . hi!" Carrie hugged her.

Uncle Jack scooped Stephie up in his arms. He eyed me sitting on the sofa. "Looks like Judgment Day," he said, smiling at me.

I pointed to the girls. "And those are the accused."

Mom touched her soft, blond waves and sat beside me. "*Now* what?"

My side of the story was scarcely out when Stephie interrupted. "She's bossing us, Daddy. We can't do anything right around here."

"How about starting with a little respect for privacy?" I suggested.

I could tell Carrie knew where this conversation was headed. She started making jerky cut-throat signs with her pointer finger when Mom wasn't watching. My sister would be in big trouble if I started to spell things out.

"This house is too crowded," Stephie whined.

"Yeah," Carrie piped up. "We need more room."

"Your mother and I *have* discussed the possibility of adding on to the back of the house," Uncle Jack said.

Mom looked at each of us. "What do you think, girls?"

"Fabulous!" I said.

"When can we start?" Carrie asked.

"Immediately, as far as I'm concerned," Uncle Jack said, studying the Psalms calendar on the lamp table. "Let's see, if we get going on it next week, we can make some good progress by Holly's birthday. What do you say, hon?"

There wasn't any question of money now that Uncle Jack was in the family. And with Mom continuing to work three days a week at the law firm doing paralegal work, there was probably plenty of extra money for things like this.

Mom nodded her head in agreement. I wanted to dance for joy. What a fabulous idea; I'd finally get my room back, along with my privacy!

Uncle Jack swung Stephie around. "The problem of overcrowding will be solved," he announced with a hearty chuckle.

"Yeah, but what about until the addition is built?" I asked. "Can't we make some stiffer laws for snoopers while the three of us are still stuck in the same room?"

"You bet we can," Uncle Jack said with a twinkle in his eyes. "And these laws *will* be enforced." He looked first at Carrie, then at Stephie as he made his point.

Yes! Finally I had the parental support I needed.

Mom pulled Carrie and Stephie over to her. "If either of you get into Holly's personal things, including her diary, there will be no TV for you for a full week."

"And double kitchen duty," Uncle Jack added.

Carrie and Stephie groaned as Mom and Uncle Jack went upstairs.

This was so fabulous I couldn't contain my excitement. I ran to the kitchen and ate a whole bowl of strawberry ice cream in nothing flat.

As I was finishing the last spoonful, Mom came downstairs and slid onto the bar stool next to me. "I understand your father called this morning." It was more of a question than a statement. "Stan left a note upstairs in our bedroom with a list of calls," she explained.

I sensed what was coming. She probably even suspected Daddy's personal invitation. "Well, I couldn't talk very long," I said. "I told him I'd call back tonight, if that's okay with you."

I paused, unsure how she'd take this news. "Daddy invited Carrie and me for Christmas." I avoided looking at her as I carried my ice-cream bowl to the sink. "What do you think?"

"As long as we have time to celebrate together here after you get back, it's okay with me," she said. "Besides, it might be the ideal time for you girls to go. Things could get chaotic with the extra rooms being built on to the back of the house." She stretched her arms, yawning.

I leaned my elbows on the bar. "Do you want to talk to Carrie about this or should I?" I remembered the last time Carrie was scheduled to visit Daddy. Last summer. She'd backed out at the last minute, so I went without her.

"I'll talk to her," Mom said, going over to the freezer. She reached for a family-size package of hamburger meat and placed it on the counter to thaw. Everything around here came in large quantities these days.

I sneaked up and squeezed her around the waist. "Sure you'll be all right spending Christmas alone with Uncle Jack and his kids?"

I giggled, knowing full well she'd have a fabulous time. Uncle Jack treated Mom like royalty. And even though everyone said they were in their honeymoon stage, I fully expected them to keep on being this happy. They were a perfect match. Uncle Jack and his hilarious humor, and Mom with her sweet qualities of kindness and patience. Made me want to be just like her, and maybe even marry a crazy guy like Uncle Jack someday.

As for Daddy, he was way too serious. Maybe I could get him to lighten up this Christmas. Besides that, maybe I could share with him the true reason for the season.

I headed downstairs to the crawl space to search for an overnight case. Suitcases of every size and shape were stashed back in the corner. Uncle Jack was a world traveler, and his collection of luggage proved it.

Blocking the path to the suitcases was a large box of Christmas wrapping paper and ribbons. Seeing it gave me an idea. Two weeks from now, before school let out for the holidays, I would present my gift to my secret pal. Last Sunday, the kids in our church youth group had drawn names. Mine was Paula Miller, but I'd traded with Billy Hill, who had Jared's name and wanted a girl instead. He was thrilled to get Paula's name from me.

I loved having Jared for my secret pal. It was so much fun to hide little notes and do special things when your secret pal was also your special guy friend, too.

I picked up one of the rolls of brightly colored wrap and decided to use it to decorate my gift for Jared. Now . . . what to buy for him?

The cool suede boots hovered in the back of my mind. If I put off buying another pair, I could afford something really special for Jared. If only I could just buy one shoe—the *right* shoe—I'd be set. The left one was perfectly fine.

With that thought, I pushed the box of wrappings and ribbons aside and headed for the suitcases. Just as I reached for the white overnight case, I heard someone behind me. I spun around to see the tail end of Carrie's long hair flying.

"Not again," I whispered. Then I realized if I acted cool, she'd never suspect my secret plan. It was perfect!

Chapter 5

After supper I called my dad in California.

"Meredith residence," he answered.

"It's Holly," I said. "Guess what? Carrie and I have decided to come for Christmas."

"That's wonderful news. Now, let's see, when is school out?" he asked.

"We go till Friday, the seventeenth," I explained, glancing at the calendar in the family room. "But Mom wants us back home before New Year's Eve—we're having our Christmas together then."

"That's great! You girls will be here for nearly two full weeks," Daddy said. "That'll give us plenty of time for a visit to Sea World and maybe a quick trip to Disneyland. It will be crowded, but I understand it's worth fighting the masses to see the Christmas parade."

"You've never seen the electric parade?" I asked, surprised.

"Too busy to take time off, I guess," he replied.

I couldn't believe it. If I lived that close to L.A., I would want to see the Christmas festivities at Disneyland *every* year. That's the difference between my dad and me. He's all work and very little play. It was a good thing Carrie and I were spending Christmas with him this year. Maybe we could keep him from working such long hours.

"Holly, do you know what Carrie would like for Christmas?" Daddy asked.

"Ask her to write a list," I suggested. "I know she'll have lots of ideas for you."

He paused. "And what about you, Holly-Heart? Is there something special you want?"

I thought a moment about asking for a new pair of boots like the one I'd ruined in the toilet, but I changed my mind. "Whatever you get will be fine."

I was reluctant to ask for anything. After five years without him under our roof, just talking to him on the phone and visiting him occasionally was a gift in itself. But there *was* something I was dying to have. It was the heart locket Daddy had given Mom thirteen years ago on Valentine's Day—the day I was born. Somehow, when Daddy moved out, the locket had been packed with his things by mistake. Mom hadn't minded that much, maybe because of their divorce. But I did. Anyway, there was no way I could gather the courage to mention it to Daddy. Only my diary recorded my true feelings about the necklace.

His voice interrupted my thoughts. "Is Carrie available? I'd like to speak to her."

"Sure, I'll get her. Just a minute." I called for Carrie. Twice. At last she came running downstairs.

She took the phone, pushing her long golden locks behind her left shoulder. "Hello?" she said shyly.

I watched Carrie as she talked to Daddy. She hardly knew him. Daddy and Mom had separated when she was only four years old. It was hard for *me* to remember much about the years before the divorce, and I had been eight when it happened.

Carrie started naming off gift options for herself. She started with brand-name dolls, then listed book titles and computer software.

"Enough," I whispered, motioning to her. I didn't want her to sound greedy.

Shortly, she handed the phone back to me. "Here, he wants to talk to you." Carrie scampered back upstairs.

"Hi, again," I said into the phone.

"I'll send the tickets well before your flight," Daddy said. "Do you want to fly out Friday night or wait till Saturday morning?"

I wouldn't think of missing the youth group party Friday night for anything! But I was hesitant to tell Daddy about it. He might think my social life was more important than spending the extra day with him. "Uh, we'll fly out on Saturday if that's okay," I said.

"I might have a business lunch that day, though I don't know for sure," he said. "If so, I'll have Saundra pick you girls up at the airport."

I wanted to beg him not to send our stepmom, but I bit my tongue. Surely Daddy would leave his lunch meeting early enough to come for us himself.

"Well, I guess that's it for now," he said. "Oh yes, Tyler says hi. He's looking forward to meeting Carrie, and he's eager to see you again, Holly."

I remembered the nine-year-old boy—our stepbrother—who lived in my father's house on the beach. Tyler was one of the best reasons to visit my dad and his new wife. Last summer when I visited, Tyler and I had made a fabulous sand castle.

Saying good-bye to Daddy, I thought about the castle on the beach. Tyler and I had designed a blueprint on paper before we ever started building. It had taken three hours, but our Castle Royale was magnificent, complete with tiny toothpick flags, tinfoil windows, and Popsicle stick balconies. A true work of art!

Tyler had marched around the castle like a soldier on guard duty. He said he was in charge of his creation. That's when I told him the story of our beginnings. Adam and Eve. It was hard to believe, but Tyler had never heard the Genesis story. Here was a kid growing up in a posh beach house on the West Coast, and he'd totally missed the creation account in the Bible! Tyler and I talked for a long time about it. It was strange discussing things like that with a kid. But Tyler wasn't just any boy. He was very bright, and I looked forward to seeing him again.

Tyler's mother, Saundra, was another story. There was something about her that made me want to turn and run. Maybe it was that bright red lipstick of hers—I never saw her without it the whole time I was there! Maybe it was the way things had to be absolutely perfect around her. Not just her makeup and hair, but everything, right down to the cloth napkins on the table at *breakfast*! I felt sorry for Daddy. Why had he chosen someone so different from Mom?

These were just a few of the many questions that continued to haunt me about Daddy and his new life. But . . . The Question, the one buried deep inside my heart, was so mixed up with the pain of lost years, I was sure I could never bring myself to ask it.

CALIFORNIA CRAZY

Chapter 6

It was two days before the Christmas party. I got up extra early and packed my backpack with textbooks, notebooks, and . . . yes, my diary. Lately I'd been taking it to school and writing in it during study hall, far away from the eyes of super snoopers.

I pulled a pen out of my bag, then tiptoed to the bathroom, letting Carrie and Stephie sleep. I felt my diary key dangling on the chain under my nightshirt. Wearing it was the only way to secure the greatest secrets of my life.

I'd changed my mind about hiding the diary in an overnight case. It was too inconvenient, for one thing, and I didn't trust Carrie not to look in the crawl space. I was convinced she'd go to great lengths to keep up with the ongoing happenings between my friends and me. So I changed my tactics. I began sleeping with my diary.

The idea had come from a dream I had. Not only was my diary beside me in bed, it was tied to my wrist with a sound alarm cued for activation by the slightest tug on the string. It worked well in the dream, but in reality I simply tied the diary to my wrist. I wasn't smart enough to wire it for sound.

In the bathroom I lowered the toilet lid and sat on it to write in my diary.

Wednesday, December 15. I can't wait to see Jared's expression when I give him my Christmas gift. It's fabulous! I bought a cool cloth-covered book with blank pages at Explore Bookstore yesterday. (I borrowed the cash from Stan for now.)

Today I'll transfer the poems from my diary to the new book during study hall. I'm calling it, A Heart Full of Poetry: At Christmas.

I keep wondering who Jared's secret pal is. He's keeping it a secret from everyone. Another big question is: What will he give me for Christmas? Even though he hasn't mentioned it, I'm sure he'll surprise me with something. It's going to be so exciting when we exchange gifts at Pastor Rob's house on Friday. There's a huge redwood deck off the kitchen with a great view of the mountains. Maybe Jared and I can give our gifts to each other outside on the deck, by ourselves. I'd feel a little less shy that way.

I closed the diary, locked it, and put the chain around my neck. Stashing my diary in my backpack, I undressed and hopped into the shower.

♥ ♥ ♥

At school, my best friend, Andie, was waiting at my locker. "Where have you been?" she demanded breathlessly.

I glanced at my watch. "Am I late?"

"No, but I have to talk to you." She pulled me down the hall and into the girls' rest room.

I leaned my backpack on the edge of the sink. "What's going on?"

"Paula Miller's up to something," she whispered, checking under all the stalls—looking for feet, no doubt. "I ran into her downtown after school yesterday."

I peered into the mirror, checking my hair. "What's so earth-shaking about that?"

Andie continued, her dark eyes flashing. "Paula said she was buying a Christmas present for her secret pal."

I hadn't the faintest clue where Andie was going with this. "Get to the point," I said, looking at my watch. Seven minutes to first period.

"Just listen," she said. "This morning I saw Paula hiding a Christmas present in her locker. I sneaked up behind her locker, and guess what I saw?"

Andie was dying to inform me; I could tell by the pre-explosive look on her face. "So, tell me," I said, playing along.

Andie grabbed my arm. "Holly, brace yourself. The tag on Paula's gift said, *To Jared W.*" She sighed. "Do you still want to rush off to first period?"

I was burning-up mad. "Jared's *my* secret pal!" I shouted. "What's she trying to prove?"

"Beats me," Andie muttered. "Maybe she's faking it—like she drew his name or something. Might just be her latest attempt to win points with him."

I shoved my hair over my shoulder. "Won't she freak when she finds out who really drew Jared's name?"

Andie turned and looked in the mirror, touching her dark, layered curls. "Jared's not dense. He'll figure it out when you give him your gift at the party." Andie's smile gave way to a grin. I could tell she was enjoying this strange turn of events. I, on the other hand, was dying to know why Paula Miller was launching another attention-getting campaign at Jared!

"I can't believe she'd do that," I said as we rushed to our lockers. "Paula's gotta be out of her mind to mess with Jared. He won't bite—not after the scrutiny test I put him through last month."

Unless . . . Was something going on between them I didn't know about?

My fears began to diminish when I saw Jared waiting at my locker. "Hey, you look fabulous," he said, using my word. "Ready for the party?"

"Can't wait." I dropped off the books I didn't need and slammed the locker door.

He leaned over and whispered, "Me too." He flashed that adorable grin of his and offered to carry my books.

"You'll be late to class," I protested. But he reached for them anyway, walking me to science, then darted off to beat the bell.

Excited, I hurried in to find my assigned seat. None of Paula Miller's foolish plans could change Jared's and my friendship!

Mr. Ross stepped up to the podium, beginning his lecture on molecules. I tried to listen, but my mind kept wandering back to Andie's latest sleuthing efforts. What was Paula thinking, buying a present for Jared and passing it off as a secret-pal gift? And why would she risk bringing it to school, when someone like Andie was sure to see?

Hurrah for Andie, the truest friend ever—always looking out for me. Maybe she would keep an eye on Paula while I was in California visiting Daddy. Who knows what that girl might pull with Jared left here all alone.

I yanked my three-ring binder out of my backpack and began to take notes, scribbling to keep up with Mr. Ross. His lectures reminded me of a hundred-yard dash. He spoke in spurts, leaning on his wooden podium. Then he took a long breath and traipsed around his desk before he began lecturing again—faster than ever. At least I didn't have to stare at his smudged glasses anymore. Ever since he started dating Miss Wannamaker, my creative writing teacher, he'd replaced his glasses with contacts. A sure sign of love.

After science, Jared rushed over to me in the hall. "Holly-Heart, what color are you wearing Friday night?"

"Probably pink," I said, my cheeks growing warm.

"Your favorite color, right?" he said.

I nodded. What was Jared up to? I imagined him presenting me with a pink corsage. "Wait," I said, changing my mind. "Maybe I'll wear red, you know, for Christmas."

Jared shrugged his shoulders. "Well, which is it?" he teased.

"Poinsettia pink," I said, laughing.

"What's that?"

"It's sorta dusty, you know, a cross between a rose color and . . ."

Just then Paula Miller bumped into Jared. Her books went flying, with a little too much assistance on her part. Jared stooped down to pick them up, and as he did, Paula leaned over and asked him to meet her after lunch. Honestly, she didn't *speak* her request. It was a definite purr. And right in front of me!

I wanted to storm off to my next class, but I stayed put beside Jared, waiting for his response.

Jared merely nodded. "I'll see you at your locker," he said, like it was no big deal. But it was to *me,* and I was determined to find out what was going on.

At lunch Jared and I sat together as usual. Danny Myers joined us later, listening as I told Jared about my Christmas plans.

"So you're going to California for Christmas," Danny said, like he was very interested.

I swallowed a bite of hot dog and reached for a napkin. "My dad's flying Carrie and me out."

He took a drink of hot tea. Probably the decaffeinated, herbal kind. "Don't forget who your friends are," he said seriously.

"Don't worry." I glanced at Jared. "It'll be fun—at least for a little while."

Jared leaned his shoulder next to mine. "It'll be fun for Holly, but . . ." and here he broke into song, "I'll have a blue, blue Christmas without her."

Danny chuckled. But his beaming eyes made me a tad suspicious. Was he happy for me because Jared and I were finally getting along? Or did he miss the days when we'd been closer friends?

"Well, I hate to leave you two alone like this," Jared kidded, "but I have to meet someone before my next class."

I swallowed hard, wishing Jared had forgotten about his pre-arranged meeting with Paula.

"See you after school, Holly-Heart," he said, winking.

My heart fluttered only slightly. Why was he running off to meet her? I was jittery inside, wishing I could hurry out and spy on Jared. It bugged me sitting here making small talk with Danny.

Finally when I could stand it no longer, I made my move. "I've gotta run," I said, excusing myself.

"No problem," Danny said with a smile. "See you Friday at the party?"

"Yep." I waved good-bye to him.

When I had deposited my tray, I noticed Danny's table was suddenly surrounded by Kayla Miller—Paula's twin—and two other girls. It made me feel a little better to know I wasn't leaving Danny by himself. Now, on to spy on Jared's locker rendezvous with Paula.

I dashed down the hall, past the main office. Hiding behind an open classroom door, I scanned the row of lockers. There they were, in front of Paula's locker. Jared's back was turned to me— thank goodness! Paula smiled up at Jared, flashing her perfect white teeth. She gestured as she spoke, and fluffed her hair.

I was boiling inside. How rude! Who did she think she was?

Paula reached up and took the gift out of her locker. It was lavishly wrapped with shiny striped paper and topped with a large green-and-white bow.

No way would Jared accept her gift. Not unless she actually lied about it. Maybe she was giving it to him early to trick him into thinking she had drawn his name. Desperately I tried to second-guess her plan. This was too weird!

Along with being angry, I was secretly amused. How would Paula react if Jared refused her gift? I was dying to know. After his refusal, Jared would set Paula straight about us. What a scene that would be.

I longed to hear their conversation. Paula held up the fancy gift, playing with the ribbon on the top, chattering incessantly. Inching closer, I noticed Jared turn slightly and glance at his watch. Yes! Just as I thought. He was going to leave her standing in the dust.

Then an incredible thing happened. Paula whispered something in Jared's ear. Then she held the gift out, and Jared actually accepted it.

Strains of Christmas music began to flutter through the hall from the school office. Someone was playing "I'll Be Home for Christmas." Probably the school secretary. The sentimental melody washed over me as Jared waved to Paula.

I wanted to cry. Instead, I turned and fled, searching frantically for my best friend.

Chapter 7

I found Andie in study hall working on last-minute math homework. "I have to talk to you," I whispered, settling into the desk in front of hers. Then I spilled out the events I had just witnessed.

She stuck her pencil in her math book and closed it. "Holly, your friendship with Jared is at stake," she said, as if I didn't already know. "Listen to me, and do exactly what I tell you."

"Okay, like what?"

She twirled a strand of hair around her finger. Trouble was brewing! "Prissy Paula has had her eyes on Jared ever since she and her twin sister moved to Dressel Hills. Here's what you do—totally ignore her."

"But how can I? She's everywhere!"

Andie's lips spread into a forced grin. "Pretend she doesn't exist."

"And then what?" I asked, dumbfounded at this ridiculous idea.

"If you act mature about the whole thing, Jared will be so impressed he'll start ignoring Paula, too."

"I, uh, don't know about this."

Andie nodded her head slowly. "Paula's trying to make you mad. I think that's part of what's motivating her." She crossed her arms deliberately and leaned on the desk. "She probably thinks you'll confront Jared about this, and that could blow your relationship with him."

"Really . . . you think so?"

"You betcha." Suddenly she looked serious. "Nobody likes to be cornered, least of all Jared. It's part of the game." She picked up her pencil.

"Andie, you're incredible!"

She relished the compliment. I could tell by the way she sat there grinning, her brown eyes sparkling.

Deep inside, I wondered about Jared. Why would he accept a Christmas gift from Paula unless she really did lie about getting his name? And if not, had he been fooling me all these weeks?

"For now," Andie added quietly, "be cool and see what happens at the party."

I rummaged through my bag and found my locked diary. It was time to transfer *A Heart Full of Poetry* to the red-and-green-plaid covered book—for Jared. As I copied the first poem in my best handwriting, I thought about Jared Wilkins. True, we'd had a parade of ups and downs in our friendship, but I thought things were settled between us. I *wanted* to trust him. And only something like this thing with Paula could make me doubt him.

I ran to catch the city bus after school. If I hurried, I could get home before the snoopers invaded my territory. I needed some privacy while I wrapped Jared's gift.

After hopping off the bus, I heard loud hammering coming from halfway down the street. I paused to listen. It was coming from behind my house. Thanks to a lack of normally heavy snows, our two-room addition was already coming along nicely.

Inside the house, I hurried to the crawl space, my backpack still slung over my shoulder. Spotting the box overflowing with Christmas wrap and ribbons, I chose the prettiest paper I could find and a bright red bow to match. I hurried to my room.

Bam! Bam! The hammering continued.

Upstairs I found Carrie and Stephie building something out of Legos that resembled a spaceship.

"What are you two doing home?" I asked.

"Early dismissal," Carrie said.

I looked at the Lego chaos everywhere. "This room is a massive mess!"

"Don't worry, we'll clean it up," Carrie said absentmindedly.

"Do it now," I said.

The girls looked up at me. "We were here first," Stephie said.

I closed the door. Stephie was wrong again; *I* was here first! Her snide remark echoed in my brain to the beat of the hammering outside. "Sassy little girl," I muttered, hurrying to the kitchen for some tape and a scissors. "I was born first, inhabited that room first, and . . ."

"Hey, Holly, you're talking to yourself again," Stan said, coming in the back door.

"Trying for some sanity," I said, hoping he'd make himself scarce and leave me alone to wrap my present in peace.

"Hungry?" he asked. He tossed his jacket on the counter beside my Christmas wrap.

I sighed.

"Not talking to me today?" He made a beeline to the refrigerator. "How about a sandwich?"

Bam! Bam! The pounding was getting to me. Really getting to me.

"Turkey and cheese okay?" he yelled over the noise, holding the refrigerator door open, waiting for my response.

"No mustard, please," I mumbled.

"Man, something's really got to you." Stan poured a glass of milk.

I didn't dare tell him what was bugging me. He might mention it to Billy Hill, or worse, Danny Myers, and it would get back to Jared. I was determined to stick with Andie's plan and pretend Paula and Jared had never met today at her locker.

I thanked Stan when he presented a sandwich to me on a napkin. Then he disappeared down the stairs to the family room-turned-bedroom.

Must be nice having the largest room in the house, I thought.

I was struggling with that old familiar feeling—jealousy. And I was dealing with it on more than one level these days. But Stan and his cozy retreat downstairs were easier to handle than Paula and her sneaky tactics.

I grabbed three grapes and popped them into my mouth as I reached for the dishcloth. Draping Stan's jacket over a stool, I wiped the top of the bar. Next, I dried the area, then began to unroll the wrapping paper, eager to make Jared's gift as dazzling as possible. No question, it would be better than Paula's any day.

Once the poetry book was neatly wrapped, I carried my school bag upstairs to the communal bedroom. I decided not to comment again on the Lego disaster as I tiptoed around the maze of tiny pieces to the closet. On days like this, I'd have given my right arm for a walk-in closet. Privacy was more important than ever, now that I had none at all.

Searching through my end of the closet, I found the rosy-pink blouse I had described to Jared. It would look fabulous with my new black pants. I whisked the blouse out of the closet and grabbed my backpack, heading for Mom's bedroom.

Closing the door, I posed in Mom's tall mirror behind the door. I held the silky blouse under my neck, staring at my reflection. If everything went well, the party was going to be so perfect. A night to remember.

Just then I heard the mail truck pull up. Peeking through the lace curtains, I saw the mail carrier climb out of the white truck and head up the walk toward the house.

I dropped my backpack and laid the blouse on Mom's bed. I ran downstairs, arriving at the door just as the postman rang the bell.

"Here you are, missy." He held out a stack of mail. One was marked Express Mail.

"Thanks," I said, eager to open the large white envelope with my name on it. I ran to the kitchen, grabbed the letter opener out of the drawer, and sliced into the envelope.

Inside, I found two sets of airplane tickets. One for Carrie, and one for me. And there was a letter from Daddy. I began to read.

> *Dear Holly,*
>
> *You and Carrie are booked to leave this Friday night at nine-thirty.*

"Oh no, he's got it all wrong," I whispered, my heart pounding.

> *I realize you preferred to leave Saturday, but holiday schedules are tight, so I took what my travel agent could arrange. Hopefully this won't cause any hardship on your end.*
>
> > *We'll see you in two days.*
> > *Love, Daddy*

"Hardship? This is horrible!" I shouted, punching the air. "How could he mess up like this?"

Carrie and Stephie came galloping downstairs. Stephie dragged my backpack behind her.

"Give me that," I said, snatching it from her. Heading upstairs, I stopped in my tracks, remembering there was no privacy to be had in my bedroom. In fact, there was none anywhere in this house.

Furious about my dad's mistake, I grabbed my jacket and fumbled to put it on. Then I dashed outside—behind the house—barging into the middle of the unfinished addition. The workers stopped their hammering and stared at me as I knelt down on the cold cement foundation and crumpled Daddy's letter. I didn't care what they thought. My estranged father had just ruined my entire Christmas—and maybe my life!

Chapter 8

"Why is this happening to me?" I sobbed into the phone hours later, telling Andie my sad tale.

She was doing her best to calm me down. "Hang on a minute, Holly. You can still go to the party. Just pack your stuff ahead of time and ask your mom to pick you up at Pastor Rob's. You can leave for the airport from there."

"That's easy for you to say," I said, sniffling. "Your guy friend's not accepting gifts from gorgeous brunettes."

"I thought we had that problem settled," she scolded.

I sighed loudly. "Maybe *you* did."

"So what are you gonna do, Holly? Confront Jared and make him mad in time for Christmas?"

Andie was right, as usual.

I blew my nose. "Okay, I'll try it your way."

"Look, I've gotta run," Andie said abruptly. "Mom needs me."

"Okay," I said reluctantly, hearing the sounds of Andie's two-year-old twin brothers in the background. "Hey, thanks, Andie," I added. "You're a good friend."

"Don't you forget it." With that, she hung up.

I ran upstairs to survey my wardrobe for California before Mom and Uncle Jack arrived home. It was going to be tight, but

I intended to get Carrie's and my clothes washed and packed in time to head for the airport directly from the party.

Mom was agreeable when I mentioned it. "You don't have to convince me of the importance of this church event, Holly-Heart," she said, touching my head. "I know."

I leaned against the sink, watching her chop lettuce for the salad. "Thanks, Mom." I hugged her. "I'm going to miss you."

She put the knife down and dried her hands. Then she wrapped her arms around me. "You're my sweetie. You know that, don't you?"

I nodded, blinking back the tears. It wasn't going to be easy leaving her. It would be my very first Christmas away from her—and Dressel Hills.

"It'll be nice coming home to my old room," I said, wiping my face.

Mom motioned for me to sit at the bar. She scooted onto the stool across from me. "Your uncle Jack thinks a lot of you, Holly-Heart. The addition we're having built isn't just to make more bedroom space for his kids. It's much more than that."

"I think I know what you're saying. It's Uncle Jack's way of showing how much he cares about *your* kids, too, right?"

Mom nodded, smiling. "Jack's a wonderful man. I'm truly blessed to be his wife." I could tell she meant it by the way her blue eyes twinkled as she spoke his name.

With Mom's help, I was packed and ready long before the party. Mom stayed home with the rest of the kids until it was time to head for the airport while Uncle Jack drove Stan and me to Pastor Rob's house.

"Feel up to driving the two of us home tonight?" my uncle asked Stan as we passed through the intersection of Aspen Street and Downhill Court.

"Sure." Stan grinned. He needed the practice now that he had his coveted instruction permit, but there weren't many times when the Patterson family van wasn't packed with passengers.

Uncle Jack turned, casting a quick wink at me. "It won't be long and I'll be giving Holly driving lessons."

"Yeah, in less than two years I'll have *my* permit," I said. Funny, I felt more confident about learning to drive than about seeing Paula in the same room with Jared.

When we pulled into the driveway, Stan turned picked up the present for his secret pal and turned around in the passenger's seat. "Hope you have fun in the sun, Holly."

"I'll try," I said, holding my gift for Jared.

"Let me know if you run out of money," Stan said. "I charge twenty-five-percent interest." He was joking, but I didn't mind. It was his way of saying he'd miss me. He leaped out of the van, heading for the party.

"Watch out for suntanned beach bums," Uncle Jack teased as I climbed out of the van. "Don't go California crazy."

"Don't worry," I said, thinking of my one and only crush. No way would I fall for some tall, tan surfer with Jared Wilkins waiting for me back home. I waved to Uncle Jack once more.

Inside, the house was bustling with zillions of kids. Pastor Rob greeted me and took my jacket. A tall Christmas tree stood in the middle of the window at one end of the room. It was decorated with red and white bows and homemade ornaments. I hid Jared's gift among the many secret-pal presents under the tree.

At the other end of the room, a crowd of kids gathered around a grand piano. Andie was playing "Jingle Bell Rock," while Stan leaned on the piano, grinning at her. Joy and Amy-Liz tossed popcorn into Andie's mouth as her fingers flew over the keys.

When Joy saw me, she rushed over. "Merry Christmas, Holly," she said, pushing a small gift into my hands. "I'm your secret pal," she whispered.

"You are?" I said, pulling tape off the side. "I never would've guessed." A white box peeked out of the wrapping. I tugged on it and opened the lid. Inside, nestled on the cotton lining, was a silver beaded necklace with a cross. "Ooh," I whispered, and gave her a hug. "I love it. Thanks!"

"Who's *your* secret pal?" she asked, her eyes bright with anticipation.

"I'm not telling yet," I said, looking around for Jared. And Paula.

"Oh, in case you wondered, Jared's in the kitchen pulling taffy with Billy Hill," Joy said, heading back to the piano, where Andie was accumulating admirers and carolers.

"Where's Shauna?" I asked, following Joy to the piano. Shauna and Joy were inseparable friends.

"She has the flu," Joy said. "She's missed out on everything all week."

"That's too bad," I said, watching Andie's chubby fingers bounce around the octaves in the bass. "Tell her I missed her tonight, okay?"

Joy nodded and smiled.

Andie stopped playing long enough to slide over on the bench. "Let's sing 'Carol of the Bells,' " she suggested, patting the bench.

I sat beside her, glancing around at the eligible vocalists. "Let's make it a round," I said.

"Good idea," Stan agreed. "But some of us need the music."

Andie rolled an arpeggio up the keyboard, holding the broken chord with the pedal. "I don't." She flashed a smile at Stan.

"Look out," Joy teased. "Andie's playing by ear again."

Stan laughed and reached for the songbook. Scanning the index, his finger ran down the page. "Found it," he said, holding the book open for Andie.

After another introductory flourish by Andie, the guys began to sing. Joy, Amy-Liz, and I came in with the repeated melody, creating a two-part harmony. Soon, Kayla and several other girls from the kitchen joined in.

Where was Paula?

At the end of our fabulous rendition, we clapped and hooted. This was going to be the best Christmas party ever!

I hurried upstairs to put my gift from Joy on the lamp table in one of the bedrooms. There, a mountain of jackets was piled on the bed. Back downstairs, I peeked into the kitchen and saw Billy and Jared pulling taffy. Pastor Rob was supervising.

"Come help us, Holly," Billy called, motioning with his head.

Jared looked up just then; his face burst into a grin. "There she is," he announced to everyone. That's when I noticed Jared's shirt. It matched my rosy-pink blouse!

I hurried to his side. "So that's why you asked what color I was wearing," I whispered.

He nodded, his arms stretched out in front of him. "Here, someone take my place." He pulled his fingers away from the sticky taffy. Then, out of the crowded kitchen, Paula Miller emerged.

She picked up the taffy marked with Jared's fingerprints and flashed her Colgate smile at me as Jared washed his hands at the sink.

Was I ever glad I'd traded names with Billy for the secret-pal gift exchange. I couldn't imagine buying a present for pathetic Paula.

Jared and I headed into the living room. We sang several more Christmas carols and helped string popcorn on the tree.

"I have a surprise for you," I said during a semi-quiet moment. "Let's go out on the deck for a minute, okay?"

Jared followed me to the Christmas tree and waited while I found his present. He held the patio door for me as we walked into the frosty night.

It was colder than I'd expected, but the view was fabulous, just the way I'd imagined it would be. We leaned on the redwood railing, gazing at the mountains, black against the moonlit sky. Pungent smells of woodsmoke enhanced the atmosphere. Perfect!

I held up my gift to Jared. "Merry Christmas! I'm your secret pal."

He looked surprised. "Really? *You* are?"

I nodded, shivering in the wintry stillness. "This present isn't for just *any* secret pal, you know."

Jared grinned down at me. Suddenly the light on the deck

flashed on. We turned to see the faces of our friends pressed against the kitchen window. Paula was among the kids waving and laughing as the light blinked on and off, on and off.

"Not her again," I muttered.

"What did you say?" Jared leaned his ear close to my face.

"Nothing," I said, disappointed that our special moment had to be interrupted this way.

Still holding the present, Jared cleared his throat. "Should I open it now?" he asked.

Suddenly I felt shy. "If you want to."

He ripped off the wrapping paper and stuffed it into his jeans pocket. Then, opening the clothbound book, he let out a low whistle. "Is this what I think it is?" He glanced at me. Then he read the title, *"A Heart Full of Poetry: At Christmas."*

"Original poetry by Holly Meredith," I said, pleased by his response. I reached up and stuck the red ribbon on his head, giggling.

That's when he caught my arm and gave me a quick hug. "Thanks, Holly-Heart. You're too good to be true."

I was thankful for the semi-darkness. It hid the blood rushing to my cheeks.

"I'll read every word tonight when I get home," he promised.

My teeth were chattering.

"Hey, I'd better get you inside. It's freezing out here."

I was reluctant to return to the loud party atmosphere. Mostly because Jared hadn't surprised me yet with a gift. And time was running out.

Pastor Rob called everyone to the family room around the fireplace. Jared sat beside me on the floor during our devotional time.

♥ ♥ ♥

Later, when the doorbell rang, I rushed to get it. Mom stood there, ready to drive me to the airport.

"Just a minute," I said, letting her in out of the cold. "I'll get my jacket."

"Take your time," she said, coming inside.

Dying for an explanation from Jared about the gift I was sure he was going to give me, I ran upstairs to get my jacket. Under the second pile of coats, I found my present from Joy. Putting it in my pocket, I headed for the stairs.

Halfway down, I noticed Paula and Jared standing in the corner of the living room, near the Christmas tree. I leaned on the railing. What were they doing? I kept watching, relieved that Mom was engaged in conversation with Pastor Rob.

My heart pounded as I observed the handsome twosome. Paula's dark, shoulder-length hair was pulled away from her face with an elegant hair clip. Her face glowed as she gazed at Jared. He held something in his hands. What was it? I stared at the small, square box wrapped in red paper and topped with a white lacy bow. Paula flashed her pearly whites as he handed the gift to her. My heart sank as he beamed down at her.

Choking back the tears, I yanked on my jacket and zipped it up. Quickly, I thanked Pastor Rob for a terrific party and, without saying good-bye to anyone, not even Andie, stumbled to the car in the cold and suddenly bleak December night.

Chapter 9

When our plane landed in L.A., I was dying to get off. Being cooped up in an airplane with a chatterbox little sister is no fun when what you really want to do is replay in your head the events of a Christmas party gone wrong. Over and over.

I waited impatiently in the aisle for the man ahead of me. He was asking the flight attendant about the weather in Hong Kong. Just my luck! I wanted to sprint down the aisle and up the ramp, but it was impossible because zillions of people were getting off.

At last, the line began to move, and we inched our way to the baggage claim area. People stood around in short sleeves and shorts, welcoming loved ones home for Christmas.

California was the place to be by the looks of things. By comparison, Dressel Hills seemed dull with its sting of cold—wintry and otherwise.

Carrie and I lugged our ski jackets, gazing at the sea of faces. One face stood out among them all. Daddy!

He waved, and soon his arms were around us both. The spicy smell of his cologne brought back a world of memories, and I was grateful, at least, for one thing. Daddy had come for us—alone—without Saundra. I was in no mood to deal with her tonight.

"Your stepmom stayed home with Tyler because of the late

hour, but I have a feeling they'll be waiting up for you," Daddy explained. "How was your flight?" he asked.

"A little bumpy," Carrie said, rubbing her eyes. It was only the second plane ride of her life. "But it went fast from Colorado to here." She continued to jabber on about the flight attendants, the snack, and the turbulence we experienced as we headed for the parking lot with the other holiday travelers.

Warm, humid air hit my face as I walked beside Daddy, holding Carrie's hand. Palm trees swayed under the lights as we found Daddy's car. I slid into the leathery front seat while Carrie climbed into the back.

Soon we were on the freeway, heading for Daddy's gorgeous beach house. An old Christmas tune came on the radio. "I'll be home for Christmas," the singer crooned.

Feelings of homesickness pricked my heart. Outside, the waves of the Pacific Ocean shimmered in the moonlight. I stared up at the moon. The same one was shining down on the mountains of Colorado. Thinking that made me feel more miserable than ever.

"It's the ocean!" Carrie said. She strained hard against her seat belt, staring out the window.

"Yes, but wait till you see the view from the house tomorrow morning," Daddy told her. He turned into a long, narrow drive. Palm trees lined the lane, casting moon shadows on the luxurious, wine-red car. "Saundra's making Chinese food for lunch tomorrow." He smiled. "How's that sound?"

"You canceled your luncheon?" I asked, hoping he wouldn't leave us alone with the wicked stepmother on our very first day here.

"It's been postponed until Monday," he replied.

I stole quick glances at him, wondering if we'd have time for a heart-to-heart talk. Then the house appeared out of nowhere.

Saundra stood outside on the porch, wearing a black-and-white polka-dot dress and black heels. She greeted Carrie and me as we came up the walk. But she hugged and kissed Daddy as though he'd been gone for weeks. I tried to remember Mom doing that. It was easy, except when the new Mrs. Meredith spoke. "Welcome to our home, girls." Heavy perfume hung in the air.

"I'm thirsty," Carrie said, waiting for Daddy to bring the luggage up from the car.

"And I have to call Mom," I told Saundra, who held open the front door. It was decorated with an enormous wreath of seashells.

A wiry boy with auburn hair and freckles zoomed past us, wearing his pajamas and bathrobe.

"Oh, there you are, Tyler," Saundra said. She turned to me. "Your stepbrother has been anxiously awaiting your arrival, Holly." She smiled broadly, her red lips glistening in the porch light. Then she introduced her son to Carrie.

Tyler grabbed Carrie's hand and pulled her into the house. I heard him say, "There's a surprise in your room that's way cool," and with that, they were gone.

I headed for the kitchen to call Mom. She would be waiting up, eager to know we had arrived safely. I glanced around at the enormous living room, brilliant with golden hues. A Christmas tree stood in the middle of an expansive wall of windows overlooking the ocean. It reminded me of another tree, a very simple one decorated with handmade ornaments—the tree at Pastor Rob's house. Then, like a roaring avalanche, the painful memories of the evening came sweeping back.

Swallowing the lump in my throat, I found the kitchen phone. No way did I want to sound sad when I talked to Mom. "We made it here just fine," I told her when she answered.

"Oh, good." She sounded relieved. "I'm praying you'll both have a wonderful time. And Holly?"

"Yes?"

"Merry Christmas."

"I miss you already," I said, aware of the lump creeping into my throat. Again.

"Me too, sweetie," she said. "I'll see you soon."

"I hope the time goes by fast," I said softly so no one would hear.

When I finished talking, Tyler appeared around the corner, ready to guide me to my room—down a long, winding Cinderella staircase, its railing adorned with evergreen. Two large bedrooms with a sitting room between graced the lower level. Just as I had remembered.

Tyler took me into the bedroom where Carrie was. "Look!" He pointed to a telescope set on a tripod across the room. It was aimed toward the ocean.

"Fabulous," I whispered. "Is this yours?"

Tyler grinned. "It's my old one, but you two can use it for now." Carrie couldn't keep her hands off it. She adjusted the lens, peering through the peephole again and again.

Then I turned to see Daddy standing in the doorway. He was piled up with luggage. Tyler dashed across the room to open the wide maple closet doors.

"There's plenty of space to hang things," my father said, bringing Carrie's bags into the room. "Make yourselves at home, girls. We're glad you've come to spend the holidays with us."

Tyler seemed impatient, shifting from one foot to the other. It was obvious he had other plans in mind that didn't include unpacking or organizing clothes.

I went into my own room to rescue my overnight case. My hair stuff and other toiletries were inside, as well as my locked diary. Saundra followed me to my room. "As soon as you're unpacked, Holly, we'll have a dish of ice cream." She stood in the doorway, watching my every move. "There are towels and linens in the bathroom closet if you want to freshen up." She motioned for Tyler to scoot.

"See you upstairs, Holly," he called.

"Okay," I said, wondering where this nine-year-old boy got all his confidence. I could've used some tonight at the party. The scene replayed in my mind. In my imagination, I actually marched up to

Jared and gleefully ripped my present—*A Heart Full of Poetry*—out of his hands!

In the bathroom, I opened a corner cupboard filled with elegant linens. I chose a thick blue towel and a washcloth to match. There were brightly colored tins filled with butterfly and bird soaps in blue and green hues. I lifted a green one to my nose and breathed deeply. Mmm! Almost pepperminty—like Mom's tea back home in Dressel Hills. I wondered if she was sipping some right now.

Glancing at my watch, I saw that it was an hour later there. Nope, she was probably asleep by now. A twinge gripped me. I was already homesick for the angel of a mother I'd left behind. I longed for her gentle ways and listening ear. Of course, she couldn't remove my hurt, no one could. But her soft voice and loving eyes would let me know I could survive—even without Jared as my friend.

After a warm shower I was too tired to engage in small talk or eat ice cream upstairs with Daddy . . . and especially Saundra. So, clad in a bathrobe, I excused myself and headed back to the huge room that was to be mine for the next two weeks. The thought of temporarily acquiring this major privacy eased the homesickness slightly.

Glancing at the strewn contents of my suitcase, I felt guilty about waiting till tomorrow to unpack. But I pushed the feeling aside and slipped between the silky sheets, reaching for my overnight case and a pen. Then I recorded the heartbreaking news of the day.

Friday, December 17. It's late and I'm so tired, but I have to write these words on paper so I won't explode. Jared Wilkins is absolutely despicable! More tomorrow . . .

I locked my diary with the key on the chain around my neck. Sliding the diary under the pillow next to mine, I reached for the massive lamp poised on the bedside table. In the darkness, I asked God to ease my pain and to please help me forget Jared Wilkins—ASAP!

Chapter 10

During lunch the next day, I watched Daddy sprinkle soy sauce on his rice. Saundra sat to his left, passing seconds to him, only to have them refused. I wished she'd back off. How many times did he have to say he was dieting, anyhow?

I decided I wouldn't call her Saundra this visit. The way she pronounced it gave me the creeps! Besides, it wasn't polite to address her by her first name anyway. Calling her "stepmom" seemed somewhat cold even though it fit her austere personality. So I resolved to avoid calling her anything. At least for now.

Tyler sat across the table from me, rolling his eyes at everything his mother said. "Sit up straight, dear," she'd say. "Lean over your plate," or "Don't poke at your food." On and on.

Carrie seemed entertained by his antics, however. And Tyler milked it for all it was worth, acting out and being rewarded with giggles from Carrie. I could see the two of them were quite a pair. And Daddy and Saundra, er, Mrs. Meredith the Second, were also quite taken with each other. As for well matched, though, I didn't see how that could possibly be.

I couldn't help it; I thought of Jared. In many ways we were opposites, too. I was loyal to the bone, but he . . . ? What he'd done was unforgivable, especially after those special moments we'd spent together on the deck . . . *"I'll read every word when I get home,"* Jared had said about my book of poetry. I wanted to wring his neck—Paula's, too!

Andie's advice rang in my ears. *Ignore Paula.*

Right! How could I when it was obvious that Jared couldn't?

Daddy reached for Saundra's hand and squeezed it. They were quite a couple. Where did that leave me? Furiously, I snapped open a fortune cookie. The thin strip of paper stuck out, but I crumpled it without reading it and stuffed it into my shorts pocket despite Saundra's disapproving look.

Tyler excused himself, and he and Carrie ran off to play. Daddy kissed Saundra and left the table, too. Saundra sat across from me, her reddish hair swept up away from her face.

Uncomfortable with the silence, I attempted to clear the table, but she interfered immediately, declaring that this was my vacation and I was not to lift a finger to help in any way.

Okay, I thought. *I can handle that.* I wandered off to find Daddy—the perfect excuse to avoid direct conversation with her.

Daddy's study was lined with wall-to-wall books, shelved in rich, glowing cherrywood. Not surprising—everything in this house was polished to a high gleam. I stared in amazement at his collection of books, ignoring the thought that some of them probably belonged to Saundra.

I tiptoed behind Daddy's chair and peeked over the back. He was reading a book of poetry. He chuckled. "Mice are quieter than you," he said, motioning for me to sit on his hassock. "What's on your mind?"

"You are," I said courageously, curious about the poetry he was reading.

He held it up, surveying the title. "It's free verse," he said. "What's your taste in poetry?"

"Rhyming's my favorite."

"That figures," he said, with a faint smile. "Your mother always preferred it over a loose rhyme pattern, too." He mentioned her so effortlessly, I wondered if he thought of Mom often.

"You remember?" I asked, feeling uncomfortable about his easygoing approach.

He nodded, touching my head as I knelt beside his chair. "There are many happy memories." His crisp, articulate voice turned suddenly soft and intimate.

Deep and dark, The Question stirred within me. *Now!* it urged me. *Ask now!*

My lips formed The Question, but the words remained locked up. Dense pain concealed it, forcing it down . . . deep into the most secret places of my being.

"I've missed so much of your life, Holly," Daddy was saying. Unexpectedly, he wrapped his arms around me. I hugged him back, feeling some of the pain of those lost years.

And then, he was reading a winter sonnet, the sound of his voice soothing me, even though the poem reminded me of cold, snowy Colorado. I didn't mind. Having Daddy all to myself like this was sweet.

Just then, Saundra broke the spell by carrying in a tray of sodas for three. She sat across the room, silently sipping hers. I cringed. The special moment had ended for me with Saundra's intrusion. I felt cheated . . . and hurt.

That night in my journal I had a few choice words to say about my wicked stepmother.

I awakened to knocks at my door the next morning.

"Yes?" I answered sleepily.

"I fixed breakfast for you," Tyler announced through the door. "May I come in?"

Sitting up, I reached for one of the many pillows piled up on my enormous bed. I pulled the covers up to my chest and called, "Okay."

Slowly, Tyler emerged, straining to balance a breakfast tray of scrambled eggs and jelly toast, a tiny glass of orange juice, and a tall glass of milk.

"You did all this?"

He looked embarrassed, but only for a second. "I'm way good at making breakfast."

"Thanks, Tyler," I said, spreading out the white linen napkin. "Does your mom know you used her cloth napkin?"

"Oh yes," he said, his golden-brown eyes smiling. "She insisted on it."

I poked a piece of scrambled egg and remembered I'd forgotten to pray. I put my fork down.

"It's safe to eat. Honest," he exclaimed.

"I believe you," I replied. "But I always pray before I eat."

"Always?" he asked, raising his eyebrows.

I nodded. "Wanna join me?"

"I don't know how," he said.

"It's not hard," I explained. "It's like talking to your best friend."

"I heard a man pray on the radio once. He had lots of thees and thous in his prayer."

"God doesn't care if our words are perfect or not. He wants our hearts," I said, delighted to share my faith with Tyler again.

"Will you pray out loud so I can listen?" he asked sheepishly.

I nodded. "Dear Lord," I began, "this breakfast looks fabulous. Thanks for blessing it and thanks for Tyler, who put it all together as a special surprise for me. In Jesus' name, amen."

"Wow, that's way easy," Tyler said.

I smiled. "Wanna try tonight at supper?"

"Nah," he said, stepping back. "My mom would freak."

"How come?"

"She's not much into God and stuff like that," he said, turning to leave.

"Where are you going now?" I asked.

"Carrie's next," he said, grinning at me over his shoulder. I picked up my fork and sampled the eggs. Suddenly Tyler was back. "Here, I forgot to give you this," he said, handing me a note.

It was from Daddy. The note said he had an unexpected

appointment, and Saundra was out doing last-minute Christmas shopping. *Do you mind watching Tyler and Carrie for a few hours while we're gone?* It was signed, *Love, Daddy.*

Tyler stood in the doorway. "Enjoy your breakfast while I plan our day." A sudden mischievous look spread across his freckled face. "The house is empty, and it's almost Christmas!"

The gleam in his eyes gave away his secret. The little sneak!

"Carrie! Wake up!" he called to her. "I'm serving you breakfast in bed." His voice trailed off, but I heard something about raiding the closets and looking under the beds for presents.

Yikes! I had my work cut out for me baby-sitting these two. I gobbled down the rest of my breakfast and found my robe. Before I made the bed, I pulled my diary out of hiding, making sure it was still locked. No one needed to know about my troubles back in Dressel Hills.

I opened the drapes and gazed out at the ocean. Sea gulls drifted lazily in the warmth of the sun. Soaking up the breathtaking view, I talked to God. It was Sunday morning in Daddy's house. Back home, we'd all be in church by now. I felt a twinge of sadness for the free and easy lifestyle Daddy was accustomed to. And Tyler . . . How could a kid make it growing up without God in his life? I blamed Saundra for her disinterest in spiritual things. I poured out my thoughts and feelings. Before long, I was soothed as I watched the waves crash in with the tide.

My gaze found a boy running along the beach, a black Labrador at his side. Every so often, the boy would stop, rub the Lab's back, and talk to her. There was no question about their relationship— they were good pals.

I leaned on the arm of the overstuffed chair for a longer look. Printed on the boy's blue sweat shirt was the number 34. Tan with sun-bleached blond hair, he was about Stan's age, I guessed. I watched till he was a speck in the distance.

Reluctantly, I turned away from the window to make my bed and then hurried off to check on Tyler and Carrie. But my thoughts curiously centered on Number 34.

Chapter 11

"Disappear!" Carrie shouted as I entered her bedroom. "This is *my* room!"

"Give me a break," I said, bending down to pick up pajamas, underwear, you-name-it.

"Sure, I'll give you a break," she snapped. "Tyler and I are going outside to the hot tub, how's that?" With a flick of her long hair, my sister flounced off to the bathroom, swimsuit in hand.

"Fine," I muttered, sitting on the edge of her unmade bed.

When she finally emerged, Carrie's hair flopped around in a ponytail high on her head, and a towel hung over her bare shoulders.

"Nice suit," I said.

"Saundra bought it for me." She pushed a pile of rumpled clothes off the chair. Then she dug into a department store bag and pulled out a hot-pink two-piece bathing suit and threw it at me.

"Where'd you get this?" I asked, holding it up.

"It's for you, from your wicked stepmother!"

Our eyes caught for a second, then Carrie glanced away, her face filled with guilt.

"Why, you little . . ." I grabbed her arm, ready to accuse her of reading my diary. But wait . . . it was locked this morning when I checked—and I was wearing the key! I glared at her. "How'd you do it?"

Carrie knew exactly what I meant. "Easy," she taunted, pulling away from me.

Tyler stood in the doorway, wearing his swimming trunks. "What's going on?" he asked.

Carrie shouted, "This is what happens when you're not the only child. Be thankful."

I wanted to shake her. "Stop avoiding the subject and stay away from my diary."

Carrie faced Tyler, still ignoring me. I reached out to grab her, but she spun away and ran upstairs as I followed her into the hallway.

Tyler shrugged his shoulders. "You two fight like this at home?" he asked. Then he turned and ran upstairs, yelling for Carrie. I stormed off to my room and sat near the window, creating a plan to catch my sister red-handed. Tonight!

After a long morning of swimming and supervising Tyler and Carrie, I should've been wiped out by the end of this day. But I wasn't the least bit tired at ten-thirty when I turned off the light.

Pulling up the sheet, I waited. I was almost sure what Carrie was doing. While I slept, she would unlock my diary with the key around my neck. I didn't know exactly how, without waking me, but I was known to be a heavy sleeper. So . . . even if it meant staying up all night, I was determined to catch her!

After what seemed like hours, I glanced at the clock on my lamp table. Only eleven. Surely Carrie would come sneaking in any minute.

In the darkness, I crept to the window and watched moonbeams promenade across the ocean. And then I saw something moving along the beach. Inching closer to the window, I spied a large animal running on the beach beside a jogger. I strained to see. Then I remembered the telescope.

Hurrying to Carrie's room, I tiptoed to the long, black tube poised on a tripod. Glancing across the room, I checked out my sleeping sister. Then, positioning the lens, I brought it into focus.

Number 34! His sleek black Labrador ran at his side. I sharpened the focus, pulling the tall, blond boy into closer range. I could see him quite clearly now in his sweats and his bare feet.

Carrie stirred in her sleep. I squatted down, holding my breath. When I was certain she was asleep again, I left quickly.

Instead of counting sheep after I slipped between the sheets, I counted the days Jared and I had been together before the Christmas party. I could still hear his voice whispering my nickname. *Holly-Heart* . . .

Tears trickled over my cheeks and landed in my ears as I stared up at the ceiling. A stream of words tumbled back into my consciousness. *You're too good to be true, Holly-Heart.*

I turned over and pressed my face into the pillow, closing my eyes and squeezing the tears out. The old days and my new Jared were gone, thanks to Paula Miller.

The next morning I woke with a start. Yikes—I'd fallen asleep! I slid my hand under the pillow next to me and felt for my diary and the lock. Both were secure. So was the key on the chain around my neck.

Glancing at the clock, I discovered it was only six forty-five. But I was too wide awake to go back to sleep. I wandered over to the windows and sat on the chair in the corner. Sea gulls screeched as they did their morning exercises over the ocean waves.

Exercise. Just what I needed. I pulled on some shorts and a T-shirt and headed outside for a walk on the beach.

The salty sea breeze energized me. I ran hard, barefooted on the wet sand, as the breakers came in with the tide. Eventually I slowed to a walk, closing my eyes, facing the first rays of the sun. Here it was, five days till Christmas, and it felt like summer. But something was missing, and it wasn't just the snow. It was much more than that. Mom was back home, and I missed her. Andie wasn't around for me to cry on her shoulder. And Jared . . . What would happen to our friendship? Thinking that thought made me teary eyed again. I was truly homesick.

I decided to take things into my own hands. There would be Christmas cheer right here on this beach, even if I had to make a snowman out of sand. I stooped down and began pushing damp sand into a large ball. Soon I had a jolly, round base, and I stepped back for a quick look.

A while later, someone called to me. "Holly!"

I turned to see Carrie and Tyler running toward my sand creation at full speed. Anger churned inside me when I saw Carrie, her long golden locks flying in the ocean's breeze. It still bugged me, not being able to keep a nosy little sister out of my very private diary.

"Wow, that's huge!" Tyler exclaimed when he saw the round sand ball. "What're you making?"

"*I* know!" Carrie shrieked with delight. "It's gonna be a sandy snowman."

"Way cool," Tyler said. "Can we help?"

"Run to the house and get something to carry water in," I told him, and off he went.

Now that Carrie and I were alone, I was dying to continue the tongue-lashing she rightfully deserved. Eyeing me nervously she said, "You won't tell Mommy, will you?"

"Of course I'll tell, and that's not the only thing I'll do," I said, thinking about how fabulous it would be to see the look on her face tonight when I reached out from under the covers and scared the living daylights out of her.

"Tell me!" she demanded.

"No way." I brushed the sand off my knees. Glancing up, I saw Tyler racing toward us, waving something.

"This just came," he said, shoving a white envelope marked *Express Mail* into my sandy hand.

"Thanks." I searched for a spot of dry sand to sit on.

"We're having brunch in ten minutes," Tyler said. "My mother said so." He made a face, laughing.

"I'm not hungry," I said, opening the letter.

"I am!" Carrie pulled off her sandals and ran, splashing into the ocean with Tyler. "Tell us when ten minutes are up," she called back to me.

"Whatever," I muttered, anxious to read my best friend's letter.

Hey, Heartless:

Do you know how expensive express mail is? Anyway, I just had to write because something weird's happening. My best friend (that's you, in case you forgot) leaves for her fancy-tancy Christmas in California without saying good-bye! Where's your heart, Holly? I mean, it's bad enough having to suffer through the holidays without someone to CON-FIDE in, if you know what I mean?

And for starters, Stan likes me. Can you believe it, your cousin likes ME? He told me so at the party. If only you were here, I could tell you everything. . . .

Now for the big, bad stuff. You are in deep water with Jared. He couldn't believe you left without telling him good-bye. Anyway, neither of us knew what happened to you. He was totally shocked that you would leave like that. I looked for you after the devotional, and poof, you were gone! That's NOT the way to treat your best friend, not to mention a guy like Jared—especially when you wrote those poems for him. (Yep, he let me read one of them.) And, hey, you're good. Jared thinks so, too. He misses you, Holly—a lot!

Would ya please write soon? Hugs for Christmas!

Love,
Andie

I refolded the letter and pushed it into the envelope. Andie didn't know what she was talking about. Jared had everyone fooled, even my best friend. If only she'd seen Jared standing in the corner with Paula, giving her that little gift all wrapped up so sweet. Pathetic Paula made me sick!

Chapter 12

I glanced at my watch. "Ten minutes are up," I called to Carrie and Tyler, who ran like hungry bandits to the house.

Carrie called back to me. "Aren't you coming?"

I shook my head as I stuffed Andie's letter into my pocket. I needed more time to sit here in the sun. Staring out at the horizon, I contemplated life and Jared Wilkins.

And then I heard Saundra's proper-sounding voice. I should've expected she'd insist I come inside for something to eat. Her vocal cords strained a bit as she called again, "Holly, dear, time for brunch!"

Here was another female who made me sick. Sick Saundra. Hmm, wasn't very nice, but oh well—it fit her just fine.

"No, thanks," I shouted. She shook her head as she went inside.

By the time Carrie and Tyler returned, I was ready to finish making Sandy, my snowman substitute. Tyler lugged a grocery bag filled with containers of different sizes.

"Perfect," I said, reaching for a plastic pitcher and heading for the ocean. It was fun smoothing and rounding out the three parts of Sandy: his base, stomach, and head. When it was time for his eyes, nose, and mouth, I let Tyler and Carrie in on the decision making.

"What about seashell ears?" Carrie suggested.

"Cool," Tyler said, grinning.

I agreed.

"How about garland for his neck?" Tyler said. "I bet my mom has some left over."

"Good idea," Carrie said.

"Don't forget the holly," a strange voice came from behind me.

We turned to see a tall, blond boy holding out a stiff, shiny leaf with a cluster of bright red berries on it. His black Labrador stood panting at his side. It was Number 34—and for a second, I thought he was saying my name.

"Hey, thanks." Tyler snatched the fake holly leaf out of the jogger's hand. He acted like he knew him! Then Tyler said, "Where should we put it?"

"Stick it in his ear," shouted Carrie before the tall stranger could answer.

In a flash, Tyler reached up and pushed the holly stem into the hardened sand above one of the seashell ears. "Fantastic," he yelled.

"All he needs now is a hat," Number 34 said with a soft chuckle. Tyler poked him in the ribs and ran down the beach toward the house.

Curious, I leaned down to pet the black Labrador. "Nice dog," I said, feeling a bit shy.

Carrie piped up. "What's her name?"

Number 34, dressed in a T-shirt and cargo shorts, responded with a grin. "Sunshine. She's my jogging partner." He leaned down to rub the Lab's side. "Aren't you, girl?" The beautiful dog nuzzled close.

"Why'd you name her that?" I asked, half wishing Carrie had followed Tyler into the house.

"Lots of people ask that." He gave a lighthearted chuckle. "I tell them you can't be fooled by her color. Underneath this black coat, there's a heart of gold."

I nodded, careful not to seem too curious. "You live around here?"

"About three miles down the beach," he said, pointing in the direction. Then he bent down and picked up a clump of wet sand, shaping it with his long fingers, tan like the rest of his body. The Lab sat at attention nearby. "You're here for the holidays, right?"

"We're from Colorado," Carrie announced as she worked on our snowman substitute.

He nodded, helping Carrie smooth out a bumpy patch of sand. "How's that?"

"What about this?" she asked, pointing to a drooping seashell ear.

Number 34 reached up to secure it, then, on second thought, stopped and leaned over to hoist Carrie onto his shoulders. "You fix it."

Carrie giggled, reaching for the ear.

"Tyler told me he was getting company for Christmas. How do you like it here so far?" the blond boy asked, balancing Carrie.

I twisted the ends of my hair. "California's nice. Uh . . . and I was here last summer for a couple weeks, but now, the winter, well, it doesn't seem like Christmas without snow." I felt tongue-tied. Why couldn't I talk to this guy?

A broad grin swept across his face. "Maybe you'll change your mind after two weeks."

Two weeks? What else did he know about us?

He turned his attention back to "Sandy." Slowly, an elf-like shoe began to take shape under his hands. He was careful to create the next shoe slightly different from the first. Soon, two clever feet stuck out of Sandy's base.

"Looks perfect," I said, still wondering why he was hanging around. But more than that, I wondered why my heart seemed to speed up when his hazel eyes caught mine.

In a minute, Tyler was back with a forest green hat. It looked like a lady's felt hat, complete with a cream-colored silk flower.

"That looks silly," Carrie said.

"It's the only one I could find," Tyler responded.

"Too risky," I whispered to myself before telling Tyler not to use it on Sandy. I had enough problems coping with my stepmom without being responsible for destroying her expensive wardrobe.

"Guess you're right," Tyler said, shaking the hat a bit too enthusiastically. "Oh, by the way, Holly, my mom wants to take you Christmas shopping this afternoon."

"How do you know?" I felt funny discussing the plans of the day while Number 34 eavesdropped.

"Because she just said so," Tyler answered, grabbing the tan boy's arm and playfully swatting at him. "And guess who's babysitting!"

"Fine with me," Number 34 said. "And are we still on for tomorrow?"

"Oh yeah, I almost forgot," Tyler admitted. "Do you two wanna go bodysurfing with Sean and me?"

Sean? I almost forgot the question Tyler had just posed as I absorbed the name.

"I'm going whether Holly does or not," Carrie announced. She ran in and out of the tide, splashing against the beach.

Sean tapped his knee, and Sunshine promptly moved to his side. "Well, that's *three* of us." Sean turned to me, waiting, it seemed, for my answer.

"Sounds like fun." My heart skipped a beat, the way it used to when Jared winked at me. I felt very strange.

"Holly, dear." It was Saundra calling from the beach house balcony. She waved her arms, trying to attract my attention.

"Coming!" I called. No sense keeping the dragon lady waiting.

"Nice meeting you, Holly," Sean said, flinging Tyler over his shoulder, then stopping to extend his hand to me.

I accepted his handshake like an adult. "Same here," I answered.

"Wait," Tyler shouted. "Don't forget the hat." He leaped out of Sean's grasp, picked up his mother's felt hat, and tossed it to me. A slight breeze caught it, and up it flew like a Frisbee.

I reached for it and missed. "Oh, fabulous," I muttered, picking it up and gently shaking it off. Now the hat thing was on *me,* and unfortunately it wasn't the best topic for opening remarks. Not Saundra's hat—no consignment shop special, for sure—dusty with beach sand.

Brushing away thoughts of the wicked stepmother, I focused on Sean and the momentary touch of his hand on mine.

The memory lingered, warm as a glove, as I headed toward the beach house.

Chapter 13

Promptly placing Saundra's hat on the deck chaise lounge, I scurried into the house.

Saundra did her scrutiny number on me first off. "I'll be happy to wait for you to shower and change into something more appropriate" was the first thing out of her mouth. "And you haven't had a thing to eat" was next. "You must be starving." She punctuated her words with a deep sigh.

I hurried downstairs to the shower. Good thing she hadn't seen the hat.

After my shower, I discovered a tray of fruit and a sandwich sliced into mini-sections on the dresser in my room. *Should've known,* I thought, reaching for some grapes.

On the bed, I spied the hot-pink two-piece swimsuit where I'd left it. "This is going back from whence it came," I protested out loud, remembering the surfing plans Tyler, Carrie, and I had made with Sean. No way would I be caught dead in this scant little number in front of a boy.

I slipped into a gray cotton skirt and a blue top. Surely *this* was appropriate enough for Christmas shopping with Saundra. After brushing my hair and applying some light lip gloss, I hid the letter from Andie under the bed pillow, next to my diary. Then, snatching up the two-piece bathing suit, I hurried upstairs.

Saundra was waiting on the deck in a smart navy-and-white dress. Red shoes and purse completed her outfit. I swallowed hard, hoping she wouldn't comment on the hat lying on the chaise. At least now it was sand-free.

"We'll head for the mall first," she announced, getting up from a white patio chair. The color reminded me of my mother's house—the bathroom cabinet where I'd hidden my diary key.

"What's that in your hand, dear?" She interrupted my thoughts, eyeing the almost-bikini I carried.

"Oh, this." I acknowledged Saundra's inquisitive look. I took a deep breath. "It's just not me," I told her flat out. "But I *will* be needing one for tomorrow, so if you don't mind, I'd like to exchange it for something a little more . . ."

"Absolutely," she said, snatching up the green felt hat as we headed inside. "You may choose whatever you like, dear."

Dear this, *dear* that. I cringed. Why did everything have to end with terms of endearment?

Inside, she hung the hat in the closet near the front door without saying a word. Then we headed for the garage. She unlocked the car doors with the touch of a button on her key. I settled into the jazzy white sports car, amazed at the super plush interior. The dashboard was almost as bright as her red shoes and purse. But I wasn't surprised. Everything about Saundra was super flashy and expensive.

At the mall, Saundra waited outside the dressing room (thank goodness) while I tried on another swimsuit. A rainbow of colors—blues, pinks, and lavender—it looked fabulous on me. Much better than the two-piece Saundra had chosen. At least this one concealed my skinny ribs and hipbones. But it did show something. I turned sideways in the floor-length mirror to admire my developing physique. Perfect! Well . . . getting there.

The swimsuit dilemma solved, I felt less reluctant about spending the entire afternoon shopping with Daddy's wife. Of course, I didn't let on to her.

Next we browsed in a candle boutique, where Saundra purchased a dozen beeswax candles, all different lengths. "Won't these look lovely on the mantel on Christmas Eve?" she commented, half to me, half to the air.

I nodded as she strolled regally to the counter. She exchanged small talk with the clerk, and I continued to survey her from afar. How could Daddy have picked her for his wife? She was so . . . fakey. I heard her say to the clerk, "Merry Christmas, hon. Keep the change."

Well, there was one thing Saundra had going for her. She was benevolent. That was okay, I guess, if she wasn't your stepmom. A faint recognition stirred within me. Yep, that was a big part of why I didn't like her. She wasn't daddy's *first* wife. She wasn't Mom—not even close.

"Do we have time for a quick stop at the card shop?" she asked, as if she actually cared about what I wanted to do.

It amused me, but I kept the smile hidden inside and the icy stare frozen to my face. "Whatever," I stated flatly. My sullen attitude didn't seem to faze her, however, and we marched to the nearest Hallmark shop. Inside, she went her way and I went mine. In the Christmas card section I pulled out a gorgeous card with zillions of hearts decorating it. "First Christmas together" was written in fancy lettering across the top.

Staring at the couple painted on the card, I drew in a faltering breath. It was obvious the twosome were in love by the way they stood, hand in hand, gazing at each other.

The card stirred up the old homesickness in me, with thoughts of Mom and Uncle Jack. Suddenly I deeply missed Dressel Hills. And I longed for my friendship with Jared. I wanted things the way they were—*before* Paula!

Oh, Jared, why did you have to go and spoil everything? my heart cried. *How could you say all those things?*

My eyes filled with tears. Out of control, they brimmed over the edge, rolling down my cheeks.

"Get over it, girl," I muttered, frantically searching for the cards that matched the one in my hand. Through the tears, things were a blur. I grabbed for a tissue, in my pocket, in my purse. Anywhere. "Get a grip," I whispered angrily, pushing the card in anywhere it fit.

Then I snatched a red envelope from another stack and shoved it in front of the First Christmas Together card, hiding it from view.

No way can I let Saundra see me like this, I thought, determined to rid myself of any trace of emotion. I pulled out a ratty tissue from my pocket and darted behind the counter display of jewelry boxes. One of them had a mirror inside its lid, and I stooped down to dry my eyes, dabbing at my cheeks.

"May I help you?" a clerk asked, appearing out of nowhere.

Speechless, I shook my head. Evidently she mistook my silence for extraordinary interest and began winding the music box of one of the most exquisite jewelry cases on display.

The song "Someday My Prince Will Come" began to spill into the air. Desperate now, I wanted to run from the store. Instead, more tears streamed down my cheeks. I was sobbing in the middle of a card shop in Southern California, five days before Christmas. It was nuts, but I couldn't help it.

Just then Saundra spotted me, and when she saw my tears, her face fell. At first I thought she was embarrassed. But as she approached, I saw something else.

"Holly, dear," she whispered, "let's go somewhere quiet." And before I could respond, she ushered me, unnoticed, out of the store.

By the time we arrived in front of a doughnut shop, my tears had subsided. I stuffed the frayed tissue into my pocket and, dying of humiliation, wracked my brain. What was wrong with me? Crying in public?

"Would you like something to eat, or would you rather I take you home?" Saundra asked gently.

It was strange. I wasn't ready for the shopping spree to end. "I'll be okay," I said.

"Are you sure?"

"Yes, thanks," I said, meaning it.

Saundra ordered two sodas and a cream-filled doughnut for me. I was amazed at her memory. Last summer during my visit, I'd chosen cream-filled doughnuts to surprise Daddy one morning at breakfast. Five months ago.

"Would you care for anything else, dear?" she asked, minus the inquisition I was sure would follow my tearful outburst. She handed me several clean tissues.

"This is fine, thanks," I replied, then blew my nose. While I sipped my pop, Saundra pulled a pad of paper from her purse. I could see three different lists printed neatly on one page. "I make lists all the time," I remarked, almost without thinking.

She tapped on the second list, smiling briefly. "This is the only way I've found I can ever manage things." She copied one of the lists onto another page and handed it to me. "Here are some ideas for your father's Christmas gift, in case you need some hints." She pulled out her wallet and handed over a wad of twenty-dollar bills. "I thought you'd want to buy something special for him, for you and Carrie to present to him at Christmas. If you'd like, we could meet back here in, say, an hour or so."

I nodded, still in semi-shock at so much money thrust into my hand. "I have my own money from home," I said. "I won't need this much."

"Don't worry about it, dear. If there's any left, feel free to spend it however you please," she said. "Who knows, maybe you'll see something you can't live without." She looked at her watch. "I have twenty minutes till two. Shall we synchronize our time?"

"Good idea," I said, moving the minute hand on my watch to match hers.

"I'll see you here in about an hour," she promised, waving her hand, adorned with bright red, fake fingernails.

"Okay," I called, feeling lighter, brighter. After all, it was almost Christmas—Jesus' birthday. If only I could focus on the true meaning of this razzle-dazzle time of year, I'd be fine. With or without Jared Wilkins.

Chapter 14

Saundra's list gave me zillions of ideas for Daddy, but there was one item missing from the list. Saundra had forgotten about his poetry obsession. I headed for the Christian bookstore with the *perfect* gift in mind. With a little help from the store clerk, I found a beautiful hardback version of the Psalms. It would be a sneaky way of introducing him to the Bible and its lyrical Psalms. Free verse—just the way he liked it.

Next I found a present for Tyler—a book on creation, lavishly illustrated and written in terms a kid could understand. Tyler had said his mom would "freak" about God and religious stuff, but today I had the urge to risk it. I hoped I was doing the right thing.

Tons of stocking stuffers took up most of the rest of Saundra's money. But there was still something I had to buy. Heading back to the card shop, I bypassed the card section and found a leather-covered organizer, the perfect gift for a list-making stepmom. A warm feeling came over me as I paid for the gift. With my own money.

The next day, Tyler, Carrie, and I ate a hearty breakfast of waffles and scrambled eggs.

"You'll have to wait thirty minutes before swimming," Saundra said, clearing off the dining room table.

Tyler protested, as usual. "But, Mom," he whined, "we're not gonna be swimming, we're using the body boards." This time it was Saundra who rolled her eyes.

Carrie pulled Tyler out of the kitchen. "C'mon, you can't play till you make your bed," she informed him.

I grinned at that. What did Carrie know about making beds and keeping a clean bedroom? I snickered as I began helping with the dishes. Surprisingly, Saundra didn't launch a protest this time. We worked in silence for a while. Then I glanced at her. "Thanks for being so understanding yesterday at the mall," I said, putting away the maple syrup.

She gathered up the linen napkins, soiled with sticky syrup and butter. "It's one of those emotional things that happen from time to time," she said.

She probably had no idea what I was really thanking her for, but I had made an attempt at least. "Christmas is a rotten time to have boy problems." I paused, feeling awkward about opening up too much of myself.

"I can certainly relate to that," Saundra admitted, pulling a chair out and sitting at the table with a cup of coffee. "My former husband decided to leave a few weeks before Christmas. Tyler was only two, so he didn't understand. Neither did I." She leaned her arm against the table.

I stopped loading the dishes and looked at her. Really looked at her. This woman—my wicked stepmom, or so I called her—had experienced some of the same feelings my own mother had years before, when Daddy left us. I didn't care to know the details of how she and Daddy met or anything like that. Not now. But one thing was certain, she seemed to understand how I'd felt in the card shop yesterday.

Without thinking, I touched her shoulder. "It must've been hard, going through that Christmas," I said, a wave of sadness sweeping over me.

Saundra reached up and stroked my hand. "All of that is in the past now," she said with a smile. "Your father and I are very happy together."

Just then Carrie came upstairs, yelling something about Tyler heading for the beach without her. "He said by the time he gets down there, it'll be exactly thirty minutes since he swallowed his last bite."

"That's fine, dear," Saundra said, pushing a stray hair into a gold clip at the back of her neck.

I excused myself, assuming our chat was over. Back downstairs, I hurried to Carrie's room and peeked into the telescope. Focusing the lens, I could see Tyler hauling the body boards toward the beach. Soon Carrie came running down the sandy slope toward him.

Slowly, I moved the telescope, scanning the area near the kids. But it wasn't the kids I was spying on. Where was Sean? I couldn't wait to see him. That wonderful laugh, and the way he treated Carrie and Tyler . . . I was sure he'd make a fabulous father someday, when he was all grown-up.

And then, there he was. In full view of this magnificent telescope. He raced over to the kids, his black Lab running beside him. When he got to Carrie, he picked her up and swung her around. *Just like Uncle Jack,* I thought.

Then I watched as Sean pointed to the house. My heart leaped up. Had Sean asked about *me?*

Hurrying to my room, I got ready for a day of fun on the beach. Before leaving, I pulled back the bedspread and slid my hand under the pillow. Grabbing my diary, I slipped the chain off my neck and unlocked the secrets of my life. As I flipped through the pages, locating today's date, I noticed sticky fingerprints on several pages. Maple syrup! We'd had waffles this morning. The truth clobbered me. Carrie had read my diary again. But how?

I scrutinized the private passages she surely must have seen, the telltale signs marking the truth. I burned with rage. "That sneaky little brat," I whispered.

At this very moment, my sister had full knowledge of my secret desire—to own Mom's heart locket, the one Daddy had given her the day I was born.

In the bathroom, I wiped the sticky smudges off the pages as my anger mixed with mounting fear. My dearest wish must be treated with reverence! Unfortunately, I knew Carrie couldn't be trusted.

Grabbing a plush hand towel, I patted the wet spots around the edges of my diary. Worry for other matters clouded my thinking. Carrie had, no doubt, read my choice words about Jared, as well, not to mention the detailed account of the Christmas party last Friday night. And, worse than any of it, she'd read about my interest in Sean.

I glanced out the window. Part of me longed to go out and ride the waves. Yet I was afraid if I went outside now, I'd yell and scream and call Carrie names. Not a nice thing for a big sister to do, especially in front of a cute guy with an obvious soft spot in his heart for kids.

I knelt beside my bed and talked to God about everything. Finally I could pray without pounding my fist against the bed. I wanted the Lord to show me how Carrie was sneaking into my private writings. "After all," I prayed, "you do know *all* things."

I stopped for a moment, contemplating the problems of the day. "And, Lord, I need your help about something else. It's Saundra. Help me forgive her for marrying Daddy and taking him away from us." It was a difficult prayer, one I'd been avoiding.

The sun was high in the sky by the time I sauntered outside and down the well-worn path. A gentle breeze stirred the tall grass on either side of the slope.

"Holly!" called Tyler, bobbing in the ocean. "Surf's up!"

I spied Sean steadying Carrie's board as she hopped on. Together they rode a medium-sized wave accompanied by my sister's squeals of glee.

I could see this was going to be a great day. Then I remembered Carrie's dreadful deed. My heart pounded as she came up to me.

"Wanna ride next?" she asked innocently.

I forced a smile, mainly because Sean was only a few feet away.

"Hey, Holly," Sean said, a dazzling smile dancing across his face.

"Looks like fun," I managed to say.

Sean came around and walked beside me. "Let's race."

I didn't have the nerve to tell him this was my first time surfing.

Carrie piped up, though. "My sister's never done this before. C'mon, Holly," she bossed, "I'll show you what to do."

Sean stepped in front of her, grabbing both her arms. "Whoa there, young lady," he said with great charm. "You'd better let me do the honors."

I felt my face grow warm. Maybe he wouldn't notice. Maybe he'd think I was sunburned. Anyway, Carrie continued to interfere playfully.

"Guess I'll just have to dunk you," he said, flipping Carrie over his shoulder and marching into the water.

"No, no! Put me down!" Her shouts mingled with laughter.

It was perfect. Carrie had it coming, and I followed to make sure she got a thorough drenching.

Jumping in and out of the shallow waves, I worked my way out to Sean. When it came time for the actual dunking, he was careful. He even held Carrie's nose shut. Then down he took her, pulling her quickly out. Carrie loved it—the attention, that is. And I enjoyed watching Sean and his playful yet gentle way with my little sister.

Swimming back toward shore, Sean leaped out of the water and grabbed a surfboard near the beach towel where Sunshine dozed. "Watch this," he called to us.

Curiously I watched as he whistled, long and low, to Sunshine. The Lab's eyes popped open. Then Sean sprinted through the foam at the water's edge, the board under his arm as he threw himself into a wave.

The sleek black dog leaped off the towel and into the ocean, swimming toward the calmer water farther out.

Treading water, I watched as Sean pushed the board under Sunshine. Standing up, the dog rode the board—rising and falling with the moving water. Then, up . . . up she went with the swell and roar of the wave, riding the crest as it pounded the surf.

Crash! The wave fizzled to foam and the ride was over.

"Fabulous!" I said. "Did you teach her that?"

Sean nodded, obviously pleased with Sunshine's performance. Then he dove under water, swimming to retrieve the surfboard. "Who's next?" he asked, grinning.

"I'll try it!" Carrie shouted.

"How about some more practice with the body board?" he suggested.

Sean was cautious, and I liked that. Reckless guys had never impressed me.

I floated lazily on my back as the warm California sun shone down. What a perfect way to spend the holidays. I'd gone California crazy, just like Uncle Jack had warned. . . .

The day sped by so quickly, and I was sad to see it end. By suppertime, I was reluctant to say good-bye to Carrie's and my new friend.

"I have an idea," he said as I wrapped myself in a towel. "Meet me here at dusk on Christmas Eve. We'll walk along the beach for a while." He never winked or flirted or anything, but in his face there was eagerness. It excited me and made me nervous at the same time.

"Sounds good, but . . ."

"Something wrong?" he probed.

"It's, uh, just that . . ." The words stuck in my throat. I couldn't tell him I was struggling with my loyalty to someone else. A jerk named Jared.

"Tell you what," Sean began. "I'll make it easy, Holly. Think about it a few days, and if you don't show by, let's say, seven o'clock, I'll know you're not coming. How's that?" He looked positively adorable as he flashed his easygoing smile my way.

It wouldn't be easy deciding what to do between now and Christmas Eve, but I nodded in agreement.

"So you'll think about it?" He wasn't being pushy like Danny Myers had been, or flirtatious like Jared Wilkins. In many ways he reminded me of a surprising combination: Attentive yet hilarious Uncle Jack—and my handsome, sweet daddy. Adding to the fact that I was still totally crushed over the master of two-time, Jared himself, Sean's invitation seemed to twinkle like the light of a zillion stars on the waves.

"I'll think about it," I said, gazing up at Sean. "I promise."

Chapter 15

Right after supper I confronted Carrie in her room. "It wouldn't be so bad if this obsession you have with snooping was a one-time shot. I mean, if I had an older sister, who knows, maybe I'd snoop, too. But you . . . you never quit!" I sighed, anger building with each word.

Carrie looked repentant enough. Her lips were pursed together; her head hung low. "It's just so . . . so much fun," she responded, attempting to sound contrite. "I'm sorry, Holly. I'll never, ever do it again."

"I can't trust you," I said. "And how are you opening my diary without the key?"

She stared at me, her eyes wide. Pulling a toothpick out of her pocket, she held it up, her lower lip quivering like crazy. "This."

I snatched it out of her hand and raced to my room. Flinging the bedspread back, I uncovered my journal. With Carrie's toothpick, I picked the lock. "Amazing," I muttered, my anger subsiding only for an instant. Then I heard a sound and spun around.

Carrie had followed me and was crying. I faced the little snoop squarely. "If you ever so much as think twice about revealing any of the contents of this . . ." I waved the diary in her pixie face, breathing hard.

"Please, don't tell Mommy," she pleaded.

"I'll do whatever it takes to make you stop."

"Like what?" She was sobbing.

"Like getting you down on your knees to repent to God while I listen," I retorted.

"Just don't tell Mommy, okay?"

I studied her hard, and then the truth dawned. "Oh, I know what you're so worried about. It's Christmas, isn't it?"

Slowly, she nodded.

"You think you won't get any presents if Mom finds out."

She was silent, wiping her eyes. Carrie didn't believe in Santa Claus, but she was still worried. Who knows, something coal black could end up in her Christmas stocking next week when we celebrated in Dressel Hills.

"Silly girl." I shook my diary at her. "Do you promise to stay away from this?"

"I promise," she echoed.

Somewhat relieved, I waved her out of my room. Then I sprawled on the bed, reaching for a pen to record the events of the day. Having someone like Sean interested in me was pretty exciting. It helped ease the snooping incident with Carrie. Calmly, I relived the day of surfing again and again. Sean's every word, every gesture was embedded in my brain.

Comparing Sean with Jared was really dumb, but strange as it seemed, my thoughts turned back to Dressel Hills. Even though Jared and I weren't actually dating, hanging out with another guy while I was still his girlfriend just wasn't my style. I mulled that idea for a while.

But he'd never find out, I argued with myself, imagining the fun of spending Christmas Eve on a beach bathed in moonlight.

Upstairs I borrowed some gift wrap, a scissors, and tape from Saundra. Then heading down the hallway, I noticed Carrie whispering to Daddy in his study. There, among his classic books of poetry, he was quietly conversing with her.

Inching closer, I smelled the magic of old books mixed with

Daddy's spicy cologne. The scent stopped me in my tracks. Then I heard his gentle laughter.

I slipped unnoticed into the room, investigating Carrie's face as an impish smile burst upon it. "What's going on?" I asked.

Daddy's face lit up like the white candles in each of the windows. "Christmas secrets," he whispered.

"Never ask questions before Christmas," Carrie protested.

"Hmm," Daddy said. "Both my girls in the same room at the same time. Can it be?" He pulled me down on one of his knees while balancing giggly Carrie on the other. I placed the wrapping paper and scissors on his desk.

"It's gonna be such a cool Christmas," Carrie announced, eyeing the wrapping paper. "I can't wait!"

"Three more days?" Daddy teased. "We open gifts around here on Christmas Eve."

"Really? Christmas Eve?" I muttered, thinking of Sean's invitation.

"That's cool," shouted Carrie, racing off to tell Tyler, no doubt.

My tentative plans with Sean were at stake. "What time are we opening presents?" I asked, concerned.

Daddy patted my hand. "Don't you worry, honey; I'm sure we can work around your schedule."

Does he know about Sean's invitation? And if so, how? I turned to look for Carrie, the little rat. "Uh, excuse me a sec," I said, getting up.

"What's your hurry?" Dad asked.

"I need to talk to Carrie about something."

Daddy cleared his throat. I could tell by the look on his face he was about to defend her. "If you think Carrie let anything slip, you're wrong. Sean called while you and Saundra were cleaning up the kitchen."

This was news to me.

Daddy continued. "He asked permission to spend some time with you."

"You're kidding." I was dumbfounded.

He leaned back in his chair as I stood up, facing him. I wondered what else he knew about my friendship with Sean. "A really terrific kid, that Sean Hamilton," he said, reaching for the newspaper. "It's good to develop friendships with lots of boys, Holly. You're awfully young to be tied down to one fellow."

I sighed. *How does he know about Jared?*

"Mom says that, too," I said, picking up the bows and paper and stuff. "I, uh, have some presents to wrap now." I fled from the study, wondering if Carrie had blabbed the entire contents of my journal to Daddy.

Closing the door to my room, I switched on the clock radio beside the bed. Christmas songs, old and new, filled the room with cheer.

I was nearly finished wrapping my purchases when I heard it. The strains of a familiar tune—"Jingle Bell Rock." The jazzy song brought back memories of the Christmas party at Pastor Rob's house. Andie had played her rendition of it while Joy presented me with the secret-pal gift. Two hours later, I had witnessed Jared's gift-giving rendezvous behind the Christmas tree.

Flipping the knob on the radio, I refused to shed another tear over Jared Wilkins, King of Deceit!

Instead, I told my diary the latest delicious facts about Sean Hamilton, Prince a la Proper.

The next day, Tyler delivered a stack of Christmas cards to the house. Three of them were addressed to me. One was from Mom and Uncle Jack, another from Andie, and the third was from none other than Jared.

I went to the kitchen, sliced the envelopes open with a letter opener, and raced downstairs to read in privacy. For some unknown reason, I pulled out Jared's card first. Enclosed was a letter.

Dear Holly-Heart,

    Hope you're having fun with your California family. You'd better be, otherwise I'm missing you for nothing. I wish we could've said good-bye before you left. Why'd you disappear like that?

    It won't be long and you'll be back in Colorado. Thanks again for A Heart Full of Poetry. *It's outstanding and so are you! Please write soon. Honestly, nothing's the same here with you gone.*

Always,

Jared

"What a con artist," I sneered, stuffing the card and its contents into the envelope. I had more important things to attend to than reading lies from the pen of Jared Wilkins.

At last, December twenty-fourth arrived. Daddy and I spent the morning running errands for Saundra. She'd ordered expensive trays and platters and things. Never in a zillion years could I imagine my mom spending so much money on prepared food. But it was interesting and perfectly lavish, Daddy's new life.

"What do you think of California so far?" Daddy shot the question to me as we waited in bumper-to-bumper holiday madness.

"*This* stuff I can live without," I said, referring to the traffic on all sides of us. "But the ocean's nice. So is the weather."

"And . . . what about the people?" he asked.

I wasn't sure what he was getting at. "The only people I really know here are you, Saundra, and Tyler."

"Tyler seems quite taken with you and Carrie." He took his foot off the brake, and the car inched forward a few feet.

"Tyler's a cool stepbrother," I said, wondering what he was going to ask next.

"And your stepmother?" He stared straight ahead.

"She's nice, actually. We, uh, had sort of a heart-to-heart talk the other day."

"I'm happy to hear that, Holly."

"There *is* something that bothers me about her, though."

He turned toward me, a question mark in his eyes.

"I understand she's not thrilled about praying." I felt hesitant about bringing this subject up. But it bugged me that Tyler thought Saundra would be upset if she caught him praying at mealtime.

Daddy took a deep breath. "Saundra was never one to entertain notions of a personal God," he said. "So she hasn't emphasized it with Tyler, either."

I jumped on that one. "But the God of the Bible *is* personal. I know Him, Daddy. And I know something else." I paused, thinking ahead. "God loved you and Saundra and Tyler, or He wouldn't have bothered sending Jesus to earth as a baby. That's the bottom line—Christmas is about a personal God."

"I can see you believe this," he commented softly.

"With all of my heart," I answered.

"Well, I've been doing a lot of thinking about a book a friend gave me," he said with a twinkle in his eye. "It's by a fellow named St. Matthew."

I couldn't keep from grinning. "You're reading Matthew's gospel?"

He nodded.

"Daddy, that's fabulous," I said, giving his hand a little squeeze. "This has to be the best Christmas present ever!"

"Ah, but the day's not over," he hinted. I had no idea what was on his mind. But it *was* something. Something he seemed to have trouble keeping secret.

After a sumptuous supper, Saundra insisted on cleaning the kitchen herself. It was part of her Christmas gift to the family, she said. Dusk was falling fast, and Sean would be waiting.

I headed for the living room, where Carrie and Tyler were shaking presents. "You might break something," I scolded.

"Right," Carrie snapped. "You used to do it, too, before you got so mature."

Tyler grinned.

"It's almost dark," Carrie said without looking up. "What a great night for a walk on the beach."

Yep, she's read that page in my diary all right.

"Sure is," I declared, leaving the holiday splendor of the living room for a peek through the telescope in Carrie's room. One quick look would tell me what I longed to know. I leaned over slightly, adjusting the focus.

Just as I thought. Sean Hamilton was definitely a reliable guy. Unlike someone else I knew.

I peered through the telescope a moment longer, bringing Sean closer . . . closer into view. I could almost reach out and touch his blue sweat shirt. The number thirty-four glowed in the moonlight.

Then I raced to my room and closed the door. Rushing to the mirror, I checked my hair. Moving closer, I checked my face. Oh yeah, he wouldn't see much color outside, even with the moonlight.

Tucking my shirt into my jeans, I dashed around the room, pulling my tennies out of the closet. Was Sean still waiting? I reached down and tied my shoes. Then I leaped up and headed for the door.

Halfway up the stairs, I remembered I'd left my diary open on the bed for the world to see. Racing back to my room, I grabbed it, but my eyes caught a phrase I'd written weeks before. *Faithful, loyal, true*—the first stanza of one of the poems for Jared. Honest, heartfelt feelings in the form of poetry—what a terrific Christmas gift from a true friend. The true friend being me, of course.

And then it hit me. If I was so loyal and true, what was I doing meeting Sean? Just because Jared had broken his promise didn't mean I had to break mine. Did it?

I flicked off the lights and turned toward the windows overlooking the beach. A tall, dark form was tossing pebbles into the ocean. "I'm sorry, Sean," I whispered in the darkness. "Please understand." A warm feeling spread over me, and deep in my heart I knew I'd made the right choice.

Turning toward the door, I scurried up the stairs. "Daddy," I called. "Let's open presents."

Carrie ran ahead of me. "Aren't you gonna meet Sean?" she asked.

"Not this time," I said. "Mind your own business."

"You'll never guess what Santa brought you," she said, giggling.

"Santa who?" I teased, following her.

"My lips are locked."

"That's a first," I muttered, heading down the hall to the festive living room.

Chapter 16

I sat on the floor beside Tyler. A few presents were already piled up around him.

"Who would like to play Santa Claus?" Saundra asked, snuggling close to Daddy.

"I will," offered Carrie, hopping up. She scooted under the Christmas tree and began delivering the mountain of presents, one by one.

When all the gifts had been distributed, Daddy did an amazing thing. He reached for a Bible on the lamp table. Silently, he thumbed through it till he found Matthew 1:18. " 'This is how the birth of Jesus Christ came about,' " he began.

I noticed the startled look on Saundra's face. Tyler pulled restlessly at a red bow on one of his presents.

When Daddy came to the verse, "She will give birth to a son, and you are to give him the name Jesus, because he will save his people from their sins," I noticed Tyler look up. He was actually listening.

Shortly, Daddy was into chapter two, the part where the Magi came. It was almost like he couldn't find a stopping place. I glanced at Saundra. She sat silently as he spoke the wondrous words about that first Christmas.

In my heart, I sent a prayer heavenward.

Daddy continued, " 'On coming to the house, they saw the child with his mother Mary, and they bowed down and worshiped him. Then they opened their treasures and presented him with gifts of gold and of incense and of myrrh.' "

"Wow," Tyler chimed in. "So *that's* how it all got started."

Daddy finished reading, and then we began opening our presents, starting with the youngest. After Carrie, Tyler opened his gifts. He tore into my present to him—the book on creation. I held my breath.

"Hey . . . cool," Tyler exclaimed, paging through the book, then holding it high. "Thanks, Holly, now I can get some big questions answered."

Saundra didn't say a word.

It was my turn. I reached for a small, square box.

"Save that one for last," Carrie objected.

Daddy agreed. Something told me this was the secret he'd hinted about earlier.

I opened a present from Tyler and two with both Daddy's and Saundra's name on them. Finally I reached for the small gift. A mini card was attached. It read: "Happy Holly-days. Love, Daddy."

Gently, I pried the ends loose and pulled off the wrapping paper. Carefully, I lifted the lid.

Inside was my mother's gold locket!

Carrie covered her mouth. I stared at her, still amazed. Then she leaned against me, whispering in my ear. "Forgive me?"

Then I knew. "So that's why you were snooping around in my diary." Instantly, I comprehended what had transpired over the past week.

"So . . . what do you think?" Daddy asked, leaning forward.

"It's the best!" I cried, crawling over to thank him. When we hugged, I spotted the Bible on the lamp table, still open to Matthew. "Well, almost," I whispered.

"Here, why don't you wear it now, dear?" Saundra said, offering to help with the clasp.

I gathered up my hair and held it while she placed the long gold chain around my neck. "It's lovely," Saundra said, admiring it.

Br-r-ing! Tyler and Carrie raced to the phone.

I stroked the heart locket, staring at the precious piece of jewelry. "Thank you, Daddy," I said. "I love it."

"And I love you," he said, eyes glistening.

Tyler ran into the living room. "It's long distance for you, Holly. Some boy named Jared."

Jared! I leaped up, heading for the privacy of the kitchen. *What's he calling about?* I wondered as I picked up the receiver. "Hello?"

"Merry Christmas, Holly-Heart." The sound of his voice made my broken heart sing.

"Thanks," I said softly, not sure how I should respond.

"Hey, what's wrong?" he prodded.

"What are you talking about?"

"Holly? Something's wrong—I can hear it in your voice."

"Everything's wrong," I blurted, peeking around the corner, checking for snoopers.

"Are you homesick? Is that it?"

"Not really," I said, hesitating. "I'm just so . . . well, surprised to hear your voice."

"It's Christmas Eve, isn't it?" he said. "I wish you were here. There's a candlelight service later. I'd rather be sitting with you at church than next to my parents."

"Or Paula, don't you mean?"

A long silence followed. I waited.

Slowly, Jared responded, "Did you say Paula?"

"She's nuts about you, but I'm sure you know that by now." Deep inside, I was a wreck. His voice sounded so good to me, bringing with it all the old memories, the good times.

"I like *you,* Holly. Nothing's changed."

Taking a deep breath, I said, "But you gave her a Christmas present. Isn't that a little misleading?"

"I didn't give Paula Miller a gift." He sounded dumbfounded.

"Yeah, I saw you at the party last week."

"You saw what?"

Then I explained, in great detail, the gift exchange I'd witnessed.

Laughter! Jared was laughing hysterically.

Finally I got his attention. "What's so funny?"

He tried to speak. "If that's all you're worried about, forget it. My secret pal, Shauna, was sick that night. I took her gift to the party for Paula to give to Shauna later."

I stood there speechless as his words sank in. What a fool I'd been. "You delivered Shauna's present to Paula? That's all it was?"

"Yep," Jared said.

"What about Paula's gift to you, the one at school?" By now, I sounded as jealous as a cat, but I was clawing for the truth.

"Somehow, Paula found out Billy Hill had gotten her name from you," he explained.

I smiled. "That's right, he and I traded names."

"Well, when Paula heard that Billy liked her, she decided to set up her own secret-pal exchange, using me as the delivery boy." Jared started to chuckle again. "In fact, at this moment, Billy still doesn't know who gave him that gift."

"Sneaky," I mumbled, feeling lousy for falsely accusing Jared in my heart, and in my diary. And Paula, too.

"Wait'll you see what I got you, Holly," Jared was saying.

"You bought me a present?"

"And you'll never guess what it is," he teased.

Daddy was motioning to me from the living room.

"I'd better not guess right now," I said, explaining that we were in the middle of our family gift-opening.

"Lucky you. I have to wait till morning," he said.

"I'll write, okay?"

"Can't wait," he said. "Bye, Holly."

"Thanks for calling, and Merry Christmas," I said before hanging up.

Still shocked at what Jared had shared, I made my way through the maze of crumpled Christmas wrap as Saundra lit the gold candles on the mantel. What an amazing Christmas Eve this had turned out to be.

♥ ♥ ♥

With the problem of Jared cleared up, the second week at Daddy's house sped by faster than the first. He took us to Disneyland and Sea World, like he'd promised. It was so fabulous.

I didn't see Sean again. Tyler said he was probably busy with his older brother and his niece and nephew, who'd come home for Christmas. *Uncle* Sean. No wonder he was good with kids.

♥ ♥ ♥

California had been lots of fun, but returning home to Dressel Hills was even better. On my first night back, I was helping Mom prepare supper when the doorbell rang.

A quartet of kids raced to investigate. Phil and Mark swung the door wide. Carrie and Stephie grabbed Jared's jacket—the visitor—fighting over who would get to hang it up.

Mom shooed everyone out of the living room, assigning table-setting chores to the door-greeters. Thank goodness for savvy moms.

"Welcome home, Holly-Heart," Jared said, holding out a large silver box with a sprig of holly on top.

"Thanks," I said. "Should I open it?"

"Why not?"

Untying the bow, I looked up at him. Jared was grinning, his eyes twinkling mischievously.

When I opened the lid on the box, I gasped and turned red. It was a brown suede boot—just like the one I'd baptized in the toilet!

"It's the right boot," he whispered. "That's the one you needed."

I stared at him in disbelief. "Who told you?"

Just then, Stan emerged from the coat closet. "Sorry, little sister," John Wayne, alias Stan Patterson, remarked. "Couldn't help myself."

"Who else knows?" I demanded.

"The buck stops here, pilgrim," Stan crooned, pointing to the two of them—Jared and himself.

Then Jared reached into the boot and pulled out a teeny red box. "Voilà!"

"What's this?" I asked, delighted.

"Open it and see for yourself," Jared replied.

Happily, I opened the lid. Inside, a bottle of perfumed toilet water awaited. The word *Always,* in Jared's own handwriting, covered up the original brand name. I turned the dainty lid and put my nose down close, breathing in the fragrance. "Mmm, nice," I said, smiling at him.

With a single wink, Jared said it all.

Quickly dabbing perfume behind both ears, I began to hum "Jingle Bell Rock."

"Nice song," Jared said. He began to hum along, harmonizing with me.

I sighed happily. "Nice blend."

"No kidding," said Jared.

Even if I *had* been the slightest bit California crazy while I was gone for Christmas, I was definitely cured. Things were going to be fabulously fine now. I was perfectly sure.

Acknowledgments

Thanks to all who have helped to make the HOLLY'S HEART series a successful reality. I'm forever grateful to Charette Barta and Sharon Madison, who believed in Holly-Heart from her earliest beginnings, as well as to my superb editor, Rochelle Glöege, whose suggestions and encouragement are so valuable to me.

Big hugs to my terrific teen consultants—Amy, Allison, Becky, Janie, Julie, Kirsten, Larissa, Mindie, and Shanna. You always have wonderful ideas, including the Meredith family cat playing the *purr*fect part at Holly's mom's Thanksgiving Day wedding.

Hurrah for my SCBWI critique group, as well as my reviewers, Barbara Birch, Barbara Reinhard, Madalene Harris, and Lorraine Pintus, for valuable assistance. Three cheers for my husband, Dave, whose thoughtful comments, loving support, and super sandwiches made this series possible.

My sincere appreciation to Del Gariepy and Carolene Robinson for their medical expertise.

And finally, my deep appreciation to my many fans who think Holly really *does* live somewhere in Colorado. I've enjoyed every minute spent writing HOLLY'S HEART just for you!

From Bev . . . to You

I'm thrilled that you've chosen to read Holly's Heart. As my first young-adult protagonist, Holly Meredith remains dear to my heart, and I laughed and cried with her as I wrote every one of these books.

Holly-Heart and I have quite a lot in common. While growing up in Lancaster County, Pennsylvania, I wrote zillions of secret lists and journal entries (and still do!). I also enjoy my many e-pals, and sending snail mail letters and notes to encourage family and friends has always been one of my favorite things to do. And I know all about the importance of having a true-blue best friend. Mine was Sandi Kline, and while we didn't have Loyalty Papers, we did write secret-coded messages to each other. Once, we even hid a few under the carpet of the seventh step leading to the sanctuary of my dad's church!

Thanks to my books, I've had the opportunity to develop friendships with people of all ages, from the grade-schoolers who love my picture books to the teens and senior adults who enjoy my novels. Through the years, some of you have even written to confide in me or share some of the difficulties you've faced. Growing up can definitely be tough sometimes. I've always found hope in the words of Psalm 139, which describes the amazing love of our Creator-God. It's comforting to know that the same God who formed us in our mother's womb, who knows the number of individual hairs we're washing and blow-drying each day, also sees the fears and concerns of our lives. Our heavenly Father sees and understands. What an enormous blessing that is!

To learn more about my writing, sign up for my e-newsletter, or contact me, visit my Web site, *www.beverlylewis.com*.